The Azanian Assignment

The Azanian Assignment

Iain Finlay

HARPER & ROW, PUBLISHERS

New York, Hagerstown, San Francisco,

London, Sydney

Grateful acknowledgment is made to David Higham Associates Limited and Macmillan, Inc., for permission to reprint lines from "Still Falls the Rain" from *Collected Poems* by Edith Sitwell.

THE AZANIAN ASSIGNMENT. Copyright © 1978 by Iain Finlay. All rights reserved. Printed in the United States of America. No part of this book may be used or reproduced in any manner whatsoever without written permission except in the case of brief quotations embodied in critical articles and reviews. For information address Harper & Row, Publishers, Inc., 10 East 53rd Street, New York, N.Y. 10022. Published simultaneously in Canada by Fitzhenry & Whiteside Limited, Toronto, and simultaneously in Australia–New Zealand by Harper & Row (Australasia) Pty. Ltd. and simultaneously in the United Kingdom by Harper & Row Ltd., London.

FIRST EDITION

Designed by Stephanie Krasnow

Library of Congress Cataloging in Publication Data

Finlay, Iain.
   The Azanian assignment.
   Bibliography: p.
   I. Title.
PZ4.F5Az 1978   [PR9619.3.F46] 823   78–1326
ISBN 0–06–011271–9

78 79 80 81 82 10 9 8 7 6 5 4 3 2 1

For Trish . . .
with whom all things are possible.

Still falls the rain—
Dark as the world of man, black as our loss—
Blind as the nineteen hundred and forty nails
Upon the cross.

Still falls the rain
Edith Sitwell, 1887–1964

Contents

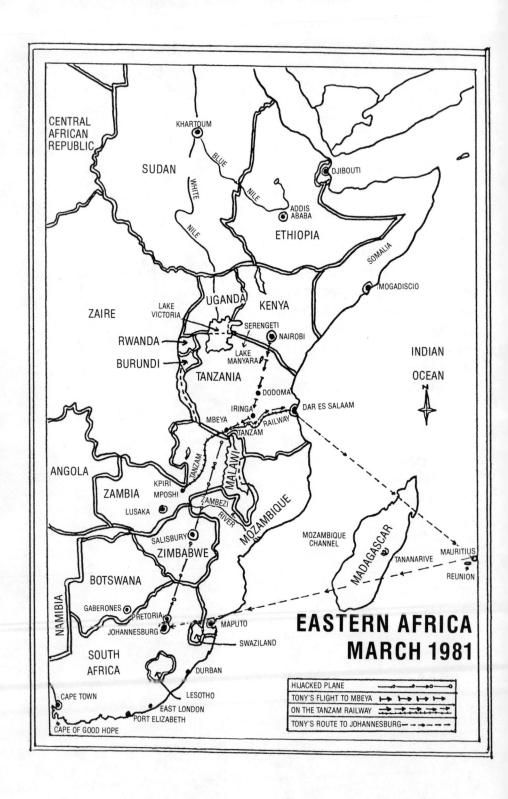

CENTRAL
AFRICAN
REPUBLIC

SUDAN

KHARTOUM

BLUE

WHITE

NILE

NILE

DJIBOUTI

ADDIS
ABABA

ETHIOPIA

SOMALIA

MOGADISCIO

ZAIRE

UGANDA

KENYA

LAKE
VICTORIA

SERENGETI

NAIROBI

RWANDA

BURUNDI

LAKE
MANYARA

TANZANIA

INDIAN
OCEAN

DODOMA

IRINGA

DAR ES SALAAM

MBEYA

RAILWAY

TANZAM

ANGOLA

ZAMBIA

KPIRI
MPOSHI

TANZAM

MALAWI

LUSAKA

ZAMBEZI
RIVER

MOZAMBIQUE

MOZAMBIQUE
CHANNEL

MADAGASCAR

MAURITIUS

TANANARIVE

REUNION

SALISBURY

ZIMBABWE

BOTSWANA

NAMIBIA

GABERONES

PRETORIA

JOHANNESBURG

MAPUTO

SWAZILAND

SOUTH
AFRICA

DURBAN

CAPE TOWN

LESOTHO

EAST LONDON

PORT ELIZABETH

CAPE OF GOOD HOPE

EASTERN AFRICA
MARCH 1981

HIJACKED PLANE	
TONY'S FLIGHT TO MBEYA	
ON THE TANZAM RAILWAY	
TONY'S ROUTE TO JOHANNESBURG	

Maps

Introduction

I hope that the catastrophic events which take place in this book never occur in reality. There is, however, the very real possibility that they will. They may not be the same incidents as those that are described here, but similar, equally horrific and destructive acts are in the wings of the South African stage, just waiting to be performed.

"Azania," the name South African revolutionaries have given to their unborn nation, is already widely used in South African underground circles and the beginnings of urban terrorism and gue-rilla warfare are being felt more and more by white South Africans.

Some of the political developments I have described with regard to the Herstigte Nasionale Party may be at variance with the real course of events and the time scale I have chosen for the narrative (a few years in the future) may not be strictly adhered to by history. However, all of the ingredients for the situations described in this book exist *now* in South Africa.

Iain Finlay,
June 1978

The Azanian Assignment

1

Hijack

If he had been free to make the choice and perhaps not such a creature of impulse, Tony Bartlett would probably not have been travelling south to Mbeya on that hot Tuesday in March. He would far rather have been spending the day resting and reading in the coolness of his flat in Nairobi, or drinking a few cold beers with the Casadys.

The concept of coolness and cold drinks occupied his mind for a period as the aircraft droned on above the vast East African plains. The pressurization system in the cabin had begun to malfunction not long after take-off and the pilot had been forced to keep the aircraft to a lower altitude than normal. He was not able, however, to fly much below about nine thousand feet, as the plateau over which they were flying was itself some seven thousand feet above sea level. Coupled with the pressurization failure, the air conditioning had hissed to a halt and the temperature inside the plane had steadily risen to hot, then very hot.

Tony had thought, when the pilot first announced the problem over the plane's speaker system, that they would turn back to Nairobi, which would have been fine with him. He'd had some doubts about whether he'd made the right decision in taking the flight the moment it left the ground, but the plane had continued on its projected route south. He felt little rivulets of sweat running down the side of his face and underneath his shirt. Other passengers mopped their brows with handkerchiefs and fanned themselves with copies of the airline's magazines. The two stewardesses, who were

1

also both in a bath of perspiration, were kept busy running up and down the aisle serving drinks. Tony ordered a Simba beer, but it was warm. He felt vaguely annoyed.

He gazed disconsolately out of the window at the immense sweep of Serengeti off to the right. The plane was flying low enough for him to make out large herds of animals on the plains. And there, much nearer, was Ngorongoro Crater, where man was supposed to have had his earliest beginnings . . . and then, almost beneath them, Lake Manyara. The dozens of tiny grey blobs by the water's edge were elephants. High above the lake, on the jungled escarpment, he could make out the lodge. He wished idly that the plane could swing around and land him there instead of continuing on this dreadful shuttle flight across central Tanzania. But at least, he thought, the airline system and schedules had regained some semblance of sanity, now that East African Airways had begun operating again after the hiatus of the late seventies.

He remembered the violent argument he'd had with Carol the last time they'd stayed at the Lake Manyara Lodge. What a place for an argument. How could anyone fight over petty personal problems when surrounded by such majesty? And yet *they* had fought bitterly there and not long after that she had left him and returned to Australia, taking Michael with her. But somehow the lodge also held fond memories. There had been better times, happier times. Michael had always loved it. The lions, buffalo, elephants, rhino. Once you left the lodge and were down by the lake, there was a wonderful primaeval quality about the place. The flat-topped Acacia trees, the thorn bushes, the dusty roads, and the high-bowled cerulean sky. For Tony it was the real Africa.

He had always experienced a tremendous feeling of excitement whenever they took off in the Land Rover, all packed up for a trip down to Serengeti or Manyara. Is all that finished now? he thought. Will it ever be the same again?

Tony Bartlett felt drained. Utterly depleted. The breakup with Carol, after nine years of marriage, had been traumatic and left him for weeks in a state of depression. Not that he really believed they should have stayed together. He knew that would have been disastrous; soul-destroying for both of them. In fact, in his more thoughtful moments he felt a sense of relief that it was all over

2

and now, after two months, he found, to his surprise, that occasionally an optimistic thought would sneak in and impinge on his consciousness. For the first few weeks he had found it difficult to think positively about anything. He had withdrawn from many of his friends in Nairobi, mainly because he found it awkward, embarrassing, or just plain boring to explain the split between himself and Carol.

The assignment in Ethiopia had come, ten days ago, as a welcome opportunity to get away from Nairobi, to immerse himself in work, and to be in situations that demanded total concentration, forcing the collapse of his private life into the background. But Ethiopia had been a shattering experience. It wasn't as if he hadn't known what to expect. He had. It wasn't his first visit to Ethiopia, and he had been confronted before by the desperate poverty and disease which has been the accepted scene there for many years. But he found that the combination of those dire conditions with a civil war presented a situation that was not only preposterous and immoral, but actually obscene.

To arm illiterate and near-starving peasants and send them off with no training and no pay—just their food and a license to loot when they got into enemy territory—was a plan of action that Tony Bartlett found hard to believe. Eritrea's continuing attempts at secession had become like a running sore for Ethiopia. It reminded Tony of Bangla Desh; huge amounts of money being spent on arms and ammunition, tanks, armoured personnel carriers, helicopters, and so on, by people who could hardly afford to feed themselves as a nation, soldiers who had nothing to their names but the rags they stood in and the Russian or American rifle in their hands, and nothing to look forward to, whichever way the war was decided, but endless, grinding poverty. It was a mad explosion of senseless violence.

Perhaps Tony's depressed state of mind at the time he had flown in to Addis Ababa had influenced his thinking about the war and the terrible scenes he had witnessed in Eritrea, because his despatches to his paper had contained a morose and horrific quality that surprised even his editor in London who had known Tony for ten years.

Tony had got off the plane in Nairobi on Tuesday morning after ten days in Ethiopia. He had puposely told no-one that he was due back. He wanted to be alone. To be quiet. He didn't normally drink a great deal, but he found himself thinking, during the taxi-ride back to his flat, that he just might drink himself into oblivion that afternoon. But apart from the one beer he extracted from the fridge as he walked through the door, he drank nothing. He lay on his bed in the darkened room, staring at the ceiling, thinking about life . . . and death.

Occasionally his mind would drift for a moment or two to completely unconnected things; like the shape of the light fitting. The room was new to him still. He found he couldn't stay in the house after Carol and Michael had gone even though it was a beautiful house and he had loved it. The garden had just the right amount of lawn and a profusion of tropical greenery had given them complete privacy. In the three years they had been in Nairobi they had made that house into one of the most attractive and comfortable he had seen anywhere. He realised he was not a little biased when he thought thoughts like that, but in any event it had been an additional trauma for him when he had decided to move out of the house and into this plain, one-bedroom apartment. He did it more or less on the spur of the moment; had he waited until his mood was more rational, he probably would have stayed in the house and, eventually, been glad of a decision not to move.

But it was too late now. He had made the move and was stuck with the apartment on a one-year lease, come what may. He had done virtually nothing to it since he had moved in. There were no paintings on the wall, only half of the crockery and cutlery had been unpacked, and there were still three large crates sitting unopened on the lounge-room floor.

There was a buzz of the doorbell.

"Oh God," Tony muttered between his teeth in despair. "Who can that be?" He began to raise himself to go to the door, then flopped back down on the bed with a determined look and lay there silently while the caller buzzed the bell twice more. A little grin flickered at the corner of Tony's mouth as the pause lengthened after the third buzz, but then he heard the rustle of paper as something was pushed underneath the door.

He got up and padded in his bare feet to the door. His heart sank when he saw the Reuters envelope. His newspaper had an arrangement with Reuters so that all of his copy could be filed by telex through their Nairobi office. All of the service messages from his editor in London also came to him through the Reuters office. He would check in there every day, when he was in Nairobi, but if there was anything urgent, the Reuters Bureau chief would normally phone him. However, with the phone still not connected in his new apartment, urgent messages were now delivered by hand.

How the hell does he know I'm back? Tony thought as he opened the envelope. He read the contents of the note inside, crumpled it and the envelope up into a ball, and hurled it across the room.

The Fokker Friendship droned on south over the great Masai Steppe. Beneath him Tony could at times follow the dusty passage of some car or truck along the sometimes mustard, sometimes ochre-coloured winding track delineated across the brown countryside by the Great North Road. Columns of dust billowed high into the air behind whatever vehicle travelled along it. He watched with brief interest from high above, while a car made repeated but vain attempts to pass through the dust cloud being kicked up by a large truck in front of it.

At Dodoma, they spent an additional hour on the ground while the cabin pressurization equipment and air conditioning were fixed. When told that there would be slight delay for this repair job, Tony immediately placed a call to the Station Hotel in the not unreasonable anticipation of having to spend the night in Dodoma. His three years in East Africa had taught him a great deal about travel in the area and one of the lessons was embodied in a little prayer he had heard once at a meeting of AA. Tony wasn't an alcoholic, nor was he very religious, but he remembered the prayer: "God grant me the serenity to accept the things I cannot change, the courage to change those I can, and the wisdom to tell the difference."

Delays in East African travel schedules of trains, buses, and aircraft fell into the first category as far as Tony was concerned. He was wise enough to know it and felt quite serene about the prospect

5

of spending the night at the Station Hotel. It was a very comfortable old colonial-style place and the more he thought about it, the more he liked it. When he had got off the plane from Addis that morning, chasing off all over East Africa after a hijacked 707 had not been part of his plans. And yet that's what he now found himself doing.

Sitting in the airport waiting room in Dodoma he wondered whether or not he might be becoming a little too jaded and blasé. After all, he thought, a few years ago . . . no, even a few months ago, I would have been onto this story like a bloodhound. I'd have been stamping around the place trying to get this bloody plane off the ground and on the way again. Now I don't seem to care. What the hell is happening to me?

But then, much to Tony's surprise, the public address system notified the passengers that the fault, which had apparently been a simple one, had been rectified and the plane was about to proceed to Iringa and Mbeya.

Tony resumed his seat and found himself, for this sector of the flight, sitting next to a Chaga woman in a bright red and yellow kitengi. Her hair was intricately braided with black cotton so that it made large loops above her head and below her ears. A child of about twelve months sat in her lap and played detachedly with the loops. Later, when it began to cry, she extracted a large, black breast from beneath the folds of her kitengi and placed it in the child's mouth.

Tony smiled at her and she smiled back and then turned shyly away. He felt a little surge of positiveness.

He forced himself to start thinking about the hijacked plane. It was a big risk he'd taken in flying to Mbeya, but if it paid off, he'd be the first one there. Maybe Steve Sumner from Dar es Salaam would be onto it, but he couldn't think who else would be there as quickly. He was well in front of any of the other correspondents from Nairobi. John Worrell might make it from Lusaka perhaps, but he would almost certainly head for Dar. But then, Tony thought again, if the damn thing isn't heading for Mbeya, I'll be in big trouble. The prospect of being professionally wrong, or being beaten to the story, seemed to dissipate some of his apathy and he began to concentrate.

Twenty minutes after tossing the crumpled telex message to the

6

floor in his flat, Tony had spoken by phone from the Reuters office to his editor, Peregrine Childers, who had given him the basic information that a South African Airways Boeing 707 had been hijacked on the ground at Jan Smuts airport in Johannesburg. Neither the identity nor the affiliations of the hijackers were known, but they were black and it was believed that they wanted the pilot to fly them to somewhere in East Africa. At the time of Tony's conversation with London, the hijack attempt was almost three hours old and the plane was still on the ground in Johannesburg.

"But what the hell can I do from here?" Tony had said. "The thing is still in South Africa and probably won't even get off the ground."

"Just be ready, that's all," Childers replied. "Get out to the airport, in case it's going to Nairobi, and also be prepared to grab a plane if it goes anywhere else . . . like Dar es Salaam. Hire a light plane if necessary."

"What about pictures?"

"See if you can get a free-lance to come with you . . . like that Peter What's-is-name who did that stuff in Angola. But if you can't, we'll just have to pick up the agency stuff."

"I'll take my camera."

There was a pause. "Well . . . yes, all right then. I suppose your stuff saved the day for us on that Burundi story, but see if you can get Peter. Nothing discouraging meant, but as a photographer, you make a good journalist."

Bastard, Tony thought.

"How did all this happen in Johannesburg anyway?" he asked. "Where was the plane going and who are the hijackers?"

"Don't know. We got the tip from a contact in the air traffic there. We were miles in front of everybody else. I tried to get through to you earlier, but you still haven't got the bloody phone on. When in God's name are they going to get it installed?"

"No idea, Perry. There's no way you can hurry them. I've slipped a little under the counter, but even that is no guarantee. All you do is get a little higher up the list. Anyway, I wasn't here. Christ, I've only just walked in off the plane from Addis. Give a bloke a chance!"

"Yes, all right. I know." A note of understanding crept into

7

Childers' voice, but only for an instant. "Look, this may not come your way, but just be on the lookout and don't get caught napping."

"Have you ever known me to?"

"No, but I know things have been a bit rough for you lately."

Tony felt himself blush—and not with pleasure. It was as if someone had suddenly peered into his private life. He bristled.

"Nothing wrong with my stuff, is there?"

"No, no. I didn't say that. There's nothing at all wrong at this end. It's just that I wanted you to understand that I know you've been working under considerable pressure."

"Thanks," Tony muttered. "Look . . ."

"It's all right, old chap, you'll come through it. We've all been through it, you know."

Tony broke the conversation off with a cursory goodbye and an assurance that he would be back in touch.

"Patronising pommie bastard," he said as he hung up the phone.

Tony made three brief telephone calls to people in Nairobi; contacts who he felt would be helpful if the hijacked plane did land in Kenya. The first was Marshall Hall, a Canadian who had been attached to the Kenyan Department of Civil Aviation for the period of the major reconstruction of Nairobi airport, which was now well under way. Next he had spoken to Lennox Sengope, the airport manager, a man whom Tony admired tremendously as he had come originally from a tiny village in northern Kenya, worked his way through secondary school, and won a scholarship to London University. He and Tony had got on well together since their first meeting and Sengope was one of the closest black friends Tony had. Not that Tony actually thought of Lennox as being black. Lennox didn't even think of himself as being "black" unless it was forced on him. He just thought of himself as a person and it came through in his personality. It was almost certainly the reason that their friendship had grown, because Tony was basically the same; he wouldn't normally think of himself as being "white," although living in Africa during times like these, it was often very difficult not to.

The third person he called was Joseph Ngala, the superintendent of police in charge of airport security.

All three of the men were aware of the hijack attempt in Johannes-burg, and were surprised that Tony knew. Ngala had asked, when Tony had phoned, where he had learnt about the hijack.

"From my paper, in London," he said. "Do you know who the hijackers are?"

"No," Ngala replied.

"Is there any indication of whether they want to fly to Dar es Salaam or to here?"

"No. All we've got is that they said East Africa."

It was difficult for Ngala not to treat Tony Bartlett with suspicion. He had a basic mistrust of journalists and particularly of white ones. He had treated Tony with what could only be described as offhand caution since their first meeting almost two years ago after an incredible crash-landing at Nairobi airport, when a chartered 747 had done a belly-landing with its undercarriage locked up.

Since then he had accorded some degree of grudging respect to Bartlett as a result of Tony's stories on the brief but ferocious little war between Kenya and Uganda which resulted in the downfall of Idi Amin. Tony's reporting of the war in the English press was reprinted in a Kenyan paper and gained him some favourable atten-tion in Nairobi. He realised that it was only because his reports had been favourable to the Kenyan side, but, under the circum-stances, it had been difficult not to lean in that direction.

The accolades had worried Tony, however. He thought that per-haps he had been too subjective in his coverage of the war, whereas objectivity was something in which Tony took some pride. But then he had thought that maybe the pursuit of objectivity was in itself subjective.

Tony had returned to his apartment, picked up the small travelling bag which he had dropped by the front door when he had first come home less than two hours ago. He threw some dirty clothes from it onto the floor, stuffed two pairs of clean slacks and a couple of shirts inside it, and grabbed a lightweight jacket, his portable typewriter, some paper, his passport, wallet, and some extra money from the drawer. He stood at the front door, looked around for a moment, and was about to leave, when he returned to the bedroom and climbed on a stool to get his Nikkormat camera from the top cupboard. He blew the dust from it as he walked back to the door.

He had driven the three miles to Peter Minotti's place and had been quite pleased to find out that Peter was not in town.

"He's in Ethiopia," Tony was told by Lolly, the very attractive half-Portuguese, half-Kenyan girl with whom Peter lived. Peter had left two days previously for Addis on a photographic assignment for *Paris Match.*

Tony had always fancied himself as a photographer, and Peter's absence was a good excuse for him to have another fling.

"All we know so far is that the hijackers were apparently hiding on the plane," Marshall Hall told Tony as they walked along the corridor of the administrative block towards Lennox Sengope's office. "They were discovered just prior to the plane's take-off and took control of the aircraft on the ground. They're very heavily armed."

"But how the hell could it happen?" Tony said. "Particularly with the way South Africa is now, like a bloody armed camp. It's almost impossible to imagine blacks being able to even get close enough to a plane to get aboard it."

"They think it's some of the airport ground crew, or rather people posing as ground crew," Hall said. "But the trouble is the South Africans seem to have clammed up on it a bit since the first report. They're not saying much at all now."

Tony was about to ask another question, but the two men had reached the airport manager's office. Marshall Hall knocked once and walked in. Lennox Sengope was on the phone. He smiled when he saw Tony, terminated the conversation and stood up, holding out his hand.

There was a brief conversation about Ethiopia and about Tony's desire to just lie in a darkened room and gaze at a blank wall, before they got onto the subject at hand. Tony found that, with Lennox, and to a somewhat lesser degree, Marshall Hall, he could quite easily speak his inner thoughts like this and that they would be taken at face value. He made the comments in perhaps a slightly jocular manner, but the two other men knew that Tony really meant them. That he needed a rest.

10

"Where was the plane supposed to be going?" Tony asked.

"That's just it," Sengope replied. "No-one seems to know. Or if they do know, they're not saying."

"So it wasn't a scheduled flight?"

"We're just not sure. There was a London flight due to leave South Africa around that time, but whether this is it or not, we don't know. All traffic at Jan Smuts has been stopped."

"Most of the European flights go through Mauritius now, don't they?"

"Yes," Sengope said. "All except the direct non-stop flights to London and Lisbon and Rome they make with their 747-SP's, which have got the range. All the rest have to use Mauritius; ever since we withdrew landing rights for South African planes. Kenya was their last card. Now there's nowhere on the African continent a South African aircraft can land."

Tony pulled up a chair. "What about passengers?"

"No clues. The South Africans have shut up completely since they first told us about it."

"So what are you getting from them at the moment?"

"Just a sporadic telex report. But the last couple of messages have said nothing more than that the plane is still on the ground and that there are some negotiations going on. Dar es Salaam has some contact too, but I don't believe they know any more than we do. Marshall spoke to them by phone, I think."

Marshall Hall nodded, but Tony noticed a vacant look in his eyes, as if preoccupied with some other thought. A phone call interrupted their conversation and Tony said that he wanted to check on flights to Dar es Salaam, in case he needed to fly there. He left Lennox Sengope's office with Marshall Hall.

"You know there's something funny here," Marshall said, as they walked back along the corridor.

"What do you mean?" Tony asked.

"Well, it's only just occurred to me. I was thinking about it in the office there. I'm convinced that the people in Dar es Salaam know a good deal more about all this than we do. And yet in theory their information should be the same as ours . . . from the same telex messages."

11

"The telex lines from South African haven't been shut down?"

"No, that was a ruling agreed to by the international telecommuni-cations people and insisted on by IATA at the time the Kenyans withdrew landing rights. But what has me puzzled, now that I think about it, is, how does Dar es Salaam know more than us from the same telex messages?"

"But do they know any more?" Tony said. "Lennox just said he thought they didn't know."

"Yes, I know, but I've just remembered that it was Dar es Salaam that told us the hijackers were heavily armed and how many of them there were."

"How many are there?" Tony asked.

At this point they reached the main concourse of the terminal building and a policeman came quickly over to talk to Marshall Hall. He wasn't wearing a uniform, but Tony picked him as a policeman for sure. Funny, he thought, as he waited for Marshall to finish speaking, how you can spot them wherever you are, what-ever colour they might be. Something about the clothes and the way they wear them. He couldn't hear the conversation clearly . . . "units one and two by runway three . . . ambulances . . . movements control . . . fire trucks."

There was already a noticeable air of activity and tension in the airport. Uniformed police were in evidence everywhere, with more arriving all the time. They were either moving from one place to another or standing talking in groups of two or three. Passengers in the concourse displayed signs of apprehension, watching develop-ments closely and talking earnestly amongst themselves. Tony no-ticed a group of three local journalists walk in through one of the entrance doors, followed, a few paces behind, by Martin Crowther of the *Express.*

Tony quickly turned his back and, as Marshall Hall had just finished talking to the plain-clothes policeman, he took Marshall by the arm and led him away from the centre of the concourse.

"How many did you say there were?" Tony asked.

"Four. Now what the hell's going on, Tony?" Marshall lifted his arm to shake it free, but Tony held on tightly and kept on walking, forcing Marshall along, but smiling as they kept walking

12

towards a large, empty reception area.

"Listen, Tony . . . "

"Let's just sit down for a moment," Tony said.

"Tony, for Christ's sake!" Marshall Hall exploded. "I don't mind if you tag along, but I haven't time to sit down and chat now. Things are going to get pretty hectic around here if that goddam plane comes in this direction."

"I know, I know." Tony smiled, and then with a sheepish look he said, "It's only that one of my arch-rivals just walked in and I didn't want him to see you."

Marshall Hall's look of irritation faded and his open mouth turned slowly to a smile. "I see," he said. And then, "But that still doesn't alter the fact that I'm getting busy."

"Couldn't Dar es Salaam have a separate telex link to Jo'burg?" Tony asked.

"No. It's been the same one. I mean they could call them separately of course, as we could, but they say that Jo'burg hasn't been replying to any inward calls. Only sending out what it wants to."

"Well, couldn't the message about the number of hijackers and the fact that they were heavily armed just be one message that Dar got and you didn't?"

"Yes, I suppose it could, but there was something else. I know it sounds stupid, but it was almost as if the two people I spoke to in Dar were expecting it all to happen."

Tony leant back in the soft waiting-room couch and looked over his shoulder towards the main concourse. "Listen," he said, grabbing Marshall Hall by the arm again, "can we go to your office and get Dar on the phone again?"

"Jesus, Tony. It's all very well for you," Marshall said with a slight tinge of desperation. "You're getting your job done, but what about me? I've got things to do too!"

"Come on," Tony urged. "There's plenty of time. The plane is still on the ground in Johannesburg. At least I hope it is."

The two men stood up and walked in the direction of Marshall Hall's office.

"Is there any way of keeping track of where the plane goes, once it's in the air?" Tony asked.

13

"Naturally we can monitor any radio transmissions once they're in range. That is if they make any transmissions, and if they stick to standard wavelengths. There's also their automatic transponder, but if the hijackers are clued up, they could easily ensure that it is switched off. The air force here can use a frequency scanner and of course radar once they're in range, but apart from those things I'm afraid it's pot luck."

"What about Zambia and Zimbabwe and Mozambique? Has there been any word from them?"

"No. And it's not surprising, really. I mean, Jesus. You know how tricky the situation is, Tony. Kenya is the most Western-oriented country in this part of Africa, and with everybody south of here leaning way off to the left, things aren't always as friendly as they could be. We're just not getting the full story . . . I'm sure of it."

An attractive young Kenyan girl came running down the corridor as fast as her ankle-length kitengi would allow her.

"Mr. Hall, Mr. Hall," she called as she ran up to Marshall and Tony, "I've been trying to find you. The plane has taken off from Johannesburg. Mr. Sengope has been calling for you."

But the only information Lennox Sengope could provide when Marshall Hall telephoned the airport manager was that the plane had taken off from Jan Smuts airport and was flying north. Its take-off time was 12.57 P.M. . . . thirteen minutes ago.

"Now will you telephone Dar es Salaam again?" Tony said.

Marshall didn't reply to Tony, but asked his secretary to get through to a telephone number in the Dar es Salaam airport office of the Tanzanian Department of Civil Aviation. Tony's mind mentally ticked off the various steps the call would take, through secretaries, phone operators, seven hundred miles of cable down to the coast and south to the Tanzanian capital, through more telephone operators, secretaries, and eventually to the man concerned. He sat and fidgeted. Many times he had spent hours waiting to get through to Dar. But in less than five minutes the call came through.

Marshall's conversation with the Tanzanian officials was disjointed. There was an increased feeling of tension. The senses of the two men had been heightened considerably by the news that the plane was on its way and Tony could tell from Marshall's attitude that there was some excitement at the other end, but it was also clear that he was not getting much cooperation.

"But don't you know where it's heading?" Marshall was saying, when suddenly a look of surprise passed over his face and he looked up sharply at Tony. He put his hand over the mouthpiece of the phone. "Mbeya," he whispered. Tony jumped up.

"Are you sure you can't tell us where they are going?" Marshall said again. Tony sat down again, puzzled.

"So that's all you've got, huh? Okay, thanks a lot. We'll keep in touch."

"What the hell's going on?" Tony said as Marshall hung up the phone. "What was that about Mbeya?"

"They're not telling us anything," Marshall said. "They obviously knew much more. They were really jumping around there. You could hear it. There were several other people in the room."

"What about Mbeya?" Tony said again.

"I heard someone in the background say they are going to Mbeya. And then the joker on the phone . . . his name's Longole . . . suddenly shouted out to them to be quiet and the rest of the room went silent."

"Are you sure it was Mbeya?" Tony asked.

"Yes. Positive," Marshall replied.

Tony was standing up. He looked for a moment at Marshall Hall without saying anything, then his face broke into a smile. He held up his fist and punched Marshall's arm lightly. "Right!" he exclaimed. "You better bloody well be right, mate, or I'll have your balls for bicycle pedals when I get back!"

Without another word, Tony ran from the office.

2

A Meeting

During the last part of the flight to Mbeya, Tony Bartlett was plagued by doubts. It would be a quarter to six by the time they landed—four hours since he had left Nairobi. An hour on the ground at Dodoma and half an hour at Iringa hadn't helped any. He figured that if the hijacked 707 had left Johannesburg when he was told it had—12.57 East African Time—then it would already have been in Mbeya for at least a couple of hours by the time he arrived. He estimated that it was about twelve or thirteen hundred miles from Johannesburg in a direct line to Mbeya, on the southern border of Tanzania, and that the jet must have averaged at least five hundred miles per hour, which would have put it down there at around 3.30 in the afternoon. He looked at his watch again.

The Fokker was losing altitude fast. Would the plane be here? Tony kept asking himself. As the afternoon had worn on he had told himself that he was a fool, an idiot, to go charging off like this just on Marshall Hall's say-so that he had heard someone on the other end of a telephone line—not even the person he had been speaking to—say that the hijacked plane was going to Mbeya. I mean, what the hell would it go to Mbeya for? Why should a hijacker want to go to Mbeya? It was a tinpot little place really.

No. That's not quite fair, Tony told himself, as he remembered the beautiful trees that lined some of the streets there and the rolling green hills that surround the town. Subtropical climate, but somehow a bit like England. In the days of British rule in Tanganyika, the town had been laid out and the trees planted to make it look as much like home as possible. Oaks and elms. Funny the way the poms did that wherever they went, Tony thought.

But Mbeya had gone downhill since then. It was tatty now. You couldn't get anything in the shops, the kids in the streets were poor, the people generally were poor . . . much poorer than in Kenya. But, Tony thought, what's "downhill"? Nobody was really starving and at least they were—he paused at the cliché—masters of their own destinies.

Tony wondered if there would be any other journalists there. He had felt extremely pleased with himself back in Nairobi when he'd been able to get a seat on the 1.45 East African flight which took off just half an hour after he had raced out of Marshall Hall's office. He had gone to great lengths to avoid being seen by Martin Crowther, who was still prowling around the terminal while Tony was trying to arrange his tickets to Mbeya.

Tony had mentally tossed a coin over whether he should, as his editor had suggested, hire a light plane, but settled on the commercial flight because at the time it seemed less complicated. However, during the flight and the delay in Dodoma, he had begun to regret his decision. He had calculated that if Martin Crowther had got onto the fact that the jet was heading for Mbeya and decided to charter a light aircraft and make the direct flight, he could be there before Tony.

Tony tried to reassure himself. Mbeya was six hundred miles south of Nairobi as the crow flies. He'd have to get a pretty nifty light aircraft to make that in four hours, taking into consideration all the preliminaries, Tony thought. Maybe that Turbo commander I went to the coast in once could do it, but not many others at Nairobi. But then, of course, there were the Dar es Salaam bods, perhaps they were on to it too. Anyway, the bloody thing probably won't even be there. If that's the case, Tony told himself disconsolately, I'll not only have *not* beaten everybody else to the punch, but I'll more than likely be looking for a new job.

But not long after they had left Iringa, Tony had an indication that he might have made the right bet. There was a sudden sense of urgency shown by the stewardesses. One of the girls had signalled from the front of the cabin to her colleague, who had been standing

17

talking to a passenger two seats in front of Tony. There had been a hasty, whispered conversation, and the girl had hurried to the rear of the plane and then back to the pilot's cabin. Shortly afterwards Tony was able to ask what was happening and was told that the plane might have to turn back to Iringa.

"Why?" he asked.

"Because there's some trouble in Mbeya."

That's it, he thought. It's there. He cursed inwardly at the prospect of the plane turning back, but there had been no change in course and it had continued on towards Mbeya.

The plane was now in its final approaches to the landing field at Mbeya. I wouldn't have thought the runway here was long enough for a 707, he said to himself. The first time he had flown in to Mbeya almost three years ago, it was just a grass strip about three thousand feet long. But last year he had seen the new, tarred runway, which he thought he remembered reading somewhere had been lengthened to around five thousand feet. Was that enough for a 707? He didn't know.

The plane banked to the right and straightened as it lined itself up on the runway. Tony turned in his seat to look out of the big oval window beneath the wing and his heart leapt. Almost immediately beneath them, in a waiting bay at the end of the runway, he caught a glimpse, for only a second, of a big, shiny, steel fuselage and a flash of the orange and blue colours of South African Airways.

He felt a surge of excitement. Now he wanted to be off as soon as possible and every second suddenly became interminable as the plane glided in to land, slowed at the other end of the runway, turned, and began its painful taxi-run back towards the terminal.

As the plane turned off the runway, Tony looked back down the other end of it and saw the hijacked aircraft. It stood alone. No vehicles or people anywhere near it. But as the Fokker neared the terminal, a hump in the field obscured most of the South African plane so that only the tail, which protruded from the ground like a shark's fin, could be seen in the distance.

Tony had wanted to barge off the plane first, but because of the position of his seat he was fourteenth to leave the aircraft. He counted the thirteen preceding him in desperate frustration, peering over their shoulders as they stood, waiting in the aisle for the doors to open.

As he hit the tarmac, he was running. Fourteenth off the plane, but he meant to be first into the terminal. He noticed immediately, as he left the plane, that the building was bristling with Tanzanian police and also the camouflage uniforms of the Tanzanian Army. There were scores of soldiers, most of whom were carrying either Chinese or Russian AK-47 assault rifles. Almost certainly Chinese, he decided.

"Stop!" someone shouted as he neared the building, and Tony realised that running in a situation like this was not the brightest thing to do. He slowed to a walk and was quickly confronted by four armed soldiers. One of them shouted at him in Swahili.

"Where are you going?" another said in English.

"Can't you see I've just come off that plane and I'm going inside this building."

"Why are you running?"

"Oh, for Christ's sake," Tony gasped, "because I am in a hurry. Look, who is in charge here? Who is the chief of police here?"

"You want to see the police?"

"Yes. Or the army. Who is the army commander?"

"Why?"

Already the other passengers had caught up and were passing him to file through the doorway into the terminal building. Tony made to move off with them, but was restrained by one of the soldiers, a large black man with thin lips and an aquiline nose. A part of Tony's mind thought, He must be a Somali. Doesn't look as if he's from this part of the world.

"Look," Tony exploded in exasperation, "I'm a journalist." He fished in his pocket for his wallet and produced a Kenyan press pass, then a Tanzanian one, issued in Dar es Salaam. It was within a week of being out of date, but it didn't matter to the soldier who looked at it. He didn't understand what it was anyway. "I'm here to see about this hijacked plane," Tony gestured back towards the aircraft, or rather its tail, which was still poking up from the ground about three-quarters of a mile away.

The soldier's face registered surprise. "You come with us," he said, taking Tony by the arm and leading him away.

"Why did you come to Mbeya?" Colonel Samere asked, after leafing through Tony's papers.

"I've just told you. Because I want to report to my newspaper on what happens to this hijacked aeroplane."

"I know that," the colonel said, his eyes narrowing, "but why do you come to Mbeya and not somewhere else? How did you know this plane was going to land here?"

Tony paused. "I heard it in Nairobi. There were several officials at the airport there who knew that this plane was coming to Mbeya." Tony told the truth, knowing it would be impossible for anyone to trace it back to Marshall Hall. And even if they did . . . so what?

"Were there indeed?" the colonel said. "You must be very well informed in Nairobi." His sarcasm was not sufficient to hide the fact that he was annoyed.

Abel Samere, at forty, was still an extremely ambitious man. In 1961, when Tanganyika had gained its independence from Britain, Samere had been halfway through a mechanical engineering diploma course at the Central London Polytechnic. He had tossed it in and returned to Dar es Salaam in the hope of climbing the power ladder more quickly under the new black government of Julius Nyrere.

Well, it hadn't exactly been a rapid climb; after all, twenty years is a lifetime in some people's books, but it had been steady. He had thought of quitting the army, at one stage, but as his authority increased, he decided to stick it. Samere held considerable power in southern Tanzania and when the guerilla training camps had first been established there in the late sixties and early seventies, the region's political importance, and therefore his also, increased. He was highly regarded back in Dar es Salaam and had been sent on training missions not only to China and North Vietnam when it was still North Vietnam, but also to the United States. He spent two years in China, most of it working as a liaison officer attached to the Tanzanian Embassy in Peking, but he also passed several months on training exercises with the Chinese Army in a number

20

of remote parts of the People's Republic. He spoke passable Mandarin.

Tony felt that somehow he had lost the initiative and that he should attempt to regain it.

"What has happened since the plane arrived? Have you been in contact with the hijackers? Are they still on board? What about the passengers?"

Colonel Samere smiled slightly. "I am afraid you are not in a position to be asking questions, Mr. Bartlett. It is I who am asking the questions."

Tony felt anger bubbling again. "Colonel, I have told you that I am a legitimate journalist attempting to cover the story of an international plane hijacking. I have shown you my accreditation with the Tanzanian Ministry of Information . . ."

"It has almost expired," Colonel Samere said.

"It is still valid at this moment, though," Tony said. "And that is all that matters. What is it that you object to in my being here? Are there other journalists here?"

"No, you are the only one."

"Well, then, at least you could be civil enough not to treat me like a criminal. I have done nothing wrong. I am not one of the hijackers. All I wanted to do was to ask a few questions, which you apparently don't want to answer, Have you got something to hide?"

The expression on Colonel Samere's face changed and Tony felt he had won a small point at last.

"No, of course not. But I am afraid you will have to speak to the police about it. I have other things to do."

The distant sound of jet engines roaring at their peak fell on their ears. The colonel smiled again.

"Anyway, I don't think you'll find much here. You're too late." He walked to the window of the small room in which they'd been standing talking. Tony sprang to his side. The hijacked jet was tearing down the runway. Its nose lifted and the wheels left the tarmac about two-thirds of the way along the strip. Tony watched open-mouthed as it climbed, then banked slowly to the east and flew off into the gathering dusk.

21

Tony turned around to face Colonel Samere. "Where is it going now?"

"I haven't the slightest idea," the colonel said.

Tony Bartlett had been in some ridiculous situations in his life, but he felt that the one he was facing at the moment could well take the cake. If the hijacked plane was going to Dar es Salaam, and that had been the direction it had been heading after it took off, then he might just as well give the game away. He had been first on the scene in Mbeya, the *only* one on the scene in fact, but he would be so far behind in Dar es Salaam, he might just as well not bother.

After Colonel Samere had left him, Tony drew blanks everywhere he turned at the airport. He had a brief appointment with the police superintendent and one of his aides, but all Tony got from them was that the aircraft had landed just before 3.40 PM, which he had calculated anyway, and that they had asked for a Tanzanian pilot to be put on board.

"And did someone go on board the plane?" Tony asked.

"Yes. A pilot," the superintendent said.

"What sort of pilot?" Tony asked.

"What do you mean?"

"Well, was he an airline pilot, or a private pilot, or what?"

"Why do you ask?"

Tony felt annoyed. "Was he qualified, I mean? Qualified to fly a 707? Not everyone can fly those things and you don't normally have commercial jet planes of that size coming in here. Where did you find a pilot who could fly it?"

The superintendent looked slightly put out and also displayed signs of annoyance. He paused. "He was an air force pilot. He volunteered."

"But you don't have 707's in your air force," Tony knew he was pushing things a little too far. "How was he trained?"

The aide stepped forward. "He was a commercial pilot before he joined the air force. He was trained in America. Look, Mr. . . . there's not much more we can tell you . . ."

"Okay, okay," Tony said. "Just one thing. You say no-one apart from the pilot got onto the plane and no-one came off?"

"That is correct," the superintendent said.

"So you don't know anything about the hijackers or the passengers on board?"

"No."

Tony didn't believe them and was about to say as much to the two men, but thought better of it.

"Thank you very much," he said, and stood up to leave.

"Where will you go now?" the aide asked, as if suddenly genuinely concerned.

"I am going to see about hiring a light plane," Tony said deliberately. "There are no flights to Dar es Salaam until tomorrow afternoon, so I am going to charter one."

Tony did not see the two policemen smile at each other as he left the room, but if he had, he would soon have understood why. There were, of course, no light planes available for charter in Mbeya.

Tony turned over in his mind the prospect of waiting in Mbeya until the following afternoon. It didn't please him, but he booked a seat at the airport traffic counter and walked from the airport building, having collected his travel bag and typewriter.

Under normal circumstances, the airport would be closed by now. It was already dark outside. His flight would have been the last for the day and usually everybody just shut up shop and went home after it had been cleared. But today was different. Nothing quite like this had happened in Mbeya in living memory and the people at the airport were still agog three-quarters of an hour after the hijacked plane had left. The lights in the small terminal building were ablaze and small groups of people stood around talking animatedly.

When Tony stepped out of the terminal building, he became aware, for the first time since he had left the plane, of the warmth. The airport terminal hadn't been air-conditioned, but there were large fans about the building and in the rooms in which he had spoken to Colonel Samere and the police superintendent. He had also been too busy to notice. Now he felt the warm night air enclose him. He looked up into a clear star-filled sky.

There were three taxis waiting. All of them had seen better days. The first one in the rank was an old Opel, fifteen years old if it was a day. Its owner, a tall, gangling man of about fifty, who had been squatting next to the wall talking to the other drivers, jumped up and hurried over towards Tony.

"Goodnight, Bwana. You want to go to hotel?"

God, how old habits die hard, Tony thought. Twenty years since independence and he still calls the white man boss.

But to Robert Ilozi, "Bwana" did not hold these connotations. He called all white men Bwana, in the same way other taxi-drivers in other parts of the world might call a passenger John, or Mack, or pal or mate.

"You English?" he asked Tony as they drove towards the town.

"No. Australian."

"Ah."

Tony wondered whether "Ah" was good, bad, or indifferent.

"You look hijack today?"

"No," Tony said. "Come too late. Plane . . ." he checked himself. What the hell am I talking like this for—as if he won't understand me? "No. I came too late. The plane was just leaving."

"Ah . . . very many soldiers and police. They capture South African people from plane."

Tony, who had been slouched in the front seat somewhat dejectedly gazing at the passing countryside, what he could see of it, in the night, and carrying on the conversation more out of politeness than anything else, felt his spine tingle. He sat up slowly, hoping his new interest would not be too obvious.

"You say they captured South Africans from the plane?"

"Yes . . . Haha!" The driver gave a little laugh, almost as if he had been personally involved. "Yes. And take all their cargo baggage too."

"But . . . but," Tony was momentarily lost. "How do you know?"

"I see it all, Bwana. Haha." He pointed to his eyes. "With my own eyes I see it, Bwana."

"But nobody else in the airport could see the plane. You can't see the end of the runway from the airport building and the police wouldn't let people out of the building."

"Haha . . . I was not at airport. I look from somewhere else."

"And you saw soldiers take the South Africans off the plane?"

"Yeh, Bwana, oh yeh. Haha."

24

"Black men or white men?"

"White men, Bwana. White men, yeh."

"How many?"

"Maybe six, maybe seven."

"And then?"

"Then take cargo baggage off. Many boxes."

"Many boxes? What sort of boxes?"

"Wooden boxes."

"Where did they go?"

"Don't know, Bwana. Go by other road. Special road. Many army cars and trucks. Haha."

Tony watched the driver's face in the dim glow given off by the dashboard lights. He was obviously getting a great kick out of being able to tell such a tale. Tony wondered if perhaps he was slightly crazy and it was all just the fabrication of a fertile mind.

On the other hand, if all he said was true, it would put a totally different complexion on things. It would indicate a fairly large-scale conspiracy. But then, Tony thought, right from the start there have been indications of something like that.

Marshall Hall's suspicion that Dar es Salaam knew more than they were saying, the correct prediction that Mbeya was where the plane was heading, the reluctance of both Colonel Samere and the police superintendent to give information and even to lie . . . and now this story. But who were the white people taken off the plane? Passengers? And what of the black hijackers? And the cargo?

Tony felt now that perhaps it might be a good idea to stay an extra day in Mbeya. But what about the plane when it lands in Dar es Salaam? That will be where the story is. I must get through to London, he thought.

He checked his watch. It was now 7.30, almost an hour and a quarter since the jet had left Mbeya. It was either already in Dar es Salaam or just arriving. Tony felt a wave of tiredness sweep over him. He booked in to the Mbeya Hotel, a low, rambling place on a tree-lined road about a mile from the centre of the town. He asked the man at the desk if he could book a telephone call to London. The man looked at him in surprise, but took the number and said that he would try.

Tony walked to the bar and ordered a beer, cursing to himself at the high prices of the beer and the fact that he had been unable to change any money on the black market before he came. Tanzanian shillings were only worth about half the value of Kenyan shillings, although Tony knew he would have to buy them at par when he paid his bill in the morning or went to the bank.

The call did not come through. Tony asked to speak to the operator, who said there was some trouble with the London line and that there would be a delay of about three hours. Tony told the desk clerk that he would wait in his room and asked if someone could call him when the line was through.

With that, he went to his room and lay on his bed, still fully clothed. He began to think over the events of the day and within little more than a minute, fell into a deep, dreamless sleep.

The light streaming through the bedroom window and the noise of birds outside the window woke him at about seven o'clock in the morning. After a moment's orientation, Tony leapt from his bed and ran from the room, almost knocking over a man who was sitting, sleeping in a cane chair outside his door. The man stood up and moved quickly down the hall after Tony.

"We are very sorry, sir," the desk clerk (a different one from the previous evening) said to Tony, "but no call came through for London. I was told about it, but it did not come."

Tony spoke to the exchange again and was informed once more that there were problems with the London line and that there would be a three-hour delay.

The rest of the morning was equally frustrating. He had tried to see both Colonel Samere and the police superintendent again. Colonel Samere was not available when Tony had called at the regional army headquarters. He was told to call back later in the morning. At police headquarters he had met with complete non-cooperation. The superintendent he had spoken to previously was apparently not in yet and the inspector he dealt with said that he had had nothing to do with the hijacked plane and that he should call back later. Back at the hotel there was still no joy with the London call. They're giving me the bloody run-around, he said to himself.

Earlier, he had become aware of a small man in a white shirt and dark trousers who seemed to be standing around wherever Tony went. Wasn't he the one who was sitting asleep in the cane chair? Tony was sure that he was, but it didn't really worry him that he might be being followed. It had happened often before on various assignments. As long as they don't start getting rough, Tony thought.

The worst thing about it all was that he felt as if in a sort of limbo. He had listened, during the morning, to the news on the little transistor radio he always carried in his travel bag. But it was not a short-wave receiver, so he could only listen to the local news, which was government-controlled. There was no mention whatever of the hijack incident.

He felt detached and isolated, without a clue as to what was going on.

At eleven, he returned to army headquarters to try to find Colonel Samere again, only to be told once more that the colonel was not there. He had gone to visit an army unit at Njombe, some 150 miles away.

"Sorry, but he is the only one who could answer your questions," the junior officer had said.

Tony thanked him over-politely . . . sarcastically. He wanted the soldier to know how he felt, and he succeeded.

He walked down the corridor, past the spit-polished guards standing with their shining rifles in the entrance lobby, and almost collided with Johnathan Kapepwe, who was emerging from another door.

"Johnathan Kapepwe!" Tony burst out. "What the hell are you doing here?"

Johnathan Kapepwe would rather not have met Tony Bartlett at this moment, although he was able to restrain himself from giving any indication, other than surprise, of his feelings.

"Well . . . Bartlett," he said. "I might ask you the same thing."

Tony had not spoken to Kapepwe for three years. It had been at least that since they had last met in London, and Kapepwe was by no means a friend. They only knew each other professionally and through occasional social meetings. Their conversations had always been polite, although Kapepwe's violent anti-apartheid attitudes had always left Tony with a slight feeling of unease. Not

27

because Tony supported the concept of apartheid, but because Kapepwe's answers to the situation seemed so brutal and bloody.

Johnathan Kapepwe, as Tony knew him, was an author and journalist. He had escaped from detention in South Africa in 1974 and, after a period of time in Europe, had based himself in London, where he had quickly become one of the most outspoken advocates of violent black revolution in South Africa. He had become something of a *cause célèbre* amongst the various anti-apartheid groups in England and, because he was a well-educated, lucid, and logical speaker, was always in demand on radio and television talk shows as well as being widely known for his articles in newspapers and magazines.

He was tall and slim, similar in built to Tony, in fact, with a reasonably pleasant appearance, except that he never seemed to smile. He was very black, although not quite the blue-black of the Sudanese or Somalis. His eyes too were black; a watery, limpid black which Tony had always found disconcerting, whenever he spoke to Kapepwe, because he could never see the pupils. Or was it that his eyes seemed to consist only of two gigantic pupils?

Kapepwe had always worn a beard; a curly, bushy, black beard with just a touch of early grey on the left side of his chin. His hair too was bushy and curly. Not quite a full "afro" style; about halfway. Kapepwe's back, so Tony had been told by an English girl who had once been Kapepwe's mistress, was covered in scars from a lashing he had received from whites in South Africa.

In the wake of the widespread riots that erupted in South Africa back in 1976, Kapepwe had made a secret visit in late 1977 to his homeland, via Mozambique and Swaziland, and, over a period of three months, under extremely hazardous conditions, using several different identities, had travelled all over South Africa for clandestine meetings with other South African revolutionaries. He took part in the establishment of a network of cells within the various major black population centres, as well as in smaller country areas. He also laid most of the groundwork for a complicated communications system, by which cell leaders in any part of South Africa could make contact or pass messages to other parts of the country or to London, which Kapepwe and others had worked hard at making the main international centre for revolution in South Africa.

28

Kapepwe was not, however, the top dog amongst the exiled South Africans living in London. Both Oliver Tambo and Potlako Leballo were bigger names in the unofficial Azanian government-in-exile. They were older and their political activities in South Africa prior to their departures had established their positions in the hierarchical structures of the African National Congress and the Pan African Congress respectively.

Johnathan Kapepwe's rise towards potential political power in South Africa had been in absentia. He had made a dramatic escape from a Transvaal prison farm and, after ten days of travelling only at night, had trekked almost two hundred miles to the Botswana border. When he arrived in London, five months later, he was nothing. But his sheer brilliance and dynamism had brought him at thirty-six to the point where in 1981 he now ranked third in the overseas leadership of South African revolutionaries living abroad.

Tony Bartlett was not aware of all these details of Johnathan Kapepwe's career. Of course he knew something of his background, but, by and large, he had only thought of Kapepwe as a rather impressive, if somewhat violent and ambitious, black intellectual. Tony had also felt on one or two occasions that he would be a dangerous man to have as an enemy.

"Well, I'm here about this damn hijacked plane," Tony said.

Kapepwe paused for only a moment. "Oh," he said. "Yes, I heard about it this morning. What was it all about?" Tony thought that he seemed unusually restrained.

"You mean you don't know? It was a South African plane, you know."

Kapepwe straightened himself up. "Look, I may be South African," he said a little sharply, "but I can't be expected to know everything about South Africa that happens inside or out of it."

"Of course," Tony said. "I just thought it was the sort of thing that might interest you, that's all."

"Well, what happened to the plane anyway?"

"Nobody seems to know . . . or rather, they know, but they're not saying . . . and the plane's gone."

"Where?"

Tony shrugged his shoulders.

"And who were the hijackers?"

"Nobody knows," Tony replied, and then, "but they were black, which should please you."   ·

Kapepwe's eyes focused on Tony's, as if attempting to read his thoughts. He was about to say something, but paused.

"Anyway," Tony went on, "what are you doing in this part of the world? It's a long way from London."

"I'm writing a series of articles on Tanzania under the new military government," Kapepwe said without hesitation. "I'm particularly interested in some of the developments in the Ujamaa villages. They've carried on the concept since Nyrere retired, you know."

There was something in the way Kapepwe said it that seemed to Tony a little too pat. "Yes, I know," he said. "I've been to several of them in northern Tanzania. But what's the army got to do with it?" He waved his hand in an arc encompassing the headquarters building in which they stood.

Kapepwe glanced down for a second. "They are involved in some major cooperative construction schemes here in the Mbeya area and also in Ruvuma Province. They're building bridges, roads, and grain-storage facilities for the villages, and they've been providing me with transport. Look, I really must go. I have a lot to organise."

"Perhaps we could have lunch," Tony said.

"No," Kapepwe said flatly. "I'm sorry, but I'm leaving for Dar es Salaam this afternoon."

"Well, that's fine," Tony said. "So am I. We'll be on the same plane." Tony was purposely polite and over-friendly, even though it was patently obvious to him that Kapepwe wanted to be rid of him.

"Sorry. I'm not going by plane. I'm taking the train," Kapepwe said. "Look, I must go. I'll see you again some time." He turned and walked quickly away down the corridor from which Tony had just come.

Back at his hotel, Tony made a decision. He knew his editor would be screaming blue murder over not having heard from him and he knew that his decision would delay that contact for a further twenty-four hours, at least, but he felt he might just as well be hung for a sheep as a lamb. The five hundred miles between Mbeya and Dar es Salaam would take just on twenty-four hours by rail, whereas the plane would have got him there in less than two hours that afternoon. He wasn't quite sure why he made the decision to take the train, other than the knowledge that Johnathan Kapepwe was taking it and that he didn't believe the story Kapepwe had told him.

Tony had travelled on the TanZam Railway once before, a couple of years ago. The 1,200-mile journey from Dar es Salaam to Kapiri Mposhi on the Zambian copper-belt, or vice versa, was more or less obligatory for new correspondents in East Africa. The Chinese-built railway was something of an engineering masterpiece and the fact that, seven years after its completion, it was still being run by the Chinese, always seemed to attract the attention and interest of foreign writers. The drivers and engineers on board the train were all blue-jacketed Chinese, as were the signalmen at virtually every station along its route.

Something like 15,000 Chinese engineers, railway experts, and labourers had been brought to East Africa in the late sixties and early seventies to build the railway at a cost of some 200 million dollars (which China provided entirely, as a loan; the first repayments were not due until 1985). Tony had found the concept of scores of busy Chinese, all dressed in Mao jackets, running a railway in East Africa, so incongruous and fascinating that he had enjoyed his first trip on the TanZam Railway immensely.

He wondered now how to go about getting on the train. Should he go openly and cancel his plane ticket, then go to the station a few miles south of Mbeya and see about the rail ticket? He thought about the little man in the white shirt, who was more than likely sitting once again in the cane chair in the hall outside his door.

Tony's window was open, but covered with mosquito wire. He eased the catches off, lowered the frame into the garden, and stepped out onto the back lawn. He moved quickly past a laundry building and over a low fence into a small, vacant field. Already he was out of sight of the hotel. He followed the line of the fence for a hundred yards and then came to a small dirt path. Shortly the path brought him to a road and he turned in the direction of the town centre. Within a very few minutes he was in the town square, which was moderately busy with stall-holders and merchants going about their business. Tony noticed a few curious stares in his direction. He asked where he could find a taxi and was directed to the bus station, where several of the decrepit cream and brown buses operated by the Tanzanian Railways were standing. Close by there were two equally forlorn-looking taxis.

Tony thought for a moment that he might meet the taxi-driver of the previous evening again, but he was not there, so he stepped into the first one on the rank.

At the TanZam station, which looked for all the world like a marble mausoleum, Tony bought a second-class sleeper ticket to the coast. There had only been three or four berths available, none of them first class. Not that there was much difference, Tony recalled. First-class had four bunks to a cabin, second class had six. Anyway, he thought, at least I've got a ticket.

The train was not due to leave for another two hours, but already the main hall was filling with early Tanzanian passengers waiting for the opportunity to be the first on board. The third-class carriages were not reserved and there you won your seat on a first-come-first-served basis. The brilliant hues of the women's kitengis made the hall a blaze of moving colour and Tony thought for a moment, as he was leaving the hall, what a shame it was that Tanzanian men had adopted, almost universally, the drabness of Western dress. He rejoined his waiting taxi, reasonably sure that he had not attracted undue attention. There had been a few other white people there; a couple of hitch-hikers with their packs and a family with two young children.

Back in the town, Tony returned to his hotel the same way he had left it, entering his bedroom, unnoticed, through the back window. He emerged a few minutes later into the hallway, heading for the front desk.

"Good afternoon," he smiled at the man sitting in the cane chair, who arose, slightly put out by Tony's politeness, and grunted, "Good afternoon."

"My plane leaves at three-thirty," he said to the man at the desk, after paying his bill and in loud enough tones for the cane-chair-man (who now stood in the lobby leafing through travel brochures) to hear. "Could you call me at two-thirty, please? I am going to have a sleep."

Tony walked back to his room and shut the door.

3

Tan Zam

The countryside between Mbeya and Makumbako, over the first hundred miles or so after they left Mbeya, was rolling and open. Only twenty-five years ago, Tony had been told by old Tanganyika hands, it had been literally full of game of all kinds: giraffe, zebra, buffalo, wildebeeste, lion, even elephant and an occasional rhino. Now there were no such animals. A human population which had exploded along the arteries of communication and then spread outwards had either killed them all off or forced them into widespread reserves.

Tony gazed out of the window at the passing landscape and, as the train rounded a long curve, marvelled at the almost too-perfectly sculptured blue-metal bed of stones for the track and the concrete rain channels running off to the side. He tried for a while to calculate how many concrete sleepers there would be in 1,200 miles of rail track.

He had attempted conversation with the four other passengers in his compartment, but had not had much success. There were two young men who could have been brothers, he wasn't sure, who were going, for the first time, to Dar es Salaam in search of jobs. The small, quiet man in his forties who sat opposite Tony next to the window was also on his way to the capital, but he was going to see his father, who was apparently very ill. Then there was a tall, rather sombre character who had said nothing to Tony in response to his few polite words of greeting and attempted conversation. He wasn't sure if it was because he couldn't speak English, or because he just didn't want to talk.

33

Tony stood up and left the compartment to walk along the train corridor. He edged past a group of young Africans who had spilled out from their own compartment and were standing in the corridor drinking beer. He thought that perhaps he would make his way to the dining car, which was for both first- and second-class passengers, and then move through the train to look for Johnathan Kapepwe.

The actual dining car was not operating when he walked into it, but there was a small bar at one end from behind which an African in a brown shirt daubed with patriotic Tanzanian slogans served coffee and tea. A vast improvement, Tony thought, on the last time, when all he could find to eat or drink on the train was a baggage car full of loaves of white bread and bottles of Coca-Cola.

He finished his coffee slowly, listening to the conversation of two men sitting at the other end of the short bar. One was obviously a Zambian and the other a Tanzanian. They both spoke English, which had become the only really universal language of all of Eastern, Central, and Southern Africa. They were apparently both connected with the Zambian copper mines, because their conversation revolved around world copper prices, the problems landlocked Zambia faced in getting her vast reserves of copper to the coast, and the shipping bottlenecks in the harbour of Dar es Salaam, once the copper got there.

Tony thought at one stage that he should join in the conversation. His paper's financial editor had been pressing him for two months for a couple of articles on the Zambian economy. He had kept putting it off, firstly because straight economics stories were not really his cup of tea, and secondly because, with his private life falling apart, he found he could only work on things that were totally demanding.

He realised, rather absently, that he had not thought about Carol or Michael or any of the depressing aspects of his life for at least twenty-four hours.

His mind switched again to the hijacked plane. Why hadn't there been anything on the news? He had listened again to the local news on his small radio before slipping out to catch the train and was puzzled that there was still no mention of the hijacked plane. Even with a state-controlled broadcasting organisation, it must be incredibly difficult to keep something like a hijacked jet quiet, if it landed at Dar es Salaam . . . *if* it landed at Dar es Salaam . . . If only I could listen to the BBC, he thought, and made a mental note to get himself a short-wave radio when he returned to Nairobi. The only thing he could be sure about the hijacked plane was that it had left Mbeya. There might be more of the story back in Mbeya. There probably is, he thought, but I could spend days there and get nowhere.

He moved along the swaying car and into the first-class carriage, stopping briefly to relieve himself in what he called the "footprint and pie-dish" toilet: a porcelain hole in the floor, with two porcelain footprints on either side. It was the standard Chinese and South-East Asian toilet which, Tony noted from the brass plaque in front of his face as he straddled the pie-dish, was Made in Shanghai.

Tony had been given to understand that there was one first-class and two second-class carriages on the train, but he had no idea where Johnathan Kapepwe might be. He started in the first-class carriage. He saw the young white couple with their two children in one compartment as he walked along the corridor. He smiled at them, but kept walking. He wanted to find Kapepwe—what for, he really wasn't sure.

Johnathan Kapepwe was in the last compartment. Alone, although there seemed to be luggage in the compartment for more than one person. He was sitting by the window with a collapsible table set up in front of him. It was covered with sheets of notepaper on which he had been writing. He was looking out of the window as Tony simultaneously knocked and slid open the door to the compartment.

"Hello there," Tony said with a smile as he entered.

"What . . . " Kapepwe couldn't have been more surprised. He first went quickly to stand up, then sat down to shuffle his papers together, then, taking control of the situation, proceeded more slowly to put them into a pile and slip them into a folder. He turned back to Tony, who was still standing in the doorway, and said with thinly disguised annoyance, "I thought you said you were taking the plane."

"I was. But I changed my mind. I thought it would be much more relaxing to travel by train. Air travel has become so frenetic."

Kapepwe looked at him silently.

"Actually," Tony said, "I had forgotten that the TanZam ran through to Dar on Mondays and when you mentioned it, I decided to switch."

Kapepwe returned to his papers and slipped the folder into a small black briefcase.

"Mind if I sit down?"

"As you please."

"Look, if I'm interrupting your work . . . " Tony said.

"No, no, It's all right," Kapepwe muttered. "I was just finishing."

"So how long will you be in Tanzania?"

"Just a couple of days. I have completed my research."

"And then? Back to London?"

Kapepwe paused, looked at Tony for a moment, then out of the train window. "No," he said. "No, I'm actually going to Zimbabwe for a few days."

"Where? Salisbury?"

"Yes, but a couple of other places as well."

"More articles?"

"Yes."

"Things seem in a bit of a mess down there right now."

Kapepwe bristled. "They're better off than they were under Ian Smith or the British."

"I'm sure they are," Tony said. "I was just thinking about the struggle between Muzerewa and Nkomo. I mean they've been at it for ages and I gather it's really slowing any progress in the country right down."

"They will sort it out," Kapepwe said. "And without any outside help, thank you."

Touchy bastard, Tony thought. "I was simply speaking as an interested observer," he said.

"Well, as an observer, you should be aware that there *has* been progress in Zimbabwe; real progress towards a revolutionary society.

The country has to shake off all the old practices and attitudes left over from the colonial days."

"Like freedom of the press and an independent judiciary, you mean?"

"Listen, Bartlett, if you wish to reduce this conversation to the bantering of puerile slogans . . ."

"Not at all," Tony said. "I only wanted to say that I was concerned about the direction that Bishop Muzerewa and his government are being forced to take. It seems that in order to hang onto political power in this part of the world, it's necessary for any leader to become more and more autocratic, which may be good in the sense that it provides firm government, but also leads to less and less freedom, freedom which you say is so important to black Rhodesians—sorry, Zimbabweans—now that they are rid of the Smith régime."

"How long have you been in Africa now?" Kapepwe spoke slowly and looked into Tony's eyes.

"Three years . . . almost."

"And what do you think you've gained? I mean, do you think you know any more about Africans, about their needs and aspirations, than you did before you came?" Kapepwe's voice had a sharp edge to it. "Do you really think you understand anything about us?" He turned and looked out of the window. "Hah!" he laughed derisively.

"Look, I may not have the right colour skin for Africa, or for you," Tony felt his temper rising, "but I bloody well know what's right and what's wrong in a place, whether it's run by people who are black, white, or brindle, and I don't give a damn who they are, I'll say it . . ."

"How would you know?" Kapepwe said bitterly, "sitting in your comfortable club in Nairobi, talking with whites, mixing with whites. How would you ever know what a black man thinks? Do you ever mix with real black people; the workers, the farmers?"

Tony felt the whole situation deteriorating rapidly. He was being put in a position of explaining and justifying himself and saw how clichéd and futile it would sound for him to say, "Some of my best friends . . ."

37

"Look, I didn't come here to get into a fight. I'm sorry I interrupted your work. I'll leave you to it."

With that, he got up and left, closing the door behind him. Had he turned back at that moment, he would have seen Johnathan Kapepwe leaning back in his seat and laughing silently to himself.

"We came to Africa to work in Zaire on a contract," the Englishman said. "But the whole thing fell through."

Tony had stopped on the way back along the carriage, to talk to the young family he had seen earlier. He did it on the spur of the moment to force his temper down; to be calm and polite.

"Yes, it was a combined thing with French, American, and Japanese money. A new copper mine. Put two hundred million dollars into it and then just scrapped the whole scheme."

"Two hundred million? What for? I mean, why did they stop?"

"Well, the original estimates were to get the whole thing producing with about a $350 million investment, but by the time they'd spent $200 million, they could see that the final cost before they reached production would be closer to $800 million, so they just decided it was uneconomic and that was that!"

"And you, what happened to you?"

"Well, there were two thousand foreigners there . . . Europeans. They gave us all three months' salary and our air-fares home. We're just getting there the slow way. We've come across through Zambia and once we get to Dar es Salaam, we're taking a ship up through the Canal."

"Three months leave!"

Tony's anger was gone. Maybe it was the thought of three months leave on full pay and what he could do with it. He stayed and chatted for a while with the Johnsons (that was their name) and then returned to his seat, two carriages back and, despite the noise made by the young men in the next compartment who were still drinking heavily, he began to doze off with his head resting against the window pane. He glanced at his watch. A quarter to five. He would have felt considerably better had he known that Martin Crowther of the *Express* had just arrived at Mbeya airport and, like Tony, was drawing blanks everywhere he turned.

When Tony awoke it was dark. The soft night-light in the train cabin barely lit the faces of his four companions. The two brothers were awake and speaking quietly to each other. The other two sat immovable and immutable. They could have been awake or asleep or dead. It was hard to tell.

Tony remained where he was for a while, letting his thoughts collect themselves. He still felt irritated with himself for allowing the conversation with Kapepwe to fall apart the way it had. He had discovered nothing about the real reason for Kapepwe's visit to southern Tanzania or about the hijacked plane. He made up his mind to have a second attempt.

Kapepwe was still alone when Tony returned to his compartment, although this time he was reading. Tony recognised the blue and white cover as it was slammed shut and placed on the folding table. He had a copy on his own bookshelves. *Ché Guevara on Guerilla Warfare.*

"Good stuff that," he said as he walked in. "Really knew what he was talking about."

Kapepwe stared at Tony malevolently. He said nothing, but Tony felt he was about to tell him to get out.

"Look, I just came to say I'm sorry. I really didn't mean to blow up like that."

Kapepwe continued looking at Tony, but still remained silent.

"It was just that you touched a nerve there before. I mean . . . sitting around in clubs is not my cup of tea. I think I've made a genuine effort to understand some of the problems of Africa . . . "

A look of mild puzzlement passed over Kapepwe's face and Tony noticed a flicker of a smile. He knew he was laying himself open and that Kapepwe would think him naïve, but he felt it was worth it, if they could get down to talking again.

"I don't know if you've ever read any of my stuff," Tony went on, "but if you have . . . "

"I have," Kapepwe said, without a hint of what he thought one way or the other.

"Well then, surely you'd have seen that, on many occasions, I've gone to some lengths to put the African viewpoint. I mean, during the Rhodesian independence war and the second round of talks in Geneva . . . "

"Yes, yes, I know. You don't have to labour the point." Kapepwe sighed and looked ahead.

"Do you mind if I sit down?" Tony asked again.

"I really don't know if all this serves any purpose," Kapepwe muttered. "We don't have that much to talk about."

"Well," Tony said, "you're the only person I know on this train and that, surely, is some excuse for us to talk to each other." I should be a bloody diplomat instead of journalist, he said to himself as he sat down.

"That's probably all we have in common," Kapepwe said, more to himself than to Tony, "the fact that we're both on this train together."

"We're both interested in South Africa," Tony offered.

Kapepwe turned to look at Tony directly. "South Africa! What interest have you got in South Africa? All you're interested in is what happens to the whites when we take over."

Tony fought the temptation to snap back. He smiled and leant against the green leather of the cushioned seat.

"You know that's not true," he said. "I've got no damn axes to grind in South Africa. It's simply that I've been there a few times and found it such a beautiful country that it would be a shame . . . "

"Shame! Shame?? Jesus Christ. He talks about shame, when the whole history of the whites' treatment of blacks in South Africa has been one of shame." Kapepwe forced a smile and spoke with bitter sarcasm, "Oh my dear, wouldn't it be a terrible shame if that beeeautiful country was spoilt by all those awful, dirty blacks taking over. I mean, really! They can't even read!" His voice became more harsh, "They don't wash, they burn their own furniture for firewood, and they even . . . " Kapepwe was almost shouting now, "they even shit in the bath!"

He slumped back into his seat, his mouth firmly set and his eyes closed.

Tony knew that he had almost lost it again and that what he had been saying had sounded trite.

"Listen," he said slowly, "I'm sorry. That seems to be all I get to say to you . . . sorry. But you're so bloody touchy. I mean, would it make you happier if I said it wasn't a beautiful country? I know it *is* an ugly place as far as human relations are concerned, but you don't give anyone a chance to finish. I know there are a hell of a lot of whites there who deserve to go under, but there are also a hell of a lot of good ones too, and all I wanted to say was that I just hope that at some stage they can do something together with blacks in South Africa, instead of being constantly against each other as they are now."

Kapepwe listened blankly to Tony and then said quietly, without looking at him, "I hope your writing about South Africa, or Azania, I should say, because that's what it will be before very long, is better than what you've been saying just now, because it's nothing but armchair liberal crap!"

"And what are you doing about it?" Tony thought, what the hell. I can only take so much from this joker. "All you do is sit back in London, talking on the BBC, writing articles for the *Statesman* and the *Guardian,* getting nice, fat fees for it all . . . and living in style in Chelsea. Hah! Why aren't you down in South Africa doing something about it, if you feel so strongly. Why don't you put your money where your mouth is and get with the bloody guerillas, instead of just talking about it on the BBC?"

Kapepwe was calm, surprisingly calm, Tony thought, considering the vehemence of Tony's abuse.

"You will see, Bartlett, you will see."

"Hah! Oh yes. I will see. I see now. I see you trotting around here in Tanzania at their expense, writing all sorts of hot-cock about the Ujamaa villages and about how the military régime here is doing a grand job for the people. You go back to London and do a snow-job on it and feed it to all those so-called armchair liberals you despise." Tony paused. Kapepwe was looking at him with calm patience. Tony found it disturbing, but went on . . . "Or were you here specifically for the hijack? Were you in Mbeya just for that? For the capture of those white South Africans on board and for the offloading of that . . . " he paused a second and put emphasis on the words, " . . . special cargo?"

41

Kapepwe's face underwent a dramatic change.

"Don't be ridiculous," he said. "The fact that four black South Africans hijack an airliner . . . "

"How do you know there were four of them?" Tony said quickly.

For the first time, Kapepwe looked slightly flustered.

"I . . . you told me this morning," he said.

"I didn't say there were four of them," Tony said. "I only said they were black."

Kapepwe looked away again. "Then it must have been Colonel Samere from army headquarters."

"When did you see him?"

"Just after I saw you."

"That's interesting. I was told that he had gone to Njombe for the day. It seems that . . . "

Tony was interrupted by the door sliding open. He turned and the look of surprise on his face was only bettered by that exhibited on the man at the door, Colonel Samere.

There was an awkward silence of a few seconds, broken eventually by the colonel.

"Good evening, Johnathan. Hello, Mr. . . . er, Mr. . . . "

"Bartlett," said Tony.

"Ah, yes," said the colonel. "I'm sorry to interrupt."

"It's perfectly all right." Tony stood up. "We were just talking about you."

"Oh?"

"Yes. Johnathan was saying that he had been talking to you this morning. I also came to see you this morning, but was told that you had gone to Njombe for the day."

"That is strange. I was in the building for most of the morning. Whoever gave you that information must have been misinformed."

"Yes," Tony said. "Something of a communication problem. But never mind, you're here now. Why don't you sit down and join us?"

"Look, Bartlett," Kapepwe said, standing up, "if you . . . "

"I'm sorry," Colonel Samere interrupted. "There are one or two things which Mr. Kapepwe and I want to discuss." He motioned towards the door. "Johnathan," he said. Then, turning back to

Tony as Kapepwe moved past him and out of the door. "I'm sorry, Mr. . . . er . . . Bartlett. Perhaps tomorrow."

Tony followed them out of the door. They turned right and moved off towards the next carriage. He turned left and went back towards his own compartment.

The porter had been along the carriages to let down the bunks and made up the beds. They were in three tiers on each side of the cabin. The bottom four had been taken up by his four travelling companions, two of whom were asleep. The other two were reading by the dim light of the small bedside lamps. One of the young brothers was reading an English comic book, while the sombre, non-speaking man read a Swahili book.

Tony stood in the semi-darkness for a moment, trying to decide whether or not to climb up into one of the two empty bunks. It was only 9.30. Too early, he thought. I'll just have a nightcap. He turned and left the cabin again. He passed the compartment belonging to the boozing youths and noted that they were still drinking—at least three of four of them were. The other two were slouched asleep by the windows. Those awake looked as though they too would soon be either asleep or passed out.

Tony made his way back to the restaurant car. He sat at the small bar again and the man with the coloured shirt grudgingly put down his cigarette and got up off a stool to serve Tony a beer and one of the pre-packaged cheese sandwiches that were sitting along the back shelf.

There were a few other people sitting, eating, at tables further along the car, and one man in a dark shirt, who sat gazing into a glass of whisky at the other end of the bar. He glanced briefly at Tony through unfriendly eyes and then back into his glass.

The train rumbled on through the night. There was absolutely nothing to see through the windows. The sky was covered with a heavy layer of clouds and the countryside that rushed past was as black as pitch.

What's bloody Samere doing on this train? Tony kept asking himself as he drank his beer straight from the bottle. The glass placed in front of him by the man behind the counter looked as if it would be better left unused.

And Kapepwe. If he's running around just looking at Ujamaa villages, then I'm a monkey's uncle. But then, he thought, if they did have anything to do with the plane, what are they going to Dar es Salaam by train for? They surely could have flown? Tony smiled at the thought of Kapepwe's face when he was caught out over the number of hijackers. But if they are involved, Tony reasoned, Kapepwe will have told Samere that I know about the passengers and the cargo being taken off. I wonder how that will affect him?

He finished his beer and sandwiches and another thought struck him. Where did the two of them go when they left Kapepwe's compartment. He had thought that there was only one first-class carriage and that there was nothing beyond it but the guards' van. Tony got up and left the bar to walk in the direction of Kapepwe's compartment again.

He passed through the connecting link between the two carriages. As he entered the first-class car, the muffled rumbling of the train's motion suddenly became louder. The carriage door at the side was open and latched back against the wall. The clickety-clack, clickety-clack of wheels on rails came sharply up to him and he felt the cooling breeze. Perhaps the guard left it open to cool the carriage down.

He continued on his way down the corridor, which was empty. Doors to the separate compartments were closed and the wooden shutters drawn down. At the end of the carriage he found Kapepwe's cabin door open, but the compartment empty and in darkness. Tony stepped back from the door and moved along towards the far end of the first-class carriage. The connecting link was there, but the doorway to the guards' van was closed. It carried a sign in Swahili and in English saying: "NO ADMITTANCE."

Tony stood, swaying back and forth in the narrow tunnel, the iron connecting plates beneath his feet shifting awkwardly with the different movements of the two carriages. He put his hand on the door handle and tried it. It was locked. Suddenly Tony felt as if he were alone. Completely alone on an empty train, travelling through the night out into space. The sound from the rails was quite soporific; hypnotic.

44

The train was not travelling fast, about thirty-five to forty miles an hour. It had remained steadfastly at that speed the whole time. Something about the track not being able to take higher speeds. He stood for a moment, undecided as to what to do next. Then he heard voices from behind the door and on an impulse, he knocked. Now there was silence from behind the door. He knocked again.

The door was opened abruptly and two Chinese men dressed in blue jackets confronted Tony. Tony was a little taken aback. He had seen several Chinese technicians at Mbeya when the train had left and there had been one or two at every station at which the train had stopped along the way. But the porters, waiters, and cleaning staff on the rest of the train were Tanzanians. The two men looked at Tony impassively and then the one standing in front spoke a few words in Mandarin. Tony didn't understand, but simply replied in English, "Colonel Samere. I wish to see Colonel Samere. Is he here please?"

Whether or not they understood his request Tony never knew. The man at the rear shouted at him and the door slammed shut in his face. He heard a lock of some sort click home.

Tony turned and began to walk slowly back down the corridor of the first-class carriage. What are Kapepwe and Samere doing in that bloody guards' van? he thought. He came to the end of the carriage and felt the breeze from the open door again. I wonder what the hell is going on back there? He stepped towards the open door to look out. Grasping the vertical railings on either side of the doorway and leaning outwards, he peered back into the night towards the last carriage.

But the train was rounding a bend in the wrong direction and only the other end of the carriage in which he was standing was visible. He would have to wait until the track began to turn in the other direction. They were passing through a deep cutting and jagged rock walls rose on both sides. The sound from the tracks was deafening—*clickety-clack, clickety-clack.*

Looking to the front, he saw the lights of the other carriages come into view as the train rumbled around another bend in the line, this time in the right direction. Tony turned back to look at the rear of the train again and saw to his amazement, first one, then two, then three carriages come into view.

"Jesus!" Tony said out loud.

Before the guards' van there were two extra carriages. Lights showed from all the windows of the next carriage down, the one he had tried to enter, but the one after that was in total darkness except for one window. Tony looked down at the edge of the track rushing past in the darkness, trying to sort out his thoughts.

At that instant, without any warning, he felt a gigantic push in the small of his back driving him outwards from the open door. The force of the thrust wrenched his left hand loose from the railing. His right hand held, though, and he swung violently out into space, pivoting on that one hand.

Before the instantaneous, heart-leaping terror of the moment had gone and while he was still in the automatic act of bringing his left hand back to try to grasp the railing again, he became aware of hands grabbing at the fingers of his right hand, trying to pry them loose from the rail. A dark figure crouched in the doorway.

Tony's left hand found a grip, just below his right, and the attacker let go of Tony's right hand to try to shift the left again. But Tony now held on like a vice in the certain knowledge that his life depended on it. He scrambled desperately to find a footing for his wildly swinging feet. The man in the doorway stood up and aimed a kick at Tony's hands. Tony screamed in pain as a heel crunched into the fingers of his left hand, which he released involuntarily from the bar again. But his feet had found the steps beneath the doorway. He pulled himself quickly upright, just as another kick was being aimed at his right hand. He shifted it and the foot connected only with the railing.

Tony's head was about level with the knees of the attacker, who now directed a kick at his face. Tony threw himself to one side and grasped the railing on the opposite side of the door, so that the kick caught him in the left shoulder. He was now standing on the steps, facing his assailant, but with both his arms spread wide, to hang onto the railings, he was helpless. The figure moved in closer to Tony and, for the first time, he saw his face. It was the man who had been sitting at the bar gazing into his whisky.

All this had taken place within a matter of seconds and Tony had reacted almost entirely on instinct. Now the man drew his leg back for a vicious kick at Tony's chest. Tony moved his body quickly to the right, dropped his left hand loose from the railing, and caught the attacker's leg under his arm. At the same instant he swung himself outwards from the train, pulling on the leg, forcing the man to lose his balance and to slide forwards. Tony loosed his grip on the leg, grasped the man by the shirt, and, without thinking of anything but his own survival, pulled him violently towards and past him, out of the train. There was a terrible tangle of bodies in mid-air for a moment and a shocking crunch, as a signal post swept by the carriage door and connected with the head of Tony Bartlett's attacker, who fell, tumbling onto the track.

Tony himself was swung hard against the edge of the carriage, his legs once again swinging loose. But for the second time his right hand held onto the railing. He clambered slowly back into the carriage doorway and lay panting and drenched with cold perspiration on the floor.

His mind was racing in a turmoil of fear and apprehension. After only a moment on the floor, he staggered to his feet in case another attack might be launched on him. But the train rumbled on with the same, steady motion as though nothing had happened. Tony glanced around the corner and down the corridor. It was still empty. Suddenly, the door from the dining car opened and he saw a Tanzanian man and woman coming through the connecting passage, laughing and talking to each other. He forced himself to try to look relaxed. He smiled and said, "Good evening," as they passed by. He peered around the corner and watched them enter a compartment, still laughing and talking, about halfway along the carriage.

What to do now? Tony felt completely vulnerable. If his assailant had been a lone psychopath who wanted to kill him just because he was white, or for any other reason, Tony would have felt much better. But he was convinced that the attempt on his life was connected to his conversations with Kapepwe and Samere and that he would remain a target, even though the first attacker was gone. If he returned to stay in his cabin, they would get him. He was sure of it. He wanted to hide.

Tony Bartlett was a good journalist. He had followed some pretty tough stories through to the end. He had also been in some pretty close scrapes in Vietnam and Bangla Desh, but nothing quite so nasty as a deliberate attempt to kill him had ever happened before. He didn't like it. He was scared. I could disappear off this train and not a soul would know I'd ever been on it, he said to himself. Then he recalled the English family with whom he'd spent twenty minutes or so talking, earlier in the day. Except for them, he thought. They might say they remembered seeing me. Maybe I should go and see them now.

Tony looked once more down the corridor. Still deserted. Then, quickly, he moved along to the Johnsons' cabin and knocked softly.

There was no sound. He knocked again, looking quickly to both left and right in case someone else came.

"Who is it?" he heard a sleepy voice say.

"It's me, Tony Bartlett," he whispered. "I was talking to you earlier today. Let me in quickly."

There was a shuffling noise and a child's voice saying, "Who is it, Daddy?" and the door slid open.

Tony said, with another quick look up and down the corridor, "I'm sorry, can I come in?" he moved past the Englishman without waiting for an answer and slid the door closed again.

"Look, what's going on?" Johnson said. The children, who were on the top bunks, had both sat up and his wife turned over, as though still in a dream, and said urgently, "Andrew, Andrew?"

"I'm sorry," Tony kept repeating.

"It's all right, dear," Johnson reassured his wife. "It's just that chap we were speaking to this afternoon. Now what the devil is this all about?" he said, turning to Tony.

"Someone has just tried to kill me," Tony said.

"Great Scott, you can't be serious!"

"He tried to push me out of the train. Just now! Just a few minutes ago." Tony's face was completely drained of colour. It was the first thing Andrew Johnson noticed when he turned on the main cabin light. Tony turned quickly to look at the door and the windows as he did so. The sliding wooden shutters were drawn across the door and windows facing the corridor, so no light would show, but he moved to the main windows to draw the blinds down to their fullest extent. He slid the safety latch across the door. Not that it would really do much good, he thought; the guard has a key which can turn it.

The children, a boy and a girl who were about nine and ten years old, were sitting bolt upright in their bunks, their eyes wide with amazement.

"They're still after me," Tony said. "Can I stay here for a while?"

"Of course," Johnson replied, looking towards the door. "But who are 'they'?"

Tony sat down on Johnson's bunk and began to tell them the story.

"And what happened to him?" Johnson asked, when Tony had finished speaking.

"I don't know," Tony replied. "As I said, we were struggling and one minute he was there, the next he was gone. It was so dark, I didn't even see where he fell." Tony couldn't bring himself to mention the signal post. The thought made him shudder involuntarily.

"Look, if I were you," Johnson said, "I'd get right out of it. I wouldn't like to mess with the army or the police in this part of the world, that's for certain. It's all very well being a hero, but there's no sense in being a dead hero. You'd better stay here for the night."

Tony thought about his travelling bag, his camera, and typewriter, which were all back in his cabin and decided to leave them there. All his important papers and money were with him. Ever since he'd had his passport stolen during his early years in South-East Asia, Tony had, whenever on an assignment, always worn a nylon security belt around his waist and under his shirt, in which he carried his passport, health certificates, travellers cheques, a couple of international credit cards, and a few U.S. $100 dollar bills. He slept with it on and only took it off in the shower. It had come in handy on more than one occasion when his baggage had been rifled or stolen.

"You can sleep in my bed," Andrew Johnson said to Tony. "I'll squeeze in with Meg."

"No, no." Tony said. "Look, it may sound silly, but I'll sleep

49

on the floor, here, under your bunk." There was a gap of about twelve inches between the bottom of the bunk and the floor, into which a couple of the Johnsons' cases had been pushed.

"Don't be ridiculous," Johnson said. "That's not necessary. I don't mind . . ."

"No, it's not that," Tony cut him short. "You see, they'll probably think I've been pushed off the train and that I've taken their man with me. They've no way of knowing, but when he doesn't come back, they're bound to start checking. They could walk in here without knocking and I wouldn't have time to move."

Johnson agreed, but Tony thought he detected a slight indication that he considered Tony was being a little melodramatic. Tony didn't care. As long as he didn't get caught, he didn't mind what Andrew Johnson thought. But Johnson must have taken Tony's suggestion reasonably seriously, because, as they settled down, with Tony sliding underneath the bottom bunk, he heard Johnson warning the two children that if anyone came to the door in the middle of the night they were not to say a word; to remain absolutely silent.

They didn't have long to wait before Tony's assessment was proved correct. None of them had gone back to sleep, although the lights had been switched off and they had lain in their respective beds in silence. Voices were heard in the corridor; muffled voices speaking in Swahili.

Several men were knocking on the cabin doors and opening them. The Johnsons' compartment was second from the end of the carriage, at the opposite end to Kapepwe's, so it was only a matter of a minute or so after the voices had first been heard that there was a knock on the door, a key fitted into the outside socket for the latch, and the door slid open.

"What the hell are you doing?" Andrew Johnson shouted angrily, swinging out of his bunk.

"Excuse me, sir. We must check the lights," a large, dark man said as he took a step into the room and switched on the lights. "There is a short-circuit somewhere in this carriage. Last month we had a fire. We must be careful."

"Good God, can't it wait until the morning?" Johnson said.

Tony could see, from under the seat, that two more men were standing in the corridor outside, but could not make out any more than their feet.

"I am sorry to wake you," the big man said, "but it could be dangerous. Thank you." He retired from the room and closed the door. Everybody remained quiet while the next compartment was checked and then, as they moved further up the corridor, Tony whispered, "Who was with him?"

"There was another Tanzanian and a Chinese standing in the corridor," Johnson replied.

"Did the black man have a beard?"

"No."

"Or a moustache?" He thought perhaps it could have been Colonel Samere.

"No."

There was some desultory, whispered conversation, before they once again attempted to sleep. Tony was not looking forward to what was likely to be a long, uncomfortable night. It was only just after 11.30 P.M.

After a while, however, the regular motion of the train and the lack of any further noise or interruption allowed them to drift off to sleep. But Tony's sleep was troubled and uneasy. He dreamt that he was in the last seat of the little open carriage on the Big Dipper—a roller coaster in some bizarre amusement park. All of the other passengers in the carriage had gruesome and distorted faces; an eye bulging here, a missing nose, a huge, pointed head, slack lips.

As the vehicle moved off to climb the steep tracks, they all turned to look and point at Tony. He felt trapped and alone and frightened. He turned away, thinking that perhaps he could escape by jumping off the back of the roller coaster while it was still climbing slowly, but behind him he saw that another carriage was following closely. This one was full of Chinese men in blue jackets and Tanzanian Army men in camouflage uniforms, all holding automatic rifles which they raised and pointed at Tony as he made a move to get out of his seat. He sat down again to wait for the stomach-churning dive down the first big dip in the railway.

51

As they dropped down the almost-vertical track, the deformed people in his own carriage all began laughing and climbing back over the seats towards him. In terror Tony stood up, noticing only at the last instant a low crossbeam in the wooden framework structure of the track. It struck him on the head, knocking him backwards onto the track in front of the oncoming second vehicle. But the track disappeared and Tony tumbled over and over into a black void.

He awoke suddenly with a start. He realised that the train had jolted and that they were stopped. He shifted his position on the hard floor and looked at the luminous dial on his watch: 2.10 A.M.

There were voices outside the carriage. Then more jolting and it became apparent that carriages were being disconnected. They had stopped at plenty of other small stations along the line, but this was different.

Tony wondered if the others were awake. "Andrew," he whispered.

"Yes."

"What's going on?"

"I'm not sure. I was just wondering myself. It woke me too."

Tony slid out from under the bunk and crouched at the window. The window had been half-open all the time, because of the need for ventilation as there was no air conditioning. Just the blinds were drawn. Tony began to slide one of the blinds upwards along its tracks.

"Oh do be careful, Tony," Meg Johnson said, sitting up in bed.

"Yes, for God's sake don't let anyone see you," her husband added.

But Tony didn't slide the blind up more than a couple of inches at first. Then, when he was sure there was no-one near the carriage who could see him, he slid the blind slowly higher. The compartment was in total darkness, so it was relatively easy to look out without being seen. Sticking his head out for a better look was another matter. If there were other people further down towards the front of the train, who were looking back in this direction, they might easily notice a head appearing from a window. So Tony slowly edged his head out. Then, after ascertaining as well as he could

52

that there was no-one standing in doorways or looking out of windows further down the train, he turned to the left to look at what he wanted to see.

A group of men were standing talking as a shunting engine slowly pushed the guards' van back towards the train. The two carriages which had earlier separated the guards van from the first-class carriage were now gone. About two hundred yards back on a siding, Tony could see them silhouetted in the glare of the headlights of several cars and trucks. There seemed to be a large number of people moving around them. He glanced quickly back towards the front of the train and out to the side. As far as he could see, there was absolutely no other sign of life. No structures or buildings. This was not a village or town. There appeared to be only flat, open fields; savannah grasslands, stretching off to a distant line of hills which shone ghostly blue under one part of the night sky that was cloudless.

"They've taken the other two carriages off," Tony said, pulling the curtain down. "I wonder where the hell we are. It doesn't seem like a station here."

"I'll go and look out the other side," Andrew offered. "But you better hop back under the seat, in case anyone comes."

Andrew Johnson surveyed the scene from the other side of the train and found it equally empty.

"There's a small hut towards the front of the train, and what looks like a water tower, but that's all," he said when he stepped back inside.

"I feel like a damn idiot," Tony said, crawling out from under the seat again, "doing this all the time."

"This is too ridiculous for words," he went on, sitting down on the bunk next to Johnson. "Why on earth would they drop these two carriages off here, in the middle of nowhere?"

For a few moments Tony had considered slipping off the train himself and following through to see just what the story of the two carriages was all about. But, he told himself, he'd look a bit of a fool if they were only left for another train to pick up, say in anticipation of heavy traffic on a particular section another day. Kapepwe and Samere would be in Dar es Salaam and there Tony would be, sitting out on some remote siding in Tanzania, waiting for the next train to come through in three days' time. Good grief!

With the guards' van reconnected, there was no further delay. The train moved off slowly to leave the two carriages sitting in the centre of a great, empty plain. They had spent no more than fifteen minutes at the siding.

Tony resumed his position under the seat, the Johnsons settled down again in their beds, and everyone attempted once more to get some sleep. The two children had slept right through the last interruption.

The morning and the rest of the next day until the train arrived in Dar es Salaam were something of an anti-climax for Tony. He decided, in the calm light of day, to retrieve his travel bag, camera, and typewriter from his compartment—if they were still there. He went with Andrew Johnson and did so without anything untoward happening. The man in the coloured shirt behind the bar in the restaurant car gave him an odd stare, it seemed, but nothing more. At his cabin, he was informed by one of the two brothers that a train guard or porter had been looking for him during the night.

He slid his bag, camera, and typewriter out from underneath the seat and said goodbye to the others in his compartment, saying simply that he would be "sitting with friends" for the rest of the trip.

About half an hour later, a uniformed train guard knocked on the Johnson's door and asked for tickets. When Tony produced a second-class ticket, the guard informed him that, as this was a first-class compartment, he would have to return to his own carriage.

"But he is our friend," Andrew Johnson protested. "He is just visiting us. We want him to stay here."

"He has not paid a first-class fare," the guard said. "He will have to return to his own carriage."

Tony pulled out fifty shillings. "Look, I don't mind paying the extra fare now, if that's all right, so that I can stay with my friends and talk to them." He pressed the money into the guard's hand. "Please see if that would be all right. If the extra fare is any more than that, please let me know."

The man was slightly lost for words for a moment, but looked down into his hand at the money, put it in his pocket, and said that he would check.

Five minutes later he was back to inform Tony that it would be all right for him to travel the rest of the way with the Johnsons, but that it would cost another fifty shillings.

Tony knew that the extra fare would not have been as much as that, but he paid the bribe willingly in the hope that the guard would say no more about it. And that seemed to be what happened. The guard had obviously pocketed the money and that was the end of it.

During the morning, Andrew Johnson walked to the end of the carriage and reported to Tony that there was no-one in Johnathan Kapepwe's compartment. It was quite empty; no bags, or indeed any sign that it had been occupied at all.

There were no further incidents. The train pulled in to the Tan-Zam terminal in Dar es Salaam and Tony disembarked with the Johnsons without seeing a sign of either Johnathan Kapepwe or Colonel Samere. Tony waited to see as many of the passengers as possible leave the train, but they did not appear. It was almost as if they had never been on the train at all.

"But where in God's name have you been?" Peregrine Childers yelled down the telephone, when Tony finally got through to London from the Reuters office in Dar es Salaam.

"It's all right, it's all right," he assured his editor. "I've got it all typed up and the girl will be putting it onto the printer here in a few minutes. You'll be able to read it all."

"Oh Jesus Christ, Bartlett! I've been looking all over for you. Why the hell didn't you phone? And where's the bloody plane?"

"Couldn't and don't know."

"What do you mean?"

"I couldn't phone, because they wouldn't put me through from Mbeya, and I don't know where the plane is. Nobody does. It's just gone into smoke."

"Don't be bloody ridiculous. Planes that size don't disappear."

"This one has."

55

Tony had been relieved to find out that the plane hadn't come to Dar es Salaam, but puzzled to discover that it hadn't gone anywhere else either. Well, anywhere that anyone knew, anyway. He found he was slightly relieved that it hadn't gone somewhere else. It meant that he wasn't going to be professionally embarrassed, as he thought he might. On the contrary, as it turned out, he knew more about the plane and what had happened to it and its contents, both human and otherwise, than anyone else in his line of business . . . precious little though that knowledge may have seemed.

Tony had checked the map and tried to figure out where the train would have been at two o'clock in the morning when they had stopped to disengage the two carriages, but his research seemed only to add to the mystery. The train would have been somewhere between the villages of Mgeta and Kidodi, but there was more than eighty miles of empty veld between them.

When Tony had finished explaining his movements of the past forty-eight hours, his editor had said grumpily, "Okay, okay. I'll get the story off the printer here. We'll make something of it, I suppose. But you'll have to get yourself down to Johannesburg now. That's where the story is developing."

Tony was taken aback. "But . . . but what about the plane? Here? I mean, don't you want me to keep following it up here?"

"Of course I do," Childers snapped, "but we can't do everything, and we've had word from Johannesburg that it's more than just a simple hijack. There's some political background to it that could be dynamite."

"What about Mulgrave?" Tony said. "Can't he do it?"

"He's down in Cape Town on a naval story at the Simonstown base, and what with the Americans shouting in the UN about what the Russian Navy's doing in the Mozambique Channel, we can't afford to pull him off it."

Typical, Tony thought; you've got one story half-finished and they push you off onto a different one. It was the same story, really, he knew that, but he felt he was being hassled.

"You know it's almost impossible to get into South Africa by air from this part of the world. I'll have to either go back to Europe and fly in direct, or try to get in through Mauritius."

"Well go to bloody Mauritius then," Childers said.

"Look, why don't you wait until you read my story from here? There might be something I . . ."

"Anthony," Childers interrupted him. Tony knew that whenever his editor called him Anthony, he was getting a little hot under the collar. "Anthony, I have told you that we want you in South Africa as fast as you can get there. Please do not make things difficult for me."

"Oh yeah," Tony said, "as fast as I can get there. You don't know what's involved."

"That's what we pay you for, Anthony." Childers said with a facetious edge to his voice.

Tony quite liked the little sod most of the time, but other times he hated him. "All right," he said. "What's this political side to the hijack story? Where did you get that? Have you printed anything on it?"

"No, we haven't got enough to go on. I can't tell you over the phone where we got it from, but, if you can get more on it, it will really stir things up in South Africa."

"As if they aren't already stirred up," Tony said. "Well, what have you got?"

"It's to do with the Herstigte Nasionale Party . . . the radical right wingers. They apparently have something to do with the hijack . . . well, not the actual hijack, but the plane. What we've got is very vague, but the HNP is up to something big. Either total power in South Africa or something else. But in some obscure way this hijack is connected with it. And what we would like you to do, Anthony," Childers' voice changed to soft and falsely felicitous tones, "that is, if you have the time . . . is to find out all about it."

Bastard, thought Tony.

4

Milton's Tower

It was Milton Molefe's twenty-first birthday on March 13, but during the whole of that day he had not thought about it once. His mother and father, who were only a few miles away, thought of Milton on several occasions, wondering and worrying about where he was. Milton hadn't seen his parents on that day, nor on any other day during the previous three years. And even now, when he was physically nearer to them than he had been at any stage during those three years, he didn't think about them. He had other things on his mind. He was lying, with five other young men, in the darkness and mud deep in a storm-water tunnel on the western outskirts of Johannesburg, waiting for the night to come.

They had been lying there since early morning, having been dropped off two at a time, at intervals of roughly half an hour, by three trucks carrying building materials to a construction site nearby. The Bantu workers in the yard who had seen at least two of the men slipping between a stack of timber and a large pile of concrete blocks to slither down the grassy verge of the storm-water channel said not a word. They were only too well aware of the consequences, not only for themselves but for their family, of breaking silence in situations like this.

The two white foremen, who had arrived at 7.00 AM to open the gates to the construction site, relieve the night-watchman, and supervise proceedings until the site engineer arrived at 9.00 AM, were too busy talking, drinking coffee, or doing other things to notice anything unusual, on this particular morning, about the workmen who came with the first three truckloads of materials. On each occasion, as the men slipped off the back of the truck, slung packs over their shoulders, and then carried what looked like a wooden tool box between them to the storm-water drain, the white foremen were either in their small office-hut or occupied elsewhere on the site.

Milton Molefe had been one of the first two men to enter the drain at shortly after seven o'clock that morning. Inside the concrete pipe, which was only four feet in diameter, the men had to crouch low or crawl into the darkness, using a flashlight to see their way. Less than thirty yards into the tunnel, there was a slight bend. Once around the turn in the pipe, the two stopped, set down the wooden box, and opened it. By the light of their torches, they extracted from it a Russian-made AK-47 rifle with a folding stock and a PPS-43 submachine gun. Milton, who was the leader of the expedition, took the PPS-43 and four extra magazines, each loaded with thirty-five rounds of ammunition. He shoved the magazines into slots in a black vest he also took out from the box.

Nelson Mifunwe, his nineteen-year-old companion, also took out two extra thirty-round magazines for his AK-47 and slipped them into a similar vest, which he put on. The two men then shoved the box further to the rear, glanced again around the corner towards the opening of the tunnel, and settled down to wait for the arrival of their four accomplices.

Nelson was nervous and kept whispering to Milton as they waited, asking what time the others were supposed to get there. Did he think they would make it? Who had chosen this tunnel as their hiding place? Could they get out any other way?

Milton was calm and impassive. If he felt any nervousness, he showed no signs of it. This was his seventeenth mission. He had raided farmhouses, blown up railway bridges and trains, destroyed power lines, launched a rocket attack on a petrol dump, and ambushed a South African Army patrol. He had killed a number of people in the past twelve months; most of them from a distance as a result of explosions or fires which he and his group had caused, but some at close range and in cold blood.

If Milton had any reason to be nervous at all, it would perhaps be that his seventeenth mission was his first in the big city, Johannesburg. His home town. All the rest had been in the northern and eastern Transvaal; Louis Trichardt, Pietersburg, Lydenburg. The nearest he had come to Johannesburg was Witbank, some ninety miles to the east, where six weeks earlier, he and two others had put out of action a large electricity substation which channelled power from the Arnot and Hendrina stations, further east, through ESCOM's national grid to the industries and mines of Johannesburg and the Rand. It had been a daring and successful raid and had earned Milton considerable kudos within the organisation for which he now regularly laid his life on the line.

Milton was a section leader in the 4th (Leopard) Company of the 15th Battalion (Northern Command) of the Azanian Peoples Revolutionary Army (APRA). He was only now, three years after he had left home, beginning to fulfill some of the ambitions he had had at that time. True, he had seen plenty of action in the past twelve months, but before that he had spent two frustrating years devoted, almost continually, to training. There had been one or two occasions in late 1978 when they had been thrown, green, into a rebel attack in Rhodesia, just before the white government collapsed there; but looking back on those incidents, he didn't count them. For one thing they were in another country, and for another, they weren't really in any danger.

Their training officer at the camp, across the border in Botswana, knowing that the white régime in Rhodesia was about to crumble, had asked if ten of them could participate in an already-planned raid on a rail bulk storage centre at Nyamandhlovu, just to the north of Bulawayo, to "taste blood, before it is too late," as he put it.

Four whites were machine-gunned in the attack, although Milton never got close enough to see that happen. The only blood he saw was his own, when he stepped on a broken bottle which sliced right through his sandal and cut his foot open. Tracker dogs had followed the trail of Milton's bloody foot for miles through the bush on the way back to Botswana, but the guerilla group was not caught.

After Rhodesia collapsed and became Zimbabwe, a large number of South African revolutionaries shifted their bases of operations from Botswana and Mozambique into Zimbabwe, because of the better facilities available and easier communications. New guerilla training camps were established and Milton, who came across from Botswana with one of the groups, spent considerable time in three of the Zimbabwean camps. His first real chance came in late 1980, when he was given the opportunity to cross the border into the northern Transvaal for a brief but important raid on the small town of Messina.

When Milton had left home, in 1978, it was not long after his eighteenth birthday. He had told his parents that he was going to become a guerilla and to fight for the freedom of his country. He had taken the train to Mafeking (there were fewer restrictions on travel then than now) and crossed the border into Botswana at night. When he left, there had been a violent argument with his father and tears from his mother, but his departure was not unexpected.

Ever since the first riots in Soweto, in June 1976, Milton had been moving in that direction. He was sixteen at the time and had been amongst the thousands of schoolchildren who had gone on strike and rioted in protest against the white government's decision to force the introduction of Afrikaans as a compulsory equal second language, with English, in the Soweto schools. The riots were so violent and extensive that the government had backed down on the issue, but it had been like opening Pandora's box. The tough police and army measures used in handling the crisis sparked off deep resentment throughout the country and the rioting had spread.

Milton was introduced for the first time to the revolutionary element in the big, sprawling African township of Soweto. The secret meetings, in defiance of the whites, the planning of riots and demonstrations, the danger and excitement and, as Milton saw it, the righteousness of the cause, all drew him deeper and deeper into the movement.

He was arrested on two occasions, but only as one demonstrator amongst hundreds of others and not as a plotter or instigator. On the first occasion, he had fought violently against the white police-men who had grabbed him and had bitten off half the ear of one of the men. But he had been clubbed unconscious with a rubber truncheon and thrown, with a split head, into the paddy wagon. In the cells he had been questioned and had had two ribs broken by the man whose ear he had bitten. He had been released only because the huge number of people arrested in that and preceding riots had swamped the system and there was no way for the courts to process them or for the jails to hold them.

But Milton learnt fast. On the second occasion he was arrested in similar circumstances, he played it very passively once the police had hold of him and was released within twenty-four hours, without a scratch.

He joined an underground cell of the outlawed African National Congress, but soon left to join a Marxist-Leninist group because he found the ANC too moderate. Their concept of non-violent pro-test lacked the appeal of the pure revolutionary ideology of the Marxist-Leninists. Milton read avidly, more so than he had ever done at school. But his reading was almost all devoted to revolution-ary theory and to urban guerilla tactics.

He worked in a succession of jobs during the day, as a labourer, a messenger boy in the city, and a packer in a warehouse, but his nights were given over completely to clandestine meetings and to the concept of total revolution. He became more and more estranged from his family and was involved continually in arguments with his father, who was a uniformed chauffeur for a diamond-mining company executive. His mother, who worked as a cook for the same family and lived most of the time in the large, company-provided house in the exclusive suburb of Sandton, begged her son to sever his attachments with the rebel groups. But Milton was committed.

His decision to leave home and to join the guerilla forces in Botswana came in late 1977 after he had met and listened, at a cell meeting, to an exiled black South African revolutionary called Johnathan Kapepwe who had secretly returned to South Africa.

Kapepwe's visit was not long after the death in prison of the black student leader, Steve Biko. Biko, the police claimed, died after going on a self-imposed hunger strike for seven days. But the post-mortem, which family doctors were allowed to attend following an international outcry, revealed that the young man had suffered brain damage as a result of a blow or several blows to the head. His body also showed signs of considerable bruising.

Biko's death was the twentieth reported case of a black detainee dying while in the custody of South African security officials. It aroused protests from around the world, and his funeral was attended, much to the embarrassment of the South African government, by ambassadors and diplomats from a host of Western countries, including the United States and Britain.

It also aroused white-hot anger in the hearts of millions of black South Africans, and Milton had participated in several violent demonstrations in Soweto and Johannesburg over what was regarded as the brutal murder of Steve Biko. Kapepwe's arrival in Soweto came in the midst of these demonstrations. He supported them, and gave encouragement; but he also delivered a different message.

"You may think you know enough about how to fight the white oppressors," Kapepwe had told the assembled group, of which Milton was a member, and not one of whom was older than twenty-three. "You may have a burning hatred for the whites over Steve Biko's death and a passionate resentment for past wrongs. You may have courage and determination. But these things are not enough. You will never win out against the sophisticated weapons and machinery which the whites can bring to bear upon you. First and foremost they have organisation. They have power, money, and materials. Individually, or in small groups . . . you have nothing. But collectively, we have the power to crush them!"

Milton listened with a degree of awe to Kapepwe, because some of his reputation had preceded him to the secret meeting in that darkened Soweto house. He had been told of Kapepwe's escape from South Africa in 1974. The danger he faced by returning like this gave him a special aura for the assembled young men.

"To have to be patient is a terrible thing when you want freedom *now* for our people, when you want to change things . . . but I am telling you that you must have patience and that you must

63

approach this struggle, not in senseless rage and fury, but with cold determination and planning, with infinite care and preparation. And the single most important thing in preparation is training. You must be trained in the art of sabotage, ambush, living off the land, and in the arts of killing and of terror."

Kapepwe then went on to tell the group of the guerilla training camps that had been established in the northern parts of Botswana and in Mozambique. "At this stage," he said, "all of their efforts are directed against the illegal white régime in Zimbabwe, but soon that will have collapsed and they will be turned to help us here in Azania."

He urged as many of them as possible to leave their homes and to join the guerillas across the border. "It is only with this training, with this expert knowledge of explosives and of sophisticated weapons, that you will properly be able to fulfill the task and the vital role that you will have to play here. It may be a year, two years or three, before we can bring the full weight of a civil war down on the heads of the racists, but the revolution has already begun and if you train yourselves properly, when the time comes, you will be among its leaders!"

Now, three and a half years after that secret meeting, Milton felt like a leader. He was well trained in all the arts Kapepwe had mentioned and as prepared as he could possibly be to bring the guerilla war in one dramatic moment to the heartland of white South Africa.

Less than two hundred yards from the storm-water drain in which Milton and his five companions sat waiting on the night of March 13 stood the 700-foot-high concrete radio and television transmission tower of the South African Broadcasting Corporation. Both the SABC tower at Auckland Park, which was also known as Brixton Tower, and the even larger Post Office Tower in the middle of Johannesburg, at Hillbrow, were sky-scraping symbols of white South Africa's dynamic industrial, economic, and material achievements on the Transvaal Highveld, which less than a hundred years previously had been only open grasslands. And if Milton Molefe and his comrades had their way, both those symbols would be lying in ruins by the morning.

64

Milton had desperately wanted to lead the attack on the Post Office Tower in central Johannesburg, mainly because it was taller (just on 900 feet), the tallest building on the African continent in fact, and because it would cause more havoc and destruction when it fell amongst the other high office and apartment buildings in the crowded Hillbrow area. But that honour had gone to Lewis Ngabe, a brilliant young man, who, like Milton, had trained in Botswana, but who had also been through special courses with Chinese experts in southern Tanzania and with the Cubans and Russians in Mozambique. If it had been anyone else but Ngabe, Milton would probably have been angry. But Milton held Ngabe in high esteem. He had been responsible for the recent car explosion in Pretoria which had killed the hated Minister for Justice, Police, and Prisons.

Milton looked at his watch . . . 10.55. It had been a long day; sixteen hours he and Nelson had been in the tunnel, the others only slightly less. Another four hours before they would move. They had all tried to doze, but the cramped and muddy conditions and the tension of waiting allowed them to do so only sporadically. At one stage Nelson shuddered and groaned, then jerked awake from a brief sleep which had brought him only a nightmare.

The calmest member of the group was Arthur Minelane, who at twenty-three was older than any of the other men. He was also the largest; in fact he was a giant. Six feet six, 275 pounds, and enormously strong. He was also a man of few words. During the whole of the period in the tunnel, he spoke not more than five or six. But his silence was not because of any diffidence or fear. He was just not a talker. Nonetheless he was held in great respect by his comrades, if not a little awe. He had a reputation within the movement of great strength and bravery and on the rare occasions that Arthur Minelane did speak, his companions listened. Arthur had lived all of his life in Soweto and had gone, at about the same time as Milton, to join the guerilla training camps in Botswana and later Zimbabwe.

Three of the other men in the tunnel had undergone basic training in Zimbabwe, but Nelson and one other youth, Joseph Mfulu, had not been out of the country to be trained. They had, however, both achieved some distinction within the underground revolutionary army as a result of missions they had been involved in in areas around Johannesburg. Nelson had participated in two daring bank robberies; one at Vereeniging and the other at Pochefstroom, which had swelled the APRA's funds by something like 80,000 Rand. But Nelson had never killed anyone.

Joseph Mfulu, on the other hand, had gained quite a reputation as a killer. He seemed to specialise in police. He had killed three, including a superintendent, only ten days previously at Kroonstad, 130 miles south of Johannesburg. He had walked through a crowd of demonstrators up to a police car in which three white police officers were sitting, talking to a black policeman outside. Ten other black policemen were shouting at the demonstrators not more than a dozen yards away. Joseph had pulled a Russian Makarov 9mm pistol from under his shirt and fired three shots into the car in as many seconds, hitting each of the three white officers in the head and killing them instantly. A fourth shot shattered the black policeman's jaw, but he lived. Joseph had melted back into the crowd and made his escape.

His action, though successful in terrorist terms, was regarded by some in the movement as being hair-raisingly foolish. The fact that he had got away with it was more luck than planning. Joseph had killed other policemen from afar. He was a crack shot and had killed two policemen on separate occasions during civil disturbances using a high-powered Dragenov sniping rifle fitted with telescopic sights.

At 2.55 AM Milton silently slipped his dark green nylon pack over his shoulders and picked up the PPS-43 from where it had been lying on a crumpled groundsheet beside him. In the absolute darkness of the tunnel beyond him, he heard the others doing likewise. He moved to the bend in the pipe and looked towards the opening. There was a faint round glimmer of grey light there, but that was all.

On a whispered command, the men shuffled silently along towards the opening. Once outside, there was a brief pause while their eyes adjusted. After sitting in pitch darkness for so many hours, the night scene was far brighter and clearer to them than to the two black security guards who were at this moment beginning their hourly walk around the inside of the eleven-foot-high cyclone fence which surrounded the gardens, car park, and administrative buildings attached to the tower complex.

It normally took the two patrolling guards six minutes to get from the small guards office, in which two white security guards now sat playing backgammon, to the point on the fence where Milton and his band lay in the grassy ditch on the other side. The area was generally lit by floodlights but the two guards also carried flashlights, which they swung randomly around into the night, sometimes along the fence, sometimes into the shrubs and gardens.

At seven minutes past three the two guards passed by. At eight minutes past, Arthur Minelane slid forward on his stomach to the fence and proceeded to cut an opening in the galvanised wire as close to the bottom of the fence as possible. With every snap of the heavy wire cutters Milton winced, thinking they would be heard, but by eleven minutes past three, a flap had been cut in the fencing and bent outwards and upwards to make an opening large enough to crawl through.

One by one the band slithered through the hole and fanned out quickly across the lawn on the other side, to crouch beside bushes and shrubs. Arthur Minelane, who was last to come through, carefully pulled the fence flap down again behind him and tied it lightly back into place with two pieces of wire. It would certainly not escape any close scrutiny, but unless someone did look closely, the cut wires could easily be missed. There were floodlights in the gardens but the dark shadows of a tall bush fell on about ten or twelve feet of the fence at this point—one of the reasons it had been chosen as the place to gain entry.

A light rain began to fall, but it had practically no effect on the six men whose senses were now so attuned to other things and the prospect of being discovered that most of them didn't notice it. Milton was glad to see it; in fact, he hoped it would get heavier. It would keep people inside. The dancing lights from the guards' flashlights had disappeared several minutes ago and Milton calculated that at this moment they should be re-entering the guard office. It was now 3.16.

He paused for a moment to look up at the giant, monolithic concrete finger towering above him. As if connected by a string, the others, who had seen Milton gaze upwards, also tilted their heads to the sky. A cloud of mist hung about the tower, obscuring the top one-third of it completely. It seemed to Milton that there must be thousands of tons of concrete suspended there.

Moving from shrub to shrub, the group passed along the edge of the open car park to a position from where they could cross the double-lane cement driveway leading from the car park to the front gate, at its narrowest and darkest point. There were, in fact, about a dozen cars in the car park belonging to the few shift and maintenance workers who stayed on in the tower through the night; but no-one was due to come off shift until at least six in the morning.

The main radio and television studios, staff apartments, and the thirty-five storey administration tower block stretched off to their right, but all they could see of them were twinkling lights through the rain. The whole complex covered some thirty-seven acres, and fortunately for Milton and his band, the tower itself was relatively isolated from the main buildings incorporating the production facilities. But the tower was surrounded at the base by a three-storey building to which they had to gain entrance. The main door at the front of the building was right next to the guard's office. There was also a steel door in the rear of the building, which provided access to the service areas of the structure—the air-conditioning plant, garbage collection area, the kitchen for the staff canteen, and an emergency power generator.

Until only a few weeks previously they had had an accomplice working night-shifts inside the building who, it was planned, would open the door for them at a given time. But, under the new curfew laws applied to blacks, only people with special clearances were permitted to work in white areas during the 9.00 PM to 5.00 AM curfew hours, and so he had first been put on day-shifts, then shifted to work at the SABC administrative offices in the city centre. But before he moved, he had provided them with an accurate plan of the building and showed them how access could be gained through

68

a bathroom window on the third floor, the catch of which he had carefully broken.

It was Zak Molako who had volunteered to enter the building through the window. He was the smallest; only five feet two inches tall and weighing only 110 pounds.

Milton had met Zak in one of the camps in Zimbabwe and soon saw that Zak's diminutive size meant nothing to him. He was filled with tremendous energy and could carry weights that would stagger men twice his size. He was like a little ferret; darting quickly here and there, gesturing nervously and glancing everywhere around him when he talked. The greatest ordeal Zak Molako had ever been through was the twenty hours he had just had to spend, sitting still in that tunnel.

Like most of the others, Zak was a killer. But his speciality was the knife. He carried a twelve-inch dagger made from a bayonet. The edges had been hollow-ground and were so sharp he could shave with either side. He had developed the art of knife-fighting as a means of surviving the onslaughts and abuse of bigger and stronger boys at school, and later in the tough life he had had to live in seedy slums and black shanty-towns with his mother and two sisters before they eventually obtained, by false pretences from the Bantu Housing Board, a small house in Soweto. At seventeen, Zak had killed his first person in a dark Johannesburg alley.

He had not really been as ideologically motivated as most of his comrades in the APRA. For much of his life he had been interested only in survival in a tough and hostile world. The concept of revolution to bring about a change in government had not been anything he really considered possible. The whites were the traditional rulers and that was the way things would always be. His life and the degree of power and influence he could exert in his own dark underworld were all that mattered to him.

But he had joined the movement because he had become aware of how quickly its power was growing. It was like the IRA in Ireland or the Palestine Liberation Front in the Middle East; its tentacles were everywhere. Even the underworld could not defy or escape the wrath of the secret army. Better to join them than to be left outside. Zak had always been something of a pragmatist.

But as he participated and listened to the messages of the leaders and learnt of what was happening in the neighbouring countries of Southern Africa, he could foresee the real possibility of white rule coming to an end in South Africa, with black rule in its place. He would be a part of it. The rights and wrongs, the morals of it all, didn't really matter much to Zak. He just wanted to be on the winning side.

In the movement, Zak was always chosen for the "silent" jobs, where someone had to be killed without a sound. And that was what could be needed now. To get from the third-floor lavatory to open the door at the back of the building for Milton and the rest of them, Zak would have to pass an office at which a white technician worked overseeing the operation of several teleprinter machines. It might be possible for Zak to slip by the office without being seen, but if he was seen, it was essential that the man be silenced before any alarm could be given.

Milton's watch now said 3.31. It had been eight minutes since Zak had disappeared through the third-floor window. He would have reached the window sooner, but part of the rainwater downpipe he had started to climb had broken away with a clatter about ten feet above the ground and he had dropped back down. There was an urgent and tense pause of a few minutes in case the noise had been heard, before Zak had climbed on Nelson's shoulders to reach the unbroken piece of pipe still remaining. It had held this time until he reached the window.

Milton and the others had remained in the shrubs on the other side of the driveway watching Zak's progress. Then the waiting began; 3.33. The guards will be doing their rounds again at four, Milton told himself for the fifteenth time. Come on, Zak.

Inside the building, Zak had reached the office on the first floor which he would have to pass to get to the rear door. For some reason known only to the architects responsible for the building, the stairway which brought Zak from the third to the first floor did not continue to the ground floor. It was necessary to walk some twenty feet along the corridor to a wider set of stairs which went down the one extra floor. But all of that twenty feet of corridor could be seen from the office, which had a glass wall and was ablaze with light.

Peering carefully from the stairway, Zak could see the lone white technician sitting at a desk, with his back towards the doorway, leaning back in his chair reading a paper and eating an apple. Zak withdrew the long knife from the leather sheath inside his shirt. But as he did so, he heard a door open down the corridor in the other direction and leapt several steps back up the stairs into the shadows. Another man had walked into the office and now stood talking to the technician.

Zak also carried a Makarov pistol, which he knew he would have to use in an emergency, but he didn't want to. It had no silencer and the noise would bring guards running from everywhere. He slipped down from the stairway while both men's backs were turned and moved along the corridor towards the door through which the second man had come. There was no point continuing in that direction as it would lead him away from the back of the building. If he stays more than five minutes in there I'll have to use the gun, Zak told himself. I'll give him five minutes.

Four and a half minutes later, Zak heard their voices raised slightly in parting. They spoke Afrikaans.

"Okay, Piet, I'll see you tomorrow . . . take it easy."

"Right man. Good luck . . . and say hello to Betty for me."

Zak pressed back into a slight niche in the wall as the white man came out of the office and walked along the short stretch of corridor towards the door. He was about to reach for the handle of the door in front of him, when he paused . . . as if he sensed something.

The pause was enough for Zak. He moved like lightning. The man was large, over two hundred pounds, but he never had a chance. Zak flew from behind and slightly to his right, and with one gigantic thrust, plunged the knife sideways through the man's throat, slicing across the jugular vein in a single motion. There was a dreadful splash of blood against the wall and the door, a gurgled gasp, and the man slumped to the floor.

Zak turned quickly and ran back to the office door. If the technician had heard anything, he would come straight out. But the clatter of the machines had covered any sounds. Five seconds passed and Zak looked cautiously around the door. The technician was back in his chair, opening his paper again. His back was half-turned towards the door, but had Zak tried to sneak along the corridor, he would have had to pass into the man's line of vision. He tiptoed into the office, up behind the technician and, with a gruesome grinding of his own teeth, grabbed the man's hair, yanked his head back, and sliced his throat open. There was no sound, except for that of the chair and the body falling back onto the office floor.

As Zak was moving to leave the blood-spattered room, he turned quickly back from the doorway at the sound of three convulsive kicks the dying man gave against the foot of his desk; after that, there was no more movement.

Zak now threw caution to the winds and ran down the remaining flight of stairs to the ground floor. Turning left at the bottom of the stairs, he ran in the direction he knew the rear door to be, through three closed but unlocked doors, to the bolted, green metal door which now was the key to the success or failure of the mission.

Outside, where Milton and the rest of the men had been waiting, there had been nothing to disturb the peace; absolute silence, except for the rain, which was slowly getting heavier. But Milton and the others had become increasingly worried at the length of time Zak had been inside the building. It was now thirteen minutes to four. If they had to wait until after the guards went by again, the whole thing would be slowed down and the crucial timing of their escape plan would be destroyed. That is, of course, if they were able to escape detection by the guards, now that they were inside the grounds.

The others had also felt the tension. They were shifting their positions and Milton saw that they were continually looking around. Nelson had slipped over beside Milton and whispered, "What's happened to Zak? Why is he taking so long?" Milton had looked at Nelson and wondered whether it was fear he saw in his face.

Eleven minutes to four. Suddenly, the sound of a bolt being slid back behind the metal door, then another, and then the door was slowly pushed open and Zak stepped cautiously out into the rain.

Within thirty seconds all six men were inside the building behind the closed door, standing silently in the pools of water forming around them from their soaked clothes.

Milton led the way. There was nothing to say. Each man knew

exactly what he had to do. Nelson and Joseph were to be the look-outs, while the other four were to place the plastic explosive charges and detonating devices in several strategic places at the base of the tower inside the building. One of the APRA's engineers had studied the plans of the structure provided by the accomplice who had been working inside the tower building. They had sent him back on a number of occasions before he was moved into town, to look for the answers to specific questions such as the width and depth of the pre-stressed concrete beams in three of the basement rooms beneath the tower proper, and details of the service access to the elevator shaft from one of the basement floors.

From all these details, a plan of action had been drawn up that was more like a time and motion study than anything else. The four trained men each knew precisely where to place their explosive charges. Each man carried three twenty-pound blocks of American C-4 plastic explosives and six detonators each. There were two types of detonators to go with each charge; one, a timing device to be set at 5.30 AM, the other, a solid-state, battery-powered electric circuit, which could override the timing device and be set off by remote control with a simple radio signal on a special frequency from a modified walkie-talkie. This could be done from a distance of up to two miles from the tower.

The six men were now all separated, four of them working fever-ishly to complete their tasks of attaching the explosives as soon as possible. The shape of each charge and the way it was placed was important. Each had to be individually shaped for the position it occupied, otherwise the effect might not be sufficient to do the job.

Nelson Mifunwe and Joseph Mfulu were at their assigned lookout posts to stand guard and, if necessary, prevent anyone from ap-proaching the four men laying the charges. Nelson occupied a posi-tion from which he could cover two access corridors to the area where the men were working, while Joseph stood guard close to the front of the building, where he could block the path of either the white or the black night-guards if they decided to move in the direction of the others.

From where Joseph stood, carrying an AK-47 automatic rifle,

he could see the lights of the guards office and hear a low mumble of voices and an occasional laugh. Standing at the end of the corridor by the stairs, dressed all in black, as were the rest of the group, he was almost invisible in the shadows.

At exactly four o'clock he saw the two black guards emerge from the office and walk briefly into the front entrance lobby, then out towards the front gate to begin their hourly check of the grounds surrounding the tower building. They were dressed in bright yellow mackintoshes and hats for the rain. Joseph thought to himself that it would be easy to just walk into that office and blast the two whites before they knew what was happening. But that was not according to plan. He reluctantly stayed where he was.

Milton paused for a second during the process of attaching his second charge to check his watch again: 4.05. In another minute the guards would be passing the point in the fence where they had cut the hole. If they discovered it, the alarm would be raised in no time. After that there would probably be a search of the grounds and then they would probably begin inside the building. In five or ten minutes, Milton thought, they could be facing a situation where they had to fight their way out. He finished attaching the second detonator to the charge and moved quickly down the hallway to another room.

Milton would have relaxed somewhat had he seen the two guards on their four o'clock patrol. Once out of sight of the white guards, they turned a corner of the building and stood, talking quietly, in the shelter of one of the overhanging concrete awnings to avoid the drenching rain. At fourteen minutes past four, the two men stepped back out into the rain and returned to the guard office, a minute later, looking respectably wet.

As they did so, Milton finished attaching the second detonator to his last charge and, picking up his PPS-43, which had been lying to his side, turned his attention to regrouping his men.

Leonard Watsese, the sixth member of the group, had finished first, at twelve minutes past four. Arthur Minelane completed the attachment of the detonators to his final charge at sixteen minutes past. Now they were only waiting for Zak.

Zak's job had been the most difficult and the most potentially dangerous. He had to mine one of the elevator shafts in three places.

It meant pressing the call button for the service lift to get it down to the basement. Once inside, a specially made key had been used to switch off the door mechanism, so that it remained open. Zak had then climbed through the man-hole in the ceiling of the elevator and into the darkened shaft, which rose seven hundred feet above him. Climbing the steel tracks at the side of the shaft he had begun placing his charges in staggered positions on both sides.

Milton had recognised the danger in switching off the power to the elevator so that it stayed in the basement; if someone tried to use it during that period, and found it broken down, it could attract attention. But the mining of the elevator shaft was, according to the engineers, essential to the success of the plan.

With three-quarters of the job complete, Milton wanted to call Nelson and Joseph back from their lookout positions, but he couldn't do so until Zak was ready.

At 4.20 AM, roughly five minutes after the return of the black guards to their office, one of the whites leant back in his chair and said, "That's all, man, I quit. I've already lost five Rand and if I go on like this, I'll lose the lot. You can play with Koos."

The other swept some small change off the table and began to pack up the backgammon board laid out on the table in front of them. "Ach no, man, he's too good. I'd lose it all to him." He put the board into a drawer of a desk to one side. "Where the hell is he, anyway? He's been up with Piet for a bloody half-hour now."

Three minutes later, at 4.23 AM, the man got up from the table. "I think I'll go up and say hello to them."

Zak had emerged from the elevator shaft just one minute earlier, having completed his task. Milton sent Arthur and Leonard off to bring Joseph and Nelson back from their separate lookout posts.

At 4.24 the white guard walked past the position where, not thirty seconds earlier, Joseph had been standing guard. He continued, after rounding a corner in the hallway, towards a stairway leading to the first floor.

By 4.25, Joseph and Nelson had rejoined the others in the basement and were ready to move off towards the steel door at the back of the building.

At precisely that moment, the white guard came upon the macabre scene in the teleprinter room. It took ten seconds for the full horror of the sight to get through to him. He stood riveted in the doorway, watching rolls of teleprinter paper overflowing from the machines, which continued to chatter automatically onto the floor and into the wide, still-spreading pool of blood surrounding the technician's body.

Reeling back, the guard rushed down the stairs, without seeing the body of his friend Koos just twenty-five feet away in the shadows at the other end of the corridor.

"My God, my God," he almost shouted as he ran, "Koos has gone mad!"

He burst into the guard room. "Quickly," he shouted, "Koos has gone crazy. He's killed Piet! He might be going to . . ."

"What the hell are you talking about?" the other white guard said, jumping to his feet.

"Just exactly what I said, man," the first guard shouted back. "Piet is dead. He's cut up something terrible!" He ran to a rack on the wall and pulled down an armalite rifle.

The two black guards stood in the centre of the room speechless. The second white began to pull a revolver from the holster on his side. "But . . . but, how do you . . . ?"

"Look, all I know is that Koos must have cracked—gone berserk, and he could be going to do more. He might even be after us. Jesus Christ, man, it's terrible—fuckin' terrible! Quickly. We've got to get to him."

The others stood immobile, stunned.

"For Christ's sake, come on! Jero," he said, turning to one of the black guards, "you go with Mr. Bouffa. Abraham, you come with me. Leon," turning back to the other white man, "you and Jero take the outside. Koos has his car parked out the back. He may be heading there. Abraham and I will go up to the studio area."

Leon Bouffa and the black guard Jero, wide-eyed with terror, ran out into the rain and around towards the back of the building.

By this stage Milton and his group had all reached the back door, opened it, and were in the process of crossing the driveway to the shrubs in the garden. Nelson and Milton were the last to go through the door. Milton was pulling it closed behind him when, at exactly 4.27, Nelson was challenged as he was crossing the drive.

"Stop!" Leon Bouffa shouted. "Stay where you are!"

Nelson peered blindly through the rain at the disembodied flashlight the black guard was shining on him. He hesitated only a second before swinging his weapon around to fire, but it was one second too long.

The white guard fired three shots in rapid succession from his pistol. At that range, not much more than ten feet, he didn't even have to take aim. The first bullet ripped into Nelson's stomach, the second passed clean through his heart, the third one missed.

Milton, who had seen all this take place within the space of two or three seconds from the darkness by the doorway, now stepped clear of a shrub and, before Nelson had even hit the ground, fired two sharp bursts from his submachine gun. Both Leon Bouffa and the black guard Jero dropped dead on the road, the flashlight clattering to the ground but still shining brightly through the rain.

Milton ran to pick it up. He shone it briefly on Nelson, ascertained that he was dead, then, switching it off, threw it into the bushes. He quickly pulled Nelson by the feet from the road into the garden, where he left him behind a large shrub.

The first guard, Solly Coetzee, who was still on his way to the third floor with the black guard Abraham, heard the shots from outside the building and turned to race back downstairs again.

"Jesus! Jesus!" he kept shouting. "That was an automatic weapon. Leon only had a pistol." He ran back into the guard office, pressed the alarm button, and picked up the telephone.

Milton and the rest of the band were halfway through the hole in the fence at 4.30 AM when the alarm went off and several extra floodlights came on in the car park area. Milton was last through the hole and, for a second, debated whether or not to wire the flap down again. Then he signalled to Arthur Minelane to retie it. He knew that every second counted from now on, but it was imperative that their escape route remain undetected for as long as possible.

By 4.32, Arthur was finished and the five men were heading off along the open part of the deep storm-water drain in the opposite direction to the tunnel in which they had waited through the previous day.

At 4.33, they heard the wail of police sirens in the distance coming towards the broadcasting centre, but they didn't slacken their pace as they ran through the darkness and the rain, sloshing and stumbling in the running water now almost a foot deep in the bottom of the drain.

By 4.42, they had travelled a mile from the tower. Three minutes after that they were underneath a road-bridge, where they stopped, panting for breath. Milton looked at his watch again. Fifteen minutes had passed since the alarm had been set off. He knew that there was no way in which the timing devices on the charges could be let run their full course, until 5.30. By then they would have been discovered. He would have to use the radio transmitter to set them off before that happened. But he couldn't do it too soon, because it might prevent their escape.

The plan called for them to be picked up precisely ten minutes after the night curfew ended at 5.00 AM. At that time a newspaper delivery van, driven by a black man, would not normally be stopped. At five minutes *before* five, however, it might be. It certainly *would* be stopped if the whole area was cordoned off or roadblocked.

If Milton fired the charges now, there would probably be ten minutes of complete confusion and then the roadblocks and police cars would start springing up everywhere. He would have to leave it until as close as possible to the pickup time and just hope that the charges were not discovered.

Ten minutes before the group reached the road-bridge, the first members of the police Flying Squad had arrived at the tower complex. It took two minutes for Solly Coetzee to blurt out what he thought had happened and that the other two guards had gone out but not returned. He told the plain-clothes inspector that because of the automatic weapon he had heard, he had thought it more prudent to wait inside until more reinforcements arrived. The inspector, Paul DuPlessis, looked at Solly strangely for a moment or two, before turning and issuing orders to his men to fan out and proceed carefully around towards the back of the building. Within a minute they found the bodies of Leon Bouffa and the black guard.

78

"He's got a machine carbine," the inspector said, looking at the row of jagged holes across the bodies of both men.

"He . . . he's got a knife too," Solly whispered from the background.

Inspector DuPlessis turned on Solly Coetzee. "Now, who is this man? What did you say his name was?"

"Henkel. Koos Henkel. He's the electronics maintenance man. Always works night-shifts. Always seemed perfectly all right to me . . . something must have snapped . . . Jesus! Jesus!"

"How do you know it was him? Did you see him?"

"No, but he went up to see Piet. I know that. And when I went upstairs, Piet was dead and Koos had gone."

"So where was this Piet killed?"

"Upstairs on the first floor. In the teleprinter room. I'll show you. Oh Jesus, it's terrible . . . awful!"

At 4.40, just as Inspector DuPlessis and his men were being led into the building by Coetzee, three more Flying Squad cars arrived. By 4.42 the inspector and three other constables entered the grisly teleprinter room; less than a minute later, one of the constables found Koos Henkel's body.

"Check everybody in the building," DuPlessis said. "How many are there?" he asked Coetzee.

"Only seven . . . sorry, five, now that . . ."

"Is there a room where I can get everybody together? No, never mind that. Just get everyone into the lobby downstairs." He turned to one of the constables. "Harry, check the outside . . . and be careful. Whoever it is is a nasty character. Take Martin and Otto with you."

Three minutes later, Nelson's body was found in the garden. Inspector DuPlessis stood in the rain again, looking down at Nelson's face which stared, open-eyed, back up at him.

"Blacks! And there's more than one of them," DuPlessis said. "The guards weren't killed with that weapon." He pointed to Nelson's AK-47 which lay near him. "But where are they now?" DuPlessis paused and then spoke slowly, "And more importantly, what were they doing inside the building?"

Suddenly he slammed his fist into the palm of his left hand.

"Good Lord!" Then he began to run towards the building, shouting. "Come on! We haven't a second to lose."

"Do it now," Arthur Minelane urged Milton for the third time since they had stopped underneath the road-bridge. "They'll be searching the place and if they find them, they'll be able to disarm them."

Milton knew Arthur was right. When the attack was first being planned they had intended to fit anti-lift switches to the charges as well, which would have prevented anyone from disarming them— they would have blown up the moment they were touched. But several of the switches had proved faulty, so they had decided not to use them.

"I can't," Milton said. "I've got to leave it as long as possible, otherwise the van won't get through."

"What's more important?" Arthur asked in the dim, dawn light. "The truck getting through, and us getting away . . . or the mission?"

Milton bristled. He felt his position as leader being slightly undermined by Minelane. He looked back through the darkness towards him and felt a surge of resentment. Involuntarily he thought, stupid Tswana. Arthur Minelane's mother was a Tswana. Milton was a Zulu. He held back from saying anything, though. Tribal differences within the secret army were one of the strictest taboos and resulted in heavy punishment; sometimes even the death penalty was imposed.

"I will make the decision," he said, staring back through the gloom in the direction of the tower. He looked down at the radio transmitter in his hands.

In the basement of the tower, DuPlessis stood for a moment staring at the sinister satchel that was taped to the underside of a reinforced concrete beam in one corner. Constable David Botha was the first to find one of Milton's plastic charges at three minutes to five. A bead of sweat broke out on DuPlessis' forehead.

"We just can't afford to wait," he said. Reaching up, he grabbed it and tore it away from the beam, wrenching the detonator wires from it. Nothing happened.

DuPlessis and the others in the room burst into a spontaneous laugh of nervous relief. "Quickly," he said, "there must be more of them. We've got to find them."

At thirty seconds past five o'clock, constable Noel Stander found the second charge, one that had been set by Arthur Minelane. He hesitated a moment in fear at the thought of what the dread package could do, then reached up and pulled it from its position with a triumphant shout.

At one minute past five, Inspector DuPlessis found the third bomb and was reaching for it when he became aware, for an instant, for a tiny fraction of a second, of a total whiteness and an immense pressure, before everything went black as Milton pressed the button on his radio transmitter.

It took roughly thirty seconds for the tower to fall. A long time for anyone who was standing watching it happen. Not that there was anyone associated with the disaster who was able to view it with that degree of detachment. The members of the Johannesburg Police Department's No. 2 Bomb Disposal Squad, who were just arriving, did see it fall and lived to talk about it, which is more than could be said for most of the others in the building. In fact, it was more than three days before they extracted the remains of the two constables who had been working closest to DuPlessis, from under tons of rubble. No trace of Paul DuPlessis was ever found.

When the ten remaining charges had gone off, a section of the tower near the base was blasted into fragments, according to the story told by the police bomb squad, who saw it. The tower had remained upright for a moment, as if suspended by nothing in mid-air, and then dropped straight down like a stake being plunged into the ground. The force of this vertical fall of about ten or fifteen feet had crumpled the rest of the tower in several places and, while the bottom half had fallen in pieces onto the building at the base of the tower, the top half had teetered and fallen to one side.

A huge section of it landed across the tunnel in which the black guerillas had hidden during the previous day, crushing the seven- or eight-foot cover of earth down into the pipe. More of it fell into the construction yard, where they had left the trucks, killing the night-watchman instantly; but by some miracle, the rest of it landed across a plastics factory which was closed for the night, and an empty field.

Milton and the others heard the explosions and for half a minute thought that perhaps the tower had survived the blasts. However, the tremendous thump and shuddering they felt through the ground, almost like an earth tremor, followed some six seconds later by the sound of the main section of the tower crashing to the ground, removed their doubts. It was all they could do to stop themselves from cheering out loud. They slapped each other and laughed silently.

Six minutes later, at 5.08 AM a newspaper delivery van pulled up on the roadway above the bridge. After a few moments there was a low whistle and the group scrambled up from the storm-water drain and into the back of the van. Once inside, they moved through a gap in the piles of newspaper bundles towards the front. There was a sliding plywood doorway across a low, concealed compartment which could just accommodate six men—or five—if they crouched low and crammed in tightly. The door was slid shut behind them and the driver shifted the bundles of newspapers across to cover the compartment. He then piled more on top to complete the job.

At twelve minutes past five, just as the van was driving off, Lewis Ngabe, in the midst of a running battle with police, pressed the button on his radio transmitter to detonate the fifteen charges he and his group had laid in the Post Office Tower in central Johannesburg. Lewis, however, never lived to enjoy the acclaim he would have received from his organisation for this extreme act of terror. Within ten seconds of having pushed the button, while the tower was still falling, he lay sprawled in the gutter in the rain, with half his head gone. A police marksman with an armalite rifle had drawn a bead on Ngabe and fired once. Had he fired ten seconds earlier, the Post Office Tower might still have been standing and more than three hundred residents of Hillbrow still be alive.

By six o'clock in the morning, Milton and his crew were safe in a hideout in Soweto. As Milton leant back against a wall to light up a cigar which had been handed him, it occurred to him

TO SANDTON   TO PRETORIA

BEREA

POST OFFICE
TOWER

AUCKLAND PARK

HILLBROW

SABC (BRIXTON)
TOWER

M1 MOTORWAY

DOORNFONTEIN

RAILWAY
STATION

BREE
TEPPE

PRITCHARD

N

MARKET

COMMISSIONER

CARLTON
CENTRE

RIOT

GUERILLA ATTACKS

JOHANNESBURG
CENTRAL AREA

PRITCHARD ST
RIOT

0   ½   1
MILES

that yesterday he had turned twenty-one and that his parents' house was less than two miles from where he was now. He wasn't sure if they were in the house or in the servants' quarters of the big house in Sandton, but they would just be getting up now, he thought.

5

Riot

"HUNDREDS DIE!"

"SOUTH AFRICA TERROR ATTACKS"

"Johannesburg towers destroyed . . . Dramatic upsurge in guerilla war!"

The Sydney *Sunday Telegraph*'s front page for March 15 was dominated by the story of the Johannesburg bombings and featured a four-column photograph of the havoc created by the collapse of the Post Office Tower in the Hillbrow area. It also carried two small photographs of what the towers had looked like before they were destroyed. The forthcoming Australian elections and a parliamentary confrontation between the prime minister, Andrew Peacock, and the leader of the opposition, Bill Hayden, were relegated to the bottom of the front page.

Tony Bartlett read the Johannesburg story for the second time with a feeling of disbelief. The hostess had brought round the magazines and newspapers shortly after they had left Plaisance Airport. It was today's paper. The South African Airways plane had left Sydney at 7.15 AM that morning with the newspapers hot off the press, so to speak.

It was now five o'clock in the evening—a full thirty-six hours since the two towers had been blasted—and yet Tony had known nothing about it until he opened the paper on board the plane. He cursed himself for not having read a paper or listened to the radio for the two whole days he had been in Mauritius. He could only keep telling himself that it had been great while it lasted;

lazing on the beach with a very attractive French mulatto girl he'd met in the casino on his first night at Trou aux Biches. Tony felt he deserved a little R & R after the traumas of the preceding couple of days. The fact that there had been no flight until this one, and the delay in getting a South African visa from the Trade Commission in Port Louis, had provided him with an ideal excuse to drop out for a brief period.

But now he felt vaguely annoyed with himself. He seemed to be continually arriving on the scenes of big stories just a little too late. He could picture his editor having a mild heart attack in London. He had telegrammed his projected arrival time in Johannesburg, but he knew that would be small consolation. He had missed the main story and the immediate follow-up.

Tony looked around the cabin of the big 747 as it lumbered into a wide turn for its approach to Johannesburg's Jan Smuts airport. It was almost empty; a little old lady sitting up near the front, a couple of businessmen behind him on either side of the aircraft, and a man and a woman three rows in front of him. Perhaps there were more in the other cabins and the first-class section, he didn't know. But for a plane that could carry 350 people, it was deserted. The South African Airline, however, was not worried by the lack of traffic, he'd been told by one of the hostesses, as they were now running five flights a week to South Africa and were filled to capacity on the return run to Australia.

Tony folded the newspaper up, noticing, as he did so, the date on the top of the front page: March 15. Great day to be arriving, he thought, the Ides of March!

On the ground at Jan Smuts, Tony was amazed by the transformation. It was no longer only a civil airport. As the 747 taxied in, he was immediately reminded of Saigon's Tan Son Nhut airport in the early seventies; several sand-bagged bays containing French Mirage and British-built Buccaneer jet fighters lined the runway. Others contained Alouette helicopters. Military vehicles moved on the perimeter of the field and there were a number of camouflaged C-130 Hercules and C-47 transport planes on the tarmac.

As the big jet nosed into its bay at the terminal building and the telescopic walkways were moved out towards the fuselage, Tony saw sand-bagged emplacements at intervals around the outside walls of the terminal and two positions at which heavy machine guns were mounted.

Inside, the health and immigration procedures were the same, but customs seemed tougher and Tony's small bag was subjected to a rigourous search. There were also considerably more soldiers and police in evidence than the last time he had been there. Most of them were carrying weapons of some sort. Tony wondered how much of it was as a result of the tower attacks and how much was now just the normal way of life.

As Tony's taxi, which was driven by a white, left the airport, it had to pass through two checkpoints, one military and one police, before reaching the freeway for the run into Johannesburg. While the driver took the route in through Edenvale and Bedford View to the eastern side of the city, Tony questioned him about the tower explosions.

"Man, it's the first time they've come right into the city like this," he said. "Up until now they've been hitting farms and power lines and things like that, but this sort of thing is very worrying . . . coming right into town like this. And mark you," he waved his finger in the air, "it's not going to get any better . . . not with the commies supplying them with all these weapons and training them."

"The commies?"

"Yes, man. The bloody Russians in Mozambique and Namibia and the bloody Chinks in Botswana and Rhodesia . . . Zimbabwe. What I can't understand is why the Americans or the British don't do something, otherwise the bloody commies will take over here, man."

"You really think it could happen?"

"Ach, I don't know, man. We've got a pretty good army, so they tell me, but what good is it against bastards like these? Look, I have been here all my life. My wife and I were both born in Nelspruit, over near Swaziland. We love this country, man. It's a beautiful place, but last night, for the first time, Hetty, that's the wife, started to talk about leaving . . . for the kiddies more than anything else."

"Where would you go?"

"Anywhere they'd have us, I suppose. Australia, Canada, America—maybe Europe. But we'd lose everything we've got, man. Already it's almost impossible to sell a house or land here. Nobody wants to buy anything."

"Why not stay?"

"What, after they took over?" He looked at Tony incredulously.

Tony smiled inwardly at the thought of how quickly things polarised into "them" and "us"—but then, he thought, it had almost certainly always been that way for this taxi-driver.

"Yes. Things would settle down after a while, surely?"

"Ach, they'd ruin the place, man. And then they'd try to put us down . . . make us into second-class citizens."

Tony glanced out of the window. There seemed to be a normal amount of traffic on the expressway, but again, far more military and police vehicles than he remembered from his previous visit less than twelve months ago. They entered Commissioner Street and drove straight along towards the Carlton Centre, well south of the area in Hillbrow which had been devastated by the falling Post Office Tower. Even if he'd wanted to, there was no way Tony could have approached the disaster area by taxi; some twenty-four city blocks, bounded by Pretoria, Twist, Paul Nel, and Fife Streets, had been completely cordoned off in the Hillbrow and Berea districts and rescue teams had been working non-stop there for two days and a night. Thousands of friends and relatives were being held back by roadblocks and only allowed to pass one way or the other if they could prove they were residents of the enclosed district, or if they were required to identify a body.

Tony's instincts told him he should head straight for the scene, but he forced himself to book into a hotel and phone London first. After all, he was some forty hours late already; another few wouldn't make much difference.

The rest of the city, what Tony saw of it on the run in, was also quite changed. It was now almost eight o'clock at night and there were very few people on the streets. The curfew for blacks came into force in one hour and another curfew for whites was enforced from midnight until dawn.

The increased military presence was obvious in almost every street, in either vehicles, soldiers, or sand-bagged buildings. Tony saw several banks, a government office, and a building owned by a major utility which were sand-bagged. The government office also had barbed wire and two guard posts outside it. He noticed a number of shops in the central district which were boarded up and saw several with smashed windows.

Tony had decided to stay in the Carlton Hotel, the plushest and most expensive in Johannesburg. Last time he'd stayed at the Landrost, opposite the park, but he had chosen the Carlton this time because, according to the taxi-driver, several foreign correspondents from the United States, Britain, and Europe were staying there. Tony always felt twinges of diffidence under circumstances like this and knew, from past experience, that getting in amongst a crowd of other journalists was as good a starting point as anywhere else; a listening post where, if something broke, he would hear of it more quickly than if he were staying elsewhere.

When he booked in, he saw, from the large number of keys hanging at the front desk, that the six hundred-room hotel was only about one-third full. He was given the key to a room on the twenty-second floor.

"I'm sorry, sir," the clerk at the desk said to Tony, "but you'll have to carry your own bag. With the curfew, we have no porters or African staff after eight o'clock."

Tony said he could manage. In his room, he booked a call to London and had a shower.

I wonder what they'll want me to do now, he said to himself, as he sat back in one of the armchairs to wait for the call, drop the hijack thing completely and concentrate on these tower explosions, or keep working on both? Both, if I know Childers!

Tony knew his editor well—too well, he sometimes thought. Their first meeting had been back in 1971, at Khe Sanh, the embattled American airstrip high in the western mountains of Quang Tri Province in South Vietnam, just south of the Demilitarized Zone. The strip was being used as an advance base for air and ground attacks across the Laotian border onto the Ho Chi Minh Trail. The "Laotian Incursion," they had called it. No American troops crossing the

89

border, just the ARVN. The Americans were only giving the air support.

The place seemed to be in perpetual chaos, with Hercules transport planes coming and going continually about every ten minutes, unloading tanks and armoured personnel carriers and troops, then ferrying the wounded back to Quang Tri and Dong Ha on the coast.

The strip, which was surrounded by sand-bagged tents and trenches, would come under rocket or mortar attack at almost any time of the day or night from the surrounding mountains. It wasn't a place that Tony had particularly wanted to spend much time in.

Peregrine Childers had been among three other journalists who had flown in to Khe Sanh with Tony, in a twin-rotored Chinook helicopter which, on the way up, had made a series of hair-raising supply drops of food and ammunition to a string of American firebases straddling the mountainous Route Nine running up to the Laotian border.

At the time, Childers had seemed an "oldie" to Tony. He was thirty-nine and Tony was still in his mid-twenties, twenty-five to be exact. They had been working for opposition newspapers, but somehow became friends. Childers was one of the best-known Asian correspondents, whereas Tony was up and coming. Childers was based in Singapore, Tony in Hong Kong. But over a period of two or three years, their paths continually crossed; the cyclone disaster in the Ganges Delta, the Commonwealth conference in Singapore, the refugee crisis in West Bengal and the Indo-Pakistan War which followed it, and of course, the seemingly never-ending war in Vietnam.

Tony admired Childers tremendously; he looked on him as the complete professional. Naturally, they never gave anything away to each other when they were together and always tried to pick each other's brains, although Childers was a little less obvious about it than Tony and sometimes treated the younger man with ill-concealed condescension.

However, Tony had brought off something of a small scoop by getting into North Vietnam in 1972 and won widespread acclaim

90

for the series of articles he wrote revealing the way of life and attitudes of the North Vietnamese people at that particular stage of the war. Peregrine Childers had been somewhat chastened. It was not until several years later, when Childers had been foreign editor of the *Herald* in London for some eighteen months, that he approached Tony with an offer to join the *Herald* and to go to Africa.

So Tony wasn't the least surprised when Childers now said on the phone, "I think you should keep an eye on both, you know. Look, we can't afford to drop this hijack business, and the tower thing is also too big a story. I did try to get Mulgrave back from Cape Town as soon as it happened, but he's gone out on a South African submarine on some bloody manouevres off the Cape and there was no way we could reach him."

"What do you want on the towers, then?"

"Well, we've had all the factual details, of course; about the size of the damn things, how many tons of rubble and how many killed . . . the ones they know of, that is. But if you could shoot off a couple of thousand words on what it all means; the implications of such a big step-up in terrorist activity, how the authorities are going to cope with it, new restrictions on peoples' lives, and so on, we'll give it a good spread. We could also do with some government reaction from pretty high up—not just to the tower thing specifically, but to the whole concept of terrorism in South Africa, to the loss of overseas business confidence in the country and that sort of thing; how it's affecting their economy and their morale . . . you know."

Tony knew.

"Also the Russian thing. How they feel about the Russians in Namibia and Mozambique . . . and the Cape sea routes . . . "

"I thought that's what Mulgrave was looking into?"

"Yes, I know. But he'll be a couple of days yet, and you don't have to go into great detail on that aspect. It would just be nice to tie it in, that's all."

"All in two thousand words?"

"Well, you know, two and a half maybe . . . see how it goes."
Tony made a face, but didn't say anything. Childers went on, "Oh,

and we could certainly use a separate colour piece on the tower situation, now that I think about it. The position as it is tomorrow . . . a follow-up piece with a couple of interviews with the rescue people, residents, and so on."

"Jesus," Tony said. "You know I can't do a damn thing until I get re-accredited."

"How long will that take?"

"Well, I've got to get a pass from the Ministry of Information and the Interior and also now, I think, from the Defence Ministry. That will all take a bit of time."

"Okay," Childers said. "Just get it moving. If you can get your first piece to us by this time tomorrow evening, we'd have it all editions. If not, well, just as soon as you can."

"And the hijack?" Tony asked.

"Just keep your ears open . . . and hopefully, by the time you've done these other pieces, Mulgrave will be back to take over and you can press on with the hijack."

"Goodbye, Perry," Tony said with exaggerated politeness. "I'll be back in touch." He put down the phone.

In the Clock Bar, just off the lobby of the hotel, Howard Goldman looked up from his Daiquiri, which he had been idly stirring with a swizzle-stick, and recognised Tony Bartlett coming through the door. He shouted across a room full of startled drinkers to attract his attention. Tony joined him and ordered a drink, realising, as he did so, that Goldman had a pretty good start on him.

Howard Goldman was with NBC. Tony had only met him on three or four previous occasions in Eastern Africa and in Lebanon.

"You're a long way south," Tony said. "You're usually based in Beirut, aren't you?"

"Yeah, but we got two crews here now and we're opening a bureau."

"How long have you been here?"

"Christ, we've been lucky. We came in just before the hijack and then, with these towers going . . . " he held his hands out wide. "Holy Jesus, what a story!"

Tony thought Howard Goldman was full of bullshit but he liked him just the same. Of course there was some professional jealousy involved at the moment. "What did you get on it?" he asked.

Goldman drained his glass and waved to the white waiter behind the counter.

"Hell, we got everything! We were at the Post Office Tower twenty-five minutes after it happened. Christ, it was still dark and raining. We were using Frezzy lamps and holding our goddam coats over the camera. We got the bodies of the guerillas . . . all seven of 'em. They got 'em all at the Post Office Tower, you know. The ones at the Brixton Tower got away, all except one. We got them carrying the bodies of people out of apartments, dozens of 'em. It was incredible, screaming and crying . . . terrible. And at the SABC tower, the Brixton tower, today . . . when they dug out those two guys who had their throats cut . . . horrible, wasn't it?"

"I . . . wasn't there," Tony said. "I've only just arrived."

A look of undisguised superiority came over Goldman's face, but then, almost as if against his will, it changed to one of sympathy.

"Hell, that's too bad. Christ, what a story to miss." Then, to make Tony feel better, "But there's plenty of good follow-up stuff in it."

"Do they know who the guerillas were?" Tony asked.

"No, none of them carried any identification on them, except for the one who was shot in the grounds of the SABC tower. He had a piece of paper, a clothing supply chit, or something like that, which mentioned the 'Leopard' Company of the 15th Battalion of the Azanian Peoples Revolutionary Army. The authorities think they are part of the same group which has been active up around Pietermaritzburg and parts of the northern Transvaal and across between the Rand here and the Botswana border."

Tony was amazed at the familiarity Goldman displayed with the geography of the place. He'd only been in the country for a few days and this was his first visit, yet he spoke as if he knew it intimately. Bullshit baffles brains, Tony thought, but at the same time he admitted to himself that he was often guilty of the same tendencies.

"It's all Russian and Chinese equipment they're carrying,"

Goldman said. "The guerillas in Botswana and Zimbabwe get it from the Chinese, and the ones in Mozambique and Namibia are supplied by the Russkies. They've captured all sorts of stuff—rockets, mortars . . . "

"Not from this tower group, though?" Tony said.

"No, from other groups in the northern and eastern Transvaal. But to the west they just hop back across the Botswana border like a flash. There's a regular little Ho Chi Minh Trail running all the way down the other side of the border from Zimbabwe to Lobatse, which just keeps the supplies running all the time. The Defence Department people have a map, we saw it yesterday, which shows those parts of the country that come under guerilla influence and those that are under complete white control—just like it was in Vietnam."

"But surely that's only confined to the border areas?" Tony said. He felt slightly out of touch, as though events had moved a little too quickly and he would have to run to catch up.

"Hell, no. Swaziland and Lesotho—and even the Transkei—are beginning to stand up to Pretoria now. There're no camps there, but they're starting to give shelter to the rebels, although they deny that they're doing it."

Tony found it hard to believe that these three tiny states, which were physically swallowed up in the body of South Africa and economically so dependent on it, would dare oppose the Nationalist government, let alone the defence forces of South Africa. Swaziland and Lesotho perhaps. They had at least been independent members of the United Nations for many years; but the Transkei? Theoretically independent, it was regarded by the outside world as only an aberrant brainchild of apartheid. Give the blacks their separate homeland, the architects of the scheme had said. Tell them it is their independent, sovereign nation, to do with and run as they wish, but leave them so dependent on white industries and business in South Africa, to provide employment for their people, that they'll have to toe the line.

When the territory of the Transkei had been formed in late 1976 and proclaimed an independent nation, not one country in the world

94

accepted it. The United Nations rejected its application for membership as simply a South African ploy aimed at perpetuating racial separation in Southern Africa.

In recent years, however, the Transkei had begun exhibiting independent traits which the white government in Pretoria did not like at all, but because of previous posturings had to sit back and swallow quietly.

But well before that, the Nationalist government had compounded its first error by pressing hastily ahead with the creation of the second "independent" state of Bophuthatswana, in the north-western Transvaal, in 1978. There were other homeland states planned— Kwazulu, Ciskei, Lebowa; nine in all, but it was only after the creation of the first two, when it was too late, that the government seemed to realise it was creating a Frankenstein monster that could be used devastatingly against its own interests.

The tiny enclave of Lesotho, for decades landlocked and isolated from the sea, was now joined to the coast by the Transkei, which met Lesotho's south-eastern border. The two of them combined, Tony thought, now seemed to form a black wedge, pointing at the heart of South Africa; an Achilles heel.

"What about the hijack?" Tony asked. "Get anything good on that?"

Howard Goldman reached down the bar for a tray of peanuts, took a handful, and then offered them to Tony.

"Sure . . . loads. 'Course we didn't get any of the hijackers. They were all inside the plane the whole time it was here. But we got the police chief and the commando group which was going to attack the plane. Great stuff."

"Did anyone find out who the hijackers were?"

"Nope. Just that they were APRA men . . . four of 'em."

"And the passengers?"

"No. Something funny there. No-one seemed to know—or at least they wouldn't say—who the passengers were. It was a chartered flight and there were white passengers on board. I got some high-powered binoculars and saw two of them by the windows."

"How many passengers?"

"That's it. Nobody knows. One of the South African Airways ground staff thinks he saw six whites board the plane, but he's not sure."

"Who was the plane chartered by?"

"Some outfit called Potgeiter Investments, but that's all anybody knows. They're not registered as a company anywhere in South Africa."

"And anywhere else?"

"We're trying to check on that, but it's a pretty difficult job."

"So that's as far as you've got?"

"Yeah. Well, we were following it up and then this goddam tower thing happened and we haven't had a chance to do anything about it since then. Not that there's much you can do here, now that the plane's gone . . . and where the hell it's gone, nobody knows. My guess is that it's crashed into the sea. It was so damn heavy loaded when it took off, it's a wonder it got into the air."

"Oh?" Tony said with interest, remembering the ease with which it had left the runway in Mbeya.

"Yeah. We all thought it was going to crash right here, it took so long on the runway. It only cleared the power lines over the highway by a matter of feet."

"And nobody knows where it was supposed to be going? On the charter, I mean?"

"Well, it was supposed to be going to Europe . . . a non-stop flight to Germany, apparently."

"Can a 707 do it non-stop?"

"Well, I think the normal maximum range is about 6,500 miles, without any additional fuel capacity. Rome and Athens for instance are only about 4,500 . . . if it flew in a direct line. But, of course, these days South African planes can't fly over African countries, so it would have to make some pretty long detours, either to the east or the west. It headed up the east coast, when the hijackers took off, and evidently it landed for a couple of hours at some little place in Tanzania—Mbeya."

"I know," said Tony with a small degree of satisfaction. "I was there."

Tony's accreditation as a visiting correspondent took only a short while to organise the next morning. It was simply a matter of renewing the permit he had been issued on his previous trip. Resident correspondents were issued with annual permits, but visiting journalists were now required to renew their cards monthly.

The Defence Department accreditation was more complicated. With the rapid increase in terrorist activity over the past twelve months, the role and status of the army had increased accordingly, as it was called on more and more to assist in suppressing violence and maintaining order. In some cities and towns, where there had been exceptionally violent and prolonged rioting, the government had imposed martial law for brief periods. In many cases it was now necessary for people like Tony to have Defence Department accreditation, as well as that of the Information Department.

But when he applied, he found that he would have to wait a day or two for the Defence pass to come through, as it was necessary for the application to be sent to Defence headquarters in the capital, Pretoria, some forty miles north of Johannesburg. Tony felt he could probably do without it in Johannesburg, but if he wanted to move around the country at all, to go to another city, he would need it.

From the Department of Information office on Market Street, Tony decided to walk to the scene of the city tower disaster. He walked along Market to Claim Street and then turned to walk up towards Hillbrow and the site of the tragedy. There was much of the normal hustle and bustle in the streets that he remembered from before, but Tony felt—or was it just his imagination?—a very real undercurrent of hostility; a sullen silence. Was it the way the black people in the streets looked at him . . . almost as if he were deformed, or mutilated in some way? There were plenty of other whites in the street, so it wasn't as if his whiteness made him unusual. The hostility, Tony realised, was directed at every white. Suddenly, he felt he wanted to make it clear that he wasn't a South African— perhaps carry a sign, or a flag.

My God, he thought, this place has so much going for it. They've achieved so much in such a short time . . . and yet they've been nothing but a dismal failure in terms of human relations. He remembered his feelings during his first visit, when confronted with the complex workings of the apartheid system. The discrimination in public places, in buses, trains, restaurants, cafés, hotels, banks, and post offices, had at first shocked, then angered him. They said it was merely *separation* of the races; that equal facilities were provided for black and white, but that they were just separate. Of course, he found that this was simply not true. He went into a bank where there was a large, modern area with several tellers to deal with the needs of two or three white customers, while off to the side, one teller was working non-stop to handle about a dozen waiting black customers in a tiny, fenced-off section for non-whites. Toilets, of course, were strictly segregated. He saw this same theme repeated over and over, wherever he went.

Blacks had been permitted, for some time, to buy food in the same supermarkets as whites and even to buy take-away food from a white restaurant (usually from a window or bar opening onto the street); but they could not come in and sit down and eat alongside whites, except at about half a dozen rather expensive restaurants, which had special dispensation to serve non-white customers, as well as white. The trendy restaurant on top of the Carlton Centre was one of them.

But these few desegregated restaurants made little impact on the overall pattern. The general indignity imposed by these restrictions and discriminations had long been accepted by most black South Africans as just part of their way of life; normality.

But what they hated most of all were the pass laws, which, in effect, made them foreigners in their own country. Blacks living in the white areas, which included all the main cities and towns and more than eighty percent of the country, could enjoy no political rights, freedoms, or privileges, and could, at any stage, be sent to a black "homeland" they might never have seen before, because their identity pass stated that it was their ethnic and cultural "homeland." You could, for instance, have a man of Xhosa tribal origin who was born and bred in Johannesburg, worked all his life in the city, but because he ran up against the system, not necessarily in a criminal sense, was sent to live hundreds of miles away in the Transkei or the Ciskei, a place he might never have been to,

98

because he was theoretically a citizen of that particular homeland; it was his ancestral "home."

And then there was the Immorality Act. Sex and marriage between people of different races was banned, and any contravention resulted in heavy fines and jail sentences; usually fines for the white partner and jail for the black. Tony passed a slim and attractive coloured girl. She looked straight through him, as if he didn't exist. That's what it has come to, he thought, the more you separate people legally, the more they come to distrust each other; to look on the other with suspicion. It was as if a glass barrier had been placed between members of the opposite sex of different races—to prevent the horrifying possibility of any "immorality."

He arrived at the first roadblock, showed his pass, and asked directions to the mobile police operations centre which had been established to deal with the disaster.

In the afternoon, Tony took a cab out to see the remains of the Brixton Tower at Auckland Park. There was not a great deal to see except rubble. The Post Office Tower had been far more dramatic, in that it had caused infinitely greater destruction when it fell. But Tony found the story of the attack on the SABC tower, as it was told to him by the superintendent in charge, interesting because of the apparently detailed planning which had gone into it. It had also, in one way, been more of a success than the other; all but one of the guerillas had escaped.

No-one living had seen any of them or knew how many there were. The police had found their escape route and estimated that five others had been involved, but they weren't sure. They figured that the guerillas had spent some time in the storm-water tunnel, but the tower had crushed it and prevented investigators from going more than twenty feet into the pipe and from discovering the weapon boxes that had been left there.

Later in the afternoon, Tony interviewed Colonel Otto Blerk of the South African Police. For the "government reaction from pretty high up" that his editor had asked for, he approached the President's Department, knowing full well that both the President and the Defence Secretary were in Cape Town for the parliamentary session, but he hoped that some other spokesman with reasonable authority would be prepared to talk. He was told that he could speak to Brigadier Christiaan Stander of the Defence Department at ten the next morning in Pretoria and to Mr. Piet Steyn of the Department of Information, an hour later.

Tony wrote the "colour" piece Childers had asked for on the towers and prepared as much of the longer article as he could without the material he hoped to get in Pretoria in the morning. He found that he felt strangely anxious to get rid of the tower story and back onto the hijack.

As he was leaving the Reuters office in the suburb of Parkwood, after sending his first piece off to London, Tony was about to enter the taxi that had been waiting for him when someone ran up from behind and grabbed him by the shoulder. He jumped with fright.

"Tony Bartlett! For Christ's sake. How long have you been here?"

It was Michael Keneally. Tony laughed with relief. "Hello, Mike. Hell, you shouldn't do things like that to me. I've had enough of that to last me a lifetime lately."

"What do you mean?"

"Oh, just some bastard trying to push me off a train in Tanzania."

"What! Didn't you pay your fare?" he said derisively. "How long have you been in Jo'burg?"

"Just since last night."

"And just in time too."

"What for?"

"A party. A big party at our place tomorrow night. You've been there before, haven't you?"

"Er . . . yes."

"Well, it's on tomorrow night for young and old."

"What's it in aid of?" Tony asked. Somehow, he didn't feel in the least like going to a party. "Somebody's birthday?"

"Hell no—it's St. Patrick's Day. I don't know whether it's his birthday or not, but it's a good enough excuse for a party, isn't it?"

"Well, I suppose so," Tony said, "especially for phony Irish bastards like you."

Michael Keneally was the Australian Trade Commissioner in

100

South Africa and in fact, he and Tony were distantly related, very distantly. Tony's wife Carol was a second cousin, once or twice removed, he was never sure, to Michael's wife Jenny.

"I wouldn't have thought anyone would be having parties in Johannesburg right now," Tony said.

"No, by God, it's getting nasty isn't it? Almost as bad as Northern Ireland was under the British," he laughed. Keneally would never let anyone forget his Irish ancestry. He was a third-generation Australian, with not the slightest trace of an Irish accent in his voice, except when he wanted to put it on. "But like oi always says," he lapsed into a heavy Irish brogue, "ye've got ter keep laffin as much as yer bleedin well can, or yer start cryin."

"How many are coming?" Tony asked.

"Oh, about fifty, I suppose. Come early if you can. You know everybody has to be home by midnight these days. About seven, if you like. There's plenty to eat and we've got Oirish whisky and caseloads of Oirish beer and Guinness."

"I thought you were supposed to be pushing Australian beer?"

Keneally's face fell, but he smiled. "Oh there's some of that too, if you really want it."

Tony lifted his foot off the accelerator and the little yellow Volkswagen slowed to the new legal limit of fifty miles per hour. He had already seen one car booked by plain-clothes policemen in an unmarked five-year-old Chevrolet, but during the last part of his drive to Pretoria the needle had crept up again. It was difficult not to travel fast on such perfect highways, but the restrictions now being imposed on speeding and car travel in general were being rigidly enforced. Ever since the Arab countries had stopped selling oil to South Africa, under the system of United Nations sanctions, things had been tight. The country's two huge SASOL plants could produce enough oil from coal to supply all of South Africa's domestic and industrial needs, had times been peaceful. But the government was stockpiling huge reserves for defence purposes, which left a minimum for ordinary domestic use. Gasoline was strictly rationed and everything possible was done to prevent the average motorist from wasting it. When Tony had hired the car, earlier

101

that morning, he had been issued with a number of gasoline coupons. On production of his passport, he was given an extra allocation, as a bona fide international visitor, but it was certainly not sufficient for him to go travelling all around the country.

He passed the brooding Voortrekker Monument off to his left, and within minutes was entering the outskirts of Pretoria. The highway ran straight into the street in which the Defence Department buildings were located, so Tony had no trouble finding it. He glanced at the street sign as he approached the army barracks. Potgeiter Street.

"Potgeiter," Tony said out loud. "Potgeiter Investments . . . who are Potgeiter Investments?"

Tony didn't stay long in Pretoria. He spent three-quarters of an hour with Brigadier Stander and half an hour with Mr. Steyn. At the Defence Department, he learnt, among other things, that within the past four weeks sixteen Russian cargo vessels had berthed and unloaded what was largely military equipment at the port of Maputo in Mozambique and at the small port of Luderitz in Namibia.

"More vessels are on their way, according to our intelligence reports," Brigadier Stander had told Tony. He also hinted that the government was considering the full mobilization of its military forces. Already all members of the army reserves, which included some 250,000 white national servicemen trained over the past ten years, had been placed on the alert and notified that they would be required to do at least twelve weeks military service a year. This had effectively increased the size of South Africa's all-white army by more than fifty thousand in one stroke.

Before Tony left the Defence Department, he picked up his Defence accreditation card.

At the Department of Information, on Church Street, he found the dapper Mr. Piet Steyn far more circumspect when discussing the extent of the threat facing white South Africa.

"Our economy is still strong," he insisted. "True, there was a considerable outflow of capital last year, but we have the resilience to withstand this sort of thing. And in any event, there are now fairly stringent controls on the movement of capital from this country."

"And the general level of business confidence in South Africa?" Tony asked.

"I think most people realise that if there is a decline, it is a passing thing," Mr. Steyn said. "We've had trouble before and we've come through. Once all this has blown over, American and European investors will be coming back. After all, we've got a lot to offer."

I wonder if you really believe it? Tony said to himself. You might be able to fool some people. I wonder if you've fooled yourself?

Tony left the Department of Information and went to the central Registry Office to check on Potgeiter Investments, but, as Howard Goldman had assured him, there was no such organization. He drove out of Pretoria on the eastern motorway which took him through Verwoedburg and Kempton Park down to Jan Smuts airport.

Peter Barbeton was the name that Childers had given him—the contact at the airport who had first informed London of the hijack. Tony located him at the office of South African Airways shortly before he broke for lunch.

He was a large, heavy-set man with a ginger moustache, but he appeared nervous as they sat over a cup of coffee in the airport restaurant. He sat facing the doorway and continually looked at the other customers coming and going from the self-service food bar.

"The problem is," he said, "that there was such an incredible clampdown on the whole affair as soon as it happened, I hardly know much more than I told them in London, right at the start. There were BOSS people everywhere within minutes."

BOSS, the ominous, all-powerful Bureau of State Security, whose original function, Tony remembered, was simply to "detect and identify any threat or potential threat to the Republic of South Africa," but whose brief had now become so broad and all-embracing that its agents could do almost anything (and often did) in order to achieve the aim of detecting and identifying the threat. It was the South African equivalent of the Russian KGB or the American CIA, and its activities were so shrouded in secrecy that the organisation attracted an aura of mystery and fear.

Since its founding in the late 1960s, BOSS had gradually gathered unto itself more and more power. Now, no organization in South Africa could defy BOSS—not even the police or the army, both of which were well infiltrated with BOSS agents. BOSS was responsible only to the President.

"Why do you think they were here so quickly?"

"The only reason I can think of," Barbeton said quietly, "is that they were involved in the flight in the first place."

"You mean in the charter?"

"Well, yes."

"Who is this Potgeiter Investments?"

"I haven't a clue . . . and probably the only thing I can tell you, that I haven't told anyone else, are two names I saw on a copy of the charter agreement before it was taken away."

"Taken away?"

"Yes, the police asked me to get the papers from the safe shortly after the hijack happened and we were just going through them on the counter, when two BOSS agents came and took them away. This was all while the plane was still on the ground here."

"What did the police say about it?"

"There was nothing they could say, or do. BOSS's actions are beyond questioning."

"And what were the names?"

"Well, these were the two signatories for Potgeiter Investments. Incidentally, the full name is Hendrik N. Potgeiter Investments."

"And was his one of the signatures?"

"No. I had difficulty at first reading them, because they were upside down, but then I saw they were printed at the side. One was Glaser—J. Glaser—and the other was Stefan Welz."

"Do the names mean anything to you?" Tony asked.

"Absolutely nothing," Barbeton replied. "Never heard of them."

Tony wrote the names into a small notebook. "Has any mention of these names come out in the press?"

"No. Nobody else knew of them."

"And do you think this Hendrik Potgeiter and the other two were on the plane?"

"Haven't a clue. Nobody knows who was actually on the plane. There were one or two BOSS people here, at least I think they

104

were from BOSS, who were almost beside themselves with rage over the whole thing. It was so frantic."

They spoke softly while Barbeton filled in some of the details of what happened in the hours between the first news of the hijack and the plane's take-off.

"And the cargo?" Tony asked at one point. "Nobody knows what the cargo was?"

"No. It was loaded up with wooden boxes. They evidently started before dawn, when it was still dark, and it wasn't until the crew and passengers boarded the plane that they discovered the hijackers. The trucks that carried the cargo—there were three of them, painted with signs saying 'UNITY CARRIERS'—were gone by the time it happened and no-one's seen them since. And of course, there is no such thing as Unity Carriers."

"What do *you* think it's all about?" Tony said.

"Well, I don't know. It's been suggested that the government, or BOSS, were trying to get a few people out of the country without it being known, or maybe they'd brought them in without anyone knowing and were taking them out again. The other possibility is that it was something BOSS was doing that the government didn't know about . . . And then there's the cargo. I just don't know."

A tall man in a grey suit, who had walked in a few minutes earlier and picked up some sandwiches and coffee from the self-service bar, now came to sit at another table close by Tony and Peter Barbeton. Barbeton glanced in the man's direction and then back to Tony, raising his eyebrows slightly.

Tony looked at his watch, stood up, and said quite loudly, "I must be off. Hell, it's been great seeing you again, Pete. We must have a few drinks together before I go." They shook hands and Tony left the restaurant.

From Jan Smuts, Tony followed the same highway back towards Johannesburg as he'd come in on in the taxi two days previously. A police car, with its siren blaring, roared past Tony in the direction of the city. Tony looked at his speedo and slowed at the same time, realising he had been doing almost sixty-five. But the police car had gone by him as if he'd been travelling backwards. Obviously they weren't interested in issuing speeding tickets at this stage.

105

As Tony approached the city centre again, he found his way to Commissioner Street, but was hoping to be able to turn left shortly to get onto Main Street a couple of blocks to the south. With the complicated system of one-way streets in the city centre, he thought it would be easier to reach the car park at the Carlton Centre that way. In the distance he heard other police sirens and the intermittent "wah, wah, wah" of the riot squad siren. Almost simultaneously two white policemen appeared in front of him, directing traffic to the right, away from where he wanted to go. He glanced to the left as he, and the rest of the traffic, turned off Commissioner Street and saw at least three police cars and a riot van about one hundred yards down the street. There were police milling around and he could hear the sound of chanting.

More sirens and two riot vans roared towards and past him. There were two cars in front of him. One of them stopped while the nervous occupant asked another policeman which direction to go. The officer pointed along the street in the direction they were already travelling and made signs to the driver to hurry. Tony followed. Two blocks further on there was another group of policemen directing traffic even further to the right and towards the Siemert Street thruway, which would start taking Tony in exactly the opposite direction to where he wanted to go.

"What's happening?" he shouted to one of the policemen as he stopped briefly at the turn.

"Just a small disturbance, sir. Keep going. You'll be all right."

"But I want to get to the Carlton Centre. It's back that way."

"I'm afraid you'll have to go all the way up to Doornfontein, sir. Then cut across to Rissik Street and come around from the other side."

Tony cursed but took off, following the policeman's directions. He was undecided about whether to stop the car and try to find out what the trouble was, or to keep going.

He looked to the left and saw that the street was clear, but kept on driving straight ahead, following the line of diverted traffic. He noticed that there were no pedestrians in sight, even though it was only early afternoon.

After passing a couple of empty streets, he decided to turn off

106

to the left to try to avoid the long, round-about route the policeman had suggested. He made a couple of turns, heading generally back in the direction of the hotel, until he found himself in Pritchard Street which ran the whole width of the city from east to west. But this was the seedy end of Pritchard Street. Most of the shops in this part of town catered for blacks only and it was rare to see a white person on the street around this area in the best of times.

Tony could hear sirens to the south, where the first policeman had directed him, but now he heard more from the west, from the direction he was heading. He could also hear chanting. The street was empty. There were cars by the side of the road, but no-one was in them.

Suddenly, about two hundred yards in front of him, a huge crowd of people swarmed out of another street and across the road, shouting and singing and waving banners. Tony braked the car and turned sharp left down a small side street. There was only sufficient room for one car to pass along it, between two rows of parked cars, and Tony felt a twinge of fear. He drove into President Street, even though the signs said it was a one-way street in the other direction, but then stopped dead with a squeal of brakes at the sight of another rampaging mob in front of him. A car had been overturned and set alight and the mob was dancing around it, screaming.

At the sight of Tony's car, several men shouted, pointed, and began running towards Tony. Tony slammed the car into reverse, but even as he moved to go back the other way, he saw that the road was blocked behind him by two other overturned cars and more people. He heard the sirens only vaguely now. His mind was turning to jelly as terror began to take over. He swung the nose of the car quickly back up toward the narrow side street down which he had just driven, but it was already blocked by a surging crowd of blacks who came running towards him, shouting and waving sticks in the air.

Tony felt his whole body go cold. The windows were wound up and he rapidly checked that the doors were locked, although he knew that neither would be of any use. He reached urgently into his pocket for his wallet. Within seconds the car was surrounded by screaming, chanting youths, hurling abuse at Tony. The car was rocked as they jumped on it and trampled all over the roof and the bonnet. The fury and venom in the faces of the rioters as they struck at the car was like the primitive rage of a cornered beast which at last turns on its tormentor and attacks him ferociously. One youth lay on the front bonnet of the car and, pressing his face close to the window, screamed insanely at the top of his lungs, his mouth wide open and covered with flecks of spittle.

Tony held his press card up and shouted back as loud as he could. "Press!" It had no effect whatever.

The crowd parted, people pulling others to one side to make way for a large, brutish man who was carrying a brick in one hand held high above his head. Without hesitation, the man hurled the brick at the front window of the car. Tony put his arm up and turned as the window shattered and the brick crunched into his shoulder.

As hands reached in to grab and tear at him, he crashed the car back into gear, but before he could let the clutch out and start it moving, the back of the vehicle was lifted bodily from the ground by the horde of rioters behind it and the wheels spun uselessly in mid-air with the engine racing. A black arm found the door handle, swung it open, and Tony was dragged out. Someone switched off the engine and the car was let down.

Tony was pushed and punched and kicked as he was manhandled from one laughing and yelling group to another. Someone grabbed his hair and yanked his head back. He felt a punch connect with his nose and start it bleeding. Someone else swung a stick and Tony saw stars. He crumpled to the ground and felt a kick in the ribs. Then another. The big man who had thrown the brick produced a flick-knife. Is this how it's going to be? Tony thought. He couldn't formulate any words. Others held his arms. His mouth hung open as the man moved in towards him. It was like one of those nightmares in which one tries to yell for help, but no sound comes.

"Hold it! Stop! Stop!" Through the crowd, someone was pushing and shouting. There was a pause. "He's not a South African," a voice was saying. "He's Australian. He's a journalist." Howard Goldman and one other white were pushing their way into the

108

crowd. His companion carried a CP.16 movie camera on his shoulder. On their jackets and equipment were big American flags.

There was a momentary lull and surprise within the rioters, at this extreme effrontery and seemingly lunatic act, then people turned and shouted abuse at Howard Goldman and his cameraman. But others sided with them. "No. They are Americans—American television. Leave them alone." The shouting raged at almost unintelligible levels for thirty seconds. The cameraman looked frightened. He remained silent while Howard shouted back and pointed at Tony. "He is an Australian—a newspaper reporter. He is not a South African. You do not have to kill him."

Someone shouted from the back, "He's a white, isn't he?" and there was roar of approval.

"Whites! Whites! Whites! We don't want them!"

"Wait! Wait! Stop!" A young man in front of the crowd shouted, holding his hands up. "We need them. They are press. If they are hurt, the rest of the world will turn against us."

Tony was, by this stage, standing up. He wiped the blood from his face and once again held up his press card, which he had crunched into his fist. "Australian," he gasped hoarsely. "I am a reporter . . . " But his words were drowned out by the shouts of the people at the back: "Kill them! They all whites . . . we don't want them . . . "

They started to surge towards the centre, but at that stage there was a fusillade of rifle and pistol shots over their heads and the crowd of blacks broke and ran in every direction, like a star-burst in a fireworks display, with Tony, Howard, and his cameraman left standing at the centre.

From the western end of Pritchard Street a line of riot police, looking for all the world like beings from outer space, moved down the roadway towards the little group of three whites and the blacks, who now formed a retreating line further down the road. The police were dressed in long, padded over-vests and fibre-glass helmets with face-masks. Some carried shields and long batons, others carried rifles and small arms. A hail of sticks, stones, and bottles came back from the blacks as they moved further away.

Tony stood, dazed and bloody, with the two Americans, while

one group receded from them and the other advanced. He was suddenly struck by the bizarre qualities of the scene. It was like something out of a Fellini movie.

Tony had had some harsh things to say about the South African police in the past, but he had to admit that this was one occasion when he was glad to see them. As the police line reached them and moved past, an officer spoke and motioned to them to move off. "Okay," he said, "you'll be all right now . . . Just move back this way."

Looking back along the street, Tony saw scores of police now pouring into the roadway, riot vans, flashing lights, police cars. It was a crazy mish-mash of sound and colour. He turned to Howard Goldman.

"Christ, Howard, I . . . "

"Shhh." Howard held his finger up to his lips and made to keep quiet. He pointed at the cameraman, who was aiming camera and microphone towards the backs of the policemen and the retreating crowd of blacks. The cameraman went to move off to follow the policemen.

"Shit, Marty, that'll do. Cut it now," Howard said.

The cameraman turned and burst out laughing.

"Goddamn! Goddamn!" Marty yelled excitedly, "I got the whole fuckin' lot! Didn't stop rolling once . . . all the way through all that shit in the crowd and everything. I kept thinking, this is fuckin' curtains for us, but I just kept rolling all the time. I got that big guy with the knife and the other prick in the back who kept yelling 'Kill'em!' Jesus Christ, Howard, this will knock 'em on their goddamn asses back in New York."

Howard slapped his thighs with both hands and then raised his arms high in the air. "Holy Jesus," he said ecstatically. "Great. Fantastic!"

Tony wondered briefly if he might, in fact, be dreaming.

Howard Goldman turned to Tony and slapped him on the shoulder. "Would you believe that, Tony? We got the whole lot . . . the whole goddamn lot!"

Tony smiled weakly. "Yes," he said. "I almost did, too. Thanks, Howard."

6
Eugene Dekker

Solomon Molefe was not happy to have seen his son. Just before Milton arrived home, he would have been overjoyed at the prospect of seeing him again after such a long absence; he was, after all, the Molefes' only son. When Milton was born, Mary Molefe had suffered a ruptured uterus during the delivery which nearly killed her and it had been necessary for her to have a hysterectomy. Consequently, Milton had become the apple of her eye and, as a young boy, he had been showered with affection by his parents. But Milton's return home now, after three years away (his parents never knew where he was, or even if he was still alive), had left both his mother and his father completely distraught. His father found himself wishing that Milton had never been born.

Milton had not seen his mother; she was still at the big house at Sandton, and he had spent less than ten minutes with his father at the family's humble little house in Soweto. But during that time he informed his father that his life and that of his wife Mary would be forfeited unless they were prepared to help the APRA in a plan to kidnap an important white man.

Milton, in fact, knew nothing about the man in question until he had been informed on the previous day, by a special planning committee, of his selection to participate in the operation. Even now he was not aware of the reason for the planned kidnapping, other than the fact that it was important for their revolution that this man be taken alive.

Milton also knew that the deadline for the start of mass uprisings throughout the country was only days away and at first he had felt that a piddling little kidnap was somewhat beneath his talents, after the signal success of his tower blast. But when the committee had informed him that the success or failure of the revolution could depend on this man, he thought differently.

Milton had been chosen for the kidnap attempt, he was told, not only because of his tower prowess but because of his parents. Solomon and Mary Molefe's employer was Clement Marais, a senior executive with the De Beers Diamond Mining organization. Mr. Molefe and his wife had worked for him and his family for twenty-three years—since before Milton was born. They had lived in several different houses in Johannesburg which had become successively bigger and more opulent as Marais gradually climbed the corporate ladder, until now they all occupied the palatial house in Sandton, covering some three acres of land next to the residence of the American consul general in Johannesburg.

When the Molefes had first begun work for the Marais family, Mary was one of the junior servants and Solomon had been the gardener. But over the years, Mary's position in the household had improved to the point where she was now the chief cook. Solomon had also gained greater seniority. At first he had worked as a general handyman around the house, then as a waiter at receptions and as a butler, and now he spent most of his time as a chauffeur to either Mr. or Mrs. Marais.

When Milton was born, the family allowed Mary and Solomon to keep the child in the ample servants' quarters provided in the rear of the house they then occupied. They also gave the Molefes a handsome array of baby clothes and helped considerably with extra money for Milton's education. As Milton had been an only child and Mr. Marais had paid the Molefes generously, Solomon and Mary were able to save steadily and, about five years ago, had bought the little house in Soweto, largely as an investment, but also as something for their retirement years.

Under normal circumstances they would live on the job at the Marais house and spend their days off, or any leave they had, at their own house in Soweto. Mary's sister, Bella, who worked in one of the new supermarkets in Soweto, stayed in the house the rest of the time and shared in with the Molefes, whenever they were all together, which was rare.

Milton's father was the only one in their Soweto home when Milton arrived with his brutal message. It was a terrible experience for Solomon, because he had begun to greet Milton with the sort of surprise and pleasure that any parent might experience at the sight of a son he had not laid eyes on for three years, but Milton had quickly crushed this expression of fatherly concern and affection.

At first Solomon had become angry and refused outright even to consider Milton's proposals. But when Milton produced a pistol and also informed his father that he had been responsible for the Brixton Tower explosion, Solomon had been shocked into silence. Milton warned him that both he and Mary would die if they did not comply with the APRA's requirements. It was simply, Milton said, a matter of taking him and two other men, in the trunk of the Marais family car, into the garage of the big house and hiding them there until dark. He, Solomon, would also have to provide them with two ladders.

Solomon Molefe knew there would be more to it than that and he thought, even while Milton was still talking, that he would turn his son in to the police. But before the thought process was finished, he realised that in the eyes of the all-knowing revolutionary army, that would be high treason and that he and Mary would surely die as a result of any action of that sort.

When Solomon returned that evening to the Marais house and told his terrified wife the story, she fainted. Even after she had recovered slightly, she lay sobbing and gasping incoherently on her bed for more than an hour.

"My God! You poor bugger! Sit down, for God's sake. Have a drink." Michael Keneally and his wife Jenny fussed over Tony, who arrived at the door with a plaster over the side of his nose and a slight black eye. The lump on his head was hidden by his thick, sandy hair but Tony knew it was there, only too well. He looked around embarrassedly at some of the other guests, who

113

turned with interest towards the commotion caused by his arrival.

"It's all right, it's all right," Tony said. "I'm well over it now."

"Look, you needn't have come, Tony, if you felt like sleeping or resting," Jenny Keneally said.

"No, truly, I'm okay. It all happened about two-thirty this afternoon, so I've had plenty of time to collect myself together and recover. I've had a couple of Scotches and a sleep and . . ." Tony gave a self-congratulatory smile, "I've even sent a piece off to London."

"But how do you feel now?" Michael Keneally asked.

"I feel fine—and a St. Patrick's Day party is just the thing to make me feel a hell of a lot better."

Michael led Tony to a group of other guests and introduced him. They began by talking about the day's riots and Tony's experience in the midst of them, and then the conversation shifted to the tower explosions.

Tony heard disjointed comments from other conversations across the room; other guests were also discussing the towers and the riots and the deteriorating security situation in the city. It seemed strange to Tony, under the circumstances, to be at a party. I wonder if the parties will go on, he thought, until it all falls down around their ears.

"It's getting to the stage," said a British businessman whom Tony had met once before on his previous visit to Johannesburg, "where one seriously has to consider leaving. I mean, it seems to me that the writing is on the wall and . . ."

"That's half the bloody trouble," a South African man standing opposite Tony interrupted, "if all the chicken-hearts who are fleeing the country would stay, we'd be able to stand up to them." "Them" and "us" again, Tony thought. "As it is now, there are hundreds leaving the country every day."

"Thousands," said Michael Keneally, joining the group. "We've been having more than two thousand enquiries a day about migration to Australia, since the towers came down."

A woman in a long black dress caught Tony's eye. It was cut so low that the halter neckline plunged almost to her waist. Tony was always quick to notice these things and she noticed that he noticed. She gave a slight smile to him from across the room.

114

She was tall; about five foot nine, Tony thought, and had long, straight, brown hair which curved under slightly at her shoulders.

"It's all very well calling people names," the Englishman returned rather hotly, "but the situation is becoming so bad that it will soon be just ludicrous to stay."

"What's ludicrous about wanting to stay in your own bloody country?" the South African said. "It might be all right for people like you—how long have you been here, ten, fifteen years?—to want to get out, but I was born here, and so was my father and his father and his father. Where do we go? And *why* should we go?"

Tony saw, from the corner of his eye, that the woman in black had moved slightly in their direction. She was with a slim, distinguished-looking man of about fifty. His thin, grey hair was brushed back from a slightly balding forehead. She, Tony estimated, would be about thirty. What beautiful cheekbones, he thought.

"Why should you, indeed," the Englishman said. "But then, if you think about it, why should twenty million blacks allow us to run their lives and keep them down indefinitely?"

"Oh don't be ridiculous, man. We're not keeping them down. We're bringing them up. South Africa blacks are better off than any other black people in the whole of the rest of Africa . . in housing, education, income. I mean, South African blacks earn more per capita than they do in any other African country."

She's also got very nice lips, Tony thought. It had been a long time since he'd seen a woman who had affected him in quite this way. I wonder who she is? And who she is with?

"It's not a matter of how much they earn," the Englishman's wife said, "or whether they can afford a refrigerator and a car, while people in Tanzania, for instance, could never even hope to. It's a matter of human dignity and freedom."

"Oh yes," the South African said facetiously, "like the sort of freedom and dignity the black people in Uganda had under Idi Amin or the Mozambiquans have under Samora Machel. Most of them haven't even the dignity of a full stomach, let alone the freedom to chose their own government. You surely don't call what's happened in the rest of black Africa democracy? I mean look at Ethiopia, Zaire, Burundi, Nigeria—it just goes on and on. And anyway," he looked directly at the English couple, "you've been here all

115

these years. I haven't noticed you doing any great things to improve the lot of your black brothers."

Michael Keneally could see that the conversation was developing along lines he didn't really feel would be productive. The thought occurred to him that things could even become "physical." Not that he hadn't been involved in a few "physical" St. Patrick's Day celebrations himself in the past, but then, they hadn't been in his house.

"Would anyone like another drink?" he said, hoping to interrupt the trend.

"I'll be the first to admit that we've done nothing in that direction," the Englishman said. "Nothing to help black people generally, other than the ones we've been personally involved with—like our servants, whom we've always paid well above the—"

"Oh, do please spare us," the South African interrupted with exaggerated condescension, holding his hand up to his brow. "What sacrifice?"

The grey-haired man and the woman in black moved across towards Tony's group and smiled at Michael Keneally, who was about to introduce them to Tony and the others.

"All right," the Englishman said, annoyed at having made himself and his wife look foolish. "It's just that I think the whole thing has gone beyond the point of saying what's right and what's wrong. The time has come to recognise the absolute inevitability of it all."

"Can I introduce Ingrid Hofmeyr and Eugene Dekker?" Keneally said, relieved by the distraction. Well, at least they're not married, Tony said to himself.

"Ingrid, I think you know Stewart and Margaret Shelby. Eugene? Perhaps not." Eugene leant across to shake hands with the Englishman. "Martin Salzman," Keneally went on, turning towards the South African, "Martin is from Cape Town—Ingrid Hofmeyr and Eugene Dekker. And this is Tony Bartlett. Tony's from Sydney, although he lives in Nairobi at present . . . Ingrid Hofmeyr . . ."

Ingrid leant forward, reaching out her hand to take Tony's. Tony caught a glimpse of the slight crease under her right breast. No bra, Tony thought, and she's got an all-over tan. Her handshake was firm. She relaxed the grip after the initial squeeze when their

116

two hands met, but then, and Tony felt a slight thump in his chest, a little extra squeeze before she let go. It was only a matter of a split second, but Tony, who had been looking generally at her face when they shook hands, focused instantly on her clear, pale blue eyes. She looked straight back at him and smiled. "Tony," she said, and then, as she took her hand away, "This is Eugene."

"How do you do. Have you been in Johannesburg long?"

"Only a couple of days, but they've been pretty hectic ones."

"Oh?" Dekker said, with slight embarrassment. "The . . . the, er . . . sticking plaster . . . is that . . . ?"

Tony explained about the riot and that he had been sent down to Johannesburg because the resident correspondent was away on another assignment.

"Yes," Dekker said sympathetically, "times aren't what they used to be, but I couldn't help overhearing you talking, as we joined you here," he turned towards the Englishman, Shelby, "about the inevitability of it all. Presumably you meant black rule in South Africa?"

His accent is British, very British, Tony thought. Eton, Harrow, Oxford, Cambridge British; but he's not British.

"Well, yes, actually, I . . . er . . ." Tony noticed that Shelby seemed slightly intimidated by the tall, non-smiling Dekker, " . . . feel that the only sensible thing to be now is pragmatic; to accept the concept of ultimate black majority rule as being inevitable."

"It's interesting," Dekker said coldly, "how quickly this way of thinking has taken over and how many whites are prepared to let a handful of black monkeys, just down from the trees, terrorize them into throwing away everything that rightfully belongs to them."

Tony glanced at Ingrid, but she was looking down and toying with a large diamond ring on her right hand.

"And not only that," Dekker continued, "but also permit these hooligans to force the bulk of the black population to accept something they don't want."

"Do you really believe the majority of black people in this country want a continuation of white rule?" Tony asked. I can see her nipples, he thought. Ingrid Hofmeyr looked back at Tony.

117

"Of course they do—the people in the countryside, particularly. Also, plenty of them in the cities—the middle-class blacks; those with good jobs and a bit of money in their pockets. They know that the whole thing would fall to pieces under black rule. Chaos like the Marxists brought to Mozambique. Not only chaos, but brutal repression, recrimination, tribal wars, and massacres. They know it as well as the whites do."

"Well, you may be right," Tony said. "I don't know. But you could hardly say they've been happy with apartheid either."

Ingrid Hofmeyr shifted her weight onto one hip. Tony's gaze shifted from Dekker with the movement, then back to Dekker again. What a body, he thought.

"We no longer use the word apartheid," Dekker said. "It is separate development." It's semantics, you mean, Tony said to himself. "But actually," Dekker continued, "when you look just beneath the surface, it's quite easy to see that a policy of integration—of racial integration—would be just as unacceptable to the blacks and coloureds and Indians in this country, as it is to the whites. The Indians certainly don't want black majority rule here. They know they would either be exterminated or kicked out. The coloureds have already indicated that they prefer a separate existence—they don't want to be regarded as blacks. And even the Bantu, the blacks, have never been a homogenous nation."

The others, who had been so vociferously involved before, now stood back in silence to let Dekker have the floor. The voice of authority, Tony thought. I must find out who he is.

"You see," he was talking directly to Tony now, "there are nine distinct tribal groups in South Africa and even the three strongest ones—the Zulu, the Xhosa, and the Tswana—differ tremendously from one and other." He looked around at the others and back to Tony. "And that is by any recognised ethnological yardstick of comparison . . . such as language, culture, tradition, even physical appearance. They don't even want tribal integration amongst themselves. That's why the Homelands Policy was developed and why, if they had really given it a chance, it would have worked."

"So you feel that it hasn't worked?" Tony said, watching the independent movement of Ingrid's breasts underneath the silky blackness of her dress.

"Well, it has worked as far as it has gone, but for the thing to be a success, it has to be accepted by all the blacks of South Africa."

"Thirteen percent of the land for two-thirds of the country's population isn't exactly a fair slice of the cake, though, is it?" Tony said. "It's hardly surprising that they haven't taken to the idea."

"It may be only thirteen percent of the land area," Dekker said with slight annoyance, "but it includes practically half of the Republic's fertile soil."

"But none of the country's major cities or industries," Tony countered, "and the black homelands, although they are supposed to be independent, have to rely on white South Africa for almost all employment; their total livelihood."

"Look," Dekker said, raising his voice slightly . . .

Ingrid took his arm in both hands and said, "Don't get worked up, Eugene. It's only a conversation."

He shook his arm free. "No. It's important," he said, and then, turning back to Tony, "All of the industry and commerce in this country was built by whites and—"

"With a little help from their friends . . . plenty of black labour," Tony interrupted, "cheap, black labour."

"Oh my God," Dekker said, turning away in exasperation, "there's no use talking at all if you adopt that attitude."

Tony didn't really want to be talking like this. He would have far preferred to have been sitting in a quiet corner, talking to Ingrid Hofmeyr. "All right," he said. "I realise that most of the dynamic development in South Africa has been because of the whites. It's just that I don't think it would have been nearly as dynamic or dramatic without that large pool of black labour. Whites here tend to dismiss that completely."

"What would you do, then?" There was a nasty edge to Dekker's voice. "Are you one of those outside experts who suggests we hand it all over to them on a platter?"

"I hate to say it," Tony said, "but I think you are past the point of having a choice. I know it's easy to speak with hindsight, but much more should have been done years ago to give black people dignity, to share the country's resources with them and to share the power. I know that, because of their numbers, they would eventually control the country once you started to share the power,

119

but if the process had been a friendly and giving one on the part of the whites, then the whites would almost certainly have a decent share of the cake, even with the blacks in charge. After all, five million whites is a lot of people."

Ingrid Hofmeyr sipped her drink and looked at Tony with a slight smile.

"The share you ended up with," Tony went on, "might be less than you have now, or had in the past, but at least it would be something. The way things are going at the moment, the radicals have got such a tight grip on the independence movements, if they get to power, you'll end up with nothing."

"Ha!" Dekker laughed derisively.

Less than fifteen miles away, in a secret, underground room in Soweto, Milton Molefe sat listening to the tense and urgent discussions of a small group of men. There was no need for them to whisper, as the room was completely soundproofed, but just the conspiratorial nature of the meeting was sufficient to induce the men to keep their voices low, almost involuntarily.

Milton felt proud to be included in the meeting, attended as it was by so many important members of the movement and the army. He knew that, at this stage, he was relatively small fry, but he also knew that his star was rising and that if he made the right moves, he would come out on top, or very close to it.

He was initially involved in the meeting because of the planning and coordination with other groups that was necessary to successfully accomplish the kidnapping. But after that was completed, he was allowed to stay and listen to the discussion and planning of several other major acts of terrorism which would take place within the next few days; the big oil-from-coal refinery at Sasolburg, just south of Vereeniging, was one intended target and the huge steelworks at Van de Bijl Park another. The explosives factory at Modderfontein would also be hit, as well as a total of four ESCOM power-generating plants at Highveld, Komati, Arnot, and Grootvlei, on one night in the Transvaal alone.

Milton realised that there were other equally daring raids planned in other provinces, but he knew little about them. He had heard that there were going to be attacks on the ports in Durban, Port Elizabeth, and East London, and that an act of extreme importance would occur in Cape Town on the night of March 20/21.

The Cape Town attack was spoken of only in very guarded terms at the secret meeting that night of March 17 in Soweto and no-one even mentioned what sort of event it would be. Milton only understood that it had been planned and rehearsed for months and that all was in readiness. The Cape Town incident, as far as Milton could see, would be the key. After March 21, everything would move rapidly towards the overthrow of the white rulers.

Milton hoped inwardly that he would be able to complete his kidnapping assignment quickly, so that he could return to the scene of the action in Johannesburg. He had been convinced by his comrades that the kidnap was important, but there were so many other things happening, he felt that he would rather be involved in the attacks on the white industrial complexes.

The kidnapping, however, would not be easy and he knew it. Once the initial grab had been made, it would require a hazardous journey from the northern Johannesburg suburb of Sandton, to a place near Brits some fifty miles to the north-west, from where they would be taken into the friendly territory of the Bantu homeland of Bophuthatswana.

The first part of the escape route would be the most difficult; they would have to make an initial dash by car, using main roads, for some fifteen miles until they reached a rendezvous in the Witwatersberg Hills. From there, using a four-wheel drive vehicle and following dirt roads and tracks, they would make their way to the west of the big Hartbeespoort Dam towards Brits.

It would, of course, be curfew time for blacks, so there would be no way they could bluff their way through if they were stopped. Their only course then would be to shoot their way out, and for such an event they planned to be heavily armed and prepared for other contingencies should they be pursued by police vehicles.

The success of the kidnap itself depended on help from inside the house they were raiding, but Milton had no fears about that part of it. The person who would provide that assistance was some-one whom Milton held in high regard. Even though he was told

121

that he would not be able to talk to this accomplice before the kidnap, Milton was still not worried; he knew that they would both be fully acquainted with the details of the plan. He took it for granted that there would be no hitches.

"What does he do?" Tony asked Michael Keneally, when they had a moment together in the kitchen. The conversation with Dekker had been broken up very diplomatically by Jenny Keneally, who called on everyone to start eating the buffet supper.

Michael's voice lowered appreciably. "He's a very big noise in the Reserve Bank. I first met him at the club—Wanderers. Started playing golf with him."

"He's pretty strong on the separate development bit."

"You were lucky. I've seen him really blow his top on a couple of other occasions. He's whiter than white and righter than right."

"What does he do at the Reserve Bank?"

"He's a director . . . there're twelve of them; six from commerce and industry and six who are appointed by the government. He's one of the government boys. Interesting really. You sort of wonder what these blokes must be thinking about all that gold they've got down there in the Reserve Bank and what's going to happen to it all, if this place goes under."

"And what about her?"

"She's an economist; pretty smart one too, so everyone says. She went to the Harvard Business School and worked on Wall Street for a few years, then on the gold market in London."

"And what about the relationship with Eugene?"

"Well, they've been on for quite a while. She's been working at the Reserve Bank as some sort of advisor and when Eugene's wife died about six months ago, he started taking Ingrid out. Not straight away, of course, but after a couple of months."

"And is it serious?"

"Don't really know. I think he probably thinks it is . . . but not her."

"Why do you say that?"

"I don't know. She just never gives the impression that she's terribly keen on him. Why? You interested?"

122

Tony laughed. "Well, I got the feeling that she was a little bit my way. Does she go out with anyone else other than Eugene?"

"I think so," and Michael smiled, "but I've heard he's insanely jealous, so you'd better watch it."

A couple of other guests entered the kitchen to get some glasses and then left again. Tony poured himself a glass of Guinness from an open bottle on the shelf and said to Michael, "There's something else I wanted to ask you about. Does Potgeiter Investments mean anything to you?"

Keneally thought for a few seconds and then said, "No. Should it?"

"Not really . . . it's Hendrik Potgeiter. Know any Hendrik Potgeiter?"

"Only the famous Voortrekker."

"What about Stefan Welz?"

"Nope." Keneally looked at Tony with a slightly puzzled expression.

"And Glaser? Do you know a J. Glaser?"

"Glaser? Yes, that rings a bit of a bell. Wait a tick—I think he's with the Transvaal Corporation. If it's the same one. I can't remember his first name. Met him once, at a reception." He paused for a moment. "Anyway, what's this about?"

"Oh, just a little bit of research I'm doing," Tony said. "I'm not quite sure what directions it's going to take yet. I'll tell you all about it when it begins to take some shape. This Glaser, what does he do with the Transvaal Corporation?"

"Well, I guess he'd be one of the top boys. Verhoef's right-hand man, I suppose."

"Verhoef?"

"Carl Verhoef. He's the chairman of the Transvaal Corporation."

"They're in gold, aren't they?"

"That's right. They're the ones who've been pulling a series of takeover bids here on the Rand. The Transvaal Corporation is second only to Anglo-American now."

"How did that happen?"

"Well, I think when you were last here they only owned African Exploration and had just taken over Johannesburg Consolidated

Mines, but since then, through some very shifty buying in London and New York, they won control of the Union Corporation, which meant another eight producing mines. I think they've got twelve now—only one less than Anglo-American—and some of the richest producers too."

"And this Carl Verhoef. What's the story with him?"

"Well, I've seen him, but never met him. He's a multi-millionaire, of course. Absolute control of the Transvaal Corporation and dozens of other companies. He's a staunch Afrikaner and one of the main financial backers of the HNP, the Herstigte Nasionale Party."

Tony's eyes lit up. Now we're getting somewhere, he thought. The HNP, he knew, had experienced a remarkable change in fortunes in the past few years. Virtually decimated in the hastily called 1977 elections, the party had risen from the ashes in a new poll only two years later, to win forty-five seats in the House of Assembly. This reemergence, after their disastrous defeat in seventy-seven proved a dramatic pointer to the rapidly deteriorating political situation in South Africa. The elections had already brought sweeping constitutional changes to the country. The parliamentary system, based on the British model although it had only ever applied to whites, was abolished, to be replaced by a system which vested supreme power in a president. The number of seats in the House of Assembly was increased from 171 to 185, and Prime Minister Johannes Vorster became President Vorster.

But although the day-to-day constitutional powers of the presidency were enormously enhanced, there were elements of the parliamentary system which were retained as safeguards so that no president could manoeuvre himself into a position of retaining the presidency for life.

President Vorster found that although he had gained power by the constitutional changes, he was steadily losing influence within his own Nationalist Party, because of his attempts at compromise with the black nations to the north. Many of the harder-line members of his own party became disillusioned and began to swing their allegiances away from the President. With Zimbabwe independent and Namibia following, the total isolation of South Africa tended to consolidate the power of the white supremacists, or to

124

convince those who may have had latent liberal attitudes to abandon them for a hard-line approach as the only possible chance of survival.

Tony recalled that President Vorster's policies of negotiation with black African leaders came under fire at home in early 1979 and that he called new elections to prove again to his critics he had a clear mandate from the white electorate to continue with his policies. The elections had been disastrous for him.

The Nationalist Party had experienced a startling drop in voter support, to gain only sixty-eight seats. This would have been sufficient to return the party to power, as the two liberal parties, the United Party and the Progressive Party, won only thirty-eight and thirty-four seats respectively. The HNP, which had come second with forty-five seats, was still not strong enough to replace the Nationalists.

But when, as the results became known, the United and Progressive parties indicated they could form a coalition government commanding seventy-two seats in the house, the National Party had been forced to turn to its radical, right-wing offshoot, the Herstigte Nasionale Party, for support in forming another coalition, with 113 seats, in order to stay in power.

President Vorster's position had been undermined. He no longer held the confidence of his party and his leadership was threatened. Within three months of the seventy-nine elections, although technically he had the right to remain in the presidency, Vorster resigned, to be replaced by the former Defence Minister, Mr. P. W. Botha.

In addition, the Nationalists had had to pay in other ways. On many issues they had been forced to accept the hard line of HNP policy, which was a bitter pill for many of the Nationalist members of Parliament.

The HNP policies called for the total territorial, political, economic, and social separation of the races in South Africa in order to safeguard the future of the whites. The party wanted to curtail the exchange of diplomatic representatives with other countries, to restrict immigration, and to promote the cause of the Afrikaans-speaking section of the community, moving towards a complete Afrikaner hegemony and the relegation of English to a "second language" status.

The party's position in the coalition government was not sufficiently strong to force these extreme measures through, but its influence tended seriously to hinder or halt any move towards liberalising reform within South African society.

Ever since the internal situation in the country had begun to deteriorate in the late 1970s, the party had been advocating tougher measures for the blacks. Ship them all to their homelands and let them stay there, was their solution. After the 1979 elections they also made it virtually impossible for the Nationalists to attempt to reach any agreement with African leaders, either inside South Africa or out, and so tended to inhibit any chances of compromise solutions being found to the racial conflict which was developing.

"So without him, the HNP wouldn't be where it is now?" Tony said to Michael Keneally.

"That's right. He and Paul Trauseld—he's another Afrikaner millionaire—put up all the campaign funds for the candidates in the '79 elections; something like six million Rand, I heard."

"Who's Trauseld?"

"I don't know much about him. He's a bit of a mystery. Lives in Cape Town most of the time, when he's not in the South of France or somewhere like that. He's supposed to have made most of his money from arms deals in various parts of Africa years ago and from diamonds in the Congo, before the Belgians pulled out in 1960. He's into diamonds here too, as much as anyone can be within the framework of the De Beers organisation. But he's evidently got a lot of money in it and gets a lot more out of it."

"So, how would I get to see these two jokers?" Tony asked.

"Well, as I said, Trauseld lives most of the time in Cape Town. Verhoef? I suppose you could try the direct approach, through his office here in Johannesburg, but I think he's pretty publicity-shy. Why don't you ask Dekker? He's like that with Verhoef." Keneally held up his hand with his index and second finger crossed.

"Dekker!" Tony repeated in amazement.

7

BOSS

Ingrid Hofmeyr was not really worried about calling Tony. She had made up her mind at the Keneallys' party that she was interested in him and now it was simply a matter of telephoning his hotel. She had to tell herself several times that she was not basically a promiscuous person; she had, after all, been involved with only two men since her return to South Africa and Eugene had been her only lover for the past three months. God, how she was sick of him. Not that he wasn't a good lover; he performed the function efficiently and effectively, but oh, how bloody dull, unimaginative, and conservative. And his politics. She had often thought, during the past few weeks, that she would explode if he went on any more with his rabid, anti-black ravings.

Ingrid, herself, could hardly be described as liberal on the subject of race relations. She was an Afrikaner and had been brought up to accept the fact that blacks were not the equals of whites; they were second-class citizens. Her opinions had gone through a considerable change, though, while she was living in the United States and Britain, where she had made several black friends.

However, when she returned to South Africa, the old feelings reasserted themselves and she found it all but impossible to stop thinking that somehow South African blacks were different from the ones in New York and London.

Ingrid had had a happy childhood, even though it had been strict and very religious. Her mother, who was Swedish, had married Ingrid's father in the Dutch Reformed Church, and from then on, became a conscientious member of that faith. Despite the constrictions of her religious upbringing, Ingrid remembered her youth with affection. Her relationships with the black servants had been loving and friendly, but they had always been on a mistress-servant basis, and that was the feeling that came creeping back over her on her return to her own country. She couldn't avoid it.

She found herself at extreme odds with Eugene though, on many occasions, because to him, blacks were all, as he described them at the Keneally's party, a "handful of black monkeys." He put a slightly better public face on it, but Ingrid, who knew him as closely and intimately as anyone, could see that it was a bitter, raging hatred Eugene Dekker felt for all blacks.

From the moment she first saw Tony Bartlett at the Keneallys, Ingrid was attracted to him. She had tried to analyse it all afterwards; why she felt the attraction. Certainly there was something physical. When their eyes had met, she almost felt as if there had been a little electric spark. Was it the way he stood or walked? There was something about his appearance. She had always liked tall men and Tony was tall. He was also slim. She found herself wondering what he looked like without his clothes on. And his face—that was nice too. There was a softness about the eyes, almost a sadness, she felt, but he had a slight air of toughness about his appearance; she couldn't explain it, probably the heavy line of his beard, which, however closely he shaved, would always leave a bluish tinge under his skin. He's probably very hairy, she thought. And there was his smile. She had only caught it a couple of times the other night and then only from a distance. It lit up his face. It was a boyish, cheeky smile and showed a set of bright, even teeth.

Or was it, she thought, just that he was obviously not South African? Was she attracted to foreigners? Or was it because Eugene was the extreme archetypal South African and, with all that turning sour, she was attracted to the opposite extreme? She didn't know.

When Eugene and Tony had had their little altercation, she had felt a combination of increased interest in Tony and embarrassment. Embarrassment that Tony might think she felt the same way as Dekker. She had said nothing and had not had an opportunity to speak to Tony again during the evening, because Dekker had left early, taking her with him. She would, perhaps, have been comforted to know that Tony felt as disappointed as she did.

Ingrid thought, as she leafed through the phone book to find the number of the Carlton Hotel, that she should be honest enough to say to him, "I'm calling because I want to see you again. I liked you when I first saw you and I want to see more of you, to talk to you." But that would probably scare him away completely. She had considered waiting until he got in touch with her and there was, she felt, a possibility that he might try to call her, but she had no way of knowing and anyway, it might take ages. No, she decided, life is too short. I'll ring him.

"It's Ingrid Hofmeyr here," she said, when the call was put through to Tony's room. "Look, I'm sorry to call you like this, but we didn't have a chance to talk again last night and I . . . well, I just wanted you to understand that I don't feel the same way about things as Eugene does and . . ."

Tony was both surprised and pleased at Ingrid's call. He had been going to call her himself and had even gone so far as asking Michael Keneally where she lived and then finding the phone number of her apartment in the telephone directory. The fact that she had called him first was only a matter of chance. Three minutes later, it would have been he calling her.

"No, please don't apologise at all," Tony said. "I'm also sorry I missed you. I didn't realise you were leaving so early."

"Oh, Eugene had to see some other people; just politics. He fancies himself as a politician, you know. I wanted to stay, but he insisted that I come with him. He's becoming incredibly possessive."

"Are you . . . er . . . are you sort of. . . ?"

At the other end of the phone, Ingrid smiled. "Engaged?" she said.

"Yes."

"Hell, no," she said emphatically, with just the trace of an American twang, "I'm just a little trapped, that's all."

"And you want to get out?"

Now, you can be open about things, Ingrid thought, and it was me that telephoned him, but he wants it laid right on the line—now.

"Well . . . I suppose so . . . yes," she said.

"Where are you now?" Tony asked, not being one to waste time once the ball was in his court. "Would you like to come over here and have a cup of coffee?"

"Look, I'd love to," Ingrid said, "but I'm supposed to be at a meeting at the office in Pretoria in an hour and after that, the day is just eaten up. But," she added quickly, "I could come around this evening, for a drink at about six."

"Great," Tony said. "I'll meet you in the Showbar, on the top floor here, at six."

Tony felt good as he put down the phone. Not just because of the sexual aspects, or rather, prospects, of their forthcoming meeting, but because of the companionship, the friendly side of it. It had been a long time since he had felt close and friendly with a woman. Oh, there had been the sexual romp with the little bird at Trou aux Biches, and very nice it was too, and a few others in Nairobi after Carol had left, but somehow Ingrid Hofmeyr emanated different vibrations. They said "Welcome."

Tony struggled to put Ingrid out of his mind and to concentrate. He had started on a train of thought, just before she called, which had begun to excite him. It was something Michael Keneally had said last night about gold. What are they going to do with all that gold they've got here in South Africa?

Tony remembered reading somewhere, when was it, almost a year ago, that the question had been raised in the South African Parliament about whether or not some of the country's huge reserves of gold bullion should not be moved out for safekeeping in the event of a military success on the part of the black Communist guerillas. The suggestion, Tony recalled, had been rejected out of hand by the Parliament and apparently nothing more had been said about the plan. Now Tony wondered who had raised the subject in the first place.

He placed a long-distance call to the parliamentary offices in the Hendrik Verwoed building in Cape Town. After a delay of

130

fifteen minutes, he was put through to George Schuman, the member for Brakpan, a constituency just outside of Johannesburg. Schuman was a member of the Progressive Party, whom Tony had met and interviewed for his paper during his last visit.

Schuman told him that the incident he was asking about had occurred in April of the previous year, and that the person who had raised the suggestion was Dirk Skotnes, the member for Stellenbosch, a member of the Herstigte Nasionale Party.

"What happened?" Tony asked him. "How was the motion put?"

"I'm not sure how it actually started," Schuman said. "I was out of the chamber when it began but I was there when they had the vote on it. It was soundly defeated by both the government and the opposition. It only had the support of the HNP and a few government members, and apparently the HNP didn't want to force the issue once they saw how much opposition there was to it."

"Where did they suggest sending the gold to?"

"Well, you can get all the details of the plan from Hansard, I should imagine, but I think the idea was to send it either to Switzerland or the United States."

"And why do you think there was so much opposition to it?"

"Well, for God's sake, man," Schuman said, "in the rest of the world's eyes, it would be like an admission of defeat, if they saw us shipping all our gold out like that. Anyway, what's brought it up now? Why are you interested?"

"Well, I was just wondering if there'd been any more said about it . . . or if perhaps there'd been any change in attitude since then?"

"Hell no, man. The Nationalists and the opposition parties were united on this and, if anything, the HNP was a little embarrassed about it all."

"So far as you know, there haven't been any large-scale gold shipments out of the country then?"

There was a pause at the other end of the phone and then Schuman answered slowly, as if he was slightly surprised by Tony's question, "Only the normal commercial shipments that are made to the London bullion market. We produce something like a thousand tons a year, you know."

"Yes, I do know," Tony said. "But what about the reserves? None of them have been moved?"

"Of course not," Schuman said testily. "Isn't that just what we've been talking about? Parliament would have to approve any change in policy like that."

"What is the level of the reserves now?"

"Man, I don't know things like that. You can get it from the Bank's annual report, or from the Department of Information. I think they are around a thousand million Rand, or something like that."

"I've heard they've been building them up, over the past few years, unofficially."

"Look, I'm sorry, Bartlett, I just don't know these things. You'll have to check with the Reserve Bank itself to find out—if they'll tell you."

"Okay," Tony said, "sorry to have troubled you, George. There's just one more thing . . . have you ever heard of Stefan Welz?"

"Stefan Welz is the secretary of the Herstigte Nasionale Party," Schuman said, "or at least he was for about a year, after the last elections. He's gone back to Cape Diamonds now, I think."

"What's Cape Diamonds?"

"It's one of Paul Trauseld's companies. Paul Trauseld is one of the financial backers of the HNP. Welz is a top dog in his organisation, but he left to work with the HNP just before the '79 elections, to help organise their campaign. In retrospect, I suppose he never left Trauseld—he was only on loan."

"How much control does Trauseld have over the party?"

"Well, to be honest, I don't think the party would last long without him. Him and Verhoef—Carl Verhoef. They're not parliamentary members of course and Van Essche is the party leader now that Hertzog has stepped down, but Verhoef and Trauseld are the main powers behind it all—certainly financially and to a large degree ideologically, also." He paused a moment. "But to be frank with you, I personally think they are fanatics."

Tony was about to ask another question, but Schuman said, "Look, I have to go. I'd like to help you more, but I really do have a pretty hectic morning in front of me."

132

Tony thanked him and rang off.

What the hell is going on? Tony said to himself, walking back and forth in his hotel room. Glaser and Welz, the two names on the air charter agreement, are connected to Paul Trauseld and Carl Verhoef, the two mainstays of the HNP, a party which is on record as wanting to move the country's gold reserves to safer places. Eugene Dekker is apparently very buddy-buddy with Carl Verhoef. What's the connection? Tony walked silently for a while and then, vocalising a thought which had been gnawing away at him for some time, he said aloud, "In other words, was that plane shipping gold out?"

And if it was, how in God's name did the hijackers know it was going to happen? Even more remarkably, how did Johnathan Kapepwe come to be waiting for the plane in some obscure little town in southern Tanzania? And where are the plane and the gold now?

Tony picked up the phone and asked to be connected to the Transvaal Corporation. When the number answered, he asked to speak to Mr. Glaser. There was a slight delay while he was connected to Mr. Glaser's secretary.

"I'm sorry, sir," she said. "Mr. Glaser is away on leave at the moment."

"Oh, I see," Tony said. "When will he be back?"

"I'm not sure. Could someone else help you?"

"No . . . . No, I don't think so, thank you very much."

"Who shall I say was calling . . . ?"

But Tony had already put down the phone. Next he made a long-distance call to Cape Town to the offices of Cape Diamonds, where he asked for Mr. Stefan Welz.

"Mr. Welz is in Europe at the moment, sir," he was told.

"Is there somewhere I could contact him there?" Tony persisted.

"No, I'm afraid he'll be out of touch for some time, sir."

"Yes, I think you're probably right," Tony muttered aloud after he'd put down the phone again. "If he and Glaser were on that plane, I think they'll probably be out of touch for a very long time."

He picked up the phone for the third time.

133

"Could you put me through to the Reserve Bank in Pretoria?" he asked the girl on the hotel switch.

"This is the English service of the SABC. The time is twelve noon. The news, read by Douglas Franck.

"South Africa's ambassador to the United States, Mr. Alex Koornhoff, has called on President Carter to institute an American naval blockade on the Mozambique port of Maputo and the Namibian port of Luderitz. Mr. Koornhoff, who had a two-hour meeting with the American President in Washington late yesterday, said that Soviet vessels carrying large quantities of military equipment and supplies, including what are believed to be tactical missiles, were being offloaded in the two ports, and that the arms buildup could soon lead to a large-scale conflict in the region.

"Mr. Koornhoff also said that elements of the Soviet Indian Ocean Fleet, including several submarines, had been observed by South African Air Force reconnaissance planes in the Cape Sea routes, some twenty miles to the south of the Cape of Good Hope. He said that only a strong American naval presence in the area could counterbalance the Russian Navy and prevent the possibility of the Russian merchant ships landing what he called 'tactical or strategic' weapons."

The car passed under a set of power lines and the static and interference continued for some time since they ran along the side of the road. Tony fiddled with the dial to try for better reception. He had returned in the morning to the car-hire firm and arranged for them to pick up his battered and smashed VW from Pritchard Street. At the same time, he picked up a new car; a VW again, but a red one this time. The radio cleared as the power lines swung away from the road.

"In Cape Town this morning, President Botha has been holding talks with the American special envoy, Cyrus Brown, on the mounting level of terrorist activity throughout the country. Since his arrival in Cape Town on Tuesday, Mr. Brown has been meeting with government and opposition leaders, as well as leaders of South Africa's various racial and ethnic communities, in efforts to try to develop a mediating role for the United States in South Africa. Mr. Brown is due to continue his talks in Pretoria and Johannesburg during the next two days."

Don't envy him his job, Tony thought. Even Kissinger would have trouble sorting this lot out. He switched the car radio off as he swung into Pretoria's Church Street and began to look for a parking space as close as possible to the Reserve Bank building in Church Square.

Tony hadn't really held high hopes of being able to see Eugene Dekker today—or any other day for that matter, after their conversation at the Keneallys' house, which had hardly been friendly. He wondered what Dekker would do if he knew that Ingrid had arranged to meet Tony that evening. Tony felt a warm sensation in the pit of his stomach at the thought of her. He wondered if he might see her now, in the Bank building.

Dekker hadn't been interested in meeting with him again, when Tony had first spoken to him on the phone. But his attitude had changed during the few minutes of their conversation, after Tony said he was interested in the safety of the gold reserves of South Africa. Tony's original line had been that his paper wanted an article on the strength of the South African economy, the effect of the flight of capital from the country, and the stabilizing influence of the large gold reserves. Dekker had initially tried to palm Tony off onto one of the Bank's economic spokesmen, but something had changed his mind.

"Now, what can I do to help you?" Dekker said, as Tony was ushered into his immense office. "Sit down over here." He waved towards a comfortable green leather lounge suite in one corner and picked up a silver box from the coffee table. "Cigar?" he said, opening the lid and proffering it to Tony. "Philippines . . . we haven't had any Cuban cigars in here for years, although I dare say there's plenty of them across the border in Mozambique."

Tony had never realised before what a terrible trauma Castro had created for anti-Communist cigar-lovers. "No thanks," he said, sitting down.

Dekker took one himself and, picking up the silver tip-cutter which lay beside the box on the table, snipped off the end of the cigar, rolled it around on the tip of his tongue, and lit it with a gold Dunhill table-lighter.

"I'm sorry about last night," Tony said. "I think I was probably rather rude—I mean, I do appreciate how complex the issue is."

What platitudes, Tony thought. But Dekker responded with similar politeness.

"Not at all," he said. "Don't worry about it. I know I'd had a pretty bad day myself, and I expect you weren't feeling too well after your little bout with the blacks during the afternoon."

He leant back and puffed a cloud of smoke towards the ceiling. As he brought the cigar down from his mouth to rest his arm along the side of the lounge chair, Dekker's hand appeared to Tony to tremble slightly.

"Now, what sort of things are you after?" Dekker said. "You mentioned that you were interested in the level of the reserves and their influence on the economy."

"Yes," Tony said. "Under normal circumstances, whenever there is a substantial outflow of capital from a country, there is generally a corresponding decline in the level of the foreign exchange and gold reserves." Tony said it as a statement, but it could also have been a question.

"That would normally be true," Dekker said. "And in the physical amount of gold in South Africa's reserves, there has been a slight decline. However," Dekker gave an odd smile, "as you probably know, our so-called 'troubles' have to some extent worked in our favour. South Africa is by far the biggest producer of gold in the world. Three-quarters of the free world's gold comes from here, so the problems we've been having with these Communist hoodlums have created a deal of uncertainty on the international money market. So, with the source of most of the world's gold being threatened—that is, in the eyes of the people involved in money and gold speculation—the price of gold has gone sky-high again. Today's price in London, for instance, is 217.35 U.S. dollars per fine ounce and it hasn't been under a hundred dollars for the past five years."

"So your reserves . . . " Tony began.

136

"Our reserves have not declined in a money value sense. They've gone up."

"What do the reserves stand at, at the moment?"

"The published figure is around 1,500 million Rand—about 2,250 million U.S. dollars."

"And is the published figure accurate?"

Dekker paused for a second and said, "What do you mean?"

"Well, it's been suggested that South Africa has, over the past few years, by judicious management been building up a sort of unofficial reserve which isn't included in the published figures."

"Where did you get that from?" Dekker said.

"I've heard it from several sources," Tony said vaguely, "including my financial editor. The true figure, I'm told, is close to double the published amount."

"Absolute rubbish," Dekker almost snapped. "Pure speculation, completely without any basis or foundation in fact. If yur paper is prepared to publish unsubstantiated rumors like that, Mr. Bartlett, I could only describe it as the yellowest of yellow journalism."

"I haven't said that it would be published," Tony said quietly, but feeling his hackles rising slightly. This bloke has a knack of irritating me, he thought. "I was just asking."

Tony asked a question about the country's balance of payments, and for ten minutes or so the two men discussed the enormous flows of money between the major industrial nations in the sixties and seventies which had led to the dismantling of the two-tier system of gold market pricing. Dekker seemed to relax considerably and to be content with the way the conversation was going.

"So do *you* think it is threatened?" Tony said, at one point.

"What? The price of gold?"

"No. Not the price—the source. You said earlier that the speculators feel that the source of gold is threatened."

The South African made an imperious, but unconvincing, gesture with the hand that held his cigar. "Of course it's not. Do you think this bloody rabble can do anything more than blow up a couple of towers and power lines? It'll take a lot more than that to bring this country down."

"Do you feel, though, that it might be prudent to move your reserves to somewhere else—somewhere safer?"

Dekker had been in the middle of blowing a cloud of smoke from his pursed lips and watching it swirl upwards towards the ceiling. His eyes shifted instantly from the smoke to Tony.

"Why do you say that?" he said slowly.

"Only because it was raised in Parliament some time ago and I wondered if the idea had gained any more support since then."

"I have no idea," Dekker said, with some relief. "Questions like that are matters of government policy and not my concern."

"It would surely be your concern, or at least you'd be aware of it," Tony said quickly, "if large quantities of gold were being shipped out of South Africa."

"Mr. Bartlett,' Dekker said, with an air of apparent exasperation, but also, Tony noticed, with renewed tension, "South Africa is continually shipping out large quantities of gold. The Reserve Bank is the sole, authorised buyer of gold in South Africa. It acts as an agent for the gold-mining companies and makes all the sales on the private market in London on their behalf. All of the gold which this country sells comes through the Reserve Bank and is sent to Europe and the United States and other parts of the world, on a regular basis."

"I'm not talking about the regular, legal shipments," Tony said, thinking to himself, here goes nothing. "I am talking about clandestine shipments like the planeload of gold under charter to Hendrik Potgeiter Investments which was hijacked last week."

Dekker's face seemed to lose all expression. He said nothing for several seconds, as he sat motionless in his chair, staring at Tony.

"I don't know what you're talking about," he said eventually. "I know of the hijack, of course, but there has been no suggestion that the plane was carrying gold. That must be a figment of your imagination."

"I can assure you it is not," Tony said. "I was there in Mbeya, in Tanzania, after the plane arrived. I saw the gold—and the white passengers taken off." Tony lied in the hope that it would draw something new from him. But he remained impassive.

"Have you told this to the police?"

138

"No, but I've written about it for my paper in London. It probably hasn't been reported here in South Africa, in the same way it hasn't been reported that the plane was chartered by a Mr. Glaser and a Mr. Welz, both of whom are employed by two of the country's richest mining magnates—one of whom is a close friend of yours, Mr. Dekker. But then," Tony's voice was tinged with sarcasm, "why should it be reported?"

Dekker stood up. "Goodbye, Mr. Bartlett," he said icily. "I hope your call has been of some use to you. As for myself, I found it most interesting."

He said no more, but simply opened the door to his secretary's office and walked through it to another room, signalling the secretary to see Tony out to the elevator.

"So there doesn't appear to be much more in the story, then?" Mulgrave said.

David Mulgrave had arrived back in Johannesburg that morning and had turned up at Tony's hotel shortly after Tony's return from seeing Dekker in Pretoria. Tony had told his colleague what he had been doing since he arrived in South Africa, but found himself holding back on the hijack story. He played it down, and told Mulgrave nothing about Glaser, Welz, Trauseld, and Verhoef— nor of his confrontation that morning with Dekker, or his suspicions about the gold. It wasn't professional jealousy, Tony kept telling himself, but whatever it was, he couldn't stop himself from being like that with Mulgrave. He just didn't like him. Ever since that time, eighteen months ago, when Mulgrave had tried to get him into a spot of trouble in London over a story Mulgrave had also been working on, Tony had gone off him. He knew that Mulgrave didn't like him and Tony found it difficult to like people who didn't like him.

Mulgrave was quite stocky—in body and in mind, Tony often thought. About five foot ten, blondish beard and hair, which was thinning on top, tortoise-shell spectacles and an unfortunate nasal whine to his voice. Reasonably attractive physically, to the right sort of bird, Tony had thought on one occasion, when wondering about Mulgrave's private life, but at thirty-seven, still unmarried

139

and unattached to anyone either male or female. A bit diffident when it comes to personal relations, Tony had decided. Works his aggressions and frustrations out in other ways.

Mulgrave was obviously annoyed at not being in Johannesburg when the tower explosions had occurred, although he tried hard not to show it. It was clear, though, that he resented Tony's presence in his territory. He told Tony that he would take over any of the new follow-up material that came from the tower disasters and then asked about the hijack story which Tony had originally been sent to cover.

Tony found himself lying and telling Mulgrave that he had not found out anything of importance so far, which had prompted Mulgrave's remarks about the story dying out.

"Well, there's something funny about it," Tony said carefully, "but I just can't seem to pin it down. I mean, it wasn't a normal hijack. The hijackers didn't make any demands and the plane has just disappeared."

"Yes," Mulgrave said disinterestedly. "Well, how long do you think you'll be here on it?" It was clear that Mulgrave didn't want Tony hanging around. "It's not much of a story now. I can keep my eye on it, if you want to get back to Nairobi."

"Oh, I'll probably stick around for a few days. There are one or two other things I want to look into, so don't worry yourself about it for the moment. Anyway, I'll be talking to Childers tonight to see what he wants me to do."

Mulgrave grunted. They spent a further few minutes in politely strained conversation, and then Mulgrave left to return to the small house he rented in the nearby suburb of Parktown.

"Potgeiter, Hendrik (born 1916–   ); Sculptor. Realistic human figures, busts, animals. Works in stone, bronze, and wood. Executed panels in Voortrekker Monument."

Tony closed the reference book with a loud slap that made several other patrons of the Johannesburg Public Library look up from their books in mild irritation.

The only other Hendrik Potgeiter of any note he had been able to turn up was the Voortrekker Hendrik who had been dead for

128 years. He was one of the most aggressive of the Voortrekker leaders, who conquered the Matabele and secured most of the northern Transvaal, laying the groundwork for the establishment of a Boer Republic in the Transvaal. But he didn't help Tony Bartlett much.

Nothing, Tony said to himself, as he returned the book to its stack. Nothing to go on, except an ageing sculptor. Hardly likely to be the master-mind of a huge gold conspiracy.

As he left the library, Tony didn't notice that one of the readers, a man in a dark suit who had been sitting nearby him, got up from his table and left also.

Tony had walked the seven or eight blocks from the Carlton to the library on Market Street and was walking back over the same route, trying to decide what he should do next. He felt, in retrospect, that he hadn't played the right game with Dekker. Tony had led with his right, but Dekker had ducked. He hadn't revealed anything. He'd looked guilty, Tony tried to reassure himself, but that wasn't good enough. It didn't put Tony any further ahead. In fact, all it had achieved was to make Dekker aware of the fact that Tony was suspicious of him.

The man in the dark suit, who was walking about fifteen paces behind Tony, was joined by another man in a brown sports coat and a polo-necked sweater. A large white car, moving in the same direction, slowed as it passed Tony and stopped, double-parked about twenty yards in front of him. The two men behind Tony quickly closed the gap between them and as he was level with the white car, one of them tapped him on the arm and said, "Mr. Bartlett?"

Tony stopped, surprised. He turned and said, "Yes?"

"We're from the Bureau for State Security. Would you mind having a few words with us?"

Before Tony could say yes or no, the two men pointed in the direction of the white car, which had its back door open and, directing him between two parked cars, hustled him into the back seat. Almost before Tony realised what was happening, the door slammed and the car drove off.

"Now just a moment," he said angrily, "what the hell's going on?" But he knew it was too late for questions like that. He had been too slow. He had been dreaming. He cursed himself for being so stupid.

"Look, what's all this about? Where are we going?" Tony said.

"Not far," the man on his left, the one in the polo-necked sweater, replied. "We just want to ask you a few questions. You're a journalist, aren't you?"

"That's right," said Tony.

"Do you have any identification on you?"

"Yes."

Tony moved to extract his wallet from the inside pocket of his jacket, then stopped. "Wait a minute," he said. "Who the hell are you? Why should I show you my identification? You show me yours."

The man smiled condescendingly. He was a big man, but he had a disproportionately thin face, with skin like stretched parchment that was creased and wrinkled abnormally around his mouth, ears, and eyes. Tony noticed that his eyes were almost completely colourless.

"Certainly," he said, taking out a plastic card bearing the name Kurt Quin, a number, a crest, and the words "Bureau for State Security" in bold letters.

"And yours?" the man said, still smiling his creased smile.

Tony showed him his accreditation card from the Department of Information. But, as he was replacing the wallet in his pocket, the car swung suddenly off the road and Tony caught only a glimpse of what appeared to be the entrance to a car park in a large office building; then they were going down a ramp in semi-darkness. Tony realised that once again he had been caught napping. He hadn't paid any attention to where the car had been going since he'd been picked up. He thought back and gathered that it had turned several corners, but, in which directions, he would never be able to remember.

All he knew was that he had only been in the car for a few minutes and that the building he had entered was still in the centre of the city. He cursed himself again and made a mental resolution to be more aware in future—if I have a future, he thought dejectedly, as the car stopped and the three of them moved out of the back seat, leaving the driver still sitting silently at the wheel.

Two or three minutes later, the two men brought Tony to a large, sparsely furnished room on the third floor. He knew it was the third floor of a fifteen-storey building, because they had taken an elevator from the basement.

There were four chairs in the room, a bare desk, and a light on a coffee table near the chair on which Tony was told to sit. No pictures on the walls. No carpets.

After two minutes of silence a man entered the room from another door at the far end of the room and sat down behind the desk.

"How long have you been in South Africa, Mr. Bartlett?"

He was about fifteen feet away and because of the position of the lamp, Tony could not see his face clearly, although he appeared to be about fifty years old, slim and neatly dressed in a suit, white collar, and tie.

"Three days . . . although I'm sure you know that already," Tony replied.

The man ignored the remark. "Have you been to this country before?"

"Yes, on several occasions."

"And what is the purpose of your visit this time?"

Tony knew they knew all the answers to the questions before they asked them, but he replied, "I am a journalist. I came here to report on the two tower explosions." He saw no reason why he should say too much about the hijack, although he sensed that that was why he had been brought here.

"What newspaper do you work for?"

"Oh come on," Tony said, "you know all these things. Why ask me things you already know?"

"What newspaper, Mr. Bartlett?"

"The London *Daily Herald*."

"Doesn't the London *Herald* have a permanent correspondent here in Johannesburg?"

"Yes, but I was brought in to help out, because he was down in Cape Town on another story with the Defence Department."

"Yes. I see."

The man behind the desk lit a pipe and puffed on it until it burned freely. He opened a drawer in the desk, took out a packet of cigarettes, and held it out to Tony. "Do you smoke, Mr. Bartlett?"

"No," Tony said. "I've given it up . . . thank you."

"Very commendable," the man commented, opening another drawer and taking a newspaper from it.

"Is this the newspaper you work for?" He unfolded a copy of the *Herald* and held the front page towards Tony.

He couldn't see the paper properly, but Tony replied, "If it's the London *Herald*—yes."

"The London *Herald,* March 13," the man read. "Is this your story about the hijacked South African plane landing at Mbeya?" He tapped the front page.

Tony's stomach tightened. "If it says so . . . yes."

"Ah, yes," the man said, "from our East African correspondent, Anthony Bartlett."

"Listen, what is all this about?" Tony stood up. So did the other two men. "If I am to be detained for any reason, I would like to call the Australian Embassy. You have no right just to take me off the street like this. I haven't done anything wrong." But Tony knew that the Bureau for State Security could do almost anything it liked and that his "rights," at this moment, were virtually non-existent.

"Sit down, Mr. Bartlett. We are simply asking a few questions. If you cooperate, I'm sure you will have nothing to worry about."

The man now spread the paper on the desk in front of him. "You say here, Mr. Bartlett, that . . . well, let me read it to you . . . 'the plane remained at the far end of the Mbeya airstrip for two hours. It was shielded from the view of people in the terminal, about three-quarters of a mile to the south, by a hump in the runway.' "

He looked up at Tony and took a puff on his pipe, then continued reading.

" 'Police and soldiers prevented anyone from approaching the aircraft or from moving to a position from which it could be seen. However, I was informed by an eye-witness, who saw the plane from a different vantage point, that dozens of wooden crates were

144

unloaded from the aircraft and placed aboard Tanzanian Army trucks and that five or six white passengers were also taken from the plane before it took off from Mbeya airfield.' "

Tony shifted uneasily in his chair.

"Did you find out who the passengers were and what was in those wooden crates, Mr. Bartlett?"

"No. You will see that, if you read further."

"Ah, yes . . . 'Tanzanian military authorities and the police, however, flatly deny that anything or anyone was taken off the plane.' "

The man behind the desk put the paper down and looked at Tony. Tony felt sensations of fear niggling at him. It was his first contact with BOSS, but he knew the organisation's dread reputation. The man stood up and walked across the room until he was standing about five feet from Tony's chair. The two other men remained seated and silent.

Tony could now see the man's face. It was round and basically featureless, except for a number of pockmarks on his cheeks. Moon-faced, Tony thought. He was balding, but what hair he had was grey. Tony noticed also, for the first time, that he had a moustache; a closely clipped grey moustache. But it appeared as if he had no eyebrows. He turned to the other two, who had picked Tony up in the street.

"All right," he said to them, "you can leave now. Wait outside."

The two rose from their chairs and left, without a word.

"In the Tanzanian military authorities, "he said, turning back to Tony, "who did you speak to?"

With the departure of the first two men, Tony, for some reason, felt slightly relieved, although he realised they were only underlings to the man he was now dealing with. But he was prompted to say, "Look, this may be the Bureau for State Security, but I would at least like to know who I am talking to."

The man smiled with his mouth. His eyes, however, showed no humour. "My name is Starcke—Colonel Starcke," he said quietly. "Now in Tanzania, who . . . "

"Colonel Samere," Tony said. He saw no reason why he shouldn't tell him that. He felt no great love for Colonel Samere.

145

"Ah yes," Starcke said, nodding his head, "Samere."

"Do you know Samere?" Tony asked.

Again the mirthless smile, "Oh yes, we know him. Who else did you deal with?"

"No-one else of any importance. A few police officials, that's all."

For some reason Tony felt reluctant to mention Johnathan Kapepwe's name. He felt bitter resentment towards him over the events on the TanZam Railway, but this was Kapepwe's own country and BOSS was surely his mortal enemy. Although why I should be doing anything for the bastard, I don't know, Tony thought.

"Do you know what was in those crates, or who the people were on the plane?"

"You asked me that before," Tony said. "And you just read out what I had written for my paper. I don't know."

"Then why did you say to Mr. Eugene Dekker this morning, that the cases contained gold, South African gold?"

For a moment Tony was lost, like a schoolboy caught at telling lies. He sought for an escape route and decided that the truth was as good as any.

"I . . . I was guessing," he said lamely.

"You mentioned the names of Mr. Johan Glaser and Mr. Stefan Welz as being involved. Where did you get that information?"

"I . . ."

"Was it from a Mr. Peter Barbeton at Jan Smuts airport?"

"Colonel Starcke," Tony said. "I have tried to be cooperative with you, but I do have some rights and, as a journalist, I do not have to disclose the sources of my information to you or to anybody else. Now, if you want to charge me, or arrest me, then please let me know, because I would like to get in touch with my embassy."

The South African laughed out loud and Tony saw that his teeth were stained with tobacco from his pipe.

"Mr. Bartlett, Mr. Bartlett, what misconceptions you have about the Bureau for State Security. We are a passive service—we have no legal powers of arrest . . ."

"No?" said Tony. "Then what am I doing here now?" He remembered the report released by the United Nations, which detailed the types of torture used by BOSS and other security organisations in South Africa—electric shocks, psychological torment, prevention of sleep. Actual powers and legal powers are two different things, Tony thought.

"You are not under arrest, Mr. Bartlett. The Bureau is only an information-gathering organisation." Colonel Starcke turned and walked back towards the desk. He sat on the edge of it, facing Tony again.

"Our job," he said, with sudden and unexpected fierceness, "is to *investigate* every source of political, economic, or military threat to South Africa."

"Are you suggesting that I am a threat?"

Another smile. "No, Mr. Bartlett, I would certainly hope not. But you are a source of information at the moment; a source that we felt was worthwhile investigating. There is probably more that you could tell us . . . and, in that context, I would like to clear up what seems to be another misconception on your part. Journalists in this country are required by law to divulge the sources of their information and there are heavy penalties for those who do not comply. In this particular case, we will not press the point, because we already know the answer, but you should bear it in mind for the future, Mr. Bartlett."

He walked back across the room again, towards the door through which Tony had entered, and then, looking at some unmarked spot where the ceiling met the wall, said slowly and deliberately, "I should also say, with regard to your future activities in this country, that you should be careful about spreading or publishing unsubstantiated rumours and you should bear in mind that in addition to the procedures laid down by law, we have . . . other means of getting the information we require."

He opened the door. "Thank you, Mr. Bartlett."

Tony noticed, as he walked through the doorway this time, that the door itself was at least four inches thick and the walls much thicker still. Soundproofed. He looked at the two men who had been sitting on a couple of chairs, waiting outside, and realised that they had heard nothing of the conversation after Starcke had asked them to leave the room.

They took him once more to the elevator, in what was a window-less corridor. In the dim light of the basement, when they reached it again, Tony could no longer see the white car. Only a small delivery van standing, with its engine running and the back doors open, near one wall. The two men and Tony clambered into the back to sit on a wooden bench along one side. The doors were closed and the van drove off. Tony felt it go up the ramp and out into the street again, but he could see nothing. There were no windows, not even one to the driver's compartment. Only a small electric bulb lit the interior of the van.

The vehicle drove for about ten minutes, stopping on several occasions, which Tony realised were for traffic lights. He tried to count the left- and right-hand turns, but when the van went straight, he had no way of knowing how many streets had been crossed, so he soon lost track completely. Eventually the van stopped again, one of the men opened the rear door, and they all stepped out into the evening light.

"Goodbye, Mr. Bartlett," the man in the polo-neck sweater said to Tony. "Your hotel is just around the corner."

Tony looked at the men. They stood there watching him, not moving. He began to walk away in the direction they had indicated. Twenty yards down the street, he turned to look back. They were still standing by the van, watching him. He continued walking until he got to the corner of the street, then looked back again. The men were still there. Tony turned the corner.

8

Ingrid

Ingrid Hofmeyr was on time. In fact, she was ten minutes early. She sat, sipping a gin and bitter lemon in the Showbar on the thirtieth floor of the Carlton, waiting for Tony. At the corner of the tiny band-stage, a pianist was tinkling his way around *These Foolish Things*. Ingrid checked the time; eleven minutes past six. She wasn't a fanatic about her men being on time, but she couldn't help feeling the first traces of annoyance. After all, if she'd been keen enough to be early, he should be too.

But before her resentment had time to develop, she saw Tony waving from the other side of the room, having come, she noticed, through a door labelled FIRE EXIT. When he reached her and slumped into a chair beside her, she saw that he was red in the face and panting for breath.

"My God, Tony," she exclaimed, "what's the matter? What have you been doing?"

Tony gasped a little laugh, panted a few more times, and then said, "Oh, just running up eight flights of stairs, hoping I wouldn't miss you."

"What on earth did you run up the stairs for?" Ingrid said. "Why didn't you use the lift?"

"It's a long story," Tony rasped, trying to smile at the same time, "but basically, I was hoping I could avoid being followed."

The waiter arrived and Tony ordered a beer. Then he sat back and began to tell Ingrid about his brush with BOSS. He told her they had questioned him about the newspaper article he had written

149

in Dar es Salaam on the hijacked aircraft, but he didn't mention his meeting, that afternoon, with Dekker.

"Have you spoken to Eugene today?" he asked Ingrid.

"No. I've had a pretty busy day. I called his office once, but he was out. Why?"

"Just wondered. I . . . they say he's a rather jealous type."

"Who are 'they'?"

"Oh, just people," Tony smiled. "Actually, it was Michael Keneally."

She laughed softly. "Yes, I suppose he is. Does that worry you?"

"Well, it all depends. I mean, what's he likely to do when he finds out that you've met me?"

"I hope that he doesn't find out," Ingrid said quietly.

Tony looked into her eyes for an instant, trying to guess her thoughts. She was wearing a brown, diagonally striped skirt and thin beige sweater. Once again, Tony noticed, she was wearing no bra and he could see the slightly darker outline of her nipples through the material.

"This is a pretty public place," he muttered, looking around.

"Yes, I know. But you chose it."

"I didn't really think too much about that side of it," Tony said. "Shall we go?"

"Yes," she replied. "But what about your friends? Are they likely to be following you again?" Ingrid felt an unfamiliar surge of excitement.

Looking around the thickly carpeted cocktail room, Tony hoped that no-one had either followed him there or recognised Ingrid. He had gone to some lengths to avoid being followed. On entering the hotel lobby, he had gone straight to the elevator and taken it to his room on the twenty-second floor, entering it and, after a few minutes, turned the cold shower on. Leaving it running, he then left the room again, using his key to close the door as silently as possible. As there was no-one in sight in the corridor, he went straight to the stairway and climbed the eight flights to the top floor.

"Listen," he said to Ingrid, "do you have a car?"

"Yes."

"Then we'll leave separately. You take your car and drive it around for ten minutes or so. Try to make sure that no-one is following you and then come back to . . . let me see, say about a block from the hotel, down that way . . . " he pointed roughly east. "What street is that?"

"Von Brandeis?"

"That's it. Von Brandeis. You just wait there right next to Main Street and I'll be there at exactly twenty to seven."

He took her hand and kissed it. She pursed her lips at him and winked, then got up and walked towards the elevator.

Tony waited, turning his glass in his hands for several minutes after she had gone. He checked his watch. A waiter asked him if he would like another drink, but he said no and moved towards the men's toilets, which were close by the fire exit by which he had entered the bar. Instead of going into the toilet, he kept going the few extra paces and walked through the exit door again, without looking back into the room. Once the door was closed, he ran, as fast as he could, down three flights of stairs and into the corridor on the twenty-seventh floor. He rushed to the elevators and pushed the button. If there was anyone in the cocktail bar who had been watching them, he would be coming down those stairs and into the corridor before long. But no-one came.

The elevator arrived. It was empty. Tony pushed the ground-floor button. The lift stopped on the ninth and fifth floor, to pick up passengers; an Italian-looking man with black curly hair and a middle-aged couple. Tony stood to the back of the elevator and watched them. I'm becoming paranoid, he thought.

When the doors opened on the ground floor, Tony walked quickly and directly towards the escalators at one end of the lobby, which he knew led down into the huge, three-storey underground complex of shops and restaurants in the Carlton Centre. He saw, from the corner of his eye, a man stand up from a couch on which he had been sitting and move in the direction that Tony was heading. Tony reached the escalator. A sign dangling from a chain barred his way: "SHOPPING CENTRE CLOSED. Open 8.30 AM."

"Shit!" Tony swore, but without hesitating, continued towards the big front doors. He turned left and walked briskly in the opposite

151

direction to Von Brandeis Street, around the corner of the hotel, across the plaza, towards the fifty-storey Carlton Centre Tower building. He glanced over his shoulder and could see, through the glass walls on the ground floor of the building, that the man from the hotel lobby was now crossing the plaza and also walking briskly after him.

Tony kept walking. He crossed Commissioner Street, up one more block. He turned the corner to the left and, out of sight of the man following him, broke into a run. He knew, though, that the man would also be running during this break in visual contact, so he probably wouldn't gain any distance. Tony reached the next corner and turned back to see his follower just coming around the edge of the building, at a run. Tony kept running. Back onto Commissioner Street again, across it and to the right, this time before the other man had rounded the corner of the last block, as he turned, so that he couldn't tell which way Tony had gone.

If I can get into Von Brandeis Street before he gets here, Tony thought, I'll be all right.

There were not many people in the streets and Tony was worried that a policeman or a soldier might try to stop him, just because he was running. But that did not happen.

As he tore into Von Brandeis Street he glanced back again, but his follower was nowhere in sight. He kept running. At the end of the next block, he found Ingrid waiting in a silver-grey Porsche, with the engine running. He opened the door, jumped into the passenger seat beside her, and they drove off.

"Wow, what a getaway car!" Tony said, and exploded with laughter.

"And this is Joey," Ingrid said, handing Tony a stuffed toy kangaroo. "Isn't he great? Complete with pouch and everything. I got him in Sydney."

"I didn't know you'd been to Australia?"

"Aha. There are lots of things you don't know about me. I worked there for six months before I came back here. It was after I left England."

"What were you doing in Sydney?"

"Same sort of thing. I was with the Reserve Bank in Sydney, working as a consultant. And Joey . . . " she took the little kangaroo back from Tony and placed him on the bookshelf in one corner, "was given to me by . . . an admirer," she smiled.

They had come to Ingrid's apartment in the Berea district of Johannesburg at Ingrid's suggestion. Tony had been worried on a couple of counts, but hadn't had any better ideas. Firstly, he thought that if someone had been watching them together in the Showbar, they might assume that they had gone to Ingrid's apartment. However, Tony felt reasonably sure that the man in the lobby was the only one interested in him and he hadn't seen the two of them together. But what Tony was most concerned about was that Eugene Dekker would turn up at the apartment.

"Eugene is going to a meeting and a dinner in Pretoria tonight," Ingrid said. "And with the curfew on, he doesn't like driving between there and here at night."

Seven people had been killed in three separate incidents on the Johannesburg–Pretoria road during the past month, when terrorists had shot up passing cars between the time the black curfew began at 9.00 PM and the white curfew came into force at midnight. Almost double that number had died on the Durban road.

Ingrid had asked Tony to "come to my place for some dinner," but now that they were there, there was no immediate move made to cook anything. Neither of them felt hungry. They sat in the lounge room, looking out through the big, sliding-glass doors, which opened onto the small balcony. Her apartment was only four floors up, but because of its position, on the hillside at Berea, and the fact that other buildings did not obscure the view, they could see a couple of miles back across the city, to Tony's hotel and the lights of the big Carlton office tower rising beside it.

Ingrid's apartment was comfortably and expensively furnished. But Tony noticed approvingly that it was not "House and Garden chic." There were a number of offbeat Asian artifacts and wall-hangings and also a couple of posters, which, although obviously inexpensive, fitted in well with everything else. It was clear that she hadn't "tried" to make an atmosphere. It had just grown that way—and it was right. There were lots of books here and there

153

and in some parts it looked a little cluttered and untidy, but it was eminently comfortable and Tony felt himself relaxing.

Despite this, their conversation remained slightly artificial for a time. They asked each other questions about their lives. Ingrid told Tony that she no longer had any relatives in South Africa. Her mother and father and her only sister had all been killed in a car crash on the ocean road along the south coast, near the Tsitsikama State Forest, about six months before she left for the United States.

"I don't really know why I came back," she said. "There was nothing here for me to come back to . . . except, I suppose, that I've always thought of it as home. But somehow it's not the same any more. I just did it on impulse." She smiled broadly and Tony thought again, beautiful cheekbones. They sat beside each other, both feeling physical attractions, but both waiting for some sort of signal—as if someone would suddenly shoot a starting pistol.

Tony saw that, under Ingrid's sweater, her nipples were standing out and showing clearly through the material. Ingrid was also aware of it and wanted Tony to see them. She shifted her position slightly.

"Like the impulse that made me phone you," she said softly.

Tony slowly moved his head towards hers. When they were almost together, she closed her eyes and opened her mouth. Their lips touched gently and while the rest of their bodies remained separate, they played with their tongues, licking around the outside and inside of each other's lips. Tony also closed his eyes and delighted in the sensuous contact of just their lips and tongues.

He moved his left hand slowly towards her breasts and found a nipple. He held just the tip of her nipple between his fingers and thumb and played with it softly through the sweater. The only other contact point of their bodies was still their mouths. Ingrid's right hand now moved across to between Tony's legs and he involuntarily pushed his hips forward towards her hand. He felt her lips move as she smiled. They both opened their eyes and smiled at each other and Tony grasped Ingrid in both arms and pulled her towards him.

They rolled onto the floor, their mouths locked together, their hands feeling urgently for each other. Tony fumbled for a second with Ingrid's skirt and found the warm little mound of hair between

154

her open legs. His finger slipped into the moist folds of skin, which parted at his touch. They both gave a soft groan as he ran his finger gently up and down, along the inside edges, experiencing intense pleasure from the sliding wetness of the movement.

Ingrid began moving her hips as Tony rubbed his finger slowly and lightly in the convoluted folds at the top of her parted lips. Her movements became more steady and rhythmic and then, in a sudden lunge, she grabbed Tony's hand and held it hard in between her legs, which she clamped together tightly and, with a series of swift, involuntary movements of her pelvis and soft gaspings for breath, brought herself to a shuddering climax.

She lay back on the thick, white rug, her face flushed and her eyes closed. "Wow," she whispered.

Tony leant up on his elbow to look at her. "Fantastic," he said. "Beautiful . . . that was really beautiful!"

She opened her eyes and smiled at him. "Sorry," she said.

"There's nothing to be sorry about," Tony said softly.

"I just couldn't wait." She reached up and began to undo his shirt. Then they both knelt up, facing and undressing each other. Tony lifted Ingrid's sweater slowly and watched her breasts tremble tantalisingly as the tightness of the sweater passed up over them and released them.

"Beautiful," he whispered again, and held out his two hands to cup Ingrid's breasts in his palms, "my favourite kind."

Ingrid laughed, "What do you mean, favourite kind? Breasts are breasts are breasts . . . aren't they?"

"Oh no," Tony said. "You've got the ones with the little extra bulge on the end," and he ran his finger up from underneath her breast. "See," he said, "it curves up and around here like this and just where the edge of the nipple starts, it bulges out again."

He bent his head down and took one nipple in his mouth, rolling his tongue around and sucking gently on it for a second or two.

"Grrrr," he growled, and pulled her bare breasts up close against the thick hair on his chest. She put her mouth on his and, at the same time, undid his belt and the zipper on his trousers, which fell to his knees. Ingrid took hold of him and, feeling Tony hard and erect, experienced a renewed tightening in her own stomach,

155

a spasm of excitement. She parted her mouth from his lips and, bringing her head down below his waist, took him deep into her mouth. She held him steady with her hand and rolled her tongue around while he moaned softly and ran his fingers through her hair.

After a minute or so, she drew her mouth slowly off Tony, keeping a strong suction on him as she did so, so that when her lips parted from him, there was a "plop."

"Mmmm," she said, smiling, "my favourite kind."

They both laughed again and rolled on the floor, removing the last pieces of clothing; shoes, socks, stockings, pants, so that they were finally absolutely naked, pressing their bodies together.

They rolled around kissing, feeling each other, and then Tony held Ingrid still for a moment and moved in between her legs. She parted them wider and he slid slowly into her. She gave a little gasp.

"You're so wet," Tony said, moving himself gently back and forward inside her.

"It's because you excite me," Ingrid said. She opened her legs more and pulled them back towards her chest. Tony felt the muscles inside her contract and hold him tighter as she did so. She relaxed and contracted them rhythmically so that he felt the slow pulsations. Now *he* said, "Wow!" He lifted himself up on his arms and they both looked down to watch the sliding movements of him entering her.

"Wonderful," she said. "I love it."

"So do I," Tony whispered. "The only trouble is, there's not enough of it and . . . "

Ingrid smiled.

". . . consequently I am in danger of becoming a premature ejaculator. I don't know if you're ready, but . . . "

"It's all right," Ingrid smiled, taking his face between her two hands and looking into his eyes, "I'll come whenever you do, so just let go. Don't hold yourself back."

Tony stiffened, almost to bursting point, and Ingrid felt her insides begin to tighten into a slow succession of jolting spasms again. Tony groaned loudly and, thrusting himself hard into Ingrid, so that their two pelvises banged together, he felt an explosive convulsion in his groin. Ingrid uttered a little scream and threw her head from side to side on the floor as she felt Tony's throbbing outpouring fill her.

"How do you get on with Eugene, generally?" Tony asked Ingrid.

They were sitting up in her double bed, sipping cups of coffee. Tony felt as though somehow he had slipped back into domesticity. He didn't really mind. He liked being with naked women—especially when they were sexy, naked women, like Ingrid, he thought.

After making love on the floor, they had wandered around, without their clothes on, in the kitchen for a short while, munching on a few snacks and making the coffee; Tony admiring Ingrid's body, which was long and slender, and Ingrid doing the same with Tony's. They were continually touching each other; she would come up and quickly take hold of him and squeeze or pull on him sharply. "Ow!" Tony would yelp, and jump away. Or he would come up beside her and, putting one hand between her legs from behind and the other from the front, lift her off the ground.

"Eugene? Oh, all right, I suppose," she replied. "We just sort of drifted into this relationship. But, as I said on the phone to you this morning, he's just too possessive." She finished her coffee and slipped down in the bed, lying on one side, looking at Tony. "But really, I think the most difficult thing is that I just don't agree with his politics or his attitude to the blacks."

"Oh?"

"Well, it's a bit of a conflict for me really. I was born here and brought up here. The way the blacks are treated here is normal to me. At least it would have been normal, if I hadn't lived away for so long. That changed me a lot. I find it terribly difficult, now that I'm back here; such conflicts. I know that it's wrong, the way we treat the blacks, but you see, deep in my heart, I really don't believe they could run the place as well as we do. I know it's a prejudice, but I just can't help it."

"Don't you think, that if the blacks had been given more opportunity, more education and better jobs, they might be able to?"

"Oh yes, I'm sure they would. But when you look around at

157

all the other African countries and see how they've screwed things up, our blacks are much better off here."

"Physically . . . materially. But what about their freedom? Their rights?"

"I know. I know. I see it that way when I am outside the country, but back here, it just doesn't seem so easy and clear-cut."

"I suppose it's because the feelings and attitudes are so entrenched," Tony said. "They're almost impossible to change." He ran his finger down from her forehead over her nose and lips and stopped on her chin. "Would you ever make love with a black man?" he asked her.

"I . . . no. I don't think so."

"Why not?"

Ingrid threw herself back on her pillow and looked at the ceiling. "Well . . . I don't know. It's just that the law and all my upbringing have constantly drummed into me that they're—well, they're—well, just that whites and blacks shouldn't make love together."

"They're what?" Tony said.

"Well—they're like . . . they're not . . . well, they're not like us," Ingrid said. She felt pressured by Tony.

"They're like what?" he persisted.

"They're not civilized," she almost shouted. "They're like animals."

"Oh for God's sake, Ingrid," Tony said crossly. "I can't believe it. Degrees from Harvard and you say things like that. I could just as easily say that a short while ago you and I were behaving like animals too, but surely you wouldn't tell me there was anything wrong with it. You seemed to like it . . . if I remember correctly."

"I know, I know, Tony. Ssshhhh," she said, putting her finger to his mouth, "Let's not argue."

But Tony wasn't going to drop it. "I've made love with a black woman—well, more than one," he said, as if it was a challenge. But even as he said it, he wondered if it had any relevance at all.

Ingrid smiled and cuddled up to him. "Was she good? Or rather were *they* good?" she asked, smiling. Then as the thought suddenly occurred to her: "All at once?"

"Of course not," Tony said. "And yes they were good," he added a little defiantly. Then, with even greater irrelevance, "And they're pink inside."

He sank down beside Ingrid, wondering whether expressing that remark was, in itself, a piece of racial prejudice. He decided to leave it.

"Pink inside where?" Ingrid asked impishly.

"Down here," Tony said, slipping his fingers between her legs again.

"Am I?" Ingrid asked.

"I'll tell you," Tony said, forgetting his crossness as he moved down under the sheets, between her legs. He felt a thrill of arousal again as he smelt her gentle but pungent aroma. It was like an aphrodisiac to him.

"It's too dark. I can't see," he said, and threw back the sheets. She lay, with her legs spread wide, while Tony crouched on his knees between them.

"Now, let me see," he said with mock seriousness, while she tried to suppress her laughter, "let me see." Tony softly opened her lips with both hands, spreading them apart. Ingrid raised herself up on her elbows to watch Tony with a smile.

"Well?" she asked.

"I can't quite see yet," Tony said, and put his head closer and closer to the open lips, until he was within about two or three inches of her. "Ah yes," he muttered, "I think I can see now. Pink!" He stuck his tongue out and ran it along the length of her parted lips.

"Oh," she cried, and dropped back onto her pillow. But she left her legs spread open as Tony continued to use his tongue, curling it and pushing it and running it over and under the folds and convolutions of the wet skin, until, once again, Ingrid's hips began to move rhythmically on Tony's tongue and lips. She groaned and held her own breasts in her hands and lifted her hips right off the bed, then suddenly she grabbed Tony's head with both hands and pulled his face hard in between her legs for several seconds, while she thrust and ground her hips and then threw herself back on the pillow again with a little orgasmic scream.

Before she had had a chance to recover, Tony lifted her legs and mounted her. Ingrid immediately climaxed again, as Tony entered her body and then, hardly a minute later, as Tony thrust himself violently into her, she came again. Tony became like a man possessed, and holding her legs back and open in the crook of his arms, while he held himself up above her on his hands and the tips of his toes, like a man doing press-ups, he plunged in and out of her. She threw her head and arms about and whispered, "Oh Christ, oh Christ . . . " and then, as Tony felt himself expanding and approaching the last climactic thrust, she reached her arms around and grabbed his buttocks, pulling them hard in towards her, and the two of them moaned in unison as they collapsed, sweating and panting, on the crumpled sheets.

"There," Tony said, when he had regained his breath, "if that's not an animal activity, then I don't know what is. It's beautiful, but it's pure animal, when you do it like that."

"Crazy, isn't it?" Ingrid whispered.

"Bloody ridiculous occupation, when you think about it; two people pounding away at each other, getting themselves into a lather, just because they've got two different things and they've got to put them together—ridiculous."

"But nice," Ingrid said. "I sometimes wonder if I'm a nymphomaniac, I love it so much."

"If you are, then you're a beautiful nympho," Tony said, and kissed her.

In the morning, they made love again, but in the wake of it, Tony realised that he had forgotten to telephone through to London. He could phone during the day, but it was generally easier to get Childers in the evenings. As the *Herald* was a morning paper, he nearly always worked until late at night and often into the early hours of the morning. Childers would have expected Tony to call last night and would probably be annoyed that he hadn't.

Tony turned over in his mind the various avenues he had pursued on the hijacked plane and how none of them had got him very far. He thought about the possible connection between Dekker and the chartered plane, through Carl Verhoef and Johan Glaser, and

160

then wondered, for the first time, if Ingrid knew anything about it all.

"Do you know Carl Verhoef?" he asked her.

"I've met him," she said. "Why?"

"I'd like to meet him."

"Why?"

"Oh, just some research I'm doing on gold."

"Eugene and I will be seeing him tonight at the American consul's place," Ingrid said. "There's a reception there for Cyrus Brown, the American special envoy who's here now."

"Verhoef is a friend of Eugene's, isn't he?"

"Yes. They've known each other for years, apparently. But Eugene doesn't like to spread that around."

"Why not?"

"Well, Verhoef is in with the Herstigte Nasionale people and Eugene feels that, if he is seen to be too close to Verhoef or the HNP, it could affect his position at the Bank."

"He's one of the government-appointed directors, isn't he?"

"That's right, and in fact, he is a member of the Nationalist Party, but I think his feelings in recent years have swung over to the HNP."

Tony felt he might as well take the bull by the horns and trust Ingrid. "Did you know that Verhoef was involved with that plane that was hijacked last week?"

"No!" She looked at Tony with genuine surprise. "What do you mean? Involved in the hijack?"

"No. He and Paul Trauseld, the other bloke behind the HNP, were involved in the chartering of the plane . . . at least I think they were. Two of their senior employees signed the charter agreement for the plane and I think that plane was carrying a large amount of gold . . . illegally."

"Gold?"

"Well, I think so. Obviously, with so many mines under his control, Verhoef's companies would constantly be handling large quantities of gold . . ."

"Yes, but it all has to pass through the Rand refinery," Ingrid said, "and then it's bought by the Reserve Bank."

161

"Yes, I know. That's what's got me puzzled. Could large amounts of gold ever leave the Reserve Bank without the government knowing about it?"

"Without the government knowing about it? No, of course not." Ingrid was now sitting up in the bed, quite amazed at the things Tony was suggesting. "There are the regular sales to the London bullion market," she said, "but they're going on all the time."

"But a large-scale shipment, say thirty, forty, fifty million dollars—they would have to know about it? The government, I mean."

"Of course."

"Does the Reserve Bank hold all of the country's reserves?" Tony asked.

Ingrid looked at Tony for a second or two and experienced the same momentary hesitation about whether to trust him with a confidence that he had felt about her a few minutes earlier.

"This is strictly confidential," she said, and smiling, she grabbed him by the throat. "Now Tony, you mustn't breathe a word of this, or publish it, because if they found out that I had told you, I'd be sacked immediately—or worse."

Tony held up his right hand, touching his thumb and little finger across his palm. "Scout's honour," he said.

"Well, over the past two months, the Bank has been moving all of the gold from its vaults in Church Square to a new, specially prepared site within the army and air defence complex at Voortrekkerhoogte."

'That's just outside Pretoria, isn't it?" Tony asked.

"Yes. It's only a few miles."

"But why have they done it?"

"Well, I'm not sure. The new vaults they've been moving the gold to are very secure. It's like the South African equivalent of Fort Knox. But then so were the vaults in the Bank building. I did hear there was going to be some reconstruction at the Bank, but I'm not sure if the gold will be coming back there or not."

"And who knows about this transfer?"

"Very few people. It's all been done under a great cloak of secrecy."

"The government?"

162

"Oh, yes . . . well no, actually. Not the whole government. I think only a few people in the President's Department and the Bureau for State Security."

At that point, the telephone rang and Ingrid answered it. It was Eugene. Tony sat in bed, watching her, as she stood by the phone, naked. He pursed his lips at her and then pushed his tongue out and wiggled it suggestively. She smiled and lifted one leg up onto a chair, exposing herself to him as he sat looking, entranced by her body.

She spoke a few moments longer on the phone to Eugene and then rang off. She ran and jumped onto the bed, rolling Tony onto his back. She kissed him and said, "I'm going to have to go now. They want me in Pretoria again today."

Tony stood up and held her close to him. He felt very much at ease with her. It was ridiculous, but he almost felt as if he could love her.

"And I won't be able to see you tonight," she went on, "I have to go to this American reception thing with Eugene. But maybe tomorrow night . . . ?"

"For sure," Tony whispered in her ear, "but maybe tonight, too, because I think I'll see if I can get myself an invitation to the reception."

She raised her eyebrows and laughed a happy laugh.

.

9

The Envoy

"This is the BBC African Service, broadcasting on frequencies of
17.8, 15.4, and 15.07 Megahertz, in the sixteen and nineteen metre
bands. Nine hours, Greenwich Mean Time. The news, read by Ali-
son Peters."

Tony settled back into the big, soft divan in David Jamieson's
den, to listen to news from London. But although the divan was
exceptionally comfortable, Tony found he was anything but relaxed.
In fact, he was worried. He'd heard the SABC version of the news
back at the hotel, when he'd returned earlier in the morning from
Ingrid's apartment, but he felt sure that it was a heavily censored
version of the events that had taken place throughout South Africa
during the night. He had also found that his shower had been
turned off and that there were six messages indicating that a Mr.
Childers had been calling him from London at various stages
throughout the night. After that, he had driven straight to the
Reuters office, which David Jamieson ran in his own house in Parkwood, just to the north of the city. Tony had checked through
the copy that David had sent out on the printer and was appalled;
with himself more than anything else. He booked the call through
to Childers, which he had been going to make the previous night,
but was now dreading, because of the prospect of having to explain
to his editor where he had been and what he had been doing.

"South Africa," the BBC broadcast began, "has been rocked by
a night of violent terrorist attacks and riots in several important
centres.

"The major steelworks complex at Van der Bijl Park, just south of Johannesburg, was subjected to a rocket and mortar attack by black guerillas last night. The attack, which lasted less than fifteen minutes, is believed to have caused almost five million pounds' worth of damage and is expected to cut South Africa's steel production by as much as one-quarter. The guerilla units taking part in the attack were engaged briefly by South African Defence forces, who report that eight terrorists were killed. However, the rest of the groups involved in the attack are believed to have escaped."

Tony groaned. "Childers is going to kill me," he said to Jamieson, who was sitting opposite him, smoking a cigarette.

"Two other major South African cities, Durban and Port Elizabeth, were also affected, late yesterday, by violent riots in which more than a dozen people died. In the port city of Durban, police riot squads and army units used water cannons, rubber bullets, and tear gas in attempts to quell a large riot which began in the city's central district shortly before six PM." Just as I was meeting Ingrid, Tony said to himself despondently.

"Two white policemen were killed by the crowd, estimated at almost three thousand, which rampaged through city streets, smashing windows and looting stores. Three rioters were killed and more than two hundred arrested.

"In Port Elizabeth, police also used tear gas to dispel mobs of students and dockworkers, who began to march through the city late in the afternoon. Eight rioters were killed when police opened fire after a white policeman had been captured by the rioters and beaten to death."

"I can't believe this," Tony said. "It's all happening and London doesn't get a word from me . . . lovely!"

"Mulgrave has been filing some stuff," Jamieson said. "That should keep 'em happy."

"I'm sure he has," Tony said. "I'm sure he has."

"In the United Nations Security Council debate on South Africa," the news continued, "the Soviet Union has vetoed an American resolution calling for the withdrawal of Russian naval vessels from the sea routes around the Cape of Good Hope and for the Soviet Union to cease the flow of arms shipments through the Southern

African ports of Maputo and Luderitz. The American ambassador to the United Nations, Mr. Andrew Oldfield, warned, after the Soviet veto, that the United States might be forced to take unilateral action if the Soviet Union continued the shipment of weapons.

"Elements of the United States Indian Ocean Task Force, including the nuclear-powered aircraft carrier *Carl Vinson* and the guided missile cruiser *Bainbridge,* are reported to be in the Mozambique Straits, heading for Maputo, while the nuclear-powered aircraft carrier *Dwight D. Eisenhower* and several other vessels of the American Second Fleet are said to be operating in the Atlantic, off the coast of Namibia and South Africa."

"But, Perry," Tony protested, when the London call came through at about 10.20, "I've been concentrating on the hijack story. I'm just starting to get close to it. I can't be expected to do everything."

Childers was in a foul mood. He had had little sleep and Tony's call, at his home, had woken him earlier than he had wanted to be woken.

"The hijack story is one thing," he had shouted down the phone, "but for Christ's sake, there've been riots and killing in Durban and Port Elizabeth and a bloody rocket attack on the steelworks and we get nothing from you!"

"Listen," Tony said defensively, but knowing it was no excuse, "Johannesburg is hundreds of miles from Durban and Port Elizabeth. I could hardly be expected to cover those riots from here."

"And the steelworks?" Childers said acidly.

"All right, all right. I was sleeping. I'm terribly sorry. Unfortunately, I do have to sleep occasionally."

"Yes, of course," Childers sounded solicitous. "Incidentally, where did you sleep last night? I tried your hotel at least half a dozen times and you weren't there."

"I . . . I slept at a friend's place," Tony said lamely. He felt swamped with guilt at having spent a night of lust and pleasure instead of working. "Mulgrave has filed something, hasn't he?"

"Yes he has—and that's just the point," Childers said. "He wants to get you out of his territory and back to Nairobi. He's already spoken to the chief editor about it and the chief has spoken to me. I said that the way things are falling apart down there, we'll need you to stay in South Africa. But I had to stick my neck out and you're not helping me much."

"Bastard," Tony said.

"Who, me?" Childers said angrily.

"No. Mulgrave . . . Look I'm just starting to get on top of this story. I can't leave it now."

Childers paused and softened slightly. "Okay, but see if you can give us a couple of other little snippets in the meantime, just to keep everybody happy . . . an interview with the president or something."

A little snippet, like an interview with the president, Tony thought, Hah.

"He's down in Cape Town."

"Oh yes, that's right," Childers said. "Well, something like that, you know."

He can be a difficult sod sometimes, Tony thought, but I like him. He felt relieved at getting off so lightly.

"I'll do my best," he said. "Don't worry, when this other story falls into place, you'll be doing backflips. It'll be a bloody ball-tearer."

But, twenty minutes later on the way back to his hotel, Tony felt at a loss about what to do next and whom he should approach. He was certain that some secret conspiracy involving immense amounts of gold was taking place. But who was organizing it? Was the government behind it? And if it wasn't, how could it *not* know about it? He felt at a distinct disadvantage being in Johannesburg. With Parliament still sitting for the summer session in Cape Town, the president and all of the cabinet members were there. Maybe he should go to Cape Town.

Then again, why not simply go to the police? But his brief encounter with BOSS tended to make him wary of that course of action. In theory, the police might be independent of BOSS, but Tony felt that, in the higher echelons, there would be close cooperation and BOSS would quickly be aware of any move he made through the police. But was that necessarily bad? After all, was the Bureau

167

for State Security involved? Yes, Tony was sure of it. Everything that Peter Barbeton had told him at the airport, about how BOSS agents had swooped on the various bits of evidence, tended to confirm his feelings that BOSS, or at least elements within the BOSS organisation, were heavily involved.

Tony suddenly felt very small and vulnerable. Why the hell was he getting into such deep water? He'd already had one brush with BOSS, and the more he thought about it and the amounts of money involved, the more diminutive and insignificant he felt. He could die a horrible death and vanish from the face of the earth, without anyone ever knowing about it.

He went back to an earlier thought. Was the government behind it? Or perhaps just a few at the very top? Didn't Ingrid say that only the President's Department was aware of the movement of the gold from the Reserve Bank to the military base at Voortrekker-hoogte? It seemed logical to think that the government might be in on it, if you accepted the fact that BOSS was involved. It would be difficult to accept an organisation that was theoretically so dedicated to the government going against its interests or doing something so incredible, without its knowledge. If all this was true, Tony told himself, then getting on the phone to the president or the Minister for Justice, or someone like that, would be of no use at all. The only thing to do, he concluded, was to give the information to the opposition; call Schuman of the Progressive Party again.

He threw himself down on the bed in his hotel room. "Why the hell am I getting myself into this? I'm a bloody journalist, not a politician or a detective. Why don't I just report the story and let all these devious bastards stew in their own juices?"

But what story have I got? Tony then thought. It's nothing but speculation—pure guesswork on my part. Jesus!

He thought of Childers' suggestion, that he go for an interview with the president. He knew how difficult things like that were to organise; appointments made through private and press secretaries, long delays at the best of times because of busy schedules. He had interviewed the previous president, Vorster, once before and the new one, Botha, shortly after the '79 elections; but with the situation as it was now in South Africa, he might have to wait weeks.

168

He picked up the phone and called Mulgrave.

"I've been talking to Childers," Tony said. "He suggests I try to arrange an interview with the president."

"Trying to find things for you to do, are they?" Mulgrave said, with barely concealed spite.

"Not really," Tony replied. "It's just that it's probably a good time to get him again. How long is it since you did him last—about three months?"

"Four."

"Yes. Well, I just thought I'd let you know what I was doing so there'd be no duplication. What's his private secretary's name? Muller, isn't it?"

"That's right. And his press secretary is Van Jaarsveld. You'll probably have to go through him."

Tony thanked him and was about to ring off, when a thought struck him. "Oh," he said, "this American special envoy—Cyrus Brown. Are there any press arrangements being made for him here in Jo'burg?"

There was a slight pause. "Yes. They're having a press conference for him at the American Consulate in Harrison Street at three o'clock this afternoon. I'm going to cover it though, if you've got other things you want to do."

You sneaky little bastard, thought Tony. You wouldn't have told me, if I hadn't asked. "That's fine," he said. "But I think I might turn up anyway, just for the background."

"Whatever you say," Mulgrave muttered. "I'm going to be there a little early. If I don't see you before, I'll see you then."

They said goodbye and Mulgrave hung up. Tony held the phone for just a few seconds longer. There was a barely audible click . . . click after a break of about three seconds. Tony smiled and put the receiver down.

Five minutes later he booked a call to the president's parliamentary offices in Cape Town. Within fifteen minutes he was speaking to Muller, the private secretary, who told Tony he thought it would not be possible to arrange an interview until March 30, eleven days away, but that Tony should first speak to the president's press secretary.

169

Van Jaarsveld was polite, but gave Tony basically the same message. He took Tony's number at the hotel and said that he would call back tomorrow with a definite time and date, but that it would be necessary for Tony to come to Cape Town to do the interview. Tony felt depressed that the date for the interview was so far off, but decided to let it stand, just in case. He felt a sudden urge to ask the press secretary if he could speak to the president directly on the phone, in order to pass on some vitally important information, but he held back. Tomorrow, he thought. I'll do it tomorrow. Maybe I'll have a little more on it by then.

When Ingrid Hofmeyr reached the Reserve Bank in Pretoria that morning, she spent the first twenty minutes in her office going through some correspondence and dictating two brief letters to her secretary. She then attended a meeting in the board room with senior Bank officials, a representative of the Bank of England, and two men from the International Monetary Fund who were visiting South Africa. The meeting lasted just under an hour and Ingrid found on several occasions that her attention was wandering. She thought fondly of Tony and of the pure sexuality of the previous night . . . but also she found that she kept thinking of what Tony had said about Carl Verhoef and the chartered plane and, more importantly, about the gold transfer from the Bank to Voortrekkerhoogte.

When the meeting was over, she began to make a few discreet enquiries about the transfer and how it had been made. There were only a few people, even in the Bank, who knew about it, so she had to be careful how she raised the subject.

But after broaching it casually, she thought, with three people, she managed to discover that the transfer had been carried out by two armoured security trucks, making two trips each night, five nights a week for four weeks. Approximately 425 tons of gold had been moved.

She was unable to find out why the gold had been moved, except, as Eugene told her, that the Voortrekkerhoogte position was extremely secure, set as it was in the middle of a large defense complex.

170

When Milton Molefe had chosen Zak Molako and Joseph Mfulu to be his two partners in the kidnapping attempt, they had both been accepted readily. They had also wanted to participate in some of the more dramatic events that were taking and were due to take place, but they looked up to Milton and respected him as a leader. If he was going on the kidnap, they would rather stick with him than change to work with some other group leader they didn't know. Milton was steady and cool . . . and clever. That was why Zak and Joseph wanted to stick with him. As for Milton, he chose Zak and Joseph because he knew they would both kill without hesitation and because of the respect and obedience they accorded him.

He could only take two men this time. The whole thing was going to be accomplished by four men; the three outside and the one man inside.

But there were parts of the scheme which were a little risky, particularly in the early stages. Not the least of these shaky elements was Milton's father, Solomon. The original plan had been for Solomon to pick up Milton and the other two in the basement garage of a city building in the early afternoon and, while his master was at work, to drive home with the three kidnappers in the boot of the car, a Mercedes 600.

However, at lunchtime, Mr. Marais had told Solomon that he would be going to the Wanderers Club at three o'clock and that Solomon should wait in town until then.

Little beads of sweat had broken out on Solomon's brow at the news and he had said to Mr. Marais that he would take the car to get some more gasoline.

Milton, Zak, and Joseph had all come to the garage in the basement of the Concorde Furniture Factory in Simmonds Street separately and dressed very differently. Milton wore a natty dark grey suit, with a white collar and striped tie. He carried a small, black aluminium-trimmed briefcase. Zak wore black trousers and a white windcheater with a pair of large red lips on the front. A tongue was poking out through the lips and the words "Rolling Stones" were printed underneath. On his head he wore a coloured woolen beanie, and slung over his shoulder, he carried a small guitar. Joseph came in the overalls of an Electricity Supply Commission repairman. He wore a soft peaked cap and carried a large, metal tool box marked "ESCOM."

There were two entrances to the garage; one from Simmonds and one from Harrison Street. Milton and Zak came in through one, about ten minutes apart; Joseph came in through the other, about five minutes after the other two had arrived.

There were two black employees working in the basement, but they were both members of an APRA cell and could be relied on. The three men were shown into a darkened back room to wait. They said nothing. At twenty minutes to three, Solomon Molefe drove into the garage in the big Mercedes. There was about thirty seconds of silence while Milton and the others looked out from the shadows, before they walked across to the car.

"Okay, open up the back," Milton said to his father in Zulu.

"Milton, I can't. He's changed his mind," Solomon said imploringly to his son. "Mr. Marais has changed his mind."

"What do you mean?" Milton grabbed his father roughly by the coat.

"He wants me to go straight back to the office now to pick him up . . . well, at three o'clock he wants me to be there . . . to go to the Wanderers Club. I can't take you."

Zak and Joseph looked at Milton.

"What's he going to do at Wanderers?" Milton asked.

"I don't know."

"How long will he be there?"

"I don't know." Solomon Molefe was sweating profusely now and wringing his hands.

"We'll come with you," Milton said vehemently. "When you drop him at the Wanderers Club, you can take us to the house."

"But . . . but you'll be in the car together," Solomon said weakly. "What if he wants to open the boot of the car, to put his golf clubs in there or something?"

"Is that what he's going to do? Play golf?"

"I don't know. I don't know. He could do anything."

Milton paused. "We'll have to take the chance," he said. And then to his father, "Just make sure he doesn't come around to

172

the back of the car, because he'll be finished if he does. Come on. Open it up."

Although the boot of a Mercedes 600 is extremely large by conventional standards, it was still cramped for Milton and his two comrades, who, once inside, with the lid closed, immediately set to assembling their weapons. Milton's was the same Russian PPS-43 submachine gun he had carried on the tower raid, but there was also a Makarov 9mm pistol in a shoulder holster he was wearing. Joseph unpacked a collapsed AK-47 rifle from his tool kit and locked the separate parts quickly into place. He also extracted four Russian-made RGD-5 hand grenades and a British Webley 9mm pistol. Zak opened the hinged back of his guitar and removed, from special clips inside the instrument, a tiny but deadly Czech-made Scorpion 9mm machine pistol and two spare magazines. Zak also carried his long, converted bayonet in the leather sheath under his arm. All of these manoeuvres they carried out in the dark, while the car was being driven by a terrified Solomon Molefe towards his master's office in the De Beers building on Main Street.

"What's the matter, Solomon?" they heard Mr. Marais say, when he entered the car, "You don't look well."

"No, sir. I'm all right, sir," the frightened chauffeur replied.

"No, seriously, man, you look quite ill. Is anything the matter?"

Milton and his crew grasped their weapons in readiness. They knew they were completely trapped if Milton's father should decide to turn them in, but Milton relied on the threats he had issued before to keep his father in line. Still, Solomon could give the game away unintentionally.

"Probably something I have eaten, sir. I feel a little sick in the stomach."

"Well, as soon as you drop me off at the club," Mr. Marais said, "you just take the car straight home and get into bed. I'll get a lift home with someone else."

The three men in the boot of the car smiled silently to themselves in the dark.

Marais had left the car and gone straight into the club and Solomon had driven directly to the big house on Marion Drive in Sandton, through the big iron gates which opened on an electronic signal from any one of the three family cars, and into the large garage at the end of the drive. The two other cars were parked in the garage; a light green Chevrolet station wagon (actually a German Opel, built under license in South Africa), and a bronze-coloured 1750 GT Alfa Romeo.

The station wagon was to be the car they would use for their escape. Solomon had been instructed to make sure that the car was full of gas, facing out of the garage, and ready to go.

The wagon was perhaps the least used of the Marais' three cars; Mrs. Marais always used the Alfa and the Chev was generally only aired on weekends, or when the family went on fishing trips—a rare thing in times like these. One never felt completely happy camping out any more. Not like the good old days.

Mrs. Marais was at home. Although she would not normally come to the garage at the sound of the car arriving, Solomon took no chances. He quickly opened the boot of the car to let Milton, Zak, and Joseph out. Without a word they made straight for the far end of the garage, where a flight of wooden steps led up to an attic that was used as a store room. It was a place Milton remembered well from his childhood. He had spent many hours playing and hiding there from his mother, although these pleasant and nostalgic memories did not cross his mind on this occasion. Milton directed Zak and Joseph up the stairs first, but stayed himself at the foot of the stairs for several moments in whispered conversation with his father, before climbing the staircase to join his comrades and settle down for another long wait.

Tony Bartlett entered the building on Harrison Street, in which the officers of the American Consulate were located, at ten minutes to three. Only four minutes earlier, the big grey Mercedes 600 with Milton, Zak, and Joseph crouched in the back had driven past on its way from the garage of the Concorde Furniture Factory, just two blocks away, to Mr. Marais' office in the De Beers Diamond Mining Company on Main Street.

Tony found the conference room, on the third floor, packed when he walked in. More than fifty journalists, correspondents, photographers, and TV crewmen were milling around, adjusting microphones on the rostrum at the front of the room, lights along the sides, and cameras, wherever they could find the space.

Tony counted eight cine-camera crews from various foreign broadcasting organizations and one video back-pack unit from the South African Broadcasting Corporation, established at different positions around the room in a maze of wires and leads. He recognised the three American networks, NBC, ABC, and CBS, a West German and a French crew, two British crews from the BBC and ITV, and a Canadian crew. He saw Howard Goldman in deep conversation with his cameraman, Marty. Marty noticed Tony as he took a seat in the back of the room and gave a wave. Howard looked up and Tony waved back. He saw the back of Mulgrave's head in the second row. The hubbub and rustling of papers died down as four men entered the room at precisely three o'clock from a door at the front. Two of them sat down, while the other two stood behind the microphones at the rostrum.

"Good afternoon, ladies and gentlemen," one of them said. "My name is Arnold Haylock, and for those of you I haven't met before, I am the American consul general here in Johannesburg. I am here only to introduce the United States special envoy to Southern Africa, Mr. Cyrus Brown. Mr. Brown, as you know, has been meeting in Cape Town with the president and members of the cabinet, as well as members of the opposition there. I'm sure you are also aware that last week he had a series of meetings with leaders of several black African nations—President Kaunda of Zambia, President Muzerewa of Zimbabwe, President Samore Machel of Mozambique, and President Mujoma of Namibia—and that tomorrow he will be leaving for more talks with President Seretse Kama of Botswana and President Banda of Malawi in the hope of preventing the widening of the racial conflict in Southern Africa. Mr. Brown's time is limited, I'm afraid. He can give you a half an hour." The consul turned to the special envoy, "Mr. Brown."

Cyrus Brown was a small man with receding brown hair, a suntanned face, and a Bob Hope nose, on which a pair of rimless spectacles had considerable trouble staying in position.

"Good afternoon, ladies and gentlemen. Thank you for giving up your time to come along here this afternoon. I hope that it

175

proves constructive for you. I will be happy to answer any questions you might have, but first, I'd like to make a brief statement about the reasons for my mission here."

He adjusted his spectacles. "The primary aim is to attempt to provide an American initiative in bringing about a peaceful solution to the problems confronting Southern Africa at present . . ."

Tony listened with interest while Brown gave an outline of his discussions with the black African leaders and some of their attitudes. He mentioned "requests" that they had made, but looking between the lines, Tony felt that these were more than likely "demands" which the American envoy had been asked to pass on to the Botha government in Cape Town. Mr. Brown gave the impression that he would be conveying the South African President's reaction to the black leaders' "requests" when he saw them during the next two days, and that he might return to South Africa to convey their reaction to the South African reaction. It was all very reminiscent of Henry Kissinger's shuttle diplomacy in the Middle East, in the early seventies; but would it achieve anything here?

"Did the African leaders issue an ultimatum to South Africa?" someone asked from the front, when Brown had finished his statement.

"No, I wouldn't say there were any ultimatums, but they were adamant on the question of eventual majority rule."

A correspondent for United Press International identified himself and asked, "Sir, everybody is aware that one of the most basic aspects of the South African government's philosophy is that there will *never* be black majority rule here. It seems then that there is a conflict between the two positions which is impossible to resolve. Can you tell us what Mr. Botha's reaction was to the President's 'requests'?"

"No, I cannot. Not at this stage. Not before I meet the African presidents again, but I can say that President Botha is prepared to make substantial concessions and to enter into direct talks with the leaders of neighbouring African states."

There were several more questions about the extent of the concessions that the South African government was prepared to make; were they in the field of civil rights? Basic liberties? Political rights?

Cyrus Brown handled them deftly, without giving any details of just what the white government was prepared to do. He said several times that he had been "encouraged by an apparent willingness on the part of the South Africans to compromise."

Howard Goldman spoke up, "Sir, we've been talking about a conflict between blacks and whites here in Southern Africa, but right now, just off these coasts, we're heading for a major confrontation between two super-powers, the Soviet Union and the United States . . . "

Tony smiled at Howard's TV sense of drama. Howard was holding his microphone, while behind him, Marty was "rolling." "Is the United States prepared to risk a nuclear war over the continued supply of Russian arms to the black Southern African states?"

Cyrus Brown smiled thinly, but then spoke seriously. "I don't think it will come to that—I certainly hope not," he said. "But there is a strong possibility that the United States will have to enforce a naval blockade of the ports of Maputo and Luderitz unless the Soviet Union diverts five ships presently on the high seas, en route, we believe, for those ports; two for Luderitz and three for Maputo. We realise that this would be a drastic step, but I can tell you now, as the American President is at this moment informing Congress and will, within the next half hour, be telling the American people, that we have reason to believe that these Soviet ships are carrying nuclear weapons for use against South Africa."

A buzz of excited conversation ran through the room and dozens of hands went up as reporters attempted to ask questions.

"Let me say this . . . let me say this . . . " Cyrus Brown tried for a few seconds to speak above the noise, holding his hands high. "These weapons are not, as in the Cuban situation of twenty years ago, ballistic missiles. They are, we believe, small-scale tactical nuclear weapons for use in the field. They could, however, wreak devastation and havoc and bring indiscriminate death to many thousands in this part of the world, particularly if they were used in heavily populated areas or near major cities. Also, and this is perhaps the most important point, their introduction here would almost certainly bring an unwanted escalation and widening of the conflict. In any event," Brown went on, "already the Russian shipments have introduced many more sophisticated weapons into Southern Africa than were here before, and their policy of training and supporting guerilla armies has aggravated the situation and continues to make any peaceful settlement increasingly difficult."

"Would the United States consider committing troops to South Africa?" a young journalist on the aisle asked.

Mr. Brown smiled; a little condescendingly perhaps. "I'm sure you are aware," he said quietly, "that the United States has spoken out consistently against the South African government's policies of apartheid. Bearing that in mind, and also the facts of our experiences in South-East Asia in the sixties, I think it's fair to say that it would be highly unlikely for the United States to commit ground forces to the defence of a white minority government in South Africa."

He made the last part of the comment with some emphasis, but went on, "This is not to say that we want to abandon the whites here to a bloody massacre. We don't believe that is the only alternative. We believe there can be a peaceful solution. The greatest danger to that peaceful solution, as I see it, is the growing influence of the Soviet Union in this part of the world. The United States does not want to see all of Southern Africa and the Cape Sea routes come under Soviet hegemony."

The questioning went on, with considerable competition from the TV crews to get an on-camera question by their own correspondent. Tony made a few notes and towards the end of the allotted half-hour found an opportunity to speak.

"Tony Bartlett, the London *Herald*," he said, standing up at the back. "What impact would it have on world financial and monetary systems if South Africa's gold reserves and supplies were cut off or diverted to the Eastern bloc?"

Several reporters turned around to look curiously at Tony. Cyrus Brown stood for a moment holding the edges of the rostrum in both hands.

"South Africa," he said, "produces three-quarters of all the gold in the free world. If this gold fell under the control, or influence, of the Soviet Union, well I don't have to tell you how serious that would be. Whether we like it or not, the monetary systems of Western countries rest very heavily on gold. If the base of that system was threatened, the entire economic order of the Western world could be pushed off balance."

He gave his thin smile again. "You don't need a crystal ball to see that it is in our interests—that is, in the United States' interests—to keep South Africa, whether it is ruled by white or black people, outside of the Russian . . . or Communist . . . orbit of influence." There was a whispered comment from the consul, who stood up to say something to the special envoy. Then Mr. Brown turned back to the microphones, to say hastily, "Let me just add that we believe that it would also be in the best interests of all of the people of *this* country, too."

In the darkness of the loft above the Marais family's garage, the luminous dial on Milton's watch told him that it was 7.42 PM. The guests were not due to begin arriving at the reception for Mr. Cyrus Brown, next door at the consular residence, until 8.00 PM. The attack was timed for 9.30, or as close as possible to that time. By then, Milton, Zak, and Joseph were to be in position, at the rear of the consul's house, waiting for the signal from within.

There had been only two interruptions in the four hours they had been lying in the loft. The first occasion was when, at about 4.30, Milton suddenly heard his name being cautiously called by a frightened voice at the bottom of the stairs. His mother, Mary, had crept into the garage, against the advice of her husband, to see her only son. In three years she had not laid eyes on Milton, nor heard a word from him or about him. She wanted to see him.

"Milton. Milton . . . It's your mother!"

Milton gave no reply. Upstairs, in the loft, he swore under his breath.

"Milton . . . please come down. It's me . . . your mama . . . *please!*"

Milton grabbed Joseph's silenced pistol angrily from the floor and hurried down the stairs.

"Get out of here. Get out . . . back to the house," he said to her harshly.

"Oh Milton, Milton." She came towards him with her arms held out, tears welling in her eyes. "My boy, oh, my boy."

She moved to put her arms around him, but he pushed her aside. "Go." He pointed the pistol at her. "Get out of this place, now!"

"Milton, Milton . . . my son."

Milton softened perceptibly, but said nothing. Mary Molefe closed her arms around her boy. His arms hung loose beside him, his right hand still holding Joseph's pistol. A surge of emotion swept through him as, for a moment, nostalgic memories of softness and warmth and love impinged themselves on his consciousness. The softness of his mother's bosom as she embraced him made him suddenly feel like a little boy in her arms and he wanted to cry.

Then he forced her arms apart and pushed her away. "I can no longer be your son," he said in a husky voice. "Now go. Go away from here. Now—and leave me." He turned and ran up the stairs, leaving his mother staring into the darkness of the garage, wishing it would swallow her up.

The second interruption came about an hour and a half later, when Milton's father had come into the garage to assure him that the alarm system around the garden walls would be switched off, as Milton had demanded, by 9.20 PM.

For many years, virtually all suburban houses in Johannesburg that belonged to whites had been fitted with elaborate alarm systems. They varied, of course, with the relative degree of affluence of the family installing the device. But in the upper-middle-class and wealthy suburbs to the north of the city, Melrose, Randburg, and Sandton, almost all houses had high walls and gates which locked, as well as alarm systems fitted to the doors and windows of the house. Many also kept dogs.

The alarm systems were usually of a type that would set off a blaring siren if anyone tried to force open a window or a door, or broke a window pane. Some were even so sensitive that they would set off the alarm even if someone—or something—simply touched a window pane. The installation of these systems was an expensive proposition, because every single window and door to a house had to be connected up with specially sensitive wires and contacts. But whites in South Africa had lived for so long with this element of

180

fear that it had become a normal part of their lives, and it was regarded as an absolute necessity to equip one's home with an alarm system. Companies manufacturing or supplying the systems, naturally enough, had been doing lucrative business for many years.

- Most of the alarms could be controlled by a master-switch, which the home-owner would normally leave off during the day or in the evenings when the family was up and about the house and windows were open. But when everyone went to bed, the windows were closed and the master-switch turned on. There were overriding switches in certain rooms which would enable some windows to be left open—on hot nights, for instance. These windows, however, often had steel bars, or perhaps a more attractive iron framework installed, as an extra precaution.

Some houses also had separate systems installed along the high walls surrounding their gardens, although this was not the case with the residence of Mr. Arnold Haylock, the American consul.

There *was* an alarm system rigged along the eight-foot wall that separated the one-acre block on which the residence was situated from the three-acre estate of Mr. Clement Marais. But Mr. Marais was not trying to seclude himself from the Haylocks; it was simply part of the total alarm net which ringed the Marais property.

There had been house-breaking incidents in the area from time to time and, occasionally, an alarm system could be heard going off at odd times of the day or night. For the most part, these were only the accidental triggering of the device by the home-owner himself, or one of his family. But in the two years that Arnold Haylock and his family had occupied the consulate residence, there had been no incidence of even attempted house-breaking or of the alarm siren being set off. Once, after being in the house for a year, he had wondered if, in fact, the siren worked at all and had tried it by placing the palm of his hand on the outside of the window pane. It worked.

Tonight, with almost 150 guests expected, there was no thought of house-breakers. The house alarm system was, of course, switched off, otherwise it would have been continually set off accidentally by the guests. The two big Doberman Pinchers were confined behind a low gate, to the bottom part of the terraced garden next to the tennis courts, so that they would not annoy the guests. If Milton Molefe had known this, he would have breathed a sigh of relief. It was one aspect of the operation he was worried about.

Two Marine guards were stationed at the front door, but as the reception was not a big, formal affair, they wore plain clothes. Two other American security men were to mingle with the guests. Milton and his crew knew that they would be there, but they had no way of knowing in advance who they were, or what they looked like. In addition, four South African police, two black and two white, were stationed in the tree-lined roadway outside the entrance to the residence. Two squad cars were parked, one behind the other, near the big entry gate, which opened onto a wide, curving driveway of red gravel leading up to the front door of the house, past it, and out an exit gate further along the road.

Milton's group knew that they were up against heavy odds, but Milton was sure that, with surprise and speed, they could pull it off. They would be coming from the least expected quarter and leaving the same way. There was a huge advantage in this for the kidnappers. The consulate residence was in a roadway which was part of a big circuit. Where it joined back onto another road, there was no easy access to the roadway serving the Marais house, unless you travelled half a mile back to a connecting road, then another mile around the winding Marion Road, to the Marais house. Had the Haylock and Marais families been close friends, they probably would have built a gate in the wall separating their two houses; but they were not. This situation meant that if Milton could get his hostage back over the wall and off in the station wagon, they would have a mile-and-a-half start on any would-be pursuers.

In the darkness of the garage loft, the three men waited patiently.

10
Kidnap

"I feel as though I've been tricked," the American consul said angrily. "Michael, when you asked if a friend from Australia could come along tonight, I took the request at face value. I didn't know he was a journalist," he waved his arm at Tony. "He was at Mr. Brown's press conference this afternoon."

"I didn't know that," Michael Keneally said, looking at Tony.

"I'm sorry, Mike, I didn't get round to . . . "

"Look, Mr. . . . Mr. Bartlett," the consul said, "the press have not been invited tonight. This is a private reception to enable Mr. Brown to meet South African business and community leaders and I would appreciate it if—"

Tony cut him short. "Mr. Haylock, I am sorry. I am truly sorry. I didn't mean to do anything underhand and I give you my word, I will not worry Mr. Brown. In fact, if you like I won't even speak to him."

"Well . . . I . . . "

An appeal for sympathy, Tony thought. "You can throw me out if you wish, but I promise that I'll remain as unobtrusive as possible," and then, with a smile, "and I promise I won't eat too many of the hors d'oeuvres."

Haylock relaxed slightly and also showed the flicker of a smile. "All right," he said, "but please keep to your word about Mr. Brown."

He turned from where they had been standing, just inside the lobby, and left to rejoin his wife at the front door welcoming the arriving guests.

"I'm sorry, Mike . . . sorry, Jenny," Tony said quietly to the Keneallys.

"You bastard," Keneally laughed. "What are you trying to do? Put me in the shit with the State Department?"

"How bloody embarrassing," Tony muttered, looking around.

"It's all right, Tony," Jenny Keneally said, "no-one else heard."

They moved into the main reception area; a large lounge room off the lobby, decorated in American period style, with New England furniture and several paintings depicting eighteenth- and nineteenth-century life in the United States.

In startling incongruity a canvas splattered, with Jackson Pollock abandon, in blues, yellows, and blacks dominated one wall above a large marble fireplace.

Another big room, which Tony thought would normally have been used as a dining room, opened off the lounge. Long tables had been placed along two walls. They were covered with white tablecloths and laden with a buffet supper of immense variety. Two French windows were open at the far end of the dining room and there was a paved terrace, lit by a string of coloured lights, beyond them.

Groups began to fill all of these areas and Tony found himself separated from the Keneallys and in conversation with people whom he not only didn't know, but wasn't interested in. He kept looking, from time to time, over peoples' shoulders to see if he could spot Ingrid, but had no luck. He noticed, to his surprise, that there were several blacks at the reception. Under normal circumstances this would be highly unusual in South Africa; for years, blacks and whites had not been permitted to mix together at private social functions where food was being served. They were not permitted to sit down anywhere where whites were eating, nor use the same toilet facilities.

The foreign embassies were the first to begin breaking down these prohibitions. Embassies being little pieces of foreign ground, they could be laws unto themselves within their own walls on these issues. It was looked on as something of a provocation at first and, for a while, blacks and whites together revelled in what seemed to be the delicious illegality of it all. But the novelty soon wore

184

off as the practice became more widespread. A white person could actually have a black person, who was not a servant, visit his home, or vice versa, without being charged with an offence.

There were, however, several nasty incidents of police interference and the all-embracing blanket prohibition on any sexual contact between the races remained.

All this was before 1976. The Soweto riots in June of that year, and the successive deterioration of black-white relations that followed, saw an increasing level of government mistrust in multiracial meetings.

Consequently, the sight of several black people at this reception was sufficiently unusual to prompt not only Tony but other white guests to comment on it, mostly in low voices.

"What about the curfew?" Tony asked Michael Keneally at one point when they were together. "How do they get around that?"

"Apparently they've had to get special dispensation from the Department of Bantu Administration," Keneally said. "The consulate had to apply separately for each individual black person and they've all been issued with special passes . . . just for tonight."

"What sort of people are they?" Tony said.

"Well, they're mainly the community leaders that Haylock was talking about . . . "

"There's none of the *real* leaders around, though, are there?"

"I don't know who they all are, but they've got the mayor of Soweto—that's him, Jimmy Maqhubela, over there now with Brown," Keneally indicated a group in one corner of the dining room and Tony saw the diminutive figure and tanned face of the American special envoy in conversation with another white and a tall, heavily set black man in a business suit.

"There are supposed to be a couple of homeland leaders as well," Keneally said. "Dr. Phatudi of Lebowa and the Gazankulu leader . . . Professor . . . Professor Ntsanwisi."

"What about Buthalezi?"

"No, he's not coming. He's playing it very cool now. Although he's officially the chief minister of Kwazulu, all the rebel and guerilla forces refuse to recognise the existence of the homelands. So if he wants to have any political power at all in a future black South

Africa," Keneally lowered his voice almost to a whisper, and looked around slightly guiltily, "he has to play down the homeland leader bit and get with the strength, so to speak."

Across the room Tony caught sight of Eugene Dekker in conversation with a group of people. Slightly to his left, he could see the back of Ingrid's head and immediately felt like running his hands through her long brown hair.

Cyrus Brown joined a group of people standing next to Tony and began an overly polite conversation with two black men standing within the group. Tony looked back again towards Ingrid.

I wish I could just go over and say hello, he said to himself, but the recollection of his confrontation with Dekker in his office made him dismiss the idea. I wonder if Verhoef is here yet, he thought. I don't even know what he looks like.

"Do you know what Carl Verhoef looks like?" he asked Michael Keneally. "You said you'd seen him before."

"Yes. I guess I'd recognise him. Why? Is he here?"

"Supposed to be."

"Well, I haven't seen him so far."

Tony moved slightly towards the edge of the small group which was talking and listening—mainly listening—to Cyrus Brown, who was doing his diplomatic best.

" . . . and we feel that a major conference of all the interested parties, including the rebel forces, should be held, to get people talking together to find a solution, instead of shooting at each other—something like the Rhodesia conferences in '76 and '78, held in an independent country like Switzerland."

"But both those conferences broke down, as failures," someone said.

"Yes, that's true," the special envoy conceded, "but the second was more successful than the first . . . and two months after the second one folded, the Smith régime in Rhodesia accepted the identical terms laid down in the conference and there was no more bloodshed, so it wasn't really a failure."

One of the black men spoke up. "You are aware, sir, that some of our most important leaders are either in prison or under banning orders? It would be necessary for them to take part in any major conference."

"Yes," Cyrus Brown replied, "and I did discuss this aspect with Mr. Botha in Cape Town." He hesitated a moment and then said, "I may be sticking my neck out, but I think we—I mean the American government—would have to support their participation in any major international conference on the future of South Africa. I think it would be foolish to do otherwise."

Michael Keneally was standing beside Tony on the edge of the group, listening. Jenny had drifted back into the lounge room in conversation with two other women friends.

"It's amazing, you know," Keneally said softly to Tony, "Nelson Mandele has been in prison since the early sixties and Robert Sobukwe has been under a banning order for about the same time and in prison for the past two years, and yet the people still look to them as their leaders—much more so than they would to even Buthalezi for instance."

"It all dates back to Sharpeville, doesn't it?" Tony said.

"That's right, 1961. No . . . 1960 it was. Mandele and Sobukwe were leading huge protest demonstrations against the pass laws and Sharpeville was one of them. The Sharpeville Massacre. Hell, that took some living down."

"They've never lived it down," Tony said.

"No, and what is it now? Twenty-one years." Keneally looked at his watch. "Exactly twenty-one years on March 21, in two days' time."

At 9.10 PM Milton, Zak, and Joseph left the garage and slipped through a side door, into the darkened back garden of the Marais house. While Milton crept silently to one side of the building and snipped the telephone wires, Zak and Joseph carried the two ladders that Milton's father had left just inside the garage doors towards the back of the garden. Milton joined them as they moved cautiously, circling around a large swimming pool and changing room, then under a huge eucalyptus tree, to the wall that separated them from the American consul's house. Several lights were burning on the ground and first floor of the Marais household, but Milton and his crew were completely obscured from the house at their position by the back wall.

Zak placed the first ladder against the wall and Milton climbed cautiously to the top, peering over into the dark. The Haylock house, on the other side, was also partly obscured from the wall by two large trees, but Milton coud now just hear the muffled hum of many voices in conversation. He glanced down at the thin wire running along the top of the wall and touched it, secure in the knowledge that his father had turned off the master-switch at least ten minutes earlier. He experienced a momentary flash of fear the instant he touched it, when he realised that he would not really have known what to do if it *had* gone off.

Joseph Mfulu passed the other ladder up to Milton, who swung it around and lowered it into position on the other side of the wall. Milton dropped out of sight into the consul's garden. Zak and Joseph followed. Once on the ground, they moved quickly and quietly towards the rear of the big house.

"That's Verhoef, there," Michael Keneally said, nodding his head toward a corner of the room where Tony saw a tall, blond man talking within a small group of other people. Keneally left Tony to get some food from the buffet table and to join Jenny and her friends, while Tony moved over to get a closer look at Carl Verhoef. As he did so, he noticed that Ingrid and Eugene Dekker were still standing talking with the other group, nearby. Dekker's back was to Tony, but Ingrid saw him and said a brief hello with her eyes; apart from that, she gave no sign of recognition.

Tony thought, as he came nearer to Verhoef, that he would be somewhere in his mid-forties. He had very strong features; a slightly hooked nose, somewhat like a hawk, with piercing, pale blue eyes. Tony also observed, after a few moments, that Verhoef had a disconcerting habit of half-closing the lids of his eyes, usually when he was listening to someone else, and peering out from under them, as if they were hoods. His facial skin, though sun-tanned, was absolutely smooth; almost as if he never had to shave. His voice was deep and he spoke English with a strong Afrikaans accent which gave it, on occasions, a harshness.

Tony stood on the edge of the small group, listening to Verhoef and the rest of the conversation. Verhoef did not say much to begin with, although, just as Tony arrived within earshot, he heard Verhoef expressing what seemed to be a combination of disgust and anger at the fact that there were blacks present at the reception.

Then Tony saw the girl. He hadn't noticed her before, because she had been hidden behind one of the other people in the group. She was beautiful; she had long dark hair, hanging straight over her shoulders, clear white skin, and sombre, dark eyes. She was tall and had an almost haughty air. She gave the appearance of being supremely sophisticated, spoilt, and snobbish. And Tony knew her. But from where? And when?

For a few minutes he churned the recesses of his memory fruitlessly. He knew he had only seen her once before in his lifetime. It was almost as if it had been in a dream . . . and it might just as well have been, because, as hard as he tried, the right links did not connect up to give him the answer. For an instant their eyes met, but she did not give the slightest hint of recognition.

Who is she? he thought and, as if in answer, Carl Verhoef put his arm around the girl and whispered something in her ear. She smiled an intimate yet somehow lifeless smile back. I see, said Tony to himself.

"What I'm really concerned about," Tony heard Verhoef saying, "is that the government should not begin to bow to any of this pressure from the United Nations, but more particularly, from the United States. I mean, the United Nations has been without any credibility as an independent or democratic organization for years. It's been dominated by the Communists and the Afro-Asian bloc since the early seventies, so I don't think anyone really takes it seriously. But unfortunately, we have to take the United States seriously as they are the key to preventing this last part of Africa from falling to the Communists." He looked across in the direction of the special envoy, Cyrus Brown. He took a large cigar from a gold case, which he produced from an inside pocket, and lit it. Everyone in the group remained silent until he resumed speaking.

"That's why it's important that this character," he nodded towards the American envoy, "gets the situation right and also that Botha doesn't allow him to sell us short with these blacks up north. I've arranged for a meeting with Brown tomorrow morning, before he goes."

189

Tony moved slightly forward into the group and said, "What sort of role has the HNP played in the talks with Cyrus Brown in Cape Town, Mr. Verhoef?"

The group parted slightly and everyone turned to look at Tony. Verhoef's eyes focused on him and, for a second, they hooded menacingly. "I'm sorry," he said, "I don't think we've met."

"Oh," Tony said, "I'm sorry . . . Bartlett . . . Anthony Bartlett."

"From?"

"I'm from Australia actually. I'm in the printing industry."

"Ah, yes." Verhoef seemed to relax slightly. "This is Marta Van Sisseren," he said, turning to the beautiful dark-haired woman beside him. Tony said "Hello," and she nodded slightly in return. Verhoef then introduced Tony to two men in the group; while the others, two men and two women, introduced themselves.

"Sorry to interrupt," Tony said, picking up the threads, "it's just that I understand you're involved with the HNP and I wondered whether or not the party had any power to influence events at times like these?"

Tony felt he was on shaky grounds with Verhoef, particularly if Dekker should come across in this direction, but he thought that if he played on Verhoef's ego, he might get some response.

"Of course it's got the power to influence events," Verhoef said. "Without the HNP, the government would collapse."

"And yet it seems," said Tony, "that Mr. Brown will be carrying the message that South Africa is prepared to make considerable concessions and to meet directly with the black presidents and the rebel leaders."

"I would think that would be more of a gambit than anything else," Verhoef said. "The HNP is certainly not in favour of any concessions. One concession leads to another and the whole thing tends to fall apart, if you follow that sort of course. Look what happened to Rhodesia."

"So you don't see any possibility of a power-sharing compromise?"

"No. None at all. Why should we?" There were slight movements among the others in the group which Tony recognised as embarrassment. He turned and smiled at them.

190

"Don't get me wrong," he said. "I'm just interested to see if the HNP has got an alternative solution to this one of talking it out, and reaching compromises, that the government seems intent on pursuing." He turned back to Verhoef. "I mean, after all, the black presidents of all the surrounding countries, plus the rebel leaders, are adamant that black majority rule is the ultimate objective."

"And I say," Verhoef said quietly, his eyes hooding again, "why should we give it to them? It was the white man who built this country up from nothing. It was the white man whose knowledge and expertise built the industries, the mines, and the factories. Man, there were no blacks here when the white man came to this part of Africa. God gave this land to the whites and said, Make something out of it . . . and we have."

Tony hesitated to raise the point again, knowing the violent reactions it usually brought, but he did. "Could you have done it without the blacks?"

"Of course we could," Verhoef said forcefully. "In fact, most of the time they're more of a hindrance than a help."

"What about in your gold mines?"

"The gold mines are the result purely of white genius! To mine for gold at thirteen thousand feet extends man's technological know-how and expertise to the limits. If it had been left to the blacks to do so on their own, there'd have been no gold coming from those mines for the past fifty years." Verhoef gave a derisive and bitter laugh. "And yet they want us to hand the whole bloody lot to them on a platter! Not if I've got anything to do with it. They'll get just what they deserve . . . which is nothing."

"Is that why you're trying to get the country's gold reserves out of South Africa?" Tony said mildly, but looking straight into Verhoef's eyes. He felt a bit as if the record had got stuck in the groove; it was the same tack he'd tried with Dekker. Did he really expect a different reaction?

Tony's voice was quiet, but the words themselves were the attack and it was obvious to the others in the group that something of dramatic importance had been said, although they weren't sure what it was all about. Apart from Verhoef himself, on whom Tony's words had a startling effect, only one other person—one of the men to whom Tony had been introduced by Verhoef, a stockily built man of about thirty-five, with crew-cut hair, whom Tony took to be a bodyguard—gave an impression that he knew what Tony was talking about. He straightened up, looked directly at Tony, then back to Verhoef questioningly, then back to Tony. The others looked at Tony with a mixture of puzzlement and hostility because the antagonism in his question to Verhoef was implicit.

When Tony had first said the words, Verhoef's mouth had literally dropped open and his face had flushed deeply. He said something that sounded like "Wha . . . " almost immediately, but then remained silent for a few seconds, staring at Tony, his mouth set hard. Marta Van Sisseren also opened her mouth in amazement, Tony noticed, and, he thought, gave a little gasp of surprise as he spoke.

"What are you talking about?" Verhoef almost whispered.

"Johan Glaser and Stefan Welz chartered an aircraft on behalf of you and Paul Trauseld in the name of a non-existent company called Potgeiter Investments and attempted to fly millions of Rands' worth of gold bullion out of the country just a week ago. Unfortunately something went wrong with your plans, which for some reason or other the government does not know about, or isn't prepared to do anything about."

Verhoef's eyes flickered. If he hadn't seemed to Tony to be such a basically sinister person, Tony might have laughed involuntarily. For a moment it struck him that the flickering of Verhoef's eyelids was not unlike that of a coy schoolgirl. It was, however, only a fleeting thought, as the malevolence of Verhoef's attitude towards Tony was now patently obvious.

"Now I know who you are," he said. "You're the crackpot journalist who Eugene Dekker threw out of his office yesterday." He drew himself up and said to the others in the group, "Which is about the level of contempt he deserves."

He turned away and began speaking to one of the men in Afrikaans. A couple of others in the group muttered abuse at Tony as they turned their backs on him and the girl, Marta Van Sisseren, also turned away with Verhoef, without a word. Only the stocky

192

man with the crew-cut remained facing Tony. He said not a word. He just stood there, staring blankly at Tony with a grim, humourless face. Tony backed away and began to weave through the crowd to try to find Keneally again. I need a drink, he thought.

But he had not moved more than a dozen steps before he came to a sudden halt. Anybody watching his face would have seen it register almost as great a degree of shock as Tony had elicited from Verhoef only a few moments earlier. There, not twenty feet in front of him, in conversation with the American consul and two other people, was Johnathan Kapepwe . . .

In the darkness outside the consulate residence, Milton had cut the telephone lines to the building and, with Zak and Joseph close behind, had edged through the shrubbery at the side of the lawn until the three men were within ten feet of the terrace, on which many of the guests were now standing talking. They crouched, pressed close against the wall in the shadows, waiting for their signal. Only a low balustrade separated them from the people on the terrace. The three men all held their automatic weapons ready in their hands.

A man and a woman separated themselves from the rest of the crowd and came across to the balustrade. The woman leant back against it, half-sitting on the low wall. The man stood slightly to one side, facing her. They were less than five feet from Milton's position in the bushes.

"How long is he going to be in Cape Town?" the man said.

"Only three days," the woman replied.

"I'll come over at nine. Will he have gone by then?"

"Yes. And the childen will be at school. It's only that damn Annie. She's such a busy-body. I'm sure she knows about us already . . . and she's such a gossip."

"Why don't you give her the day off?"

"I've a mind to sack her for good measure. She's hopeless anyway. Ever since we've had her, the dishes haven't been done properly and she's totally unimaginative when it comes to cooking. I might just as well do it myself."

"Where did you get her?"

"She was with the Jenkinses and, when they went to Canada, they gave her to us."

"I think they're all getting a bit difficult now . . . bloody uppity. That boy I sacked the other day was getting too big for his boots, resentful. He actually threatened me when he left . . . told me my time would come . . . Ha!"

In the bushes, Zak gave a grim smile.

"Never mind," the woman said. "I'll make sure that Annie's gone by the time you come and we'll be able to spend the whole day in . . . "

"Sshhh!" the man whispered. "Here comes Jerry."

"Hello, Jerry," the man by the balustrade now said aloud, "we've just been talking about your domestic problems."

"Oh?" Jerry said cautiously, looking at his wife.

"Oh no, not those problems, darling," she laughed. "Annie. I was telling Peter about Annie and what a dreadful bore she is."

"Here's your drink, darling," he handed his wife a glass of rum and Coke. "Sorry, Peter, I didn't get anything for you. Didn't know you were out here."

"That's all right," he said. "I've still got some left, anyway."

"Annie," the husband said thoughtfully. "Yes, she is a bore. I think we'll have to get rid of her."

. . . Or was it Johnathan Kapepwe? Tony stood rooted to the spot for a few moments, staring at the black man in the long robes talking to the three other men. He had so far not seen Tony. Was it one of those situations where the first impression is the right one? Tony was a little confused, because now that he looked more carefully, he realised this man was quite different from the man he had seen just over a week ago on the TanZam Railway. This man was beardless, whereas Kapepwe had a large, full beard. The Kapepwe on the train had also had a fuzzy, afro-style hair-do, whereas this man's hair was short and closely cropped all over.

But when Tony saw that it was only the hair and the beard that were different, he started once again ticking off the similarities. The height appeared to be the same, but the loose robes prevented

194

Tony from seeing what sort of build the man was. The general impression was one of slimness, though.

The men began to move in Tony's direction. He stood where he was and looked at the black man. Their eyes met briefly and Tony thought he saw a flash of recognition, but it passed instantly as the man continued talking to the consul, as if nothing had happened.

As the group came closer to Tony, crossing the dining room, he realised he would have to move to let them past, but he remained where he was and said to the black man, as the group stopped, "Excuse me," and then to the consul, "I'm sorry, Mr. Haylock, it's just that I think we have met before." Tony gestured towards the man in the long robes.

"I don't think so," the black man said, in quite a strong American accent, "your face is not familiar to me." He smiled what seemed to be a genuine smile and held out his hand. "Henry Lobosane. How do you do."

Tony found himself slightly nonplussed by the man's disarming openness. He took his hand and shook it.

"Bartlett," he said, "Tony Bartlett . . . I . . . ."

"Professor Lobosane has just spent five years at the University of Wisconsin," the American consul said. "He returned to South Africa only yesterday on sabbatical leave."

"Courtesy of the State Department," Lobosane said, smiling at the consul, who gave a smug grin in return.

"Yes. The professor is here on a State Department fellowship grant to look into ways of improving language teaching in small country townships."

"What do you lecture in at Wisconsin?" Tony asked, chastened but still suspicious.

"English Literature."

"And have you been away from South Africa long?"

"Seven years altogether. I left in '74."

"Do you have family here? Relatives?"

The professor maintained a relaxed and interested manner. Tony, on the other hand, felt stiff and formal. He couldn't relax. There

195

was something about Lobosane which he felt was inescapably Kapepwe.

"Sure." The professor smiled. "My mother and father live in Cape Town—and two brothers also. I'll be seeing them within a few days."

"So you only arrived yesterday? Which way did you come?"

"From the States? Via Europe. Spent a day in Lisbon to pick up the direct flight. It's quite a hop. Eleven hours non-stop." The professor looked directly at Tony.

It's his eyes, Tony thought immediately. His eyes. The professor's limpid black eyes were identical to Johnathan Kapepwe's.

"You said I reminded you of someone," Professor Lobosane said, still smiling. "Who was it?"

Tony collected his thoughts. For a second he had been lost and the professor's voice had gone into the background.

"What? I . . . Well, I suppose it was someone who looked very much like you. He was a writer I knew in London. I must have been mistaken. Extraordinary likeness."

"Yes, well, if you'll excuse us, Mr. Bartlett," the consul said, taking the professor by the arm.

"Nice to meet you," Lobosane drawled as they moved off.

"Yes," Tony said. "Sorry to interrupt you."

He turned and watched them negotiate a path through the crowd of guests in the direction of the special envoy, Cyrus Brown, who was now talking to another set of people on the far side of the dining room. Tony noticed also that Verhoef and his friends had moved their position and were standing near to Cyrus Brown, and were apparently about to serve themselves some food from the table.

Tony found himself drifting slowly back in the same direction, watching the consul and the black professor talking to one or two people for a few minutes and then moving on, also evidently heading for the food table. Tony held a glass in his hands and, looking at it, realised that he had been going to get a drink. He moved towards the small bar at the end of one of the food tables. The barman poured him a Scotch and, taking a sip, he began to walk thoughtfully towards the terrace. Through the crowd, just to his left near the French windows now, he saw Verhoef lean over to whisper some-

196

thing to the dark-haired girl, Marta. She turned her head slightly and, in a flash, he knew where he had seen her.

"My God!" Tony said under his breath, and turned back to look at the black professor.

In the garden, underneath the shrubs, Milton held a small radio receiver close to his ear. Zak and Joseph crouched behind him. Suddenly, there were three quick little bleeps on the receiver and Milton turned and whispered to his comrades: "That's it . . . let's go!"

As if in a dream, Tony saw the professor reach into his long robes and withdraw a long-barrelled pistol which was fitted with a silencer. He pushed the consul and the American special envoy, who was standing close by, to one side and shouted a few words of command, which Tony missed, because of the screams made by several women at the sight of the gun.

Simultaneously there was a commotion on the terrace, as Milton, Zak, and Joseph broke from their cover and, in one movement, leapt over the balustrade onto the tiled floor of the terrace amongst the guests. Milton and Zak moved quickly through the parting crowd towards the door of the dining room, issuing sharp, urgent commands as they did so: "Up against the wall . . . quickly . . . up against the wall!"

Joseph, who was carrying his AK-47 slung over his right shoulder so that it nestled under his arm in such a way that he could comfortably handle it with one hand, also carried his pistol, which was fitted with a silencer, in his left hand. He remained on the terrace to see that the orders were carried out and, in less than thirty seconds, all of those on the terrace, except one, were facing the wall of the house with their hands held high against it. The one exception was Jerry Kendall, who already lay dead on the floor, a pool of blood spreading from beneath his body. He and his wife and their friend Peter had been almost bowled over when Milton and his crew came bounding over the balustrade. After the initial shock, Jerry had not obeyed the orders to move up against the wall.

"Why, you dirty little kaffir," he had snarled as he lunged at Joseph.

The little "phutt, phutt!" sounds made by Joseph's silenced Webley had been almost inaudible amongst the general noise and confusion, but the impact of the 9mm snub-nosed shells striking Jerry's chest had stopped him in his tracks and hurled him backwards, with a look of surprise on his face, to land him in a crumpled heap at the feet of his wife and his friend Peter.

By the time Zak and Milton came through the doorway from the terrace, the professor—or Johnathan Kapepwe, as Tony now knew him to be—was ordering everyone to move up against two of the dining-room walls.

Everything was happening so quickly. In one move, Kapepwe bounded to where Carl Verhoef was standing and, without hesitation, shot the stocky, crew-cut man standing beside him in the face at point-blank range. He pulled Verhoef violently to one side and waved the pistol at Dekker, Ingrid, and Verhoef's girl-friend, Marta. "Up against the wall!" Kapepwe shouted, and pointed to where Tony and a group of others, including the American consul, had backed up against one wall.

Tony saw a man on the other side of the room, probably one of the Marine guards, draw a pistol. A burst of fire came from Milton's PPS-43 and the man with the pistol fell dead on the floor. Another man and a woman, who were standing next to him, were also killed instantly by the same burst.

Kapepwe now stood behind Verhoef, pushing the pistol hard into his back. Milton and Zak were standing watching the crowd up against the walls. The whole operation had so far taken just over a minute.

"Come on," Kapepwe said, "that'll bring the police from outside." He pushed Verhoef. "Move," he said. "Out there." Verhoef moved.

As they were passing through the doorway onto the terrace, Kapepwe said, "Stop!" From the terrace, Joseph covered Verhoef with his AK-47. Inside the dining room, Milton and Zak covered the crowd up against the walls.

Kapepwe looked quickly at the group of people standing beside Tony next to the door.

"Dekker!" he shouted. Eugene Dekker looked up from his position by the wall. Kapepwe raised his pistol, as if he were about to say, "Come over here," and shot Dekker between the eyes, without a word. The pistol went off not five feet from Tony's face. Again, because it was silenced, it seemed deceptively harmless. But Eugene Dekker now lay dead on the floor with half his face missing.

The room was a din of screams and some of the terror of the guests seemed to transfer itself to the four armed men, who now made moves to escape.

"Get going, quickly!" Kapepwe jabbed Verhoef in the back and moved rapidly out onto the terrace and over the balustrade. Inside the dining room, Zak and Milton backed as quickly as they could towards the door. Zak went first and while Joseph covered him from the terrace, he ran and jumped the balustrade to go with Kapepwe and Verhoef to the wall at the back of the garden.

As Milton was about to follow, one of the uniformed white policemen from the front gate came bursting into the room from the lounge reception area, with a pistol in his hand. Before the policeman could even see what was happening, Milton had pressed the trigger of his PPS-43 for only a second, during which time ten rounds had left the barrel in a stuttering roar. Six of them found the policeman's body, dropping him in his tracks. One of the other bullets hit a woman in the back of the head, killing her outright. Another passed through the hand of the American special envoy, Mr. Cyrus Brown, as he held it high against the wall. The other two missiles embedded themselves harmlessly in the same wall.

Milton turned and ran through the doorway to the terrace. As he did so, Tony, almost without thinking, stuck out his foot and Milton fell sprawling on his face on the terrace floor, his automatic weapon sending off a volley of bullets into the air, narrowly missing Joseph who was standing near the balustrade. At the same instant, a large man in a grey suit stepped quickly from the crowd near Tony, taking a pistol from under his left shoulder inside his jacket. He jumped into the doorway, through which Milton had just fallen, and pumped two shells into his back as he was getting up from the floor. Then he quickly fired one shot at Joseph, but it missed and Joseph was already returning the fire. Hit by three shots from

Joseph's assault rifle, the big man also crumpled to the floor. Joseph leapt the balustrade and ran as fast as he could across the darkened lawn towards the wall.

With the terrorists gone, confusion had full rein inside the Haylock house. The rest of the police charged into the room. Two women fainted. Ingrid threw herself into Tony's arms. She was splattered, all over her face and hair and the top of her dress, with Eugene's blood, as were several other people. Three policemen and another of the consulate's Marine guards ran out into the night, all carrying weapons. Fifteen seconds later there were some pistol shots and another burst of submachine gun fire from the back of the garden.

Tony sat Ingrid down against a wall. He stepped out onto the terrace and looked down at Milton Molefe. Milton had twisted and fallen back onto the tiled terrace floor on his back. His head, which was turned a little unnaturally to one side, lay in the large pool of blood that had spread from Jerry Kendall's body. A small trickle of blood came from Milton's mouth. His eyes, though open, were quite vacant.

As Tony looked down into those empty eyes, he had no way of knowing that it had been Milton Molefe who had led the raid on the Brixton Tower less than a week earlier, that Milton had just turned twenty-one, and that his mother was lying, sobbing—terrified for her son—on her bed only a few hundred yards away. All Tony knew was that, whether he was a bad man or a good man, less than two minutes earlier this man had been alive and, simply because Tony had tripped him, he was now dead.

Kapepwe and Zak, bundling and pushing Verhoef in front of them, had reached the garden wall within about thirty seconds of leaving the house. Zak went up the ladder first and straight down the other side. Kapepwe pushed his pistol hard into Verhoef's back and shoved him to the ladder.

"Move, whitey!" he spat out the words with undisguised hatred. "Get up that fuckin' ladder . . . fast!" He jabbed the pistol painfully into Verhoef's kidneys. Verhoef climbed up and over. On the far side Zak covered him, while Kapepwe followed, but once over the

200

wall, Kapepwe remained, on the Marais side, to wait for Milton and Joseph.

"Take him to the car, quickly," he said to Zak. Within seconds, Joseph came running through the darkness and was up the ladder.

"Milton's dead!" he panted.

"Get over, quickly," Kapepwe said, taking Joseph's AK-47, while the two precariously shared the top of the ladder on the Marais side of the wall, so that Kapepwe could cover Joseph as he struggled to raise the ladder from the consul's garden.

A shot rang out, then another. The second one tore through the sleeve of Joseph's shirt, grazing his arm. Kapepwe let loose a burst from the AK-47 and the second white policeman fell dead. One black policeman was also hit in the shin. He fell to the ground, gasping. Joseph hurled the ladder down on the Marais side of the wall and the two men leapt to the ground to run for the garage.

Seconds earlier, lights had flashed on in the ground floor of the Marais household and, just as Kapepwe and Joseph reached the side door of the garage, Clement Marais, who had been in the front den watching television with his wife and had been disturbed by the shooting, ran out of the back door of his house.

"Hey!" he shouted.

Joseph whirled around, firing blindly as he did so, and Clement Marais fell to the concrete pathway, hit in the leg and shoulder. He was quite conscious, but he had the presence of mind not to move once he had fallen and to make no sound. He remained there until the three terrorists and their hostage had roared off in the station wagon, down the drive, out the front gate and, with a scream of tyres, turned into the roadway and disappeared into the night.

Within minutes of the escape, the Marais backyard was a blaze of lights and full of people. The remaining Marine guard and the black policeman had climbed the back wall and now came into the Marais garden. Mrs. Marais was the first person to come out of the house after her husband had been shot. A minute or so later, Solomon and Mary Molefe also ventured outside to render assistance to the injured Mr. Marais.

In the car, Zak sat alone in the front seat, driving. Kapepwe and Verhoef sat in the back, as widely separated as possible, with Kapepwe holding his pistol so that it pointed across the seat at Verhoef's stomach. Joseph was in the rear part of the wagon with the back window wound down. He had his own weapons, plus Zak's Scorpion machine pistol, the RGD-5 grenades, and his tool box, which held several plastic containers, open beside him.

Verhoef sat grimly and silently against the door. At a couple of stages he had contemplated opposing the men, but when he had seen his bodyguard disposed of in cold blood and then Dekker shot, apparently for no reason, he realised that in the hands of these men, his life was cheap.

If there had been light enough in the car, Verhoef's face would have appeared like that of a ghost. It was completely drained of colour. For the first time in many, many years, he was frightened. He realised that the longer he delayed any action, the less likelihood there would be of his ever escaping from these men. The thought had crossed his mind of opening the door of the car and hurling himself out, but the car was going too fast. They were on a reasonably open, main road now and it would be suicide to attempt it.

The three terrorists did not know it, but they had an even bigger lead on any possible pursuers than they could have hoped for. The confusion at the consulate residence and the policemen they had killed there helped enormously. With the telephone lines cut, the only possible communication with police headquarters was through the two-way radios in the squad cars parked at the front of the consulate residence. But two of the policemen were dead, a third injured, and the remaining black policeman had climbed the garden wall with the others attempting to follow the terrorists.

By the time another ladder had been found and the first pursuers, including the black policeman, had climbed over the wall, a vital two minutes had passed since the car had left the garage. More precious time went by while they established that Mr. Marais was only wounded, and that they couldn't use the phones in the Marais house either, then the black policeman had got back over the wall and out to his squad car to give the first urgent and slightly garbled message of the kidnapping to his headquarters. A total of six minutes had elapsed before the alarm was raised. By that time, Johnathan Kapepwe, Zak Molako, and Joseph Mfulu were more than five miles from the Marais house.

But their position had been made even better by the fact that, in his rush to get back to the squad car to report the killings and the kidnap, the policeman had forgotten to find out the make and registration number of the car used in the escape, and to inform headquarters that it was taken from the Marais house and not from the consulate residence. Consequently, another three minutes' lead was gained by the kidnappers while the policeman returned, over the wall, to the Marais house to find out the relevant details about the car. Three more squad cars arrived within eight minutes of the first call, but at the consulate residence and not the Marais house. Another two minutes were taken up while two of the squad cars followed the roundabout route from the Haylock house to the front gate of the Marais estate and, from the tyre-marks on the road, established which way the car had gone.

This meant that nine minutes had elapsed before a description of the car was received and immediately broadcast, but sixteen minutes before the police had established in which direction it might be heading.

The three kidnappers heard the first police broadcast of the description of their car on a small, short-wave radio in Joseph's tool kit. But, by that stage, they had left the main highway north of Randburg and were tearing along a secondary road heading north-west towards the Witwatersberg. By the time the police found the tyre-marks outside the Marais gate and knew that they had turned north instead of south, the car was some eighteen miles away and had crossed so many roads and made so many turns that there was nothing the police could do but guess—and they guessed wrongly. They surmised that the vehicle was heading in the general direction of Pretoria.

There was a slight relaxing of tension in the car when the police conversation informing other squad cars to concentrate on the network of roads linking Johannesburg to the capital came across. There was, of course, a general alert, but the route the escape car

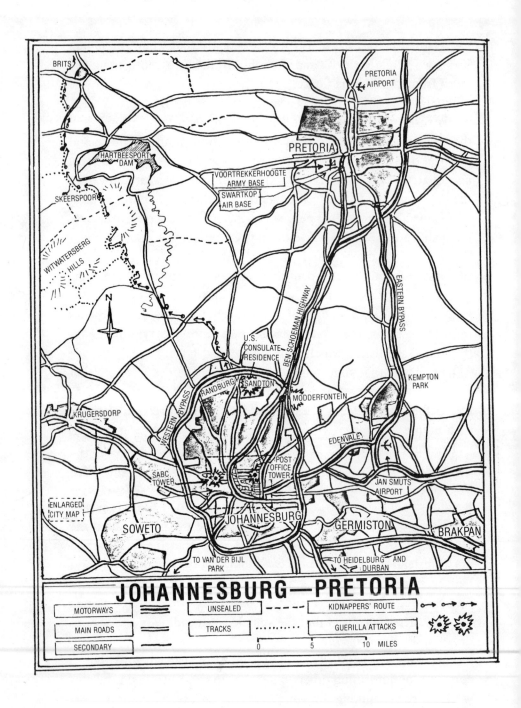

BRITS

PRETORIA
AIRPORT

HARTBEESPORT
DAM

PRETORIA

SKEERSPOORT

VOORTREKKERHOOGTE
ARMY BASE

SWARTKOP
AIR BASE

WITWATERSBERG
HILLS

N

EASTERN BYPASS

BEN SCHOEMAN HIGHWAY

U.S.
CONSULATE
RESIDENCE

KEMPTON
PARK

RANDBURG
SANDTON

MODDERFONTEIN

KRUGERSDORP

WESTERN BYPASS

EDENVALE

SABC
TOWER

POST
OFFICE
TOWER

JAN SMUTS
AIRPORT

ENLARGED
CITY MAP

SOWETO

JOHANNESBURG

GERMISTON

BRAKPAN

TO VAN DER BIJL
PARK

TO HEIDELBURG AND
DURBAN

JOHANNESBURG—PRETORIA

MOTORWAYS	UNSEALED	KIDNAPPERS' ROUTE
MAIN ROADS	TRACKS	GUERILLA ATTACKS
SECONDARY		

0   5   10   MILES

was following was now less likely to come under scrutiny. In the back of the wagon, Joseph almost felt disappointed that he might not get the opportunity to use some of his special devices on any following cars.

Kapepwe spoke his first words to Verhoef since they entered the car.

"You don't like black people, do you, Mr. Verhoef?"

Verhoef said nothing. He simply stared ahead.

"It can't be very nice for you to know that your life is in the hands of people you despise so."

Verhoef still remained silent.

"Do you know why you're here, Verhoef?" Kapepwe asked.

Still no reply.

"DO YOU?" Kapepwe shouted, lunging across the seat and pushing the pistol hard against Verhoef's temple.

"Uhh . . ." Verhoef flinched away. "N . . no."

"Oh yes you do! You know why you're here. Your days have been numbered in this country for some time, and you and your white cronies have known it. But if you think that you are going to destroy our chances of liberating Azania and running this country ourselves . . . then you're wrong."

Verhoef turned his head slightly to look at Johnathan Kapepwe. Kapepwe returned the look with a gratuitous smile. "Oh yes, Mr. Verhoef, you are wrong, because you are going to help us. We have some interesting questions we would like to put to you about gold and," Kapepwe's voice was low and menacing, "when we have more time, I have some interesting marks on my back I would like to show you."

11

A Death

"This is the BBC. The news, read by Noel Collins.

"The American special envoy to Southern Africa, Mr. Cyrus Brown, was wounded in a terrorist attack last night on the home of the American consul in Johannesburg. The attack coincided with widespread terrorist action involving several major industrial targets in different parts of South Africa."

"God, what a mess!" Tony slumped back into David Jamieson's couch. It was ten o'clock in the morning. He had just woken up. What a terrible night, he thought. The news broadcast continued:

"Ten people, who were among more than one hundred attending a reception at the home of Mr. Arnold Haylock, the American consul, were killed and three others injured by four terrorists who also kidnapped the millionaire South African industrialist, Mr. Carl Verhoef. One of the terrorists was killed, but the other three escaped with Mr. Verhoef as hostage.

"According to reports, one of the terrorists had been attending the reception as a guest, disguised as an American university professor.

"The American special envoy, Cyrus Brown, was hit in the hand by a bullet fired by one of the terrorists. Mr. Brown, who is due to leave South Africa today to continue talks with black African leaders on the South African independence issue, is reported to be in a satisfactory condition and says he will not delay his departure for the Botswanian capital, Gaberones."

"I'll bet he wants to get out of the place as fast as he can,"

206

David Jamieson said. He was again sitting opposite Tony in exactly the same position he had been twenty-four hours earlier, and again lighting up a cigarette.

"In other attacks," the announcer went on, "the major oil-from-coal refinery at Sasolburg, forty miles south of Johannesburg, was subjected to heavy mortar and rocket fire during the night, and four power-generating plants supplying the industrial complexes of Johannesburg and Pretoria were attacked. Two of the plants, at Grootvlei and Komati, are believed to have been so badly damaged that it may be several months before they can be made operational again."

Tony sat forward to listen more closely.

"No estimates of the damage to the Sasolberg refinery have been made available, but our South African correspondent points out that, as there is a total United Nations embargo on all foreign oil shipments to South Africa, the country relies entirely on its ability to refine fuel oil from coal at the Sasolberg plant and one other near Trichardt in the eastern Transvaal. Last night's attack, which comes only twenty-four hours after the partial destruction of the major steelworks at Van de Bijl Park, could, our correspondent says, severely limit South Africa's fuel oil production capacity.

"In Washington, President Carter has warned the Soviet Union that five Soviet merchant vessels, believed to be carrying tactical nuclear weapons, will be prevented from landing their cargoes in Southern Africa. Following an emergency meeting of the American Congress yesterday morning, Mr. Carter said that he has ordered the American Indian Ocean Task Force to intercept three Russian vessels, if they attempt to enter any Mozambique ports. He said that elements of the United States Second Fleet, operating in the southern Atlantic with the nuclear attack carrier, *Dwight D. Eisenhower,* had been given similar instructions regarding two Soviet vessels reportedly heading for the Namibian port of Luderitz."

The news continued for a minute or so more on the South African crisis, giving some details of the emergency session of the South African Parliament in Cape Town, before going on to other items.

"God, what an unholy mess this is turning into," Tony said, getting up to stretch his legs.

He had not returned to his hotel that night, but had spent it at David Jamieson's place, working until three in the morning, filing his stories to London, before collapsing to sleep on the divan in Jamieson's den.

It had been more than an hour before the police had let him leave the Haylocks' house. All of the guests—at least those who were not wounded or hysterical—were questioned for various lengths of time; some only for a few minutes, some quite thoroughly. There were ambulance men and morticians removing the bodies and cleaning up the mess.

Tony desperately wanted to get out of the place. He wanted to be with Ingrid; to comfort her and hold her; but other people, friends of Dekker's and hers, were doing that. He felt it might create difficulties if he appeared to be too close to Ingrid. After half an hour she was allowed to leave. She glanced briefly and sadly at Tony as she walked from the room with two other couples, but she said nothing.

Michael Keneally and his wife were told they were free to leave at about 10.45. Michael offered to stay and wait for Tony, but Tony assured him that he would be all right and that he should go.

The consul, Mr. Haylock, was of course questioned at length about Kapepwe, or Professor Lobosane, as he knew him. He assured them that there had been nothing prior to the attack which might have aroused his suspicions about the professor. He had received a telegram from the State Department in Washington, advising him of Mr. Lobosane's return visit to South Africa, and the consulate had been involved in deciding his itinerary. His attendance at the reception had been planned for some time, in fact—well before his departure from the United States. The police asked several questions about his stopover in Lisbon on the way to South Africa and it seemed they would pursue their investigations about the twenty-four hours Lobosane spent in Lisbon, with the Portuguese police.

For some reason, the consul did not mention Tony Bartlett's conversation with Lobosane/Kapepwe. It apparently slipped his mind completely.

208

Tony also decided not to mention it, when the police questioned him. He had a nasty feeling that his omission of this information would catch up with him, but, for the moment, he wanted to get away from the place as soon as possible. At ten past eleven he was told he could go.

As he settled behind the wheel of his hired car in the shadow of the trees outside the front gate, he noticed another car draw up and three men leave it, to walk hurriedly towards the gate. Two of them were the men from BOSS he had encountered on the previous day. He decided not to return to his hotel, but to go straight to David Jamieson's place and to stay there for the night.

Jamieson's home was divided in two; one half was his office, complete with teleprinter machines, telephones, maps, filing cabinets, and desks; the other was his home, soundproofed and separate. When Tony arrived, Jamieson was on the point of going to bed. Of course, he had not heard a word of the terrorist attack on the consulate reception.

He was astounded when Tony told him the news, but professionally there was nothing he could do until Tony had filed his own story. Tony extracted a promise from him to this effect, even though he knew it wouldn't be necessary. They had a standing arrangement. All the same, Jamieson was hovering around in frustrated anticipation while Tony worked at getting his story together.

He had contacted the *Herald's* night editor on the printer at just after midnight, about 10.00 PM in London. Tony was told that Childers was still there. When he gave them the bare outlines of the story on the printer, their amazement and excitement could be felt, just from the printed words coming up in front of Tony. Tony was told that they would hold the front page open for him.

He then sat down to work solidly on the story, getting the last takes off on the printer by 2.00 AM—midnight in London. It took him an hour to wind down before he could even think of sleeping. He kept wondering about Kapepwe. Tony had named him in his story, but now he had doubts about whether he should have done so or not. He needn't have worried. Childers dropped the name from the story, referring to him only as a "well-known South African writer who has been living in London."

But the story had been splashed across the front pages of the *Herald,* which had a two-edition lead over all the other British dailies. Childers was ecstatic and Tony was, for the moment at least, vindicated.

At three in the morning, just before he began to doze off on Jamieson's divan, Tony had also wondered whether or not he should call his colleague, Mulgrave, and tell him of the developments, but he decided not to. I also have the ability to be a bastard, Tony said to himself, smiling as he settled back further into the soft cushions.

Now, at a quarter past ten in the morning, as the news finished, Tony began to try again to sort out what he should do next.

"What do you know about Marta Van Sisseren?" he asked Jamieson, who had just handed him a cup of coffee.

"Nothing much, except that she created a real scandal here last year, when she took up with Verhoef . . . broke his marriage up."

"Where's his wife now?"

"In Europe somewhere, I think."

"What about Marta? Where does she come from?"

"She's Dutch, I think."

"But how long has she been in South Africa?"

"Haven't a clue. She just sort of appeared from nowhere."

"Do you know where she lives?"

"No. I suppose she's been living with Verhoef. I could probably find out."

"How?"

"Well . . . I'm not sure that I can . . . except that I have a friend who works in one of Verhoef's companies. He might have some of that sort of gossip. I could ask him."

After a brief telephone call, Jamieson sat down again with Tony and said, "He says he believes she's been living with Verhoef, but that he thinks she also has an apartment of her own in the Hillbrow area. He says it might be Bellevue Towers or something like that. Skyview, he said also."

Tony borrowed a razor from Jamieson, shaved and showered,

and, by ten to eleven, left to drive in the direction of Hillbrow. Before he left, however, he tried unsuccessfully to contact Ingrid. There was no answer from her apartment and when he telephoned the Bank's offices in both Pretoria and Johannesburg, he was told that she had not come in to work, so far.

"There's no Van Sisseren staying here," the woman said huskily. She was a dumpily built white woman of about forty-five or fifty. She wore a frowzy, floral-print rayon dress and too-high wedge-heeled shoes, from the front of each of which poked two or three rather distorted toes with unevenly painted red nails. Her skin was pallid and her hennaed hair hung in thin strands on her shoulders. She spoke with a heavy central European accent.

"Definitely no Van Sisseren."

"Are you sure?" Tony said. "She's very attractive. She has long dark hair and very pale skin."

"Look, mister, we see a lot of very attractive women around here with long black hair and pale skin. But there is no girl with that name living in these apartments."

"Well, can you tell me where the Skyview apartments are, please? Perhaps I got the name wrong."

"What? Her name?"

"No, the name of the apartment building."

"Well, there's no Skyview apartments in Hillbrow."

"Are you sure?"

"Of course I'm sure. I been here thirty years. You think I don't know, or something?"

"Of course," Tony said, rapidly losing patience. "I'm sorry. It's just that . . . "

"There's a Starview Towers over on Claim Street, but that was one of the buildings that was hit when the Post Office Tower fell."

"Thanks," said Tony. "I'll go and check over there."

Tony walked two blocks after leaving the woman and encountered the first roadblock cordoning off the disaster area around the fallen tower. It had been four days since he had first visited the scene, which was still in a state of chaos. Bulldozers and rescue workers were still clearing the rubble, and only yesterday he had heard that a family of four had been brought out alive from under the crushed remnants of their apartment block. One of the children had been trapped under a fallen beam, but the others had been free to crawl around in a confined space and were able to collect water dripping from a broken main and give it to the trapped boy. They had heard the sounds of the rescue teams and had shouted themselves hoarse, but no-one had heard them until yesterday.

Along the path of destruction lain by the falling tower, the bodies of other less fortunate victims of the tragedy continued to be found as more of the wreckage and debris was cleared.

Tony had no trouble this time in passing the roadblock. A limited pedestrian access was now allowed into the area, although vehicular traffic was still prohibited. Whites were only required to give some reasonable explanation for wanting to enter the area; being residents, or wanting to visit friends for example, to be allowed immediate entry. Blacks, on the other hand, were subjected to much more stringent requirements.

On Claim Street, Tony found the remnants of the Starview Towers. It had been a very modern fifteen-storey block. Most of the building was still standing. It had not received the full impact of the falling tower but had been struck from the side by another building, which had crumpled under the terrible impact of the tower itself. Tons of concrete had exploded sideways into one wall of the Starview building, causing the top four floors and most of one side of it to fall. The rest, however, remained standing. How precarious the building's position was, was something a team of structural engineers was trying to establish at the time of Tony's arrival. All the surviving residents of the Starview Towers had been shifted out.

"Yes, there was a Miss Van Sisseren staying here," Tony was told by the caretaker of the building, when he eventually located him. He was an ageing Englishman who had taken up residence in the basement of a block of apartments across the road from the Starview Tower block and was responsible for the security of the remaining unoccupied apartments.

"She wasn't in the building the night the tower fell, but I saw her twice after that."

"Where?" Tony asked.

212

"Here. She came back a couple of times to get some of her things out of her flat."

"What floor was she on?"

"Tenth."

"Did she take everything . . . or did she leave some in the flat? I mean, do you think she's going to move back here eventually?"

The man looked at Tony as if he were crazy. He waved his arm at the building. "You think anyone's going to move back into *that?*"

"Where did she go, then?"

"I've got her new address written down," the old man said. "She gave it to me in case we wanted to contact her about the rest of her furniture and so on."

"So she has left some things here?"

"Of course. There's no way of getting furniture and heavy stuff down. There are no elevators working."

"So you have her address?"

"Yes . . . just a moment and I'll get it." He disappeared down a flight of steps leading from the pavement towards his new residence in the basement.

"Here it is," he said, emerging a few moments later. "There are several more addresses I've got to get . . . the other residents, you know. I've got most of them. Now. Marta Van Sisseren? Yes, that's her . . . very pretty young woman." He looked up and across the road, "You know, I remember when she arrived . . . "

"Yes," said Tony, leaning forward. "Do you have the address?"

"Oh, yes . . . of course," and then, as if slightly affronted by Tony's impatience, "you're a friend of hers, are you?"

"That's right," said Tony. "I've just come up from Cape Town. I've been worried sick about her. Thank God she's alive."

"Yes," the old man said. "Well, all right then," and he looked down again at his scrap of paper. "She's moved to Flat 32F, Savoy Regent, down on Jager Street."

"Thank you very much."

"Hello, Marta," Tony said, as the door was opened to him.

"I . . . I'm sorry. What do you want?" She kept the door open only a fraction. Tony slipped his foot into the crack.

"Listen!" she said with immediate annoyance. "What are you doing?"

Tony pushed the door quickly open and stepped inside.

"Get out of here," she shouted angrily, "I'll call the caretaker. I'll call the police." She moved towards the telephone.

"Yes—you do that," Tony said. "I'm sure they'd be very interested to hear from you—and from me. I'd like to talk to them about our last meeting."

"What do you mean? I spoke to the police last night."

"That was last night. I'm talking about our first meeting, a long time ago. You probably don't remember me, but I remember you."

"I don't know what you're talking about," she said. "I saw you last night, but I've never seen you before that in my life."

"Oh yes you have." Tony smiled. "It was five years ago . . . more than five years ago."

Tony moved across the room towards the large windows and then sat down on a plush velvet sofa. The girl remained standing in the centre of the room, staring at Tony. She said nothing.

From his position on the sofa, Tony could see into the bedroom, where two open suitcases were sitting on the bed, half-filled with clothes.

"Moving again?" Tony said.

"That's none of your business. Now please just tell me what *your* business is and get out . . . I've got a lot to do."

"I'll give you a clue. It was in London."

"Oh come on," she said. "Get to the point and get out."

"All right." Tony smiled again. "It was at a meeting in London of the external wings of the Pan African Congress and the African National Congress at the Young Communist League's offices in Holborn. All the various anti-apartheid groups were there. I was there too—as an observer."

"Yes?" Marta Van Sisseren said quietly. Her eyes narrowed imperceptibly and she let her arms hang loose by her sides as she stood staring at Tony. "And presumably you observed something?"

"I did," Tony said. "I observed you there . . . with Johnathan Kapepwe!"

214

She brought one hand up in front of her and began to examine her fingernails for a few seconds, apparently thinking.

"I don't know where you came from, or where you went," Tony went on, "but I remember that on that occasion, you gave the impression of being very close to Johnathan . . . and yet you disappeared completely from the scene after that. What happened?"

She turned and walked towards the big window and stood, staring out over the city.

"It must have been quite a surprise for you to see Johnathan last night at the reception—or *was* it such a surprise?"

Marta Van Sisseren's face was completely expressionless as she turned back from the window. She walked towards the bedroom slowly, saying as she went, "You interest me, Mr. Barton . . . I think that . . . "

"Bartlett," Tony said.

"Whatever you say. I don't quite know what to make of you. You attacked Carl last night, and now you come to resurrect a section of my past that could be damaging to me." She reached inside her suitcase and turned back towards Tony with a small black pistol in her hand.

"I think," she said softly as she took a few steps into the lounge room, pointing the weapon at Tony, "that you are a very dangerous person—dangerous to me, anyway, and that is all that matters. I would have to admit that if what you have just said became known to others here, I would be in a very awkward situation. Therefore, I am unfortunately going to have to kill you." She raised the pistol and pointed it directly at Tony's head.

Tony held his hands up. "Wait!" he almost shouted, all of his cock-sureness gone, replaced by a sensation of cold fear in the pit of his stomach. "You . . . you'll never get away with it. You'll go to jail."

"Don't be ridiculous," she said. "After the aggressive way you behaved last night towards Carl, one of this country's leading citizens, it will be a simple matter for me to say that you attempted to continue the conversation in the same vein with me today and that when I refused to talk to you, you attempted to rape me. I shot you in self-defence."

Tony realised that she was working the whole thing out as she talked, but he also knew that there was a chance she could get away with a story like that and that she almost certainly wasn't fooling with the gun. She would shoot him.

He stalled desperately. "I . . . I've already told someone else. If you kill me, they'll tell the police."

"Who?"

"Well, I'm not going to tell you that, am I?"

"I'm sorry, but I don't believe you, and anyway . . . "

Two pigeons fluttered noisily up to land on the window sill next to Marta Van Sisseren and she turned, with a start, to look at them for an instant. Tony dived at her. With one hand he went for the gun, grabbing at her wrist. They went rolling onto the floor with the pistol falling to one side. The girl screamed and scrambled wildly with Tony, biting and tearing and struggling to get at the gun. Tony yelled in pain as she bit into his hand. For an instant he was on his back and she rolled across his stomach reaching for the weapon on the floor. Tony swung his fist around awkwardly and caught Marta hard on the side of the face. She went sprawling off him and screamed again. Tony pulled her head up by the hair and hit her once more on the jaw with his right. She fell back unconscious. Tony picked up the pistol, stuck it in his pocket, and stepped quickly across to the door and out into the corridor, closing it behind him. A few seconds later, as he was walking towards the elevator, a man and a woman came running around the corner of the hallway.

"It was down this way, I think," the woman was saying, and then, when she saw Tony, "Did you hear someone screaming?"

"No," Tony said. "I didn't hear a thing."

Bruno Van Wyk regarded himself as a perfect physical specimen. He was a big man, about six foot four, but there was not an ounce of fat on his body because he worked so hard at keeping himself fit. He never smoked or drank and he ate only good foods, but he wasn't a vegetarian because he knew the value of protein from rich, red meat. He did long, daily workouts in a gymnasium, concentrating not on muscle-building exercises, but on routines to make

216

his muscles elastic and supple; stretching exercises to keep him loose and agile. He would also run at least a mile every day and try to find time for a sauna and a massage. You might say that Bruno Van Wyk was something of a fanatic about physical fitness. It was, if you like, an obsession with him. He was more interested in the state of his own body, for instance, that in members of the opposite sex. He had never been interested in girls, even as a teen-ager—nor in boys, for that matter. He was the complete narcissist.

But Bruno Van Wyk was not only obsessive about his body . . . but its colour too. He liked swimming and the sunshine, but he was always careful not to get too much of a suntan. He was proud of the whiteness of his skin. He had blond hair and blue eyes and there was not a blemish on his body. A few scars perhaps, but no natural blemishes. The most notable scar on Bruno Van Wyk was one which ran, for three inches, diagonally across his right cheek. It had been given to him by a black man who had slashed at him with a knife during an interrogation session. The man had somehow untied his hands and reached a knife which had been lying on the table. He had paid dearly, though. Bruno had personally emascu-lated him and when his "interrogation" was finished, the man simply disappeared from the face of the earth.

Several other black subjects of Bruno Van Wyk's distinctive style of questioning had also come to unfortunate ends. Three of them, on separate occasions, "threw themselves" from the window of the eleventh-storey office in which Bruno and one or two of his col-leagues were asking them questions. When examined after their death leaps, the bodies were found to be extensively battered. But then, one can't expect to fall eleven floors without some damage.

Whenever Bruno was involved in one of these question and answer sessions, he wore surgical rubber gloves. He found he could not bear to touch black skin. It repelled him. He regarded blacks as unclean and somehow subhuman. If you asked him, he would not hesitate to say that he hated blacks. But then, there was nobody whom Bruno Van Wyk actually loved—black or white—except him-self and perhaps his mother, and she was long dead.

Bruno joined the Bureau for State Security in 1971, two years after it had first been formed, and quickly realised that he had

217

found his niche. It gave him the degree of personal power he had always wanted, without the limitations imposed by the army or the police department, both of which vocations he had tried previously. He found that BOSS tended to turn a blind eye to individual idiosyncrasies like his fetish for physical fitness and pathological hatred of blacks; in fact, to some extent, they were an advantage for him. In the eyes of his employer, anyone as single-minded as Bruno could invariably be trusted.

Bruno had been sitting, waiting in Tony Bartlett's hotel room, since two o'clock in the morning. With him was the tall, thin, parchment-faced Kurt Quin; the man in the sports coat and polo-neck sweater who had picked Tony up on the street two days earlier.

They had taken it in turns to doze while they waited. But when the morning came and wore on into the afternoon, they began to get impatient. They had ordered breakfast to be brought to the room and then lunch. They had phoned to headquarters where they learnt that the Australian had spent the night at the Reuters office, but that by the time this was discovered, he had left and gone somewhere else. The two men were told to continue waiting in Tony's room.

When Tony left Marta Van Sisseren's apartment, his mind was reeling. He had realised, the moment he remembered who she was, that she must be deeply involved in the whole intrigue, but he hadn't expected her to pull a gun on him! And there was no doubt, he thought with a slight shudder, that she had meant to use it.

At first, after he dashed out of the entrance lobby of the building, he began to hurry back towards his car, which he had parked several blocks away when he first started looking for Marta Van Sisseren's apartment. But when it became clear that he was not being chased or followed, he slowed to a walk. She's obviously been in cahoots with Kapepwe and double-crossing Verhoef, Tony said to himself. He snapped his fingers—and that's why Kapepwe was waiting in Mbeya for that plane . . . Jesus! She'd be mincemeat if that got around.

Tony felt reassured by this thought. It meant that she dare not tell the police about him, for fear that he would tell them about her. But it also meant that because Tony represented a danger to her, he would have to be careful of her—if he ever saw her again. He wondered whether she would think that he would go to the police about her anyway and then he thought, should I? Wouldn't that just be lending support to Verhoef and Trauseld and the HNP and maybe BOSS, all of whom, he was now convinced, were involved in a self-seeking conspiracy to steal a vast amount of gold.

Whose bloody side am I on? he asked under his breath as he walked along. Do I have to take sides at all? Jesus, what a mess! Why am I getting into it?

He stopped at a phone booth and tried again to telephone Ingrid. He was missing her. He felt that if he could just lose himself in her arms and the sweet, woman-smell of her body, everything else would go away. But he was unable to even talk to her on the phone. No answer from her apartment and she had not gone to work at all today.

As he stepped from the phone booth, deep in thought, there was a shout from a car passing him in the street and a screech of brakes as it came to a halt. "Hey, Tony!" Howard Goldman called, as he jumped from the car.

"Hi," he said, running up. "Jeez, I've been trying to find you all day, Tony. Where the hell you been?"

"Oh, chasing up a couple of things."

"Chasing up a couple of things," the American said derisively. "Jeeesus, listen to him! After a goddam story like that! You know all the American papers are quoting you! How the hell did you get into that reception, anyhow? We couldn't get our noses near the place."

Tony smiled a little self-consciously, "A bit of subterfuge, I suppose."

Marty, the cameraman, parked the car just ahead and walked back to join them.

"For Christ's sake, Tony," Howard said, "you've got to tell me about this thing. I mean, they didn't touch Brown at all?"

"He got a bullet in the hand," Tony said.

"Yeah, yeah, I know that . . . but they didn't take him . . . they weren't interested in him?"

Tony gave a little laugh. "Does that hurt your national pride, Howard?"

"No, but . . . well, you know. Hell, if you're going to kidnap someone, you'd think you'd go for the high stakes—and Brown was the most important guy there."

"Maybe he wasn't as important to them as Verhoef." Tony said.

The two Americans looked at Tony blankly. "Come and have a coffee," Goldman said, taking Tony by the arm and walking a short distance down the street towards a small coffee lounge. Tony knew that Goldman wanted to pick his brains, but somehow, he didn't mind at all. For one thing, he liked Howard—and Marty— and secondly, he owed them both a very big favour for rescuing him from the rioting mob on his second day in Johannesburg. Thirdly—he went over the points, rationalising a decision that was forming in his mind, to tell Howard about his theories—thirdly, he wasn't in direct competition with Howard; an American television network and a British newspaper; two different audiences, no real clash. At least that's what he hoped. Finally, Tony told himself, it would be a relief to share it with someone else.

They sat for an hour, talking. Tony began at the beginning and told them about the plane landing at Mbeya, Kapepwe's suspicious role there, the murder attempt on the train, his research here in Johannesburg which had led to the confrontations with Dekker and Verhoef and the interrogation by BOSS. But for some reason— he wasn't quite sure why—Tony didn't mention Paul Trauseld's name or Marta Van Sisseren. He thought, at one stage, that he had said enough. He felt a little like a virgin who has just lost her virginity. He had given all this information away and there was no way he could take it back. Was he being unprofessional? I haven't got enough of the killer-instinct in me, he thought. He knew dozens of journalists who would never dream of giving that much of a story away before anything had been made of it, but he felt greatly purged by his revelations to Howard and Marty.

"But there's no way of proving any of it, so far?" Marty said, after their third cup of coffee.

"No, that's the whole problem," Tony agreed. "The gold is going out. I'm sure of it. That plane was only one shipment, where things

220

went wrong. But the rest of it? Well, Verhoef knows what's happening—and before long I should think Kapepwe and his crowd will also know . . . from Verhoef."

"Holy Jeeesus," Howard Goldman whispered. "How much gold do you figure is in it?"

"At least two and a half, maybe three billion dollars," Tony replied.

Marty gave a long, low whistle and made goggle eyes. Howard Goldman just shook his head slowly from side to side.

Tony tried, from the restaurant, to phone Ingrid's apartment again, but there was no response. He began to worry about her. He telephoned the switchboard at his hotel to see if there had been any telephone calls for him and the operator confirmed that a woman had phoned, asking for him on four separate occasions during the day, but she had not left her name or a number at which she could be contacted. It was now almost five o'clock in the afternoon.

"Where are you going from here?" Tony asked Howard.

"We were just driving out towards the Witwatersberg," Howard replied. "The police say they've found the car the terrorists used last night. It had been abandoned in the bush and they apparently transferred to a four-wheel drive vehicle; one of those little Suzukis to follow some narrow trail across the hills."

"What time will you be back?"

"About seven."

"Can I come with you?"

"Sure."

At twenty minutes past seven, Tony walked into the lobby of the Carlton Hotel. Howard Goldman had dropped him back in the Hillbrow area, where he had picked up his own car and driven back to the hotel, parking it, purposely, some two blocks away.

Out in the Witwatersberg, Tony had seen the Marais family's station wagon and been along some of the trail the kidnappers had taken. He spoke to police on the scene and learnt that they had followed the trail right up to a spot near the small township of Skeerspoort, to the west of the Hartbeespoort Dam, but that the vehicle had gone back onto tarred roads for at least a short distance and they had lost the track. They surmised, however, that it had been heading in the direction of Brits.

At the desk of the hotel, Tony checked again to see if there had been any more calls for him. According to the switch, there had been two more calls from the woman who did not leave her name and a message that Childers had phoned him from London.

When Tony walked into his room, he was immediately confronted by the sight of Bruno Van Wyk sitting in one of the armchairs at the far end of the room, by the window. Bruno smiled at Tony.

"What are you doing here?" Tony said. "Who are you?"

The door slammed shut behind him and he turned to see—and recognise—Kurt Quin.

"Oh, I see," Tony sighed, "it's you again. What do you want now?"

"Where did you spend last night, Mr. Bartlett?" Quin said.

"None of your business," Tony said. "Where did *you* spend it?"

"Here, Mr. Bartlett. Waiting for you."

"Well, I'm terribly sorry you had such a long wait. Now, what's it about this time?"

"Where did you go when you left the American reception?"

"Oh, for God's sake, I went to the Reuters office. I'm a journalist, you know," Tony said facetiously. "I have to work. I have to write stories, and that's what I was doing last night . . . all right? Is that against the law or something?"

Bruno Van Wyk remained seated and silent, although he kept smiling, as if amused by what Tony was saying.

"That depends on how well you know Johnathan Kapepwe."

Tony looked at Quin for several seconds. "How did you know I know him at all?" he said.

"You spoke to him last night and you wrote that you had recognised him as Kapepwe."

"How do you know that?"

"Please, Mr. Bartlett, at least give us some credit. We monitor the Reuters despatches . . . it is standard procedure, not only here, but in many other countries."

"Well, if you monitored my stuff, how come you didn't know I was at the Reuters office?"

222

"Oh, we knew," Quin said. "It was just that the despatches weren't read and it wasn't realised that it was you, until after you had left the Reuters office. A slight communications problem, that was all."

"Yes, I see," Tony smiled. "And that's probably why I don't give you any credit."

Quin looked puzzled for a moment and his parchment face knotted into a frown. Bruno Van Wyk stood up and said, "He's a smart one this one—I'm going to enjoy talking to him." He came across and stood in front of Tony, smiling blankly into his face.

"There's nothing to talk about," Tony said.

"Oh yes there is, Mr. Bartlett," said Quin. "You are reported as having spoken aggressively and provocatively to Mr. Carl Verhoef, one of this country's most prominent businessmen. A few minutes later you are observed in close conversation with Mr. Johnathan Kapepwe, one of this country's most dangerous and wanted criminals. A few minutes after that, this criminal and his crew of kaffirs kidnap Verhoef and kill ten people, including Mr. Eugene Dekker, whom you have also verbally attacked in the past few days. Oh yes, Mr. Bartlett, there is a great deal for us to talk about."

Bruno took Tony's arm in a vicelike grip. "You are going to come with us," he said.

Tony tried to shake his arm loose, but Bruno just held on and smiled at Tony.

"Look, let me . . . "

Suddenly there was a knock at the door.

Tony shouted "Hello" just an instant before Bruno's hand clamped hard over his mouth.

"Hi . . . Tony. It's us again . . . Howard."

Bruno still held his hand over Tony's mouth. Tony struggled.

"Let him go," Kurt whispered, and then to Tony, "Be careful."

"Hang on," Tony called. "I'll be right there."

"Get rid of them," Kurt said to Tony. But Tony had no intention of getting rid of them. He went to the door and opened it wide. "Come in," he said.

"Hi," Howard said, "we just decided to have a Chinese meal

and we thought you—" he saw the two other men standing in the room. "Oh . . . er, sorry," he said. "I didn't know you had company."

"That's quite all right," Tony said happily. "I'm glad you arrived. I was just coming around to your room. These gentlemen were just leaving anyway."

The two Americans looked at the two men from BOSS and recognised them immediately for what they were. Tony was about to continue, when the phone rang. He picked it up.

"Hello . . . Tony?" It was Ingrid.

"Yes," Tony said, "it's me. I've been trying to call you all day."

"Oh, Tony, thank God I've found you." She sounded distraught and spoke urgently. "I've been looking for you all day, too. You must come quickly."

"What's happened?" Tony desperately wanted to talk normally to Ingrid; to comfort her, to find out what was the matter; but with the two security men standing glaring at him, he was anxious not to give anything away.

"I spent the night and most of the day with friends of Eugene's. I didn't want to. I wanted to get away. I wanted to see you, but I couldn't. But this afternoon, Eugene's solicitor gave me a letter which Eugene had left with him with instructions for it to be given to me, if anything happened to him. Oh Tony . . . it's terrible. I can't tell you over the phone. Can you come to the apartment?"

"As soon as I can," Tony said.

"Oh please come quickly. I'm frightened."

Tony put down the phone. He had his back to the door, but he was closer to it than anyone else. The two men from BOSS were in the centre of the room. Howard and Marty were between them and Tony.

Tony half-turned to Goldman and said, "Howard, I'd like you to do me another big favour." He winked. Howard saw it and so did Marty. "I'd like you to keep these two gentlemen entertained for a while, so that I can go and see a friend."

With that, Tony whirled and dived for the door.

"Stop!" Quin shouted, making a lunge after Tony as he turned and fled. Marty stuck his foot out and Quin sprawled onto the

224

floor. As Bruno tried to charge past them to the door, Howard tackled him and they landed in a heap on top of Quin. Bruno's immense physical strength enabled him to literally hurl Howard aside, but Marty was behind him and brought an old-fashioned bronze lamp down hard on Bruno's head, knocking him senseless. With Bruno out and the two Americans standing threateningly in front of him, one brandishing the lamp, Kurt Quin lay still. Howard felt under the man's coat and withdrew a pistol. He took another from the prostrate form of Bruno Van Wyk. Quin was directed to move to the far end of the room. He went quickly and sat in a chair, glowering.

It took Tony roughly twenty minutes to reach Ingrid's apartment in Berea. Once again, he had followed a circuitous route to his own car, then spent several minutes driving in a random way to make sure he wasn't being followed.

It had begun to rain and although there was a parking space right in front of Ingrid's building, he parked the car around a corner, in a side street. As he ran back across the road toward the block of apartments, he glanced up at the fourth floor and saw the light shining from Ingrid's lounge-room window behind the balcony. He felt a warm, comfortable sensation at the thought of the night he had spent there. But he was worried. He stepped into the elevator and pushed the button for the fourth floor. What had happened to make Ingrid so upset? This letter— "It's terrible," she had said. What was terrible? The elevator doors opened and, as Tony was stepping out, a man wearing a dark raincoat and hat brushed rudely past him to enter the elevator. Tony turned crossly to say something, but the doors shut quickly behind him and the only impression Tony was left with was one of pallid skin and bushy black eyebrows.

At Ingrid's door he knocked, but there was no answer. He knocked again . . . and again. He called softly, "Ingrid, it's me . . . Tony." He tried the door handle. Locked. Something's wrong, Tony thought. A light showed further along the hall from a small window that was not locked. He pushed it open and looked through. It was not a window to Ingrid's apartment, but opened into a wide light-well, which went from the top of the twenty-six-storey building to the basement. Across the well, some fifteen feet away, a light shone from another window, which Tony decided must be Ingrid's bathroom.

He thought, for a moment, of trying to climb around the well on the plumbing pipes, but dismissed the idea. I'll go and check downstairs, he said to himself. There was a small delicatessen open on the corner. He thought perhaps Ingrid had gone there to buy something.

As soon as he left the elevator on the ground floor he could tell that something had happened. He saw two men run past the front entrance to the building and there were noises and shouting from the street. He ran across the lobby of the apartment building and out of the door. A crowd was gathered on the sidewalk. Tony ran up.

"Don't move her," he heard someone say. "Has someone called an ambulance?" "Yes," said another voice.

Tony pushed his way through to the front of the group and, with a great choking sensation, recognised Ingrid lying in a crumpled heap, half in the gutter and half on the sidewalk. Her face was turned to one side and a slow trickle of blood ran from her mouth, mingling with the rain that was now soaking her hair and her clothes. She was moaning softly and repeating a word which sounded like "Tony."

Tony stood, unable to move for several seconds, looking down at Ingrid. Small tears began to form and to run down his cheeks. He lowered himself slowly onto his knees to look at her face.

"Ingrid," he whispered.

Her eyes were open, but there was no way of knowing if she saw Tony; they stared blankly ahead. Tony put his hand out to rest it softly on her shoulder. "Ingrid," he said again softly.

"Don't touch her, pal," a man said from somewhere in the crowd, "leave that for the ambulance boys."

"Joey," Ingrid whispered. Tony put his head down closer to hers. "Joey," she said again, and then she closed her eyes. Her body seemed to relax slightly and her face turned slowly up into the rain.

Tony softly ran his fingers down her cheek. He felt huge sobs welling up inside him.

226

"Don't touch her," the same man said again from the crowd.

"She's dead!" Tony shouted back angrily at him. "Can't you see that? She's dead." He stood up and pushed his way through the crowd. Across the road, the man in the dark raincoat and hat stepped into the back seat of a car, which drove off into the night. Tony wandered vacantly off down the street.

"Joey?" he said to himself twice, before he remembered.

He ran past the back of the crowd and into the apartment building again. As he entered the elevator, he heard the wail of police sirens in the distance.

On the fourth floor he ran back to the door to Ingrid's apartment, but this time he didn't even try it. He went straight on to the small window which opened onto the light-well, pushing it open and climbing quickly through, then pushing it closed again behind him. He clung to a heavy steel pipe which ran from the top of the building to the bottom. Several branch pipes ran off from it. He heard the sirens slow to a stop outside the building.

Tony lowered himself down so that he could stand on a brick ledge above the window on the floor below, then found that he could edge his way around the walls of the well, clinging to the lateral drainage pipes which ran to the outside walls of all the bathrooms on every floor. There was another vertical pipe running up alongside the bathroom windows and when he reached it, he began to climb up again to the level of Ingrid's bathroom. There were lights in the bathroom immediately below and a woman was humming softly to herself as she splashed in the warm water.

"Oh Jesus," Tony moaned softly, tears streaming down his face as he climbed towards Ingrid's window. How precious life is, he thought desperately and violently.

As he stepped from the bathroom into the main part of the flat, Tony saw immediately the signs of a terrible struggle or a ransack search—probably both. However, he had no difficulty finding what he was looking for. He went straight to the bookshelf in the corner and lifted the little toy kangaroo from its position there. He put his fingers into the pouch and pulled out a folded piece of paper. He was about to open it, when he heard voices in the corridor.

"This must be her room," a man's voice said. "It's the middle flat on the fourth floor."

Tony slipped the paper into his pocket and darted quickly for the bathroom.

"Who's got the keys?" another voice said.

"The caretaker's coming just now."

Tony climbed back out through the bathrom window, clinging again to the down pipe just outside. Standing on one of the joints of the pipe and hanging on with his right hand, he reached back into the bathroom and pulled the window to, as well as he could.

Through the opaque window onto the hallway, across the well, he could see blurred figures moving backwards and forwards and hear voices. Then the front door to Ingrid's apartment was opened and people came inside, talking. Tony began to lower himself quickly into the darkness of the well. The rain was falling heavily now and, on two or three occasions, because his hands had become slippery, he almost lost his grip and fell.

He had no idea what he would find at the bottom of the well. Upwards was a tiny square of grey light at the top of the building and, in beween that and him, a vertical, black tunnel, studded by occasional yellow lights from windows that opened onto the well. Below him was only darkness. There were no other bathrooms lit below the third floor.

Within minutes, he was at the bottom of the well, at what he judged to be the basement level. There was a concrete floor, so he cautiously let go of the pipe and felt his way around the walls in the darkness. Eventually, he came to a window, but it was locked. It seemed to him that the only way out was to smash it and hope that there would be a catch inside. But what about the noise? He looked back up to the fourth-floor level of Ingrid's bathroom. The light was still on, but he could hear no sound coming from anywhere within the building—only the rain spattering onto a piece of corrugated tin in one corner of the well. In the dim light, to which Tony's eyes were slowly becoming accustomed, he saw that the piece of tin was actually a sloping door-cover, resting at an angle out from the wall, like the lid over old-fashioned coal shutes. He moved across to it and lifted. With a rusty creak, it opened to reveal an utterly black hole.

Tony put his foot in and felt a step. He began to go down into

228

the hole, closing the sloping roof over his head. After seven or eight steps downward, he found the floor but was in absolute darkness; not the slightest chink of light showed anywhere, and still the only sound was that of the rain pounding onto the tin roof he had just closed.

He felt his way along the side of the steps until he found a wall. Then slowly he began to edge along the wall. His way was barred by packing cases, or something similar, but eventually, after slowly negotiating them and passing along two more walls, he found a flight of concrete stairs going upwards. He felt on the sides of the walls at the bottom of the stairs until his hands encountered a light switch.

The sudden glare of the lights blinded him temporarily, but within seconds he had adjusted and saw that he was in a large basement, filled, as he had expected, with packing cases and assorted junk. Up the stairs was another room which had an even greater collection of packing cases and old and broken furniture. From behind a door in front of him came a soft, humming noise. He opened it cautiously to see what appeared to be part of the air-conditioning system for the building. There was no-one in sight, so Tony moved across the room and around the humming machinery, to another door which, after quietly slipping back a bolt, he opened carefully.

The cool, damp air of the night blew in on him again. The door opened into a covered alleyway at one side of the building. At the end of the alleyway, Tony saw the rain bucketing down onto the concrete yard at the back of the building. Without hesitating, he stepped out into it, clambered over the back fence surrounding the yard, and started running.

Once Howard Goldman and Marty had overcome the two men in Tony Bartlett's room, Goldman was not really sure what to do. He knew these men were plain-clothes policemen or BOSS agents, or something like that, and he knew that he would not be able to hold them for long. He looked at the unconscious form of Bruno Van Wyk and whispered a few words to Marty.

"Listen, man," Kurt Quin said from the chair at the end of the room, "you're in big trouble. We are from the Bureau for State

Security. We are government agents and you will be arrested for obstructing us in the course of our duties."

"Oh yeah," said Goldman. "Sure, sure. And we're FBI agents." He laughed. "Do you really expect me to believe that? I've seen standover men before. You were trying to rob our friend. You can explain it to the police."

Howard stepped to the phone and when the switch answered, he said simply, "Could you get the police to come urgently to Room 2217? There are two armed men here, who tried to threaten Mr. Bartlett. We are holding them here."

Bruno Van Wyk started to regain consciousness.

"Look," Quin said, reaching inside a pocket. "Hold it," said Howard, pointing the pistol at him. Quin slowly withdrew his wallet and opened it. "Look," he said again, "here's my identification." He held it out to Howard, who inspected it.

"Hmm, how do I know this is genuine? Anyone could have one of these made. No, we'll just have to wait for the police to arrive."

Howard Goldman then put in another call to the American Consulate, where, on an after-hours number, he was connected to a third secretary he knew. He told him that he and his colleague might be in a spot of trouble with the police or with the Bureau for State Security, and could he please send someone to the hotel quickly.

Within minutes of the phone call, there was a banging at the door. It wasn't the police, but two more BOSS agents. Monitoring Tony's telephone from a room on the floor below, they had heard Howard's call to the switchboard asking for the police and realised that something must have gone wrong.

Hardly more than three minutes had elapsed since Tony had run from the room, but Howard felt sure that would have been sufficient. Now he had to concentrate on extricating himself and Marty from the situation. After the arrival of the second BOSS men, the two Americans allowed themselves to be convinced of the authenticity of the credentials of Kurt Quin and Bruno Van Wyk and were profuse in their apologies.

Bruno, who was gradually regaining his awareness of what was going on, suddenly became aggressive towards Howard and had

230

to be restrained by the other security men. The four BOSS agents then insisted on the two Americans coming with them to their headquarters for further questioning, but they refused.

"We're not going anywhere until the man from the American Consulate arrives here," Howard said, and when Bruno became threatening with his regained pistol, Howard said, "Shoot us if you like and carry our bodies out the back door, but you'll have a lot of awkward questions to answer from my government and yours, now that I have spoken to our consul."

The police arrived shortly and, when they heard the details, left the matter in the hands of BOSS. Then the consular official arrived and listened to Howard's story.

The BOSS men continued to insist that the Americans should be questioned further, so the man from the consulate agreed that they should go to the Johannesburg office of the Bureau for State Security, but insisted that he would also come along to sit in on the questioning.

Two hours later, at about 10.00 PM, Howard and Marty had been released and allowed to return to the hotel. They were, however, to be placed under close surveillance from now on, and they knew it.

12
The Letter

At twenty minutes to midnight on the night of March 20, the view from the lookout on Table Mountain in Cape Town was a singularly beautiful one. A myriad lights twinkled, some three thousand feet below, from the great city spread out beyond the base of the sheer mountain. It was warm and there was not a breath of wind. A brilliant moon, surrounded by countless stars, shone down from an almost totally clear sky. Almost clear—except for a solid band of cloud moving slowly down from the north. It was, however, sufficiently far away that it in no way detracted from the beauty of the panorama.

The last cable car from the peak had been empty on its final run down to the city for the night. Now, there were only two night-watchmen left on the craggy mountain to appreciate the scene. They had been sitting, smoking and talking, for a quarter of an hour in the deserted waiting room of the cable car station; then they got up to walk together along the pathway that connected the station to the various lookout points and the nearby restaurant.

Far below, the waters of Table Bay rippled and glistened in the moonlight, like sequins on a piece of shimmering material. About ten miles to the north, out in the middle of the wide, sweeping bay, Robben Island with its low prison buildings interrupted the pattern of the light reflected up from the sea. It sat like a dark spot on the silver waters.

The two men stood at the first lookout for some minutes, continuing their conversation. The thick band of cloud and the moon moved

232

closer together and, for a brief, dramatic period, the moon sat as if balanced on the edge of the long cloud, lighting its entire length across the whole night sky. For a few moments, there was the impression of a straight strip of light cutting the sky in two; twinkling stars on one side, blackness on the other. Then, slowly, the moon disappeared behind the advancing band of cloud and the sea slid into total darkness. The two men moved off from the lookout to continue their rounds.

Seven miles beyond Robben Island, in the waters of Matroos Bay, Dmitri Bessonov smiled with satisfaction as he watched the moon slip behind the cloud.

"Malyi Vperiod," he said and the order for "half ahead" was repeated by his second officer a few feet away. Almost immediately, the great bulk of the new Alpha class fleet submarine, one of nine attached to the Soviet Indian Ocean Fleet, began to move slowly forward under the water. Commander Bessonov did not take his eyes from the periscope. His stomach was tight with excitement. He was thirty-four years old, but during his sixteen years in the Soviet Navy, he had never come close to seeing anything like real action. There had been plenty of exercises in different parts of the world, a couple of brushes with American destroyers in the Gulf of Tonkin during the Vietnam War, but not a situation which could, by any stretch of the imagination, be called dangerous. Now, for the first time, it was happening.

It had been a slow buildup over the past four days; ever since they had picked up the twenty-five black commandos north of Maputo. There had been the long run south until they slipped around the Cape.

Three other Russian submarines had been accompanying Bessonov as he approached the Cape Sea lanes, when they first came under the surveillance of Shackleton aircraft of the South African Air Force's maritime reconnaissance wing. But by the time the tracking of the submarines had been taken on by two destroyers of the American Second Fleet and one of the South African Navy, Bessonov's craft had dropped away from the other submarines, which were intended as decoys anyway, and slipped, fully submerged, into the deep waters that run off the southern tip of the

African continent, close in to the coastline, well within South African territorial waters.

He rounded the Cape of Good Hope, less than two miles from the steep and ragged cliffs, during the night of March 19. From the Cape, he had cruised about sixty miles north, until he was opposite a comparatively deserted stretch of coastline between Matroos Bay and Bok Bay, and then allowed the submarine to settle to the sandy bottom, in some sixty fathoms of water, where it lay, quietly waiting for more than twenty-four hours.

The twenty-five black commandos who were taken aboard Dmitri Bessonov's submarine, under cover of darkness near Joao Belo, were all South Africans. They had been trained in a variety of different camps in Mozambique, Tanzania, Zimbabwe, and Botswana. Seven of them had undergone special training in either Russia or Cuba, while four had been to China for similar training. They had all come together under the Azanian Peoples Liberation Army during the past eighteen months and had been chosen as a separate group some three months prior to their submarine journey.

The men underwent intensive training of the most rigorous kind, under conditions of absolute secrecy. They were all chosen to take part in the mission on the basis of their intelligence, leadership qualities, physical fitness, and ideological motivation. They were given no knowledge of the exact nature of their mission until one week before it began, when it became necessary to acquaint them with the exact tasks they would have to fulfill and the people they would have to recognise.

Up until that time, they had only been able to guess at what they would be required to do, from the type of exercises they were continually being called on to carry out. They were taken to the remote Ilhas do Bazaruto, about 130 miles south of Beira on the Mozambique coast, and shown a prison, or rather, a mockup of a prison, from which they had to extract seven prisoners. The prison was surrounded by high, wire fences and guard-dogs patrolled behind them. They were told that the position of the fences and the single-story buildings in the mockup prison approximated those in the real one.

The island of Bazaruto was considerably bigger than the island on which the real prison was situated, so the training authorities had accurately marked out the shape of the real 1,300-acre island around the mockup prison.

Over a period of several weeks, the commandos carried out simulated attack after attack on the prison, using a variety of different approaches, and they were always met by real opposition. Only blank cartridges were used in their weapons, but they did make use of detonators to simulate explosions and on one occasion, one of the defenders was killed. The death, however, only served to remind the men that when it came to the real thing, they would not be playing games. They were equipped with the most modern infantry weapons, and many of the rifles were fitted with night-scopes. They also carried gas masks and cannisters of both CS and tear gas, as well as two fragmentation grenades per person.

By the end of their training period, they were all superbly fit and ready for the mission. They felt confident that they could do it and extremely proud, once they had been told the exact nature of the operation, to have been chosen for so important a task. But they had no illusions as to the size and difficulties of the job in front of them. There were 370 prisoners on the island. They had to find seven special prisoners and get them out.

During the last week before they left the island, they rehearsed the procedures they would have to go through to leave and rejoin the Russian submarine in inflatable rubber dinghies. For many of them, this was the most dangerous moment because it was the time they would be at their most vulnerable. Now, Robben Island and that first part of the mission was only minutes away.

After leaping the fence at the back of Ingrid's apartment, Tony had run blindly through the rain, with only the thought of putting distance between him and the building uppermost in his mind. But after a short while, when he noticed that one or two of the few people in the streets were turning to stare at him, he slowed to a walk and then continued, aimlessly stumbling along the sidewalks, sobbing like a child. A policeman suddenly stopped him at a corner. Tony jumped in surprise and fear.

"You drunk, pal?" the policeman said.

"Wh . . . ? Huh . . . oh, no. No, I'm not drunk."

"What's the matter, then? What are you walking around in the rain for? You're getting yourself all wet, man."

Tony looked at himself. "Yes," he said. "Yes . . . I . . . I suppose I'd better go home."

"Where do you live? You don't look well. Do you want me to take you home?"

"No," Tony replied. "No. I'll be all right. I don't live far from here. I . . . I just . . . my girl-friend just left me."

The expression on the policeman's face changed. He smiled and slapped Tony on the back.

"Ach, man, don't worry about it. You'll get over it. There's plenty more about. Now just take it easy, eh?" He slapped Tony again on the back and continued to walk on down the street.

Tony stood for a moment, staring at the pavement. The rain was soaking through his clothes and running in little trickles from his hair, down over his face.

"Jesus, what a terrible mess!" he said to himself, aloud. "What the hell am I going to do now?" He considered the options open to him. He couldn't go "home" to the hotel. They'd be waiting for him there, with open arms, for sure, and he knew that any future session with Colonel Starcke and his cohorts wouldn't be quite as gentlemanly as the first.

His mind kept jumping back to Ingrid, beautiful Ingrid, lying there in the rain, crumpled on the road. Two minutes earlier he had run across the same piece of roadway, looking up at her apartment. Two minutes! Two minutes, three minutes, four . . . what did it matter? She was dead now—killed by these bastards. Christ! Why? Why? Why?

The image of the pallid face and bushy eyebrows came back to him and he felt fear again. Fear for himself.

"This is madness," he said aloud. "I've got to get out!"

Then he remembered the folded piece of paper he had taken from Ingrid's toy kangaroo. He pulled it from his pocket and began to open it, but seeing that it was getting wet, and noticing at the same time that the policeman who had spoken to him was returning in his direction on the other side of the street, he slipped it back

236

into his pocket and turned to walk slowly away down the hill.

I'll have to try to get the car, he thought. But he was now lost. He knew he had not run more than several blocks, but in which direction? From the back of the apartment building, he couldn't remember where he had gone, except that he had run uphill nearly all the way. So he continued the way he was going, downhill, and came, within six or seven minutes, to the street in which he knew Ingrid's apartment to be. Looking to the right, through the still falling rain, he could see the flashing lights of police cars parked outside the entrance to the apartments, about two blocks away.

Tony walked slowly along the opposite side of the street, under the trees which lined the road, to the side street where he had parked the car. As he turned the corner, he took one last look at the building and the piece of roadway where he had last seen Ingrid. A police car was now parked there. A wave of uncontrollable sobbing swept through him. He walked quickly to his car, got in, and drove off.

As soon as he did so, he thought, Am I being followed? Was I watched? But, he reasoned correctly, if he had been watched, they would have taken him there and then, rather than following him.

As he drove along, Tony once again began to analyse his situation. His typewriter, camera, and the rest of his clothes were all back at the hotel. He still had his passport, wallet, and travellers cheques in the nylon security belt under his shirt, so, at least to that extent, he was still independent and free to move anywhere he wanted to. But where to move? He *did* want to get out now. Of that he was certain. All this killing was not for him, especially when it started to come as close as it had been.

"It's not bloody well worth it," he said aloud. "Let these nasty bastards kill each other off. People like me and Ingrid don't think the same way. Oh God, Oh God . . . Oh Christ, why?"

On three previous occasions, twice in Vietnam and once in Bangla Desh, Tony had seen death at close quarters and missed it himself by only a small margin. On each occasion he had sworn not to allow himself to get into that sort of situation again. It wasn't that Tony Bartlett was a coward, it was simply that he placed a high value on his own life. Life was infinitely precious to Tony, basically

237

because he had enjoyed being alive for most of his thirty-five years and there were a great many more things he wanted to see and do during the next thirty-five years.

He found himself driving out on one of the roads heading north from the city, towards Belrose and Alexandra. He passed a convoy of army trucks going in the opposite direction, towards town. A police car drew up alongside him as he drove along. The two men inside it looked across at Tony and, without a smile or a hello, moved on to the next car, two hundred yards or so further along in front, to do the same thing again. Looking for blacks I suppose, Tony said to himself. Oh, God, I want to get out of here.

But how? All the international flights would be booked out for weeks ahead. He knew that. But most important . . . where should he go now? He couldn't just keep driving forever. But if he returned to the hotel, he'd be nabbed—and he knew it.

A new, more frightening thought now struck him. They might even be able to say *he* killed Ingrid. He could easily be identified as the person who was beside her as she lay dying in the road and they could certainly find plenty of his fingerprints in her apartment. He began to feel like a fugitive.

He thought of contacting Howard Goldman, but knew that he would also be in trouble himself and that his phone would be tapped anyway.

Then there was Mulgrave. Christ! Fancy entrusting your life to that bastard, Tony thought immediately, and dismissed the idea.

No. Mike Keneally's the best bet, he decided. They'll probably figure out that I might go there, but at least, if they grab me, there'll be someone who will shout and jump up and down on my behalf.

Having made up his mind, Tony continued driving north, looking now for signs indicating the turnoff for Sandton, but after only a few minutes, he remembered the folded piece of paper again. He pulled off the main road into a suburban street and, stopping underneath a street lamp, opened it up. Another piece of paper dropped into his lap. He put it back into his pocket and began to read Eugene's letter.

It was written on two sheets of plain foolscap typing paper in

238

a small and precise back-hand style. In the top right-hand corner it said simply: "March 9th." The day before the plane hijack, Tony thought, and then read on:

> My Darling Ingrid,
>
> I write, hoping that you will never have to read this, but, being the sort of person I am, I cannot but prepare for the worst. I have a number of enemies, of which I am sure you know nothing, and should anything untoward happen to me, I would like you to be aware of the reasons for it happening and the people concerned, so that by contacting the authorities, they might be brought to justice.
>
> As you well know, I have grave doubts about the future of South Africa. Despite what I have said in public, I have long believed that the blacks will take over here eventually and that, as much as we love this country, we and millions of other whites will have to leave, or be killed . . . or if we remain, live some degraded, subhuman form of existence. I am not willing to see this beautiful country handed over to a bunch of ignorant savages, who will destroy what we, the white race, have built. My family like yours has lived in Africa for generations . . . one of my ancestors arrived in Cape Town in 1693. Without the whites, this country would still be nothing more than open veld and bush. The blacks would have done nothing for it and so they deserve nothing from it.

Tony wound the window down slightly to prevent the glass fogging up inside. He glanced around outside the car to see if there was anyone else about, but there was no movement. Only the rain and an occasional car passing on the main road a hundred yards or so behind him.

> Consequently [Dekker's letter went on], I and several associates have taken steps to ensure that this country's most precious treasures, its gold reserves and many of its diamonds, will be transferred out of South Africa to Switzerland, so that they will never fall into the hands of any black terrorists who try to take over here. There, if all goes well, this vast wealth can be used, if necessary, to guarantee the proper treatment of whites remaining in South Africa or those wanting to leave. They could also be used to finance a white counter-revolution and return to South Africa.
>
> This was a policy put forward some time ago by the HNP, but vetoed by the Nationalists and the opposition, so we have had to go

239

it alone. In some peoples' eyes it could be seen as the biggest robbery in history; however, I like to think of it not as a robbery, but as a precautionary step; the safeguarding of our rights, our heritage . . . not just for the few people involved in the project, but for all of the whites of South Africa.

He's crazy, Tony said to himself.

But there are problems. I mentioned that I have enemies. There have been many people involved in this project and in case one—or several—of these persons tries to circumvent our ultimate goals, I would like you to be acquainted with some of the details of my plans.

I must say that the only person I have been able to trust, absolutely, in all of this is myself, because I know, in my heart of hearts, the strength of my own ideals, my standards and my conscience. I have to admit that I cannot say the same for Carl Verhoef and Paul Trauseld, who have been my main associates. Verhoef perhaps, but of Trauseld I have never been entirely sure and there are several things which have recently given me reason to believe that he may be planning independent actions in his own interest with regard to the gold.

I can put down the details of the gold transfer here in the sure knowledge that unless something goes terribly wrong, this letter will never be read. However, I must take this precaution simply as a safeguard, so that if I were disposed of, at least something could be done to prevent the gold from falling into the wrong hands.

During the four weeks in which the reserves were transferred from the Bank to Voortrekkerhoogte, under my supervision, we were able to substitute false bars of gold-plated lead in their place, at least for seventy-five percent of the reserves. The substitute bars were prepared secretly over many months at one of Verhoef's mines. The changeover required the participation and cooperation of several highly placed people in the Bank, the Rand refinery, the security forces, and the government. Under normal circumstances, it could be many months before the substitute bars are discovered.

The first shipment of gold is due to leave by air tomorrow, with two other flights shortly after. But the bulk of the gold will leave Durban in one of Trauseld's ships and, hopefully by the end of this month, be well on its way to Europe.

If the country does go under to the blacks, Verhoef has made secret arrangements for all of his gold mines and most of the other major mines on the Rand to be mined with explosives, so that they can be destroyed and thereby deny the blacks the benefits of the main economic strengths of South Africa which were developed by whites. I was against this move at the start, but when I thought more of what these murdering terrorists have done, and how they will destroy this country, I changed my mind.

All these plans have been very carefully laid, but should they go wrong, there has been another thought constantly on my mind and that is that I would very much like you to be able to have some of the benefits of what I had hoped to share with you in the future. As you will see, I have enclosed a copy of the form which I have sent to the Union Banque Suisse in Zurich, bearing a copy of your signature, which I took from one of your files at the Reserve Bank. It will give you access to a numbered safety deposit box in Zurich.

My darling Ingrid, I hope that you will never have to read this and that we will be able to share together the future I have planned. But, if by some sad misfortune, you do one day read this letter, please do not think badly of me. In all of this, my motives have been pure.

I love you,
Eugene

Good God, Tony said, throwing his head back against the headrest at the top of the seat. Good God almighty! The biggest robbery in history . . . and the bloody mines too! What a bunch of fanatics! Oh Christ, what in the name of God am I going to do? He again felt small, insignificant, and helpless; like an ant clinging to a matchbox as it is swept by a raging, flood-swollen torrent towards a waterfall. He can swim, but the sides and safety are too far away.

Tony pulled the second piece of paper from his pocket. It was a form transferring the ownership of a numbered account deposit box from Eugene Dekker to Ingrid Hofmeyr. There was no indication of what the box contained. Fat lot of use that's going to do anyone now, Tony muttered to himself bitterly, with both Dekker and Ingrid dead. The gnomes of Zurich win again. But then he noticed, with a degree of puzzlement, that not only was the second piece of paper a photocopy, but so was Eugene's letter.

Why would Eugene send Ingrid a copy of the letter, instead of the original? Tony wondered. Of course he wouldn't.

So Ingrid must have made the copy during the afternoon. That meant that the original letter and envelope—and perhaps the original bank form—had been left in the apartment. No. The bank form was already a copy, Eugene says that in the letter.

241

Perhaps her killer found the original letter. If he did, then they won't expect me to have a copy. A small advantage, Tony thought, but better than none. He folded the pieces of paper and put them back in his pocket, realizing, as he did so, that Marta Van Sisseren's pistol was still there. He had forgotten it.

He started the car again, slipped it into gear, and turned back onto the main road.

The news of the commando attack on Robben Island and the escape of six of South Africa's best-known political and revolutionary leaders swept the country like a bushfire. The SABC carried only a brief reference, saying that an attempt had been made to attack the prison on Robben Island by a group of terrorists who had been landed, it was believed, by a Russian submarine. It made no mention of the fact that any of the prisoners had escaped—only that four terrorists had been killed during the raid and that South Africa was protesting to the United Nations against what it termed a "flagrant violation of South Africa's national sovereignty by an armed Soviet vessel."

But the clandestine rebel radio stations within the country and those stations which beamed their broadcasts into South Africa from the surrounding countries, Botswana, Zimbabwe, Namibia, and Mozambique, were all euphoric in their description of the successful raid and graphic in the details of how the "brave freedom fighters," as they put it, had carried out their daring task. These radio stations, of course, made no mention of the means by which the guerillas had arrived on and departed from Robben Island.

The story of the raid dominated the air-waves on the rebel stations all day long. They made the point many times that the freeing of these six heroes of the revolution was an event of immense significance in the struggle for freedom in Azania and that it took place on a date of tremendous symbolic importance to black South Africans; the twenty-first anniversary of the Sharpeville Massacre.

These radio stations, which were heard, or could be heard, by the vast majority of the twenty million blacks living in South Africa, also issued the call for a general uprising against the white oppressors. "The time has come," the broadcasts all said, "the hour of freedom is at hand." They warned all black South Africans to be prepared for a general uprising and to be ready to obey any commands. The first step would be a nationwide general strike, to begin immediately. The broadcasts called on all blacks to stay away from their jobs, or if they had already started work, to leave and go home.

They instructed listeners to keep tuned to their radios. Within hours they would hear the voices of the leaders who had been freed from the Robben Island prison; the sixty-three-year-old African National Congress leader, Nelson Mandele, who had spent the past seventeen years on the grim island, and two of his top aides, Walter Sisulu and Govan Mbeki, who had been sentenced with Mandele at the same time back in 1964 to life imprisonment under the sabotage and suppression of communism laws. In 1960, Mandele had founded "Umkhonto we Siswe," the Spear of the Nation, a militant wing of his own ANC, aimed at forcing a general uprising in South Africa. Now, twenty-one years later, it was happening.

Robert Sobukwe, the leader of the Pan African Congress, was also among those taken from the prison. He had only spent some two years on the island, having been sent there in 1979 for contravening the restrictions on him under the banning orders which had effectively placed him under house arrest for more than fifteen years. Two other senior members of the Pan African Congress, Gerard Dumile and Ezrom Zondi, were the last of the six escapees. No mention was made of the fact that the attackers had hoped to bring seven prisoners out instead of six. But in the overall context, that was of no importance; the operation could only be seen as an unqualified success from the guerillas' viewpoint.

The BBC also carried news of the raid in its early morning bulletins on the African Service, but to begin with, they were somewhat behind the Southern African rebel stations, which, understandably, had slightly easier access to the sources of information concerning the raid.

It was this short-wave service that Michael Keneally and Tony Bartlett sat listening to in the Keneallys' home at 7.00 AM next morning.

"The South African Parliament," the BBC broadcast went on,

"will continue its emergency session in Cape Town today and, according to our correspondent, will be considering declaring a state of emergency throughout the country.

"The South African president, Mr. Botha, is due to make a nation-wide radio and television address on the crisis later today. However, Mr. Botha's position as leader of the coalition government is now apparently in doubt. In an extraordinary development, a motion of no confidence in the president was put last night in the Parliament, by the vice president, Dr. Hugo Van Essche, leader of the Herstigte Nasionale Party, the Nationalists' own partners in the coalition government. The move is seen, our correspondent says, as an attempt to bring stronger, more conservative forces to power in South Africa. If the no-confidence motion succeeds, then it is understood that Dr. Van Essche will almost certainly assume wide-ranging emergency powers as an interim president."

The BBC broadcast continued with details of a number of guerilla raids in different parts of South Africa. Rocket and mortar fire had hit the huge explosives factory at Modderfontein, just to the north of Johannesburg. Modderfontein, which for years had produced all the TNT and dynamite for the vast underground workings of the gold mines on the Rand, had long been described in South African official publications as "the biggest explosives factory in the world." The attack had started fires which in turn set off explosives that destroyed many of the buildings on the eastern side of the big complex, but firemen, who were either extremely brave, or crazy, Tony thought, managed to bring the fires under control before they reached the main explosive storage facilities. Still, almost a quarter of the plant had been destroyed.

Jan Smuts airport had also come under attack from rocket and mortar fire. A Hercules transport plane, two helicopters, and part of an administration building had been hit.

Michael Keneally stood up as the news broadcast finished and paced up and down the sun-room in which they'd been sitting. "Well, whatever happens in Cape Town today," he said, "I still think you should report it to the government as soon as possible."

"But the HNP is involved in it all, I'm sure of it," Tony said. "BOSS certainly is. What hope have I got of getting through to

244

anyone who'll do anything about it?" He poured himself another cup of coffee from the stainless-steel thermos on the low table in front of him. "And the moment I call someone in Cape Town, BOSS will know that I'm here—that is, if they don't already know it. I might try to call Schuman again, though."

"Incredible! Incredible!" Michael Keneally said for the fifth time since Tony had recounted the events of the previous night. "You're in a spot of trouble, I'd say, Tony. As long as you stay here, you'll probably be okay, but the moment you leave, they'll have you." He stood by the window staring out onto the sloping lawn. "I've never had to put it to the test before, but I think you're safe within these grounds; that they're covered by the embassy's diplomatic immunity. But what happens next, or how you get out of it all, I just don't know."

"I'd like to try to call Howard Goldman and his cameraman," Tony said, "to see how they got on with those two BOSS agents. I feel guilty now about letting them in for all that."

"They'll be tapping their phones for sure," Michael said. "They'll trace it here as quick as a flash."

Tony sat silently in thought for about a minute and then said, "I've got to get out. I can't just stay hiding here like a criminal. I've also got to ring Childers, my editor, and write the story before someone else does. I've already told Howard Goldman most of it." He stood up and joined Keneally by the window and they both stood for a few moments saying nothing. Then Tony slammed his fist into his other hand, "But also . . . somehow . . . I'd love to see that bastard that killed Ingrid get it in the neck."

"You're crazy, Tony," Keneally said. "These guys aren't fooling around. The country's falling apart and they know it. They've got nothing to lose, and anyone who stands in their way will get the chop. These are nasty times and they're getting nastier every day. We're already talking about getting several special flights in here for all Australian citizens. The Yanks are planning to do the same. If you stick around here, we'll probably be able to get you out on one of them. They've only just suggested it, but I wouldn't be surprised if it starts happening within a week. If things get any worse, I'm sure it will."

Tony turned away, as if certain cogs and gears had suddenly shifted into place. "No," he said, "I'm going to try to head for Durban."

"Durban!"

"Yes . . . I'm going to try to find out what ship that gold is going on, or has gone on . . . and maybe I'll be able to get on another ship out of there, myself. There's no planes available from here right now anyway."

"How would you get there?"

"By car, of course."

"But that bloody road to Durban is a deathtrap lately," Keneally said. "There've been guerilla attacks and fighting in some parts. It's over four hundred bloody miles, man!"

"I know that, but I read a couple of days ago that the army was running daily convoys and that civilians can travel in with them if they're heading in the same direction. I'm going to try to get in one of them."

Keneally sat down again in his armchair with a sigh of desperation. "You're mad—nuts! They'll pick you up straight away."

"No, they won't. I'm sure the army won't be looking for me and, unless someone from BOSS is there on the spot, waiting for me to join the convoy, they won't get me. Anyway, for one thing, I'm going to change my car, and for another, they won't expect me to be heading for Durban. I'm pretty sure they don't know I have Dekker's letter. As far as I can see, the only dangerous parts are as I leave here—if they've got onto me being here—and when I change the car over if they're watching there. But I doubt that they'll be expecting me to change it."

Tony took his car keys from his pocket and twirled them around.

"The longer I stick around here, the more likely it is that they'll get onto me. As it is, they've probably already tried Mulgrave's place and the Reuters office. I'm going to go."

Tony pulled a pen from his pocket and, tearing a corner off a newspaper on the coffee table, said to Michael Keneally, "There are only two things I'd like you to do for me. First, ring my editor in London on this number—make it a collect call, he won't mind—and tell him that I'm closing in on the hijack story and that I'll be out of touch for a few days. You won't have to tell him any more than that." Then Tony wrote down Howard Goldman's name. "I don't know if you've met Howard, or the other guy in his crew, Marty, but I'd like them to know what's happening. They've been great to me. You can tell them everything I've told you and that I'm heading for Durban. Don't tell them over the phone, though: just call them up and ask them to come out here for lunch or something like that. They'll understand. You could also ask them to see if they could get hold of the rest of my gear from the hotel." Tony looked down at the clothes he was wearing. "This is going to wear a little thin after a while."

When he'd arrived, drenched to the skin, at the Keneally house the previous night, Jenny Keneally had put his summer-weight suit and shirt—the same clothes he had worn to the American reception and had not had a chance to change since—through the washing machine and drier. But these were the only clothes he had now; what he stood up in. Michael Keneally offered, and Tony accepted, some extra clothes: "A pair of slacks and couple of sports shirts would be fine," Tony said. But Keneally also put some socks, hand-kerchiefs, a light sweater, and a bottle of Scotch into the small overnight bag he handed Tony just before he left.

"I really think you're crazy, Tony. The only advice I can give you is *not* to go. Look, you'll be completely out of touch. There is absolutely nothing I can do for you at that distance. You could disappear down there and no-one here would be any the wiser. I think it's very dangerous, what you are doing . . . and foolish!"

"Thanks, Mike." Tony smiled. "It's great to get a little encourage-ment from time to time."

"What about this call to Cape Town, to try to tell someone in the government or the opposition about the gold?" Keneally said. "Are you still going to do that?"

"Yeah," Tony said. "I'll probably try to put a call through from a post office call booth or something like that, so they can't trace it back easily."

With that, he took Michael's hand, shook it, and turned for the door. "Goodbye," Tony said.

"Good luck."

As he opened his car door and got in, Tony called back to Keneally, "I'll try to call you from Durban. I might need a seat in that plane."

By the time Tony was back in the city centre, it was just after 8.30 in the morning. He had felt conspicuous driving the bright red little Volkswagen the ten miles or so back from Sandton into town. He had avoided the main highway and travelled from one suburban street to the next. It had taken him at least an extra quarter of an hour to make the trip, but he didn't feel like taking any chances. The fact that there was no BOSS car waiting outside the Keneallys' house was blessing enough.

At the hire-car office in Hillbrow, he was nervous, but kept telling himself that there was no reason for BOSS to be there, unless they expected him to change his car. But then, he thought, surely they *would* expect me to change it. Whatever they expected, there was no-one there and Tony made the change to a new model, a fast-back Chevrolet—iridescent green. He liked the colour and felt his spirits lift slightly at having passed a couple of hurdles with no apparent problems.

He noticed, now that his mind was free to focus on things other than his own predicament, that the streets were more empty than usual and that many of the shops were closed. True, it was only just nine o'clock, but the place did seem quiet. No blacks! That was it. No black people anywhere. It was weird. It seemed as if the call for a general strike was going to work.

Tony wanted to ask the girl at the hire-car company about the army convoys to Durban, but thought better of it in case someone from BOSS came around asking questions about him later. He drove a couple of blocks to a service station and was told that the convoys had been leaving at 9.00 AM from Heidelberg, about twenty five miles south-east of the city.

Tony cursed. It was 9.03 now. He could catch them up, but he wanted to phone Cape Town first. He drove to the Hillbrow post office on Van Der Merwe Street and placed a call to the parliamentary offices of George Schuman. He was told there would be a slight delay. Within six minutes, the call was connected and he heard Schuman's voice at the other end say to the telephonist, "Who is it calling?"

248

"A Mr. Bartlett," she replied.

"Oh, Bartlett," the voice said to the operator. "Look, I'm sorry. I am very busy now . . ."

Tony cut in to talk to the telephonist, who had not yet connected him, "Operator, please tell Mr. Schuman I will only be two minutes. I only want to talk to him for two minutes. It's important!"

The operator spoke again, and then Tony was put through.

"Hello, Bartlett, look I'm terribly busy at the moment, all hell is . . ."

"Yes, I know," Tony said, "but I have some important information for you—extremely important. Now listen. I have sound evidence that the bulk, if not all, of South Africa's gold reserves have been shipped out of the country, or are about to be, without the government's knowledge. The reserves which were transferred to Voortrekkerhoogte—you probably don't know about that yet—are false."

"What are you talking about?" Schuman said. "Do you know what you're saying? And what's this about Voortrekkerhoogte?"

"Listen," Tony said urgently, "I haven't much time. Say that I'm crazy or whatever you like but it should be easy enough for someone to check it out. Eugene Dekker, you know, the man from the Reserve Bank who was killed the other night, and Carl Verhoef are behind it all. Also Paul Trauseld."

"Trauseld? Don't be ridiculous. Behind what? Look, Bartlett, where did you get all this . . . ?"

"All right, don't believe me. Just check on it, that's all. Check the gold that has been transferred from the Reserve Bank to Voortrekkerhoogte."

"What gold has been transferred to Voortrekkerhoogte?" Schuman's voice was ringing with disbelief.

"All of the reserves! And the other thing is that all of the Johannesburg gold mines have been set with explosives. They are ready to be destroyed."

"Listen, Bartlett, you don't really expect me to swallow all this, do you?"

"I don't care if you swallow it or not," Tony said harshly, feeling anger rising within him. "It's not my gold. I really don't give a damn. All I'm trying to tell you is that there is a conspiracy between

249

the HNP, BOSS, and God knows who else, to lift all of South Africa's gold. Now if you get onto it and do something about it, you'll find that I'm telling the truth."

Tony noticed, through the window of his booth, that one of the female assistants at the front desk was talking on a telephone, looking towards Tony and nodding. He stopped what he was saying to Schuman and said, "Sorry, George, I've got to go now. Good-bye."

He walked out of the booth and asked the girl how much the call would be. She told him to wait a moment and disappeared through a door at the back of the counter. Tony fidgeted and waited impatiently. A minute went by. He moved further along the counter, so that he could see through the door. The girl was in conversation with two other men inside. She saw Tony and looked embarrassed. One of the men, a post office official, came through the door to speak to Tony.

"What's the trouble?" Tony asked.

"Oh nothing at all, sir. We've just been checking on the toll for your call to Cape Town."

"Yes?" Tony said, "and how much is it?"

"Oh, er, it's seven Rand fifty. Yes. Seven fifty."

"Thank you," Tony said impatiently. "Here you are." He handed the man a ten-Rand note.

"Oh, er, I don't think we've got any change at the moment. Our floats haven't come through. Can you wait a moment? I'll go into the next offices and get some change."

"Don't worry," Tony said. "Keep the change." He started walking for the door.

"Oh, don't go . . . sir. Wait. I'll have your change in just a second or two."

"Never mind," Tony called back and continued walking.

He walked around the corner, slipped into his car, and drove off quickly, convinced that within minutes a carload of BOSS agents or police would arrive at the post office.

Tony drove straight through the city, heading south-east towards Alberton, where he joined Route 3 to Heidelberg. It was already 9.27. It would probably be ten o'clock before he reached Heidelberg.

The convoy would have an hour's start. He'd have to do some fast travelling to catch up.

As it happened, the convoy's departure from Heidelberg was delayed until 9.25, so its lead on Tony was considerably shorter than he imagined. At Heidelberg, he established that the convoy had taken the highway through Standerton, Volksrust, and Newcastle; the continuation of Route 3. Tony knew that Route 16, which ran straight down to Harrismith, was a good 25 to 30 miles shorter, but it covered more than 120 miles of open countryside in which there was not one major town. He decided to stick to Route 3, the safer of the two, and just try to catch up.

The convoy travelled at roughly forty miles an hour, whereas Tony tried to average sixty, hoping he would not be picked up for exceeding the speed limit. By eleven o'clock he had caught them . . . about ten miles before Standerton. He slid into a gap at the end of the convoy, to which he was directed by a white soldier riding on top of a French-made Berliet VXB armoured personnel carrier that was bringing up the rear of the convoy. Tony settled back for the long, monotonous drive southward.

13

Crisis

By eleven o'clock on the morning of March 21, Carl Verhoef was near death. During the past twenty-four hours he had been subjected to so much physical pain that his mind had almost snapped. He had spent many of those twenty-four hours in what had become blissful periods of unconsciousness, but during the moments when he was awake, his interrogators had applied a succession of primitive and brutal tortures in order to try to force the information they required from Verhoef.

At first, never having experienced real pain, Verhoef was arrogant and defiant; but when they took the tip of one of his fingers and smashed it underneath a hammer, he collapsed, writhing in agony. After that, he attempted to pursue a policy of silence—teeth-grinding, determined silence.

Johnathan Kapepwe was there, as were Zak and Joseph. Their escape across the Witwatersberg, past the Hartbeespoort Dam, and up into Bophuthatswana had been successful. Now, in the safety of a secure hideout in the small town of Heystekrand, about twenty-five miles north of Rustenburg, there were others to handle Verhoef.

There was no doubt that their hostage was an important prize. Zak and Joseph were impressed to see two very senior APRA unit commanders amongst the seven other people present for the questioning of the white South African. Zak and Joseph, who had not met Kapepwe before the actual kidnapping, felt slightly lost without their usual leader, Milton, and weren't quite sure where Johnathan Kapepwe fitted into the overall scheme of things. They were interested, for instance, to see that although Kapepwe took no part in the torturing or actual questioning of Verhoef, the others showed obvious deference to him.

The only occasion when Kapepwe participated in the proceedings in any direct way was right at the beginning when, while Verhoef was sitting in a chair facing the group, Kapepwe removed his shirt and, kneeling in front of the white man for a few seconds, bared his back. It was a mass of ugly weals—huge scars which crossed his back from top to bottom.

The others in the room were obviously surprised to see Kapepwe kneeling before the white man, but then Kapepwe stood up.

"Did you see that, Verhoef?" Kapepwe said. "Did you see my back?"

Verhoef said nothing.

"Did you see it?" he shouted, holding his face only inches from Verhoef's.

"Yes."

"That was done ten years ago by three white men, Mr. Verhoef. Three white men who tied me down in a kneeling position like that and laid my back open, because I had dared to make love to a white girl . . . a white girl who had wanted me."

Kapepwe paced up and down in front of Verhoef. "They were like you, Verhoef—white supremacists who think that the black man is shit; nothing but a jungle bunny, a nigger, a coon, a kaffir, a munt. Do you know what it is like to kneel in front of someone and to be totally and absolutely in their power? To have no legal rights whatsoever, to be unable to fight back, to be spat on, demeaned, humiliated, abused, tormented, crushed?" Kapepwe's eyes dilated as he shouted. Zak and Joseph and the others stood silently in the background watching.

"You will soon know, Verhoef. Your time has passed. You and your kind are finished. Now the wheel turns . . . It is our time now, and you will have to swallow the dirt that you have kicked in our faces for so long. We will rule this country, and you will not take the wealth that belongs here away from us!"

Verhoef's eyes flickered up to meet Kapepwe's.

"The gold that has been taken from the Reserve Bank will not leave Azania." Verhoef's head turned slightly to one side, a look of puzzlement crossing his face briefly. Kapepwe leant forward again, bringing his head close to Verhoef's. He spoke slowly and deliberately, "Because you are going to tell us how you plan to get it out."

Verhoef smiled at Kapepwe and said, "I don't know what you're talking about. You jokers are all crazy."

Then Kapepwe had held out his left hand. "Do you see that?" he said to Verhoef. "Look closely."

The tips of his index finger and third finger were missing; only a quarter of an inch from each one. The nails still remained, but they were smaller than on the other fingers and somewhat distorted.

"It doesn't look very much does it?" Kapepwe said. "It was done in a South African prison, eight years ago. Soon you will understand what this means, Mr. Verhoef," Kapepwe shook his hand in front of Verhoef, "and then I'm sure you will know what we are talking about when we ask you again about the gold."

Johnathan Kapepwe had then turned and walked away from Verhoef, past the others without a word, and into another room.

Verhoef had held out, through a nightmare of excruciating pain, while five of his fingers had been crushed over a period of as many hours. His hands were strapped down on two tables on either side of him. The pain from the bloody stumps of three fingers on his left hand and two on his right had amalgamated into two giant balloons of pain at the end of his arms. He no longer felt any distinction between his thumbs and his fingers; in fact, his hands could have been cut off at the wrists and he would have felt no worse. On several occasions, while he was conscious and wishing to be unconscious, he had felt sure that it would have been better to have both his hands cut off.

Whenever he was conscious—and they were continually throwing mugs of water over him to bring him around—they would question him.

"Where did the gold go from Voortrekkerhoogte? Are you flying it out? Is it going by ship? Who handled the transfer? Has it gone to Cape Town? Has it gone to Durban? How many bars are there?"

Verhoef's face was bloodied and bruised from continual slapping and pummelling. There were members of the questioning team who

254

were impatient and in whom the hatred for Verhoef was hard to suppress.

But somehow, Verhoef had held on. Perhaps it was because he was so close to the edge of insanity that he was able to continue defying such abominable pain. He had never studied Yoga, but almost involuntarily, his mind had gone into a sort of "alpha" state, in which everything around him became a haze and the pain he felt was a detached thing that he could look at and study with interest, as though in a dream; as if his pain was unreal and didn't really belong to him at all.

At 8.30 on the morning of the 21st, after a night of unbearable horror, Carl Verhoef looked up from his chest to see Johnathan Kapepwe standing in front of him again.

Kapepwe was concerned that no progress had been made with Verhoef. He had told them nothing. Kapepwe was about to try a different tack.

"I just thought you would like to know," he sneered at the battered prisoner, "that Nelson Mandele, Robert Sobukwe, and four other Azanian leaders have been liberated from Robben Island by black freedom fighters and that blacks throughout the entire country are in a general strike—that the uprising has begun and that within a week . . . "

Something stirred within Verhoef; a remnant of defiance. "You couldn't run this country," he whispered. His lips were cracked and torn from biting them himself in pain. "You're just a bunch of bloody kaffirs."

A man stepped forward angrily with the butt of a rifle raised in the air. Kapepwe stopped him.

Verhoef continued, "You'd make nothing but a bloody mess of it. You bloody kaffirs can't do anything properly."

Kapepwe smiled cruelly. "There are some things we *can* do properly, Mr. Verhoef. Like Marta Van Sisseren, for instance."

Verhoef's head jerked up. He looked directly at Kapepwe.

"What? What do you mean?"

Kapepwe laughed out loud. "No, you didn't know, did you? You didn't know that Marta loves black cock. She can't get enough of it. I've fucked her myself many times."

"You dirty liar," Verhoef hissed. "You dirty, stinking liar."

"Oh yes, Verhoef. Many times," Kapepwe taunted him. "What does it feel like to know that I've had my black cock right up inside your lovely little Marta? Eh?" Kapepwe burst into peals of harsh laughter. The others joined in.

"You can say what you like," Verhoef shouted. "I don't believe you."

"Oh no?" said Kapepwe. "What if I tell you that she has a little mole, under her pubic hairs, just at the top of her crack and that she likes it best with her legs up over your shoulders . . . it goes in deeper that way . . . and . . . "

"You bastard! You fucking bastard!" Verhoef shouted. "You lie! You lie!"

"How else do you think we knew about the first planeload of gold you tried to get out and about the plans to shift it from the Bank to Voortrekkerhoogte? She told us. She's told us everything, right from the beginning. The gold is safe with us now. The plane, unfortunately, met with an accident—the passengers also. Were they friends of yours?"

Verhoef's face twisted in anger. Despite the pain, he struggled to free himself.

"If only you'd kept talking to Marta about your plans," Kapepwe said, "none of this would have been necessary. We wouldn't have had to take you away at all."

"You dirty black bastards," Verhoef summoned all his energy to shout the words, "you filthy coons. There's no way you'll ever get hold of that gold. I'll see you in hell first!" He spat, and a small gob of phlegm landed on the chest of the man with the rifle.

The man's face contorted and he lunged forward past Kapepwe and drove the butt of his rifle hard into Verhoef's solar plexus, forcing a great, gasping scream from his lungs. Kapepwe pushed the man aside roughly and others pulled him back, restraining him from hitting Verhoef again.

Verhoef lapsed almost immediately into unconsciousness. With his spleen ruptured, he began to bleed internally and to slowly die.

He drifted back and forth from moments of relative clarity to semi-consciousness and total blackness and all the time, Kapepwe and two of the others hung close to him, whispering, "The gold . . . where is the gold?"

But Verhoef said nothing. It was no use applying any more forms of torture or intimidation. He was clearly past that. The men stood in the room, watching, waiting, listening for the slightest word; but Carl Verhoef was beyond them. His breathing began to rattle and then it slowly became weaker and weaker. At seven minutes past eleven, it stopped. As far as Carl Verhoef was concerned, the guerillas had lost.

At eight minutes past eleven, 184 members of the South African House of Assembly began to cast their votes in the chamber of the Parliament buildings in Cape Town, on the motion of no confidence in the president.

The vote had been delayed for half an hour while the stunned house had been given the sensational news that one of its members had apparently committed suicide. The Progessive Party's member for Brakpan, Mr. George Schuman, had just thrown himelf from his own eighth-storey office window, dying instantly on the pavement of the courtyard below.

There had been no note left to explain his action and, to a man, his party colleagues would not believe that he had taken his own life. Yet no other explanation was immediately available. The telephone operator in the building said that Mr. Schuman had taken a phone call from a Mr. Bartlett in Johannesburg, shortly before his death, but that she had not overheard any of the conversation.

By thirteen minutes past eleven, the no-confidence motion had been passed and President Botha was no longer in office. His defeat came as a stunning and unexpected blow and was only brought about because of massive defections from within his own Nationalist Party.

The president had felt reasonably confident that a significant number of the liberal opposition members, from both the Progressive and the United parties, would vote for him, since the alternative of elevating the vice president, Dr. Hugo Van Essche, leader of the Herstigte Nasionale Party, to power, was not something they wished to contemplate. In this assumption, President Botha was

257

correct; fifty-one of the seventy-one United and Progessive party members voted for him on the basis that they considered him the lesser of two evils.

But Botha lost when thirty-two of his own party members, almost half of the sixty-eight Nationalists in the Assembly, crossed the floor to vote against him. With the forty-five HNP votes and the twenty remaining liberals against him, the tally came to 87 for and 97 against. He was gone.

Under the terms of the constitution, the vice president automatically assumed the presidency and would have held it until the next elections, which, in this case, were not due for another three years. But, because of the extraordinary circumstances, where the vice president was leader of a party which did not command a majority of seats in the Assembly, Parliament was dissolved and new elections would be called in three months' time. Dr. Hugo Van Essche took the reins as an interim president only; the leader of a caretaker government.

He was, however, in full command, and no-one who was present in the House of Assembly on that dramatic morning of March 21, 1981, expected anything but dramatic action from Dr. Hugo Van Essche, whether they were for him or against him. He was the rightful successor, as leader of the HNP, to its founder, Dr. Albert Hertzog, who at eighty-two had been forced to retire from politics as a result of the infirmities of age.

Van Essche, like Hertzog, had been a member of the Nationalist Party until 1969. In February of that year, the then prime minister, Johannes Vorster, had dismissed Hertzog from his post as a senior cabinet minister, following a series of speeches in which he stated that English-speaking, white South Africans were generally too liberally inclined to be entrusted with South African affairs. When Hertzog resigned from the Nationalist Party later in the year and founded the Herstigte (reconstituted) Nasionale Party, Dr. Hugo Van Essche left with him, and during the seventies right up to the old man's reluctant departure from politics, worked as Hertzog's right-hand man.

Now, during a time of national emergency, Van Essche assumed sweeping powers with the presidency.

258

At 12.25, after the vote had been passed and he had spent more than half an hour in consultation with the country's defence chiefs, he stood before the House of Assembly to speak.

He was a small man and, in many ways, looked very similar to his former leader, Dr. Hertzog. He had grey hair and a small, grey goatee, which was almost identical to Dr. Hertzog's beard. Dr. Van Essche had sad blue eyes, but he was not sad this morning. There was an air of triumph about him as he addressed the members in Afrikaans.

"We meet today in the midst of the greatest crisis this country has ever faced," he said in strident tones to a hushed chamber. "We are surrounded by enemies on our borders and sabotaged by enemies from within.

"I don't have to tell you of the dreadful atrocities that have been committed in recent weeks by terrorists in all parts of the country. You all know now of the raid, in the early hours of this morning, on the detention centre on Robben Island which resulted in the escape of several important political prisoners. You have heard of the attacks last night on Jan Smuts airport and the Modderfontein explosive factory near Johannesburg, the explosions in the dockyards of Port Elizabeth and East London, and of the call for a general strike.

"The Robben Island raid clearly involved the use of one or more Soviet submarines, and our ambassador at the United Nations has already been instructed to lodge the strongest possible protest with the Security Council." Van Essche paused to look around the chamber. "Not that I believe it will do any good."

There was a ripple of cynical laughter from several parts of the room.

"That is right, my friends. We are alone now. And the greatest test is yet to come." He paused again and waited until there was absolute silence in the chamber.

"We have information that, in both Mozambique and Zimbabwe at this moment, two well-equipped armies—one of approximately fifty thousand men, the other of around forty thousand—are mobilized and ready to cross our borders. This is in addition to the guerilla forces already operating within the country."

There was not a sound in the big chamber as Dr. Van Essche continued.

"Our security forces have never been better prepared. But, as you know, the permanent forces, that is, the army, navy, and air force, consist only of some fifty thousand men. Up until now the government has only ordered the partial mobilization of the citizen forces and the commandos, which has added a further fifty to sixty thousand to our forces, but only on a three-month, rotational basis."

Once more he paused. "However, the situation facing our Republic is now so grave that I have, after consultation with our defence chiefs, signed, not fifteen minutes ago, a paper authorising the total mobilization of all our citizen forces. This will . . . " Van Esche's voice was momentarily drowned out by a burst of spontaneous applause in the chamber, "this will involve an immediate military call-up of upwards of 250,000 men. I have also issued instructions that a state of martial law will be proclaimed throughout South Africa as from one o'clock this afternoon."

This information was greeted with a chorus of cheers and "hear, hear's," but also low murmuring from the benches of the opposition parties.

"There may be some among you who consider these actions precipitate," Van Esche continued, "but I can tell you that there is every possibility that, within a matter of days—hours, even—this country could be at war, not only with Mozambique and Zimbabwe, but with Botswana and Namibia also.

"I cannot stress strongly enough that this is now a matter of survival—the survival of the white race in Southern Africa. It is a time for unity. We must shelve our differences and stick together to prevent the black hordes from overrunning our fatherland."

He thumped the desk in front of him.

"The greatest traditions of our forefathers, the Voortrekkers, involved the overcoming of insuperable odds—the defeat of the Matabeles and the Zulus. In those days, when brave farmers and their families were surrounded by hostile blacks, they formed themselves into protective 'laagers' inside the circle of their wagons. We need a modern laager, to close our wagons in around us . . . and we can do it! I assure you we can do it!

260

"It will require many sacrifices, some of which I am not yet in a position to ask of you or of our people, but if our understanding of the situation is correct . . . accurate . . . then there will be a need for further drastic action, and we will not hesitate to take it."

President Van Essche continued to speak for another fifteen minutes, explaining the details of the possible military threats from Mozambique and Zimbabwe, of the logistics involved in the mobilization of the citizen forces, and some of the technicalities of martial law. He left the chamber at ten minutes to one, in possession of greater powers than any other South African leader in this century.

The road south to Durban was not a particularly scenic route, except for the section through Volksrust, Charlestown, and the mountain passes beyond it. There was also some very attractive country below Estcourt and Mooi River, where the vegetation started to become more lush because of the higher rainfall, but Tony's convoy would pass through that area just after dark.

For most of the day, Tony found himself travelling, in a fixed position in the convoy, through country that reminded him very much of Australia. An open, rolling landscape; dry-grass, cattle country. And there was nothing more likely to make him homesick than gum trees. Ever since the late nineteenth century, Australian eucalypts had been transplanted in thousands all over South Africa. The trees had an exraordinary ability to survive in some of the harshest and driest of environments as well as in damp and more temperate climates. Consequently they thrived here and many an Australian, driving through parts of South Africa, had felt, as Tony did, that he was driving from one town to another in his own land.

Tony experienced this sensation very strongly during the drive to Durban. He had travelled extensively through South Africa on his two previous visits and each time had been awed by the great physical beauty of the place. Much more dramatic than Australia, he had thought. Much more varied. All the browns and ochres of the outback, the vast, open panoramas, wonderful beaches along the coast, as well as tropical beauty. But there's more here; the

261

flat-topped mesas of the Karoo Desert and the incredibly beautiful and dramatic mounains in the Drakensberg.

And yet Tony couldn't help feeling infinitely depressed. What a place this could be, he kept thinking. If only . . . If only there was love instead of hate. But the hatred and bitterness was now too deeply ingrained. Was it, though? Was it really? Had the black man suffered too many indignities, too much abuse and discrimination at the hands of the whites, throughout all of the three-hundred-year history of white habitation in the land, for there to be a simple solution like—love?

I'm going home, he told himself. At least we only have a few strikes and union problems to worry about there. Nobody gets bloody violent like this. But then, he thought, how long will it last? Could something similar happen there? People only start to get really violent as a last resort, when they can see no other way, when they can't wait any longer.

Would the blacks in South Africa get anything if they waited, or if they gave love instead of hate? Or would they be condemned to another three hundred years of serfdom and subservience to the whites? Tony laughed out loud.

But what will they get, if they take the country over by force? Chaos? Of course it'll be bloody chaos! Democracy will go out the window and . . . but what's democracy? Was there ever democracy here? Maybe for the whites . . . but there's never been democracy for the blacks. They have never experienced it. They've effectively lived under a white dictatorship; the dictatorship of every white man, woman, and child in the country. What does democracy mean to them?

To hell with it all, Tony thought, I'll go and buy that little piece of land I've always wanted up on the north coast. Grow a few avocadoes and mangoes and paw-paws. Have a little boat and sail through the Barrier Reef. Christ, what am I messing about over here for? This place is a bloody madhouse!

He thought again of Ingrid and their brief encounter. It really was like ships passing in the night, he said to himself sadly. He wondered if they ever could have loved each other, could have been something together. Sexually they had been great. But, he thought, what about the rest? Maybe. He shook his head, concentrating again on the road and his surroundings. No sense thinking thoughts like that. Like chasing rainbows.

Tony's convoy was due to arrive in Durban around 9.00 PM that night. During the drive south, the average speed had dropped to around thirty-five mph as a result of two brief stops at Volksrust and Ladysmith and, in fact, the convoy commander would normally have called a halt to spend the night at Estcourt, but there were military elements of the convoy which had to reach Durban urgently.

The new martial law regulations introduced a universal curfew for both blacks and whites from 9.00 PM to 6.00 AM, and only police and military personnel and vehicles were permitted on the roads between those hours. The convoy commander was informed of the government's new martial law decision at about four in the afternoon at Ladysmith and passed it on to the drivers and passengers in the forty-three civilian cars in the convoy.

Because the civilian cars were part of the military convoy, there would be no problem for them if they did not make Durban before the curfew started; but in any event, they expected to arrive before nine o'clock.

By nightfall, at 7.00 PM, the convoy was about ten miles past Mooi River. They had been on the motorway for some time now and were averaging about forty. Just the spot for a land-mine explosion, Tony thought as they cruised along, but nothing happened. At Pietermaritzburg they were joined by additional saladin scout cars and two Berliet M3 VTT armoured personnel carriers for the two-hour run down the highway to Durban, which passed without incident.

Arriving in Durban just as the curfew was about to come into force created problems. The civilians could not be allowed to leave the convoy and travel to their private destinations, because not only would they be breaking the new laws, but they would be placing themselves in considerable danger of being shot by the security forces. Tony and the rest of the civilians therefore had to spend the night at the Natal Command Headquarters army barracks on Snell Parade, before leaving in the morning to go about their own business.

It was during that evening at the barracks that he learnt that George Schuman had "committed suicide." One of the other civilians in the convoy had heard the news on an afternoon bulletin on his car radio. Tony's car was also fitted with a radio, but he had not listened to it once during the drive south. The news of George Schuman's death plunged Tony into an even deeper depression and he sat, for almost an hour, in one corner of the big communal room in which a group of people from the convoy had congregated. To an observer, Tony appeared to be reading; underneath, his mind was in turmoil, thinking about what he should do next.

Basically, Tony admitted to himself, he was afraid. He realised that the people involved in the gold conspiracy would stop at nothing. He was also very aware that he knew no-one in Durban. Where would he start? And what was he doing here anyway? He was swept with a desire to get out; to get on a ship and go . . . somehow . . . anyhow!

In the morning he felt slightly better, and at 8.30, he drove into Durban's central district.

Tony was amazed by the scenes in the city. Again, there were practically no black people to be seen. Shops were closed or boarded up, others carried big signs: SALE, CLOSING DOWN SALE, or ALL STOCK MUST GO! He saw several jewellery shops carrying similar signs: CONVERT CASH TO DIAMONDS, DIAMONDS THE ONLY SAFE INVESTMENT, HURRY WHILE STOCKS LAST!

The larger office buildings were open, but there seemed to Tony to be an air of unreality about the place. He saw white people doing jobs that normally in South Africa would be done by blacks. Garbage collection, though, was not one of the tasks that any white had been prepared to take on immediately and there was already evidence in the streets that two days' waste had not been cleared away. The promise that things would get worse was clear.

In the offices of Safmarine, which Tony found in John Ross House on the Victoria Embankment, he asked about the schedules of passenger vessels travelling in any direction. It took him fifteen minutes before he could even get to speak to someone, there was such a crowd of people trying to book tickets. He was told there was not a single berth available on any of the company's passenger ships for the next five months. When Tony asked about other lines, the white clerk behind the desk said that every other passenger line was also heavily booked, but he could try.

"What about cargo lines?" Tony asked.

"Well, you could try them all," the clerk said. "I know that most of them don't carry passengers, but they might be changing their policies now—the way things are going."

Tony was about to ask the man if he knew of a shipping line run by Mr. Paul Trauseld, but, glancing around at the crowd of people standing behind him, decided not to. Creeping paranoia reared its head again.

He thought, as he walked from the shipping company's office, that he would try the public library instead.

"Trauseld, Paul Clement . . . " Tony found the entry in a copy of *Who's Who in Southern Africa:*

"BA (Stell.), D. Phil (Oxon), LLD (Leiden), Mging Dir. & Chief Executive Cape Diamonds (SA) Pte. Ltd., Chairman & Mging Dir. Trauseld Investments (Tvl) Ltd., Continental Bitumen (1966) Pte. Ltd., Chairman & chief exec. Southern Sugar (Ntl) Ltd., Cape Chemicals (CT), memb board Transvaal Corporation Ltd., African Exploration (1970) Ltd., Johannesburg Consolidated (Tvl) Ltd."

"But no bloody shipping lines," Tony cursed under his breath. He read on:

"B. 29 Jan. 1928, C.T., S.O. Rev. Johannes Paul Trauseld, Educ. Diocesan Coll., Rondebosch, Stellenbosch University. Served 4th Armoured Car Regt., 1940–45. M.1959, Maria Stern. 1S. Carl Pieter. Clubs: Rand, Union, Kim, Inanda, Salisbury, Brooks. Rec: Tennis, sailing, golf, horseracing. Add: c/o Union Club, Cape Town."

Great! Tony said to himself. That gets me just about nowhere. He sounds incredibly boring. Just like any one of thousands of chairmen and chief executives. You close your eyes and stick a pin in. They're all the same.

Tony asked the librarian for a company directory.

"Do you mean for companies registered in South Africa?"

"Yes, I suppose so," Tony replied. "Do you have a directory for all the companies registered in South Africa?"

"Well, we do, but they're all registered separately," she said.

"One for the Cape, one for the Orange Free State, one for the Transvaal . . . Don't you know where the company is registered?"

"Not really, although I think it might be registered in Cape Town. Could I have the directory for the Cape Province, please?"

She gave him the reference and directed him to the shelves where he could find it himself. The library was all but empty. Only two or three people in the silent, mahogany-lined chamber.

Of the companies listed under Trauseld's name in the *Who's Who,* Tony decided to check out four first; Cape Diamonds, Continental Bitumen, Southern Sugar, and Cape Chemicals, only because, as they all involved products that would more than likely be exported, he thought they might have some connection with a shipping company.

But only Cape Diamonds and Cape Chemicals were in the Cape Province Directory and there was no reference, under their listing, to any shipping company. He was about to return the Cape Directory to its shelf and try the Natal Directory, when he decided to check the reference for Trauseld Investments. It was there, and Tony noted that one of the company's investments was apparently in another company called simply P.C.T. Holdings. He turned to the index for P.C.T. Holdings only to find that it was not registered.

But in the Natal Directory, which Tony quickly pulled from the shelves, P.C.T. Holdings was registered, and amongst the companies listed as coming under the control of P.C.T. Holdings was one called Cape Trading. Tony felt a degree of excitement as he turned back through the alphabetical listing to the reference for Cape Trading, only to find that there was no reference to any shipping company. Cape Trading was described in the directory as a company whose primary function was the export of South African manufactured specialist machinery to various European countries. It listed the company's products as "precision instruments" such as pressure and vacuum gauges, industrial hydrometers, and high-temperature control mechanisms.

Tony slammed the book shut in annoyance. At this rate, checking all of Trauseld's companies would take days. He was about to return the directory to its position on the shelf, when he noticed the gold-embossed cover: *Natal Companies Directory—1978.*

"Do you have a more up-to-date edition?" he asked the librarian a few moments later.

"We haven't got the 1980 edition yet, but there should be one for 1979," she said, walking with Tony back to the shelves. There was no copy there, but she assured Tony that there would be a second copy in the store room and she returned, a few minutes later, with it in her hands.

Tony thanked her and immediately turned again to Cape Trading.

This time, the entry included reference to a newly acquired company called South Cape Shipping. The company, Tony read, was formed in 1978 and, at the time of the directory's printing, had three ships; the *South Cape Mariner, South Cape Trader,* and *South Cape Aurora.*

It seemed, from what Tony read, that the *Mariner* was a bulk cargo carrier, possibly used, he thought, to carry either bitumen or chemicals for Trauseld's other companies. *South Cape Trader* was a bulk sugar carrier, obviously carrying Southern Sugar's exports to Europe and probably the United States. *Aurora* was more a general purpose cargo vessel, which Tony figured would more than likely be used to carry Cape Trading's machinery exports, as well as other commercial cargoes.

Tony slipped his notebook back into his pocket and again felt Marta Van Sisseren's gun. He had already grown used to the extra weight and its small bulk, so that he no longer felt conscious of it at all. On one or two occasions he had thought of getting rid of it, but, although he would not have liked to have admitted it, he found that it gave him a slight sense of security and, as everything around him was so insecure, he held onto it.

At the Marine Office of the Department of Transport, Tony asked for details of what ships were in the port of Durban at the moment. He purposely avoided any mention of South Cape Shipping Lines, telling the officials that he was a journalist (they wanted to see his accreditation) and that he was researching an article on how South Africa's trade had been affected by the emergency and now, more particularly, by the general strike. Were foreign ships staying away? Were imports still coming in and exports going out? What about the Russian and American naval ships and the confrontation which was looming between them—was that inhibiting the passage of merchant vessels? Could South Africa continue to operate its ports and harbours?

The two white men to whom Tony directed these questions were only too willing to give him as much information as possible in an effort to convince him that it was "business as usual"; that a little emergency like this wasn't going to upset the whole pattern of trade on which so much of the country's livelihood depended.

The general strike had already caused big problems in only twenty-four hours, they admitted, but there were whites operating the docks and in some cases the army had been called in to perform the manual work in loading and offloading merchant vessels. "Oh no, my friend, South Africa will be able to continue very nicely thank you."

They chatted for a while and Tony took some notes. They gave him a list of all the vessels currently in or expected in port, their wharf positions and estimated dates of departure or arrival. Tony thanked them and left.

Outside the office, he studied the photocopied list: "*South Cape Aurora*," the words stood out towards the bottom of the page, "Salisbury Island Pier No. 1. Departure 23/24 March, Genoa."

Nearby, at a camping goods store, Tony bought a pair of 10-power binoculars, the strongest available in the shop, and drove from the central district to the beachfront and then southwards along the esplanade towards the bulk oil storage facility at the end of the point. Turning into a side street, he found a parking space and began to walk towards the harbour, looking as he went for a suitable tall building that might give him the vantage point he was seeking.

He found one or two apartment blocks that he thought might have been suitable, but there was no access to the roof, either because none was provided or it was locked or because the caretaker would not allow Tony onto the roof. One caretaker had begun throwing awkward questions at him when he asked permission to go up to the roof. He left and continued looking.

Eventually, he found a five-storey building, rundown in appearance and without a caretaker in sight. There were a few grubby children playing in the street. It was a white area, but definitely a second- or third-class white area, for some of the not-so-well-off whites who came down from Johannesburg once a year for their three weeks annual leave and who couldn't afford the jazzy hotels on the beachfront. The building was drab, seedy, and, Tony guessed, only one-third full—if that. The growing state of emergency throughout the country had all but killed the tourist industry.

Tony took the shabby elevator to the fifth floor and found, without trouble, a door and steps leading to the roof. Squatting down and resting his arms on the low wall surrounding the roof, he peered through the binoculars across the railyards and the naval berths on the point, out across a stretch of harbour water to the new Salisbury Island piers. He focused the glasses and tilted them down along the vessels lined up on Pier One. There were three that he could see and the *South Cape Aurora* was in the middle, between the *Safocean Albany,* which was berthed in front, and another vessel with its name obscured.

He could see the cranes working and activity on the wharf as the front hold of the ship was being loaded with large wooden crates. The crates, Tony saw, had printing on the sides, but he was too far away to make out what the words said. There seemed to be a considerable number of people on the wharf beside the ship, either supervising operations or just standing around. He made up his mind to try to see the proceedings from closer quarters.

He left the building, made his way back to the car, and drove again to the offices of Safmarine, where he asked for a boarding pass for the *Safocean Albany* on Pier One.

"A boarding pass?" the clerk said, slightly puzzled. It was a different clerk from the one Tony had spoken to earlier in the morning.

"Yes. A boarding pass . . . a visitor's pass," Tony said.

"We don't issue visitors' passes to merchant vessels . . . only passenger ships."

"But I have a friend on board," Tony said, "I've only just discovered he's in port. It's important."

"Oh, there's no trouble in getting you into the docks, but getting

269

on board the ship is another matter. There's customs and the skipper. You have to get their permission. But I can give you a pass to get to Pier One." He tore a slip of paper from a pad and began scribbling a few words on it. He handed it to Tony, "Try your luck once you're over there."

"Thanks," Tony said.

It was a long drive to Pier One, which was on the opposite side of the harbour. It meant circling right around to the south side of the harbour and then coming back up towards the city again, but the highway was good and there was little traffic, so Tony covered the distance in good time.

He drove up to the sand-bagged entry gate, but was told by two soldiers manning it that private vehicles were no longer permitted. He parked a short distance away and walked back, showing his dock pass, and gained entry without any questions asked.

He walked along past the railway siding and goods sheds to the beginning of Pier One and followed it along the western side, the opposite side to where the *South Cape Aurora* was berthed. He followed the pier to the end of the storage sheds and turned right, walking along beside a Japanese freighter. As he turned the next corner, he saw the bow of the *Safocean Albany* and beyond it, three hundred yards or so back down the wharf, the *South Cape Aurora*. Both vessels were busy loading.

Tony took out a notebook and pen and began scribbling meaningless nothings in an effort to appear busy. He moved slowly along the wharf beside the *Safocean Albany,* glancing at the ship and the cargo being steadily swung aboard, appearing only to be interested in what was happening to that particular ship, the *Albany.* But every now and then, as he moved further towards the stern of the *Albany,* he would look casually and disinterestedly at the *South Cape Aurora.*

Over a period of several minutes, Tony built up a picture of what was happening there. There were several dockside cranes working on the job of loading the ship with a variety of general cargo, but Tony's interest was caught, although he dared not show it, by the cargo being loaded into one of the forward holds nearest to him as he stood by the stern of the *Safocean Albany.* They were

270

large wooden crates bearing the markings in English, German, and Italian: "HANDLE WITH CARE, PRECISION INSTRUMENTS, THIS SIDE UP."

In large, red stencilled letters Tony read the address: "POTGEITER INSTRUMENT CO., Helverstrasse 145, ZURICH."

Tony had seen enough. There were a couple of men dressed in business suits standing by the wall of a wharf shed who were looking in his direction. Without turning again toward the *South Cape Aurora,* he began moving slowly back along the wharf beside the *Safocean Albany,* continuing all the while to take notes. He stood for a while watching the proceedings at the forward hold of the vessel, then walked off in the direction of the main gate again. Turning the corner of the shed, he immediately quickened his pace and then broke into a jogging run. But no-one was following him. He slowed down and walked directly, without interruption, back to his car.

Tony now drove slowly back towards town. A car behind him tooted and he realised he was going too slowly and speeded up slightly. Again, his mind was in a tumult of indecision.

Here was the biggest robbery in history, as Dekker had put it, about to be pulled off and Tony was powerless to do anything about it. George Schuman had been killed because Tony had told him about the plot, and Tony knew that he himself would almost certainly be quickly disposed of if BOSS knew where he was—and that wouldn't be long. Once they pieced together the details of the phone call to Schuman, they'd know that Tony had seen Dekker's letter and would probably head for Durban.

Tony wondered if he could make another attempt to get the information to the government. But, he thought, the government is now the HNP, which is almost certainly mixed up in the thing anyway. Who can I tell? Why should I tell anyone? Why not just let the whole thing go? But then he thought about the mines and the act of bitter spite that would destroy them. If the mines were blown up, it would be a terrible setback to any efforts at reconstruction made by any new government, whether it was black, white, or multi-racial. A few whites would benefit from the gold that was spirited away, but the ones who chose to remain, or who stayed because they had no alternative—and that could be millions of people—wouldn't benefit from it. And they certainly wouldn't benefit from the destruction of the gold mines, the richest source of South Africa's foreign income.

But how could he stop it? The only course open to him, to tell people about the conspiracy, seemed to place him in danger. He made up his mind to type up a series of letters that evening and to send them off in the morning to various people in positions of influence in the government, the opposition, and in industry. But how much time was there? He turned on the car radio and caught the tail end of the news and a special announcement.

"Just repeating," the newsreader said, "that the interim president, Dr. Van Essche, will deliver an important special message to the nation this evening at six PM. The president's message to the nation, tonight, 6 PM on this and all radio and television stations."

Tony followed the expressway onto Alexandra Street which would have taken him back onto West Street and the city centre, but he took the exit that led down to the Victoria Embankment. He had in mind to head back to the beachfront and try to find some accommodation in a small holiday apartment for the night. He thought it best to avoid hotels—certainly the major hotels, where it might be easier for him to be traced.

As he drove beneath the underpass and onto the Victoria Embankment, with Albert Park stretching off to his left, Tony caught a glimpse of a group of five or six whites in the park, in what at first looked like a rugby game on the grass. They were a couple of hundred yards away, towards the far end of the park. Several trees and shrubs obscured Tony's view for a few seconds as he drove on, but there was something unusual about the group that prompted him to keep looking. Then, suddenly, as the road curved to the left around the park, he saw a black man break from the group and run. He was tackled in seconds and brought to the ground by two of the whites, who proceeded to beat him with their fists and to kick him on the ground as he rolled over and over, trying desperately to escape. Two other whites left the first group to join in and Tony saw that another black man was struggling on his knees, while the two remaining whites hit him continually in the face.

In a reflex action, without thinking, Tony swung the car off the road onto the footpath beside the park, jammed on the brakes, leapt out, and ran towards the two groups. By the time he reached them, the man on the ground was unconscious, but the whites were still kicking him. The other, whose face was bloody and battered, was being held up by the arms by two men, while the rest took turns to punch him in the stomach. He had been hit more than once and was gasping for air.

"Stop! Stop!" Tony yelled, as he ran up. "Leave them alone. You'll kill them!"

"What the fuck do you think we're trying to do, man?" one of the whites said, "Play pussyfoot? Piss off and leave us alone. We're just teaching these bloody coons a few lessons."

The beating had stopped temporarily when Tony arrived on the scene. "What sort of chance have they got?" Tony shouted angrily. "There's six of you and only two of them—three to one! You don't even give them a fair go." He looked down at the one lying on the grass, who began to regain consciousness, but then started writhing in agony and groaning.

The whites were all young men in their late teens or early twenties. The one who had spoken, a tall, dark-haired youth, stepped across to Tony and grabbed him by his jacket. "Listen, smart-arse, what are you? A nigger-lover or something? Just keep your nose out of other people's business," he said, "or you'll end up getting the same treatment as these two." His right fist came round too quickly for Tony to avoid it. It connected with Tony's left cheek and sent him sprawling on the grass.

Tony stood up, rubbing his jaw. "All right," he mumbled. "All right. I'll go." He made as if he was about to leave and then, without telegraphing his moves, let loose a sharp left jab to the dark-haired man's stomach. As the man doubled over, Tony brought his right fist up hard to his jaw, snapping his head back and laying him out flat on his back. "But not unless I take them with me," Tony said, reaching quickly into his pocket and pulling out Marta Van Sisseren's pistol. The whites stepped back in unison at the sight of the gun.

"Let him go!" Tony shouted at the two men holding the black man who was standing.

"Try to get your friend on his feet," Tony said, motioning to the other black on the ground. He estimated them both to be only about eighteen or nineteen years old.

"All right," Tony said now to the five whites, "start walking . . . that way." He pointed across the park in the opposite direction to where he had come from.

"What about him?" one of them said, pointing to the dark-haired one lying senseless on the ground.

"Leave him there. He'll be all right in a few minutes. Now walk!" They walked.

The young black who had been kicked unconscious staggered to his feet with the help of his friend and hobbled, groaning, between him and Tony, back towards the car. They put the injured boy in the back seat to lie down. The other sat in beside Tony in the front seat.

Two other cars had stopped ahead of Tony's car to see what was happening and three whites were walking back in his direction. Tony slammed the car into gear and drove off.

Taking the first turn off the Victoria Embankment to the left and manoeuvring quickly through several side streets, he suddenly found himself back on the main road heading for the expressway to the south, out of the city again.

"Which way do you live?" Tony asked the young man at his side.

"This way," he said, pointing straight ahead.

14

A Decision

Tony drove for several minutes in silence before he spoke again. He had the distinct feeling of having grabbed a tiger by the tail. I'm in for it now, he thought. Just getting deeper and deeper, instead of getting out—right out.

"Where is your home?" he said again to the youth beside him, who had been trying to clean up his face with a handkerchief, but was unable to stop his nose from bleeding.

"Put your head back," Tony said and then, once more, "where do you live?"

"Near Umbumbulu."

"Where's that?"

The young man turned and looked at Tony. "It's in the hills up on the Umbogintwini River."

"Is that far from here?"

The boy paused a few seconds. "It's about fifteen miles from Isipingo . . . but . . . but you don't have to take us there. We don't need your help any more."

"Does your friend live there too?" Tony asked, looking over his shoulder at the other boy, who was conscious, but unable or unwilling to talk.

"No," said the boy in the front. "But he is coming to stay at my village."

"And Isipingo's only about ten miles or so from here, isn't it? To the south? We're on the right road, aren't we?"

"Yes," the young man said quietly. He looked at Tony again. "Are you from Johannesburg?"

"No. I'm from Australia," Tony said, and smiled at the boy, who turned back to the front, opened his mouth as if about to say something, but instead simply nodded his head slowly.

"What's you name?" Tony asked.

"Ben," the boy said. "Ben Mbatha."

"And your friend?"

"Marcus . . . Marcus Saoli."

"What happened back there?" Tony said. "How did you get into that fight?"

"Well . . . I . . . we . . ." he shook his head. "It doesn't matter."

"It does," said Tony. "Please tell me. I want to know."

"There is nothing to tell," Ben said, still shaking his head. "They just came up to us and started abusing us and pushing us around. It is quite normal."

"Normal?" Tony said in surprise. "Normal to half-kill someone?"

"No. That was because we answered back and told them to leave us alone." Ben stuck his chin out stubbornly and looked straight ahead, almost as if he expected Tony to turn on him. "I . . . we . . . we told them that they had better enjoy their power, because they would not have it for much longer."

Tony sat quietly for a few minutes, just concentrating on the road.

"Do you work in Durban?" he asked eventually.

"No. We both go to university—the University of Zululand."

"That's up at Richards Bay, isn't it?" Tony said.

"Yes."

"But that's a hundred miles to the north . . ."

"Yes. It's been closed because of the general strike and martial law and we've been hitch-hiking home today. A sugar truck dropped us off at the sugar terminal near the park and we were just walking across to the Berea Road station to get a train to Isipingo, when they stopped us."

"How old are you?" Tony asked.

"Twenty—almost twenty-one."

"And what are you studying at university?"

"Law." The young man looked again at Tony and, as if to say, that's enough, now it's my turn, said, "And what is your job?"

"I am a journalist. I work for a newspaper in London."

"And your name?"

Tony told him and then noticed, up ahead on the highway, a police car. It was travelling in the same direction, but Tony slowed the car slightly and allowed a couple of other cars to pass him.

"I think," he said, "that if we see any police cars coming close to us, you should get down, so as not to be seen."

Ben Mbatha said nothing.

Shortly they reached Isipingo and turned east to drive into the low green hills that spread back from the coast. As they made the turn, Tony saw the police car ahead, continuing on its way south. Had it been any other time but this, Tony also would have liked to continue south, as Isipingo, he remembered, was just at the start of a ninety-mile stretch of magnificent sandy beaches, backed by a profusion of tropical growth; a resort area of great beauty, which had only been marginally spoilt by the inroads of the tourist industry. Ninety miles, with more than fifty beaches where, with the long, Indian Ocean swells rolling in, there was always somewhere to catch a wave or two. The last time Tony had been down this road was on his second visit to South Africa almost two years ago. He had been with his family, Carol and Michael, then. They had hired a surfboard in Durban and a couple of inflatable mats and had spent a week surfing on the beaches at the southern end of the strip, between Margate and Hibberdene.

His thoughts were confused. It had been a good time, really. Carol and Michael had enjoyed it . . . and so had he. No arguments. No traumas, just swimming, lying in the sun . . . loving. Loving? It all seemed so long ago. He found Ingrid creeping into his thoughts. Ingrid. We never got around to lying on beaches in the sun, to swimming, or to loving. Only briefly . . . so briefly. I wonder if she ever came down here?

He remembered the beaches. Amazing, really. Beaches with names like St. Michael's on Sea, Southport, Sunwich Port, interspersed with other beaches called Uvongo, Umtentweni, Uzumbe. Black and white names, but no blacks on those beaches—whites only. Oh, the blacks had places to swim; segregated places, well away from the whites, but there was no doubt who had the best beaches.

And yet, at that time, along those beaches, Tony had not been tremendously conscious of racial discrimination. It was as if it were a completely white country, with a few blacks in evidence at the right moments to provide service when it was required. It was easy to put them into the background, to say that they didn't really exist. In thinking about it later, Tony had realised that that was what most South Africans did with the blacks—also what white Australians did with the aborigines, and Americans with their Indians—shuffled them into the background of their minds, where they wouldn't have to think of them, nor have to be confronted with inequality and the darker side of their own souls, which perpetuated the black man's subservience to the white.

Oh, to be sure, the black man was better off here than in any other African country—better off materially. That was what you were constantly told here, but few whites could ever accept that this was not the point. By economically, politically, and spiritually subjugating the blacks, the whites also subjugated themselves, brutalised themselves, without knowing it. Maybe the knowing of it was the only terrible thing, Tony thought.

And what about me? Here I am, an outsider, sticking my nose in.

"Oh, you haven't lived here long enough," was the standard comment. "You can't possibly understand the situation . . . not unless you actually live here. It's too complex. The tribes all hate each other anyway. They'd massacre each other if there wasn't law and order here . . . white law and order. That's the only thing that keeps this place running!"

And Tony knew there was considerable truth in that. Yet he found himself now heading deeper into a dangerous situation where he would be in conflict with that white law and order. In the white man's eyes, what he had just done made him a "nigger-lover" as the white youth in the park had said—a traitor.

But Tony didn't feel he was either. He also had no guilt complexes about being white. There were a great many things the white race could *not* be proud of—the Hitlers, the slave traders, a thousand inhuman and barbarous acts committed by Europeans down through history. But every race has that sort of record; the Chinese, the Japanese, the Indians, the Pakistanis, the Arabs. We've all perpetrated horrific and inhuman acts and that's basically what it's all about, Tony thought. We're *all* human, but we've also *all* got the capacity to be inhuman, whether we are English, Cambodian, South African, black, white, or brindle. Field Marshall Idi Amin didn't do too badly in the inhumanity stakes and that was black against black. No, Tony told himself, the only thing you can possibly do in all of this is to try to keep your own personal integrity . . . to be a "human" and not an "inhuman" individual.

There was a groan from the boy in the back seat, Marcus. Both Tony and Ben Mbatha turned to look at him.

"Are you all right?" Tony said.

"I . . . I think so," the young man replied. "My chest hurts."

"We should be taking him to a hospital," Tony said. "He could have some ribs broken."

"There is a mission not far from us," Ben said quietly. "We will take him to our village first and then, if necessary, we can get him to the mission."

Marcus shifted his position slightly and closed his eyes. "Is he also studying law?" Tony asked Ben.

"No . . . political science."

"Political science? What sort of political science do they teach?"

"I am not doing the course," Ben replied, "so I am not sure exactly what is in it, but I know that they concentrate a great deal on the politics of the homelands; the political structure and development of Kwazulu, for instance, as a separate and independent state like the Transkei and Bophuthatswana."

"But do most blacks really accept the homelands?"

"Of course not!" Ben looked vehemently around at Tony. "The Transkei and Bophuthatswana are independent now—theoretically independent. But in the hearts of all black people they are all part of one country . . . of Azania." Again the look of stubbornness and defiance.

"What about the tribal differences?" Tony suggested. "The Transkei is all Xhosa, Bophuthatswana is for the Tswana, and Kwazulu is for the Zulus."

"Hah," Ben sneered, "the whites try to tell us that the homelands will preserve our tribal heritage and customs. But really, the only

279

reason they push these homelands on us is to divide us. Divide and rule! It's easier to control three or four million Zulus here, a couple of million Tswana there, and three million Xhosa somewhere else, than the whole lot together as one black nation."

It occurred to Tony that, if the views held by Ben Mbatha were shared by the rest of the black students in South Africa, the policies of separate development pursued by the white government could not possibly last forever. He also felt sure that Ben would not have spoken so openly to him if Tony had been a South African.

"Some blacks are in favour of the independent homelands," Tony said.

"They are just the arse-lickers," Ben said. "They feel they can gain a small degree of power through the white man's manoeuvring."

"What about Buthalezi? He goes along with the political structure they've set up for Kwazulu, even though it's not independent yet: the Legislative Assembly, the Executive Assembly, and so on, and yet as chief of the Zulus he still has enough independence to stand up to Pretoria on many issues."

"Yes, I know. I'm not saying they are all stooges. Buthalezi tries to achieve his aims—freedom and dignity for us, firstly within the framework of the white man's system, but . . ." Ben paused, looked at Tony for a second or two, and then back to the front again. ". . . But after we have won, then Kwazulu, Transkei, Bophuthatswana, Ciskei, Lebowa, and the others will all join together to form one country. We will be a United States of South Africa—a United States of Azania."

Tony sat quietly, wondering for a few moments about idealism, ingenuousness, and his own cynicism. But was it cynicism or just pragmatism? Tony thought that perhaps pragmatism was the lesser of the two evils . . . If it was an evil. But then, you can be too pragmatic.

In the distance, a quarter of a mile away, an army convoy rounded a bend and came rolling towards them, truck after truck.

"Hop down," he said to Ben urgently. Ben slid as far down as he could under the dash, on the passenger side.

They had seen very little traffic since they had turned off the main coast road at Isipingo and Tony had thought, once or twice, that the road could be dangerous, but he consoled himself with the thought that Ben and Marcus could say a few words in his favour if they were stopped by blacks. If they were stopped by whites, on the other hand, particularly the police or the army, Tony felt he would be in for some trouble.

The convoy came down on them so fast that there was no way they could do anything to cover up Marcus on the back seat. Tony just hoped that no-one in the convoy trucks, or on the motorcycle escorts travelling with them, would be able to see into the back seat.

The twenty-five vehicles roared past and Tony glanced in the rear vision mirror to see if any motorcycle outrider or vehicle would turn back, but none did. Two miles further along the road, they came to the small township of Umbumbulu. At Ben's direction, they turned off the road to the right and began to follow a dirt road. A number of blacks stood and watched with some amazement as the car passed through the township. Umbumbulu dropped behind them, obscured by the pall of dust rising from the car as it trundled down a long, winding hill.

"The river is only about three miles from here now," Ben said.

Shortly, they saw more signs of habitation. Village huts—small, round, mud-walled rondavels with thatched roofs—dotted the surrounding hills on both sides of the road. Tony caught a glimpse of the Umbogintwini River winding down through dense foliage along its banks. The dirt road ran down the hill towards the river, but as they came near a small building standing on its own by the side of the road, Ben motioned for Tony to stop. By the signs hung on the verandah and painted on its sides, it was obviously a small general store. Three black men, who had been sitting on the verandah, stood up when they saw the car and then, seeing Tony at the wheel, began to move towards the car.

"Wait here," Ben said, getting out of the car.

At the sight of Ben, the faces of the three men all broke into smiles and they shouted greetings in Zulu to the youth, shook his hand, and slapped his back. But when they noticed his battered face, their looks became serious. They stood in earnest conversation for several minutes, looking across at Tony a number of times.

Then the four of them disappeared inside the small shop and, after three or four more minutes, emerged again with two other men. The group walked towards the car. Tony had no idea what to expect.

"This is my father and my uncle," Ben Mbatha said to Tony, as he came up to the car. Tony stepped out, smiled, and said hello and then shook their hands. Ben turned to the original three. "This is another uncle," he said gesturing to one of them, "and these are two of my friends." Tony shook their hands also.

"We must take Marcus out," Ben said, and the others moved to help the injured youth from the back seat.

"Are his family near here?" Tony asked.

"No. He lives at Nongoma, further north from Richards Bay. He was coming to stay with us. You will stay with us too," Ben said.

Tony was surprised. "No," he said, "I can't. I must go back to Durban. I have work to do."

"It is almost five o'clock," Ben said firmly. "Soon it will be dangerous for you to travel. No. It is better that you stay here with us. My father has said so. Our house is there," he pointed to a small but substantial house, a hundred yards or so away, on a hill. It was made from concrete blocks and had a shiny tin roof.

Ben's father, a large man with commanding features and curly hair that was slightly greying, stepped forward and said in broken English, "Yes. You stay. Friend of my son. You stay night time here." He grasped Tony's shoulder and smiled.

Inside the house on the hill, Tony met Ben's mother, a large, full-bosomed woman of about forty-five. She registered surprise at the sight of a white man coming into her home, but after a short explanation of the afternoon's events, she smiled and welcomed Tony. "I'll make some tea," she said. She gestured to a wooden chair. "Sit down and I'll make some tea."

Marcus was helped into a small bedroom and examined all over by Ben's father and one of the uncles, who had been a nurse's assistant at a Durban hospital. They were not sure about his ribs. Marcus told them he felt severe pain on one side, under his arm, but they could feel no break. He was a mass of bruises. There were several nasty lumps and cuts on his head and face. His nose was apparently broken and two teeth had been kicked out.

The men strapped his chest with a piece of torn sheeting and laid him down. While they were caring for him, he talked and managed an occasional smile. He was sick, but showing considerable improvement, Tony thought, from when they had first bundled him into the car. They decided to wait until morning to see if it was necessary to take him to hospital or to the Adams Mission station, back down the main road, which ran a small clinic.

The Mbatha house was simple and rustic. Ben's parents were poor by Western standards, but reasonably well off by comparison to the majority of other people in their area, who were mainly subsistence farmers. Ben's mother had worked for many years in Durban as a domestic servant. His father, who was ten years older than Ben's mother, had had a score of jobs; labourer, office messenger, gardener. He even worked as a rickshaw puller for the white tourists on Durban's beachfront for several years before he became a taxi-driver. But through all of his and his wife's various jobs, the two had saved diligently. Nine years ago, they had returned to the district where Ben's father had been born, bought the little wooden store on the road, and begun building their house.

Ben had two brothers and a sister, but they were all working in Durban.

Over a cup of tea, they all sat around in the main room on a variety of sofas and chairs, going over the whites' attack on Ben and Marcus. At first they spoke rapidly in Zulu, none of which Tony understood, although he could tell by Ben's gestures basically what was being said. Then Ben's father turned to Tony and said, "I am sorry. We talk Zulu. You do not understand. Ben," he said to his son, "we speak English."

Tony protested that he did not mind them speaking Zulu, but they insisted, even though it tended to slow the conversation down considerably, and consisted for several minutes of Ben's father, whose name was Lucas, and his mother, Nellie, thanking Tony profusely.

Tony asked them what they felt about the general situation— the breakdown of communication between blacks and whites and the introduction of martial law. He found the older adults reluctant to speak, either because Tony was white and they were embarrassed, or for some other reason. Ben, however, was not deterred from speaking and Tony soon saw that there was a divergence of opinion between parents and child.

Mother and father represented a generation which had grown up within a system, accepting the things they could not change and doing the best they could for themselves, which was not insubstantial. They had achieved a lot, were comfortable, relatively independent, well clear of any interference from whites, and happy.

Ben, on the other hand, was a member of a generation which had been made aware that South Africa was alone in the world as a country where a white minority completely controlled the destinies of the black majority, simply on the basis of the colour of its skin. He had been exposed to the radical ideas of his fellow students and, although not accepting the Marxist line of terrorism and anarchy as a prelude to revolution, Ben strongly believed that the whites must somehow be forced to accept the principle of majority rule.

"Did you hear the broadcasts of Nelson Mandele and Robert Sobukwe?" Ben asked his parents and Tony together. His mother, father, and uncles all nodded, but Tony said, "No. I knew they were going to speak, but I didn't know when or where to listen." He checked the time: 5.45. "There is a special broadcast by the new president in fifteen minutes," he said. "Do you have a radio here?"

"Of course."

"The broadcasts by Mandele and Sobukwe—they were on the secret radio stations?"

"Yes," Ben said with a smile. "They were broadcast yesterday and last night. They told us that it would not be long before the white government fell, that all blacks were to stop work completely, to refuse cooperation with whites, and to help one another with food and money until the aim was achieved."

"And anyone continuing to work, or assisting the whites?" Tony asked.

"Will be regarded as a traitor," Ben said.

"What about you having me here, now?" Tony then said.

"That is different, of course. You have more to fear from other whites than you have from us."

"Did they both call for an uprising . . . to fight?"

"Sobukwe did. He said there were arms and ammunitions in plenty already in the country and that we were to fight the white man at every opportunity. Mandele was more moderate. He called for basically passive resistance and non-cooperation. But that any violence on the part of whites should be met by violence."

"So there is something of a split between the two of them already, is there?" Tony said.

"There always was. Mandele was always a little more moderate than Sobukwe. I don't think it matters. Both of them called for unity, for trust between the tribes, and for a combined war against the whites."

"What would you like to happen to the whites after you won?"

"Well, there are many people I know who would want to kick them out—or even worse. But there are many others who feel that they should be allowed to stay and be given a chance to participate in a multi-racial society . . . if they could take it . . . if they could accept it."

"Which way do you think?"

"I think the second way is right. After all, what the whites say is true. They were born here. It is their home too. And anyway, there are too many of them to kick out. Five million is a lot of people. The thing is to get them to accept the fact that they can no longer be the rulers. They can only be a significant minority in the future. How significant, depends on them."

"Are you at all worried that the whole thing might just deteriorate into chaos?" Tony asked.

"Naturally. I personally am not a Communist. I would like to see a democratic government here, not a dictatorship, whether it be a Communist one or whatever. But I am convinced that the only way to get majority rule is through revolution. We cooperate with the Communists to get it done and hope that in the end we are able to make it a democracy rather than a totalitarian rule."

"Dangerous," Tony observed.

"Yes, but not all revolutions have resulted in Communism. Look at the French Revolution and the American Revolution."

"Communism wasn't around then."

"I know, but we have to take the chance."

It was three minutes to six. Ben's father shifted a chair and put the Mbatha family's small black and white television set on the table, where everyone could see it. He switched it on.

At precisely six, after an introduction by a studio announcer, the image of President Van Essche came up on the screen. It was a pre-taped message in English. An identical message, recorded in Afrikaans, went out simultaneously on the Afrikaans channel. The president's speech was also broadcast on all English and Afrikaans radio stations and translations were transmitted at the same time over the seven Bantu radio services in the Sotho, Zulu, Xhosa, Tswana, Venda, and Tsonga languages.

Van Essche looked strained, serious, and pale, although you couldn't really tell with television.

"Fellow South Africans," he began. "I speak to you tonight at a time of grave crisis for the Republic. During all of our long history as inhabitants of this part of the African continent, no threat has been greater than the one which we now face.

"The Zulu and Matabele wars and the Anglo-Boer War will pale into insignificance when compared to what is about to confront us. I have to tell you that this afternoon, the frontiers of the Republic were crossed by hostile forces at several places in the northern and eastern Transvaal and in Natal, and that this country is consequently at war with Mozambique and Zimbabwe."

Tony glanced up from the set. Everyone in the room looked around at each other in a stunned silence.

"Units of the South African Army have repulsed two armoured columns which crossed from Mozambique in different areas of the Kruger National Park and another force driving south from Zimbabwe on the Messina road towards Louis Trichardt. However, a strong armoured force which crossed at Ndumu into Natal has reached Jozini, about fifty miles inside our borders. It has been contained there by South African forces and will shortly be driven back.

"The South African Air Force is at this moment carrying out

preventive air strikes on strategic targets in the port and industrial areas of Maputo and on military supply depots in various parts of Mozambique and Zimbabwe."

The president, who had been addressing the camera directly, looked down for a moment at the papers on his desk, and then went on.

"Let me assure you, we have the ability to crush each of these armies utterly and completely. However, our military intelligence has confirmed that within hours, we can expect similar invasions from across the borders of both Botswana and Namibia. As I have said, we have the ability to crush these aggressors, but . . ." Van Essche paused and looked piercingly from the screen, as if he were trying to look into the eyes of every white person watching, ". . . only if we have the total and unqualified support of everyone in this country. We cannot fight a guerilla war within our borders at the same time. That is clearly impossible!

"The government has therefore reached a momentous decision that will affect the lives of every man, woman, and child in South Africa. In consultation with the National Security Council, the Bureau for State Security, and our defence planners, the government has decreed the immediate institution of a policy of multi-lateral national partition!"

"My God," Tony whispered. The others again stared around the room in blank amazement.

"Successive South African governments," Van Essche went on, "have pursued the policy of separate development for the black and white races, by different degrees. The concept of the Bantustans, the homelands, was to give the various tribal and ethnic groupings of South Africa independence and autonomy from the white government. But while nominally they have been self-governing and two of them have become independent, they have remained, to all intents and purposes, economically part of South Africa, and millions of black people have remained living and working in the white homelands. This can no longer continue. It has become increasingly apparent that black and white are incompatible in South Africa and the mounting threat of internal subversion and murderous terrorist attacks by black guerillas has only tended to confirm this.

"Consequently, a programme of transmigration will be put into effect, beginning tomorrow morning, under which every black person living or working in areas designated as part of the white homelands will be required to move to the tribal homeland shown on his pass. All Zulus will be moved to Kwazulu, all Tswanas to Bophuthatswana, all Shangan to Gazankulu, all Basotho to Qwaqua, all Venda to Venda, Swazis to Swazi, Xhosa to the Transkei, and Ciskei and northern Basothos to Lebowa. These territories already have the political infrastructure of internal self-government, such as legislative and executive houses of Parliament, and presidential proclamations will be issued granting immediate independence to those territories which do not already have it. Any black person defying or obstructing the moves, or not producing his or her pass when required, will be imprisoned. This also applies to any white person who obstructs the programme."

The president, who had been reading the last few paragraphs from his notes, now looked up again into the camera.

"My fellow countrymen, these are drastic and terrible steps to have to take, but we are faced with the question of survival and I am convinced that, without these drastic measures, there can be no survival for white democracy in Southern Africa.

"I accept the fact that this decision will bring great hardship to many black people—and to many whites also. So the government has today appointed a Commissioner of Compensation who, with a newly formed department, will study any claims for compensation made by black people moved from their homes. The government will also undertake a programme of economic assistance to the independent nations formed by this partitioning of South Africa and for the cost of establishing temporary accommodation and transmigration camps once the programme has begun.

"In the meantime," the president went on almost sternly, "if you are black and living in any part of the white homelands, you must prepare yourself to be moved to your own homeland as part of the transmigration scheme. It will be against the law for you to remain where you are now living. Further announcements will be given on all radio and television stations telling you details of the transport arrangements being made for you."

Dr. Van Essche paused, shifted slightly in his seat, and clasped

288

his hands in front of him on the desk in what presumably was the president's office in Cape Town. "I will end this broadcast on a note of assurance," he said. "I stressed the fact earlier that we have the ability to crush the invaders. God's help and these additional, non-military steps we are taking will ensure our success. Goodnight."

Tony stood up. "They can't do it," he said. "They just won't be able to do it." He looked around at the Mbatha family. They were all still sitting down, not saying a word.

"It won't affect us," Ben said eventually. "This is already part of Kwazulu. We won't have to move anywhere."

"But what about all the people living close to the white cities— like Soweto, for instance? There's more than a million black people living there alone. Are they going to shift them all?"

"It seems so," said Ben.

"It'll never work! The more you think about it, the more ridiculous it seems. Obviously, they think that if they can separate all the blacks from the whites, they'll be able to contain the blacks more easily."

One of the uncles said something in Zulu and the conversation went on for several minutes amongst the family. Tony sat silently in one corner of the room thinking.

It was an amazing decision for a white government to come to, he thought, because it meant that finally white South Africans would have to forego forever all of the luxuries provided for them for generations by an ever-present pool of cheap black labour. No more housemaids, cooks, gardeners, chauffeurs, butlers, boys, general handymen, and man Fridays, on the domestic scene alone.

The impact on the commercial and industrial world could be catastrophic. Who for instance would dig the ditches, clean the sewers, collect the garbage, serve in restaurants, sweep the floors of offices and factories? Who would work the production lines of industry, and who would sweat on a jackhammer, 13,000 feet below the surface of the earth, to bring up the gold?

The answer, of course, was simple. The whites would have to do it—as they do in Europe, North America, Australia, or any other basically European country. For South African whites the

289

partitioning programme would obviously bring traumatic adjustments.

Tony was overcome by the desire to rush out and phone a story through to London. It was the sort of dramatic development that his editor would be screaming for. But of course, Tony realised, Mulgrave would be filing something from Johannesburg—and anyway, he was in no position to do anything. For a start, there was no phone in the village, secondly he'd be on the spot again the moment he picked up a phone, and thirdly, wasn't he supposed to be doing something else; chasing gold conspirators, preventing the mines from being destroyed? For the past few hours, he told himself, you've done precious little about that.

He thought again about how to get a message to someone about the gold and the mines. He had been going to type up all those letters. Now, stuck out in the hills, he had no facilities to do it. In the morning, he thought. But then, it would already be the 23rd. The *South Cape Aurora's* sailing date was set for March 23/24. By the time his letters reached anyone who could do anything about it, it would be too late.

He mulled over something in his mind for several minutes, while the Mbatha family continued their discussion. The president had said it was time for momentous decisions. Tony now came to one of his own.

"Do you have any contact, or know of any way of reaching someone in the APRA?" he said suddenly to Ben.

The family went silent and Ben looked at Tony with an expressionless stare for several seconds. There was a note of caution in his voice when he answered, "Why do you ask?"

"I have some important information . . . some very important information, which I should give to them."

Lucas Mbatha, his wife, Ben's two uncles, and their two friends all looked steadily and silently at Tony. An atmosphere of suspicion had suddenly fallen on the room.

"Why should you want to give them any information?" Ben asked.

"I don't really know," Tony replied. "It's just that I'm beginning to think that there's no-one else who'll be able to do anything about it." Tony paused for a moment or two, thinking. "And I suppose,"

290

he went on, "it's also because I don't believe that the government is doing the right thing now."

"What is the information?" Ben said quietly.

"Do you know anyone in the APRA?"

"Yes."

"Can I talk to him?"

"You can give the information to me."

"Are you in the APRA?"

Ben looked around at his mother and father and his uncles. "No," he said, "but what is it you want to tell?"

"Let me just tell you that it concerns a vast amount of gold . . . most of this country's reserves. Just pass that on to whoever it is . . . and . . . and see if they could come here as soon as possible to talk about it."

"But it might take time," Ben said.

"How long?"

"I don't know."

"Well, just see what they say."

Ben left the house and did not return for almost three-quarters of an hour. His mother, in the meantime, served plates of spiced meat and hot mealies to the men sitting around the main room and to Marcus, who sat up in his bed to eat some of the food.

Tony's conversation with the others was now sporadic and strained. Their English was not as good as Ben's and this introduction of the APRA into the conversation had changed Tony's status as a visitor. He was no longer someone who had saved Lucas Mbatha's son from being beaten to death. He was suddenly something different now; someone over whom there was a question mark, someone to be wary of, perhaps. Ben returned with the news that a member of the APRA would come, but he would not be able to be there until very early next morning.

Mrs. Mbatha produced coffee for everyone, but there was an awkwardness in the group. Before long, Ben said to Tony, "There is an extra bed for you in the same room as Marcus. You can sleep there."

Tony took the hint and excused himself, saying goodnight to the others; but when he lay on the bed, he found he could not sleep. Marcus dozed fitfully a few feet away, occasionally groaning softly. The light from the lamps in the main room was reflected off the ceiling over the partition that separated the two rooms and the low murmur of voices continued in the next room for what seemed like hours.

Tony lay on his back gazing up at the ceiling. Would he, in fact, be a traitor to his race by giving the information about the gold to the black rebels? Wasn't it simply a matter of preventing a wrong from being done? It was wrong, wasn't it, for a small group of whites to take the gold out without the consent of the people? After all, George Schuman had said that the Parliament had rejected the idea conclusively—the previous Parliament, that is. And they were all whites. But Tony was rationalising it all and he knew it.

And the bizarre plan to blow up the mines! He couldn't see any excuse for that. But what also troubled him was that the rebels, it seemed, were no better than the whites. They were brutal killers. He had seen that. And many of them, probably a majority, were either Communists, or Communist-led, and he was not a Communist—never had been. But then neither were the bulk of South Africa's twenty million black people, and Tony hoped that if the result of the present crisis was black majority rule, then the non-Communist elements in the various revolutionary factions would be able to hold their own against the Communists. Anyway, what damn difference would his two-cents-worth of information make? He drifted slowly into a troubled sleep.

At five in the morning, as the eastern sky began to lighten, two members of the southern wing of the Natal Command of the Azanian Peoples Revolutionary Army arrived at the Mbatha house. There was a soft knock at the front door and the two men were admitted by Ben Mbatha. His father and mother stayed in bed, awake and silent, as Ben led the two men to Tony, who, having slept in his clothes, was now sitting on the edge of the bed, waiting.

One of them, a man of about thirty years old, Tony thought, was obviously the leader. He was tall and thin and had an almost haggard look about his face. He wore gold-rimmed spectacles and had closely cropped hair, which tended to baldness at the front.

The other man was about the same age as Ben Mbatha, Tony guessed, about twenty. He was short and plump and had a big, fuzzy crop of hair on his head. A picture of Laurel and Hardy kept coming into Tony's mind, but, at the same time, he couldn't avoid a feeling of fear in the presence of the two men, who looked at him, throughout their meeting, with cold, suspicious eyes.

Only the older man spoke, and then only to ask brief questions. He was not in the least interested in why Tony wanted to give the information—only in the information itself. They talked for little more than five minutes, during which time Tony told him about the plan to destroy the mines and the fact that the country's gold reserves were being smuggled out of the country on board the *South Cape Aurora,* which was due to leave within thirty-six hours. Tony also told him that the information had come from a note he had received that had been written by a director of the Reserve Bank, Dekker, who had been killed on the night of the 19th, in the raid on the American Consulate residence. He mentioned Johnathan Kapepwe's name and urged the man to check with his headquarters as soon as possible, as they would have to act quickly.

When Tony had finished speaking and said, "Well, that's about all there is to it . . ." the two men simply stood up and left, almost without a word. The tall man turned at the door to the main room and said an emotionless, "Thank you. Goodbye."

When Tony arrived back in Durban, at around seven in the morning, he found the city in a state of far greater confusion than when he had left it, little more than fifteen hours previously. He had said goodbye to the Mbatha family at six. Although the twenty-five-mile drive should only have taken forty minutes on the expressway, he found the road congested, even at that early hour, with army vehicles, buses, and private cars, all heading for Durban. The army vehicles, he assumed, would be passing through the city and heading north towards Swaziland and the Mozambique border, where some of the rebel army units the president had spoken about were concentrated.

For part of the trip into Durban, Tony tuned to one of the frequencies for the clandestine, rebel radio stations which Ben Mbatha had told him about and heard part of a message urging defiance of the new moves to partition the country. It was repeated in several tribal languages, as well as in English.

The announcer's voice, quoting the words of rebel leaders, including Mandele and Sobukwe, instructed all Africans to refuse to be moved to their so-called homelands. "All of Azania is your homeland. Do not accept the white man's schemes. Go to jail if necessary. They cannot possibly jail everyone. We will fill their jails until they overflow. You must refuse to show your passes. They must be thrown away and destroyed. Now is the time to defy the white racists. We have them running. Soon freedom will be ours. But to gain freedom, it is essential that you do not obey the government's orders. If you go to jail for refusing, you will soon be free again. You will be heroes of the revolution."

Tony could not see a black man anywhere in the streets of Durban. There were a few Indians about, but the majority of them were staying in their homes in the Indian townships sprinkled around Durban. What would happen to them in the new order of things had so far not been said. But it was clear that they were in a parlous position. They enjoyed only a slightly better status than the blacks in white South Africa, yet they were hated by the blacks for their success as merchants and traders and their control of the lower and middle-level business world. With a total population of just over a million, the Indians were South Africa's smallest significant racial group. The number of Chinese and Cape Malays was too small to have any great impact.

Most Indians were sure that their position would deteriorate markedly under a black government. Consequently, some Indians had tended to support the policies of the white government, thinking perhaps that, as far as Indians were concerned, these racist policies represented the lesser of two evils. But this attitude had only tended to heighten any feelings of antipathy amongst blacks for Indians.

As Tony drove through the streets of Durban, almost all of the shops and stores in the central business district were closed. Whites swarmed to and fro like bees, all intent on doing something to organise their lives. He stopped at a small café to eat a breakfast of sorts; toast and coffee.

294

A car pulled up outside laden down with a family's belongings. It had a roof-rack piled high and was pulling a small trailer which was also crammed with an assortment of household goods—even a lawn mower. The essentials of life, Tony thought. The driver left his family waiting in the car and came into the café to ask the proprietor if he could buy several loaves of bread and some butter or margarine. He was told he could have two loaves of bread, but no butter or margarine. While the owner was getting the bread, Tony, who was sitting at the counter, asked the man where he was going.

"We're heading for the Cape, man," was the reply. "That's the only place that'll last. Even if Natal and the Transvaal and the Free State go, they'll never take the Cape."

"But how will you get there?" Tony said. "You can't pass through the Transkei, down the coast road."

"We're going north first—up around Lesotho. There are convoys going from place to place. It's a longer way round, but we'll get there." He took his bread and walked out.

Tony was reminded in an obscure way of the refugees he'd seen coming over the border from East Pakistan into West Bengal almost ten years previously. Of course, they were totally different, in that the East Pakistanis were starving, desperately poor, and travelling for the most part on foot, whereas these people (and he saw many more as he left the café) were affluent, well fed, and driving cars. But there was the same basis of fear as the reason for their travel. They were carrying the trappings of their relative affluence with them, but the disruption of their lives was just as absolute.

There was considerable evidence of looting in the city, even though, under the martial law regulations, looters could be shot on sight. Anyone breaking the curfew now would also be shot. Blacks were not permitted to congregate anywhere in white areas in groups of more than three people, and weapons of any kind were forbidden to be carried, including any form of knife or solid stick.

At the bus terminal on Pine Street, opposite the railway station, Tony saw scores of buses of all different types being assembled, presumably to begin the task of moving blacks to their homelands. Buses would be used to take Zulus to the various parts of

295

the Kwazulu Homeland, while anyone of another tribal origin who had to travel to the Transvaal or the Free State would be moved by train. The idea of building and running refugee camps for these scores of thousands—hundreds of thousands—of people was almost too enormous to contemplate, and yet, Tony thought, that's what they're going to have to do. It's going to be a bloody disaster.

He was swept again with the desire to run . . . to get out as quickly as he could. He could see no way he could function properly as a correspondent, with BOSS after him the whole time. He was sure that if they got their hands on him again, he wouldn't last long. He made up his mind to try to get on a freighter going any-where . . . anywhere away. At the first port of call, he thought, I'll take a plane back to Nairobi, or Europe. He had thought that if the *South Cape Aurora* was heading for Europe, he could easily beat her there by flying. The cargo was destined for Switzerland, but the ship would land first at Genoa. He could organize a reception committee.

He looked down the list of ships on the piece of paper the man at the Marine Office had given him. There were three merchant ships due to leave today, the 23rd; a German freighter bound for Hamburg via Lagos and Accra, a Norwegian container vessel head-ing for Singapore via Mauritius, and a Japanese bulk sugar carrier destined for Yokahama.

Tony considered the three. The German ship might be all right. She was headed in the right direction, but he doubted if he would be allowed off the ship in either of the West African ports, having boarded in South Africa. It didn't show in his passport, because he had asked for a separate visa before he had flown in to South Africa. But you never knew what sort of difficulties might arise. In fact, Tony was surprised that a vessel trading with South Africa at the present time would even be allowed to land in Lagos or Accra. Maybe it wouldn't.

The Japanese ship listed no ports between Durban and Yokahama, so he dropped that one. The Norwegian ship, which was stopping at Mauritius, looked as though she might be the best bet.

296

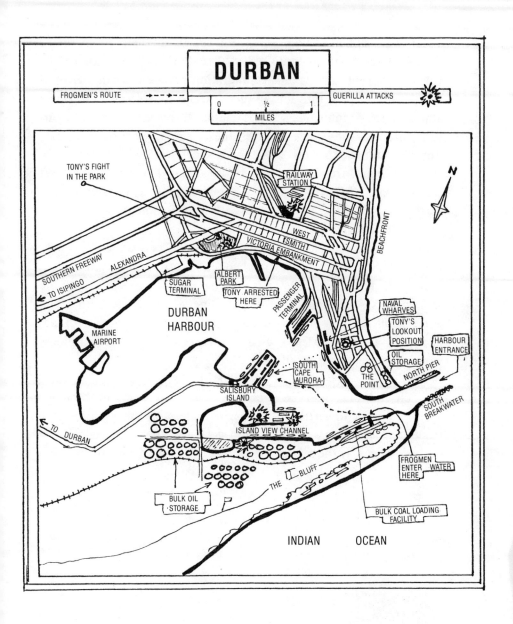

DURBAN

FROGMEN'S ROUTE →-·-→-·→ GUERILLA ATTACKS

0   ½   1
MILES

TONY'S FIGHT
IN THE PARK

RAILWAY
STATION

N

BEACHFRONT

WEST
VICTORIA EMBANKMENT
SMITH

SOUTHERN FREEWAY
ALEXANDRA

TO ISIPINGO

SUGAR
TERMINAL

ALBERT
PARK

TONY ARRESTED
HERE

PASSENGER
TERMINAL

NAVAL
WHARVES

DURBAN
HARBOUR

TONY'S
LOOKOUT
POSITION

HARBOUR
ENTRANCE

MARINE
AIRPORT

OIL
STORAGE

SOUTH
CAPE
AURORA

THE
POINT

NORTH PIER

SALISBURY
ISLAND

TO DURBAN

ISLAND VIEW CHANNEL

SOUTH
BREAKWATER

THE   BLUFF

FROGMEN
ENTER   WATER
HERE

BULK OIL
STORAGE

BULK COAL LOADING
FACILITY

INDIAN   OCEAN

The most difficult thing, Tony realised, would be to get on board the Norwegian ship—or any ship, for that matter—without the South African Customs and Immigration people knowing. Even if he talked a skipper into letting him travel on a ship, it would take a hefty bribe to influence a ship's captain to contravene regulations like that. Still, these were strange times. It might even be necessary, Tony continued, to stow away for a short while. In that respect, the Norwegian freighter would be ideal. He'd be discovered and thrown off at Mauritius, then fly straight out again. But he felt sure he would have to slip a large bribe to someone, even to be able to stow away.

He checked the money in the wide nylon belt under his shirt. He had U.S. $650 in travellers cheques, mostly in fifties, and three U.S. $100 dollar bills; $950. Even if he had to give it all away, he still had his American Express and Diners Club credit cards. The great panacea; he smiled. Fly now, pay later. Anyway, if I get away with it, I'll give 'em such a ball-tearer of a story that Childers won't hesitate to pay it all back.

He decided to try the Norwegian freighter. Even if there's no luck on this one, there're a couple more tomorrow, he thought. He drove back towards the Safmarine offices on the Victoria Embankment again, to see if he could get another wharf pass. As he parked the car by the side of the road, a police car drew up alongside him and two white policemen stepped out.

"Excuse me, sir," one of them said, "is this your car?"

15

A Private Hospital

The big Grumman E2-C Hawkeye droned on, relentlessly closing in on its two "targets" 1,850 miles north-west of Cape Town. The AN/APS-120 radar antenna, turning slowly inside the 24-foot-diameter rotodome, carried like a flying saucer above the aircraft, had long since pinpointed the two Russian freighters. The radar officer and combat information centre officer sitting in the ATDS compartment of the plane had watched the two blips become slowly clearer on the screens. But now the five-man crew of the American surveillance aircraft were peering ahead for a visual sighting.

Jerry Steiner, the pilot, was the first to spot the *Taseyeva.*

"There she is! That's her," he yelled.

"We have visual contact," he radioed back to the carrier. "We're closing on her now."

A few minutes later, Pete Mathews, the air control officer, spotted the *Berdyansk,* which was travelling about thirty miles astern of the *Taseyeva.* The pilot reported back again to the carrier and began to lose altitude, aiming to bring the Hawkeye down from five thousand feet to sea level by the time they reached the two ships, which at the moment of sighting were on the horizon.

The two Russian merchant ships were about three hundred miles north-east of the island of St. Helena in the South Atlantic at the time they came under the electronic eyes of Jerry Steiner's Hawkeye and they were travelling on a south-easterly course for the coast of Namibia. They had been under continuous surveillance, of course, from American military satellites, ever since they left Rostov and sailed out through the Black Sea and the Bosporus into the Mediterranean. But now that they were entering the outer defence perimeters of the United States South Atlantic Naval Task Force, they would be under constant watch from all-weather Hawkeye patrols from now on.

Nine hundred miles to the south-west, just above the Tropic of Capricorn and some four hundred miles off the coast of Namibia, Jerry Steiner's home base was ploughing through the water at just on thirty knots.

Her two A4W nuclear reactors, powering huge steam turbines, were pushing the 90,000-ton attack aircraft carrier *Dwight D. Eisenhower* through the low swell with effortless ease. On board, the crew of over 6,000 men (3,000 sailors and 3,000 men of the air wing) all knew that there was the possibility of real trouble ahead. Not many of them had any real worries, though. It's difficult not to feel confident when you're riding in two billion dollars' worth of equipment.

Two nuclear-powered guided missile cruisers, the *Texas* and the *Mississippi*, were accompanying the *Dwight D. Eisenhower,* while three Charles F. Adams-type destroyers remained cruising in a holding pattern, 150 miles to the south.

The commander of the task force, Admiral Marvin Stone, had been instructed directly by the Chief of Naval Operations in Washington (following urgent meetings with the Joint Chiefs of Staff, the National Security Council, and the President) that the *Taseyeva* and the *Berdyansk* were to be prevented from landing their cargoes at the Namibian port of Luderitz and anywhere else on the West African coast south of the Congo River—at all costs.

"Sink 'em?" the admiral had asked the Chief of Naval Operations when he spoke directly, over the scrambler, to Washington.

"If that's what's necessary—yes!" was the reply.

The two Russian freighters continued on their course and the three American warships continued on theirs, towards them. In less than eighteen hours American naval vessels would stop or attack Soviet merchant ships on the high seas.

There were no Russian naval ships close enough to be able to do anything to prevent it. Several were located on the other side of the Cape of Good Hope, off the east coast of Southern Africa, but they were preoccupied with a similar confrontation looming between the American Indian Ocean Task Force and three other Russian arms freighters heading down the Mozambique Channel towards Maputo.

The American President spoke on the hotline to the Soviet premier in Moscow and he addressed the American people on national television, reminding them of the Cuban missile crisis of 1961. It was a difficult point to make—that tactical nuclear weapons, some eight thousand miles away, could be as dangerous to America as strategic missiles had been less than one hundred miles away—but that was basically the message. Soviet nuclear weapons in Africa, he said, would lead to an automatic escalation of the whole conflict and inevitably involve the major powers. The President told his vast television audience that there would be no backing down. The Russian freighters would not be allowed to land.

The Soviet Union protested vehemently at emergency sessions of both the General Assembly and the Security Council at the United Nations and put its armed forces throughout the world on full alert.

Meanwhile, the carrier *Dwight D. Eisenhower* and her accompanying cruisers moved nearer and nearer to direct confrontation with the *Taseyeva* and the *Berdyansk*.

After two hours of relatively formal questioning at Durban's police headquarters, Tony began to feel that he might have a chance. When the two policemen had picked him up, he had been crestfallen, but their questioning at the station had been confined purely to the incident in Albert Park and the fact that he had used a firearm to threaten the white youths. The whites had lied to the police, saying that Tony had held them at gunpoint while the two blacks had beaten the dark-haired white boy senseless. That would be a problem to overcome, but Tony, who had been left alone now for half an hour in a cell, began to hope that perhaps the liaison between the municipal police departments and BOSS was not close. If the police were as good as their word, and allowed him to contact his embassy, Tony felt his chances would improve considerably.

If he could get through to Michael Keneally, then there was hope that some pressure could be brought to bear from outside. Without that, he was on his own. He had given the police his version of the story and there was no indication that they disbelieved him, although the fact that he had sympathised with the blacks against the whites was definitely not in his favour. They treated him as if he had just crawled out from under a stone. Had he been a South African white, Tony felt his treatment would have been far worse. It was almost as if they expected foreign whites to behave like that. From one of their own, however, actions like Tony's would be more than reprehensible.

Tony was also concerned about the gun. It was not licensed in his name—obviously—and when questioned about where he had obtained it, he had lied, and lied lamely. He couldn't think of a believable story quickly enough and so simply said that he had found it.

"Where?"

"Under the seat of the car. It's a hire-car."

Naturally, they didn't believe him and Tony knew it would only be a matter of time before they traced its registration back to Marta Van Sisseren, which would only complicate things further. His one hope was that she also had had the gun illegally and that they would not be able to trace it to her.

As he sat in his cell contemplating these things, a face appeared around the edge of one wall and peered in through the bars that separated the cell from the corridor outside. A three-inch scar ran down the right side of the face. Tony looked up and recognised the blond hair and piercing blue eyes of Bruno Van Wyk.

The South African tilted his head slightly to one side, smiled thinly, and closed his eyes for a second. "Good morning, Mr. Bartlett. What a pleasure to meet again."

Tony said nothing.

Bruno produced a key and proceeded to open the barred door to the cell. Two of the uniformed policemen, to whom Tony had been speaking, appeared beside Bruno and then another man in plain clothes, whom Tony took to be one of Bruno's colleagues

302

from the Bureau for State Security, walked up to join the group.

"You're coming for a little ride with us," Bruno said patronisingly. "Come along now."

Once again, Tony had no idea where he travelled with the men from BOSS. In the yard of the police headquarters, he had been led to an ambulance and ushered into the back of it. Unlike the previous BOSS van, it did have windows, but you couldn't see out of them. As they drove from the yard, the policemen by whom he'd been questioned during the morning stood and watched, without a word.

The ambulance drove for about fifteen minutes before coming to a stop. Tony heard the sound of a large gate being swung open and the vehicle moved forward over what he thought sounded like a gravel driveway. He guessed that they were in one of the suburbs of Durban, by the lack of traffic sounds. They had travelled for almost ten minutes on an expressway, then a series of turns and three or four minutes driving down what seemed to be very quiet streets to their present position, which Tony was willing to bet was a large suburban house.

The doors of the ambulance were opened and Tony stepped out onto a concrete parking area at the rear of a large old house. Looking back along the driveway, he could see part of the front lawn, a high, brick wall separating the grounds from a street lined with elm trees. Slightly to the right he could also just see the large iron gate through which they had passed.

"This way," Bruno said harshly, taking Tony by the arm and pushing him forward. "We thought we'd find you here somewhere," he went on. "You're not really very clever, Mr. Bartlett."

Tony was led through a back door and into a series of corridors. A couple of white-coated men stepped aside to let him and the others pass. It was like a hospital, a private hospital. It had that all-pervading hospital smell about it; Tony had never known what it was . . . lysol, chloroform? Whatever it was, he had always hated it.

"What is this place?" he asked.

"Never mind, Mr. Bartlett, never mind. You will find out soon enough." The same patronising but menacing tone.

He was led up a flight of stairs to another corridor lined with absolutely plain white walls and a series of white doors set into recesses along the hall. They entered one of them and a sense of horror and fear clutched at Tony's innards.

The room was almost totally white, not unlike the one in which he had been questioned in Johannesburg. There were three light, kitchen chairs in one corner and a solid, wooden chair which sat ominously in the centre of the room. It was bolted to the floor and, Tony noticed immediately, there were leather straps on the arms and the legs.

"Sit down, Mr. Bartlett." Bruno waved his hand towards the chair.

"Now, look," Tony said swiftly, "this isn't necessary, I . . ."

"Sit down!" Bruno shoved Tony hard across the room. The other men who had been at the police headquarters with Tony and the driver of the ambulance spread out in the room. One of them picked up one of the chairs in the corner, swung it around and sat, leaning over the back of it, looking at Tony as he slowly lowered himself into the big wooden seat.

"Look, there's no need to tie me up," Tony said, as Bruno walked towards him.

Dammit, he thought, I'm not just going to bloody well give in without some sort of fight. As Bruno bent down towards him, Tony brought his foot up hard into the big man's stomach and pushed with all his strength, sending Bruno flying back across the room. At the same instant he leapt up and dived for the door. He was out and had slammed the door shut behind him, before the others could stop him. In the corridor he ran for the stairs, colliding, as he turned the corner, with two more white-coated attendants. The three of them went sprawling down the stairs in a tumbling heap of bodies. As they hit the first landing, Tony was up in an instant and leaping down the remaining steps.

Two more attendants suddenly blocked his path to the back door. Why the hell do they always come in twos, he thought. He charged headlong towards them. They both crouched ready to stop him. Tony's fist connected with terrible force with the cheek of one of the men, laying him out instantly. The other simply grabbed Tony in a bear-hug around the waist and clung on. Tony could not pry

304

him loose. He pummelled him in the head and, at the same time, tried to move forward, but the man made himself an absolute dead weight. Within seconds, the two men from the stairs and then Bruno and his two colleagues were on him and Tony was ploughed under by weight of numbers.

Four minutes later he was back in the white room, securely strapped down in the big chair and looking steadfastly back into the ice-blue eyes of Bruno Van Wyk, who held his face only inches from Tony's. It was obvious that he was furious, but somehow he restrained himself.

"I can't do anything to you just now," he hissed. "I have to wait. But I know that my time will come, Mr. Bartlett . . . and I will wait. It will be a pleasurable anticipation for me. There are so many things I can do to you—simple things. Your ears for instance . . ." he took one of Tony's ears and began to twist it until it burned, "and then, of course there are your eyes." He placed his forefinger on the outside edge of Tony's right eye and began gently pressing it across towards his nose. Tony went cross-eyed and felt a blinding pain building up in his head. He let out a gasp and Bruno took his finger away slowly. "Yes, Mr. Bartlett, it will be a pleasurable anticipation."

Bruno Van Wyk then left the room. The other two remained. They sat in the corner ignoring Tony and speaking quietly between themselves.

Tony tried to think sensibly, constructively. But he found himself unable to come up with a single positive thought about his predicament. He was, he told himself, in the classic idiom, "up shit-creek in a barbed-wire canoe, without a paddle!"

He felt sure that the police had not been in touch with Michael Keneally or anyone else in the consulate or the embassy. So no-one, literally no-one, knew where he was except BOSS. They could do what they liked with him and no-one need *ever* know. Tony Bartlett could simply disappear.

Tony was still thinking on these things, some twenty minutes after Bruno had left the room, when the door from the hallway opened and a man in a neat grey suit entered. Tony recognised Colonel Starcke.

"Mr. Bartlett," he said, walking across towards Tony, "good morning. How nice to see you." Starcke stood looking at Tony for a few seconds, then said, "It seems that you have become involved in something that is too big for you. What a pity."

The balding head, pock-marked face, and bristly white moustache appeared suspended before Tony like an apparition. On the one or two occasions he had thought about Colonel Starcke since their unpleasant meeting in Johannesburg, Tony had been slightly consoled by the thought that they would never meet again. But here they were, facing up again for a repeat performance, only this time under vastly less opportune circumstances.

Colonel Starcke took his pipe from a pocket and, striking a match, puffed away until the tobacco began to glow and clouds of smoke issued from both the pipe and Colonel Starcke's mouth. He put the box of matches back into his pocket and smiled, with the pipe still clamped between his teeth. Tony noticed again how stained they were.

"Situations like this are best left well alone by amateurs," Colonel Starcke said. "Well alone."

"Are you a professional gold thief, then?" Tony said.

Starcke took his pipe from his mouth and laughed out loud. "Ha ha," he chuckled, "I see you're prepared to get right down to business. Right, Mr. Bartlett," Starcke's countenance suddenly became serious, "we won't play at games. We will start right into it. You are obviously aware of some aspects of this operation." He took a piece of paper from his pocket and opened it out. "Tell me. This letter from Eugene Dekker to Miss Ingrid Hofmeyr . . . how did you get it?"

"Look, I don't feel inclined to answer any of your questions. If I have done anything wrong, then I should be charged and tried. I want access to my embassy and to a lawyer." Tony knew inside himself that it was futile to say it, but he said it for the hell of it.

Colonel Starcke smiled at Tony around the edge of his pipe stem.

"Mr. Bartlett, you may be an amateur, but I'm sure I don't have to explain to you in words of one syllable what will happen to you if you do not cooperate with me." His voice became slightly higher pitched, hard and cutting. "You have absolutely no rights here and it is within our power to do what we like with you." He paused and walked around Tony's chair. "I believe in coming straight to the point, Mr. Bartlett. Your position is a very bad one. If you do not tell us what we want to know, it will become extremely bad. If, on the other hand, you are prepared to answer our questions and to cooperate fully, then your position could improve considerably."

He turned away and walked over to speak to the two men in the corner. One of them got up and left the room.

"Now," Starcke said, returning to stand in front of Tony, "where did you get that letter?"

"You should know," Tony said bitterly, "since it was one of your hatchet men who killed Ingrid Hofmeyr to get it."

"And we did get it," Starcke said slowly, "the original. This is a copy. I repeat, where did you get it?"

"From her apartment."

"When?"

"Just after you killed her." The words came out as an accusatory sneer, but had no effect on Starcke.

"The apartment was locked when you arrived. Did you have a key?"

"No. I broke in."

"How?"

"Through the bathroom window."

Starcke lifted his eyebrows and turned away from Tony, pacing a few steps back and forth, puffing on his pipe. There was a knock on the door and the man in the corner moved to open it, but Bruno Van Wyk walked in before he got to it. Bruno nodded at Colonel Starcke and crossed to the corner to sit down.

"How well did you know Miss Hofmeyr?"

"Not very well. I'd only just met her a couple of days previously."

"And yet she telephones you, asking you to come to her, so that she can give you this information?"

Tony shrugged his shoulders and said nothing.

"How is it that, at the American Consulate reception, Eugene Dekker is shot in cold blood, while Miss Hofmeyr, who is standing right beside him, is not harmed at all? How is that, do you think?"

307

"I would think it was because your little secret is not quite the secret you thought it was," Tony said.

"Probably true, Mr. Bartlett. But we won't try to get too clever, will we?" Starcke relit his pipe. "There are some very interesting questions arising from that observation, Mr. Bartlett. Firstly, the fact that those terrorists singled out Dekker and Verhoef as their targets on that raid. Then there is the fact that you were observed in close conversation with Mr. Johnathan Kapepwe at the reception. The fact that Mr. Kapepwe was in Mbeya at the same time as you were, when the hijacked plane landed there—a fact you conveniently forgot to mention at our last meeting. Our intelligence sources have informed us that Kapepwe went to Tanzania on March 5 and is believed to have been in Mbeya from the 8th until the day after the hijack. On checking our files on him, we find that you have written articles previously about him and that you have known him for some time."

"Only as a journalist!" Tony said vehemently. "I knew him as a journalist, that's all. I had no other connection with him. If you read through those articles properly, you will see that they were not entirely sympathetic to Johnathan Kapepwe and his ideas."

Another thin smile with the pipe still clamped between his teeth. "That means nothing, of course," Starcke said. "Was Ingrid Hofmeyr passing information to you or Kapepwe?"

"No, of course she wasn't. She had no idea about any of this," Tony said. "And anyway, I told you that I only met her a few days ago."

"Our records show that she was in Sydney at the same time that you went home on leave from Nairobi last year."

"Oh for God's sake," Tony shouted, "and so were three million other people! I tell you I didn't know her until just a few days ago . . . the 17th, to be exact . . . St. Patrick's Day."

There was a slight movement from the corner and Tony glanced across to see Bruno Van Wyk staring silently back at him.

"Where was that?"

"At a party at the Australian Trade Commissioner's house."

"Ah, yes . . ." Starcke paused a moment and then, "What are you doing in Durban, Mr. Bartlett?"

"I came here to see if I could arrange a boat passage out of the country. There are no plane bookings available for weeks."

"I see. And where have you been staying since you have been here?"

Tony hesitated a second and then said, "I came down in a motor vehicle convoy. I stayed at the army barracks."

"Last night?"

"No. The night before."

"And last night?"

"Well, you already know that I picked up those two black boys who were being beaten . . ." Tony looked into Starcke's eyes. They were looking unblinkingly back at him. "Well," Tony went on, "they were heading to some village down the coast, so I drove them as far as Isipingo and dropped them off."

"Do you remember the name of their village?"

"No."

"Where did you stay in Isipingo?"

"Ah . . . in a little guest house close to the beach. It was a small place in amongst the trees," Tony lied. He gave a description of one of the places he and Carol and Michael had stayed in two years ago at Southport, some seventy miles further south from Isipingo. He knew it was ridiculous for him to lie like that, because it would be relatively easy for them to check out. But still, he thought, it all takes time. "I can't remember the name of it," he said. "Very nice, though."

"What were the names of the two men you dropped off at Isipingo?"

"They didn't tell me their names."

"And you had never met them before?"

"No."

There was another knock on the door. This time Bruno went. Starcke turned to see what was happening. A whispered conversation between Bruno and the other man at the door and Bruno turned to Starcke, who walked across the join them. Tony felt an itch in his nose. He moved involuntarily to scratch it, but was immediately restrained by the strap. The itch suddenly became unbearable because he couldn't scratch it. It made him realise how helpless he was. Slowly the itch went away, while at the door there was more whispering, none of which Tony could hear. Finally, the man who had come to the door left, Bruno returned to his seat, and Starcke walked back to stand in front of Tony again.

"This becomes more and more interesting all the time," Starcke said. He pulled out Marta Van Sisseren's gun. "Where did you get this?"

"I told them before, at the police station," Tony replied. "I found it in my car, underneath the seat."

"Strange," Colonel Starcke said sarcastically. "It happens to be registered in the name of Mr. Carl Verhoef. What an incredible coincidence!"

Tony felt a desperate sinking sensation.

"I . . ." he started, but words failed him.

"Yes, Mr. Bartlett? You . . . what?" Colonel Starcke asked solicitously.

He stood waiting. Tony was dumbfounded. Nothing could have been more incriminating.

"How *did* you get Carl Verhoef's gun, Mr. Bartlett? It would seem to me you have more to tell us than I had imagined."

Suddenly a thought struck Tony.

"All right," he said. "All right. I didn't find it in the car."

"No?" said Starcke sarcastically. "Really? Then where did you find it? Under a cabbage?"

"I found it during all the chaos of that night at the American reception. Verhoef, or his bodyguard, must have dropped it on the floor."

"Why didn't you tell that to the police in the first place?"

"I don't know. I suppose because I didn't want to admit that I had stolen it."

Starcke sucked on the bitter juices of his now-extinct pipe.

"Hmmm," he muttered; "a bit more plausible than the last one, but . . ." He looked at Tony for a full ten seconds without saying anything. "But I'm afraid I don't believe you, Mr. Bartlett. I am afraid there are several things you have been telling me this morning which I do not believe. I think you know where Carl Verhoef is. We shall see. I will talk to you later, but in the meantime I will leave you with Bruno."

Starcke turned to Bruno van Wyk and nodded slightly. Then

310

he walked from the room. Tony felt his stomach harden into a tight knot as he saw Bruno stand up and slowly move towards him.

Bruno stood in front of Tony for a moment, then slapped him hard across the face, knocking his head to one side.

"This is purely for my own satisfaction, Bartlett," Bruno sneered, as he brought his hand back again in the opposite direction and then forward again, slapping Tony's face back and forth until it was red and his nose began to bleed. Bruno stopped when his own hand began to hurt. "I don't like being made a fool of, Bartlett, and you have done that to me twice."

He walked slowly around the chair, looking at Tony, who kept looking straight to the front, without saying a word. From the corner of his eye, Tony saw that the other man was still leaning over the back of the chair in the corner, watching.

Tony now had an awful fear of what he might have to expect from Bruno. The horrible prospect of torture confronted him. Until this moment, it had been only a word to him. Like everyone else, he had read of people being tortured, but there had always been a remoteness about it, an air of unbelievability, like something from the Dark Ages; it didn't happen any more. And yet, he recalled, he had himself written about torture—about the tiger cages in Vietnam, about the brutal atrocities committed by the Pakistan Army in Bangla Desh, by Idi Amin in Uganda and General Mengistu in Ethiopia. Somehow, he thought, when you wrote or read about it you never, ever thought that it could happen to you.

Tony found that, as he sat in that wooden chair, it was impossible for him to contemplate the immediate future, beyond what was happening at that moment. He could only live from minute to minute.

Bruno walked around to the front of the chair into Tony's line of vision again. He held a clear, plastic bag in his hands.

"This is just to give you a taste," he said, "a taste of what to expect—of what we can do—and of the pleasures in store for you, if you do not answer our questions properly."

With a sudden twitch of his upper lip, Bruno moved swiftly to slip the plastic bag over Tony's head, holding it tight around his throat. Immediately, Tony's normal breathing sucked the bag in close around his nose and mouth and, as he breathed out, he felt his breath spread warmly over the front of his face instead of dissipating in the outside air. He knew that within a short while all of the oxygen in the bag would be used up and he would be breathing in only the stale, carbon-dioxide-laden air he had already breathed out. But he also knew that Bruno was not going to kill him on this occasion . . . at least he hoped he knew. Even with that knowledge, there was a little flower of stark terror growing inside him.

For the first few breaths, there was no discomfort whatever, just the crackling sound of the bag collapsing around his face as he breathed in and then ballooning out, when he exhaled.

Bruno crouched in front of him, holding the bottom of the bag around Tony's neck; not tightly, but securely enough so that no appreciable quantities of fresh air could enter the bag. Tony could see clearly through the bag and found himself looking into Bruno's eyes. Bruno stared impassively back. Tony found that he wanted to give Bruno as little satisfaction as possible and determined that he would not show fear or panic. But as the oxygen content in the bag dwindled to nothing, Tony's breathing became more rapid. He desperately wanted to gasp in a big breath of air, but if he took a really deep breath, the bag simple closed off both his mouth and nostrils completely. And yet, having done it once, he could not go back to an easy, quiet rate of breathing.

He began to struggle frantically, to try to move his head, to shake it loose from Bruno's grip, but Bruno just moved his hands easily with Tony's movements. Tony strained at the leather bonds on his wrists and legs, but to no avail. His lungs began to cry out for air. He tried to scream, but there was not enough air in his lungs to scream with. Only a grunting gasp came from his throat. He was conscious of Bruno's face and loud laughter. Tony's chest began to burn and then it felt as if a fire inside him was pushing his chest outwards to immense proportions. His head reeled, a myriad halucinatory images raced frantically through his mind, then suddenly, with a swirl of stars, everything went black.

A splash of cold water brought Tony sharply to his senses. He gasped and gulped at the air and licked at the water running down his face. He had no idea how long he had been unconscious, but it was probably not more than a minute or two.

"Ah, there we are," Bruno said. "Back again in the real world. How did you like that?"

Tony said nothing.

"Would you like some more?" Bruno held up the plastic bag in front of Tony.

Tony shook his head.

Bruno slapped Tony viciously across the face again. "Right," he said. "Then let's see what we can achieve."

Somehow Tony felt infinitely more able to cope with the physical pain of being beaten than the prospect of facing the plastic bag, but either way, he could now see the real possibility of not coming out of all this alive. He would have to convince them of his innocence.

"Look," Tony said to Bruno. "I have never been involved with anyone over this. I'll admit I've been following up the gold, but only as a reporter . . . just a reporter chasing up a story."

"There are too many coincidences for that to be true, Bartlett. You are a kaffir-loving swine and you have been helping these fuckin' coons all along. White trash like you don't deserve to live. It is people like you who would have us intermarry with these dirty apes and eventually wipe the white race off the earth. If you love them so much, why don't you go and live with them in their filthy hovels, instead of the way you do, eh?"

In the face of such warped fanaticism, Tony was momentarily at a loss for words.

"It . . . it's not like that," he whispered. He felt almost like crying at the hopeless communication gap that existed between them. "It's just not like that . . . I . . ."

Tony had been looking at the floor. Suddenly he felt his head jerked up and his hair almost torn out by the roots as Bruno yanked his head back, slapping him backwards and forwards across the face again.

"Piet," he called to the man in the corner, "untie his hands."

The man who had been sitting in the corner ever since they had first entered the room hurried across to the chair and unstrapped Tony's hands from the arms of the chair.

"Stand up!" Bruno said.

Tony stood uncertainly to his feet, feeling the restraining ties of the straps that still held his feet tightly against the legs of the chair.

Bruno nodded to the other man, who moved behind Tony and grabbed his arms, pinning them behind him and twisting him slightly sideways.

"That's better," said Bruno. "I can't get at you while you're sitting down." He let loose a powerful punch into Tony's stomach. Tony gasped and doubled up in pain, struggling at the same time to loosen his arms, but they were pinned tight. Tony tensed his stomach muscles to take the next blow, but Bruno aimed it directly at his solar plexus and Tony found himself once again gasping agonisingly for air.

"Please," he whispered, "Please!"

Bruno brought his knee up with brutal force into Tony's groin and Tony screamed aloud in pain and terror. His legs doubled up underneath him and he collapsed on the floor.

The two men hauled him back into the chair and strapped his arms back up. Tony groaned and writhed as the sharp, shooting pains spread from his groin up into his stomach and blossomed out into a terrible, throbbing ache. Slowly it became thicker and duller and Tony shifted himself in the chair, looking back at the two men with a mixture of fear, horror, and the first touches of resignation.

Minute to minute, he thought again. We pass through one thing, to face the next—and so it goes on, until, somewhere along the line, it becomes too much. That was it, wasn't it? How many times had he read it? Every man has his breaking point, just the same as every man has his price. And these macabre and cynical experts knew it. How many times had they been through this routine before? How many times had they driven men—and women?—to their breaking point and beyond it? What happened at your breaking point? Tony wondered. You died, or went crazy. Which was better? he asked himself.

"Who have you seen here in Durban?" Bruno asked softly, after a minute or two of just sitting watching Tony. He had brought one of the other chairs over from the corner and positioned it close to the right side of Tony's chair.

"No-one," Tony said. "Only the shipping companies to try to get a passage out of the country."

"What companies have you tried?"

"Only Safmarine so far."

"And did you make a booking?"

"No. There was none available. I was hoping to get out on a freighter, but if that hadn't worked, I would have gone back to Johannesburg to leave on a plane the Australian Embassy is organising."

"Why did you telephone George Schuman to tell him about Dekker's letter."

Tony looked back at Bruno for a moment, trying to understand what was going on in his mind and to estimate just how much of the truth he would take before he laid into Tony again.

"Because I thought he could help to stop the gold from being stolen."

Bruno said nothing. Silence for several seconds.

"It *is* being stolen, you know. It's not for the good of the white race, as Dekker says in the letter. It's for the good of a few people like Verhoef and Trauseld and people in BOSS like Colonel Starcke who'll be able to get their grubby little hands on it, once it gets to Switzerland. But *you* and the rest of the white people in South Africa won't see any of it. You're kidding yourself if you think you will."

Bruno slapped Tony's face again, but said nothing.

"That's why I told George Schuman about it," Tony said, "and you killed him because of it . . . just like . . . ."

"Who else have you told about that letter?"

Tony was about to say "no-one," but something inside him told him that that might be the only thing that could keep him alive.

315

If they really believed he had told no-one else, they could simply dispose of him and that would be that. If he left some doubt in their minds, he might stay alive longer. But he couldn't say he had told Michael Keneally, who was also to tell Howard Goldman. That could mean the end of them too. The thought flashed through his mind that he should tell Bruno that he had sent dozens of photocopied letters to all members of the opposition and of the Nationalist Party, including the former president—the plan he had thought of two days ago, but had not followed through. But it was too complicated a lie to be able to back up convincingly on the spur of the moment.

"No-one," he said.

But the pause was sufficient. Bruno did not believe him.

"Where is Johnathan Kapepwe? Where is Carl Verhoef? Is he in Durban? How did you get his gun? You have been involved with the kidnappers, haven't you? Where is Marta Van Sisseren? How long had Ingrid Hofmeyr been passing information?" The questions came over and over again and Tony gave the same answers again and again. The hours wore on into the afternoon. Tony was slapped continuously. His face was bruised and bloody. On two more occasions he was given the plastic bag treatment until he passed out through lack of oxygen. By the end of the afternoon, he was in a state of mental and physical collapse. He could no longer talk coherently. His mind and body had been traumatised to the extent that he felt, in a sort of fantasy, as if he were sliding down a black, icy slope into a bottomless chasm and there was nothing he could do about it. He relaxed, let his body go limp, and gave up.

"There's nothing more we'll get from him at the moment," Bruno said to Colonel Starcke, who appeared at about five in the afternoon to see what progress had been made.

"All right, Bruno," Starcke replied, "get yourself cleaned up and we'll meet for dinner at seven. Piet," he said to the other man, "you come too."

"And Bartlett?" Bruno asked Starcke.

"There's a room at the end of the hallway for him. It's the only

316

one open. We'll come back and have a word with him later in the evening."

Starcke left and Tony was untied from his chair to be dragged down the hallway. The different handling and the movement stirred his consciousness, but something told him to remain as if he were still senseless.

"This is it," he heard Bruno say, "in here." They dumped Tony through the door into a crumpled heap on the floor, closed the door, and locked it. Then Tony heard their footsteps moving off down the corridor.

Tony's brain and body cried out just to lie where they were and drift off to sleep without moving, but something in the inner recesses of the same brain urged him to wake, to pull himself together, to fight back somehow. He struggled up into a sitting position and felt his whole upper body wracked with pains.

From where he was sitting in the room he could see that it was, like the other room, absolutely plain and white. The walls were about ten feet high and the room was a simple box about nine feet long by six feet wide, with the door at one end and a tiny window, roughly a foot wide by eighteen inches high, set at the top of the wall at the other end. The dim, late afternoon light filtering through this window was the only illumination by which Tony could assess his surroundings. It was sufficient, however, because there was nothing much more to assess, except a thin mattress lying in one corner, a plastic laundry bucket (which Tony assumed was to be used as a toilet) in the other, and a plastic bowl full of water next to the mattress. That was all. There was a peephole in the centre of the door, but no handle on it. No other feature in the room—nothing but blank whiteness.

Tony dragged himself across to the mattress and lay down on it, stretching his body out straight, moving tenderly and gently so as not to aggravate his bruises and pains. He lay on his back, staring up at the ceiling as the gloomy light gradually faded away to blackness.

16

The Ultimate
Solution

At 5.30 of the same afternoon, the new president, Dr. Van Essche, met with his cabinet in Cape Town to discuss the latest developments. The situation had deteriorated rapidly during the day—not so much in a military sense, but on the civil front, where it appeared as if the programme aimed at partitioning South Africa was already heading for disaster. It could, several of the cabinet ministers thought, drag the whole country into chaos and turmoil.

Many thousands of black people had obeyed the call of the rebel leaders and destroyed their passes, refusing to participate in the mass transmigration programme. There had been literally thousands of arrests throughout the country and already the jails were full. But the arrests had not been straightforward or easy. Riots had erupted wherever white police or officials of the Department of Bantu Administration had attempted to begin the process of assessing people's tribal origins and moving them to assembly points. There had been physical clashes with the police and the army, which had been called in to help in many areas. In some centres, police had been forced to use tear gas and to fire on crowds in order to escape being beaten to death.

One policeman was killed in the East Rand town of Witbank, and throughout the country, some thirty-seven blacks died in the riots; twelve in East London, seven in Durban, fifteen in Johannesburg, two in Pretoria, and one in Bloemfontein.

There had also been several disastrous guerilla raids during the previous night. Two more major power-generating plants at Camden and Hendrina in the eastern Transvaal had been hit by rocket attacks and severely damaged. The new Sasol plant near Trichardt on the eastern Transvaal high veld, which had taken five years to build and was only now coming on line with its fuel oil production from coal, was also hit by rocket fire.

The attack on the other Sasol plant at Sasolburg, three nights earlier, had swung tremendous responsibility for the country's fuel oil needs onto the Trichardt plant. Sasolburg's production capacity had been reduced by almost a half and now Trichardt had been hit. The damage had not been as bad as in the Sasolburg raid, but there was the possibility that it could happen again.

On a nationwide basis, March 23 had been the worst day of violence in South African history, and although the police and army had contained the riots, it had strained resources to their limits and shaken them to the core. An estimated one and a half million blacks took part in the riots and demonstrations in almost every major population centre throughout the country.

In addition, the general strike had been almost completely observed and many industries and community services had been brought to a standstill. It had been necessary to call in the army and the Civil Defence Corps, to operate essential services in centres all over the country, and this seriously depleted the manpower that was needed, not only to contain the violence in the cities but to fight the enemies crossing the borders.

Both Namibia and Botswana had entered the war and sent armoured columns and troops rolling into South African territory. On the north-western coast, a force had crossed from Namibia at Orange Mouth and captured the big alluvial diamond-mining complexes at Alexander Bay and Port Nolloth. The main force column, including dozens of Soviet-built T34, T54, and PT76 tanks, had driven down Route 11, the main road to Cape Town, and taken the town of Springbok, some seventy miles inside South Africa. From Botswana, two forces had crossed the border; one near Mafeking, the other near Grobler's Bridge in the northern Transvaal.

The South African armed forces had, as the new president had made clear in his radio and television broadcast, the ability to crush each of these military incursions into South Africa. But the operative word was "each." Had the South Africans been able to deal with them one by one, without also dealing with an internal guerilla war, riots, and a general strike, they certainly could have crushed them. But that opportunity was denied them. By launching concerted attacks in widely separated areas, the revolutionary forces split South Africa's defences into several fragments. The need for military assistance in the cities meant that the South African Army could not put the manpower it required into the various military engagements it found itself involved in around the country's borders.

From the beginning, the defence forces relied on the fact that they would have air superiority. Had it not been for that fact, then the revolutionary forces would have advanced even more rapidly on all fronts. As it was, they suffered heavy casualties on the Mozambique border and in the northern Transvaal, but managed to hold their ground in northern Natal and to push some thirty-six miles further south towards Durban, taking the small township of Hluhluwe, near Lake St. Lucia. The revolutionary units which crossed near Mafeking also took a pounding from air strikes, but both of the units crossing from northern Botswana and from Namibia suffered few casualties and were reported to be still advancing.

Although the South African Air Force could claim much of the credit for containing the rebel advances, they had suffered heavy losses in doing so. South African pilots, flying Mirage III and Buccaneer aircraft, had been surprised on three of the war fronts to suddenly encounter MIG 19 and MIG 21 fighters. A total of thirty of the Russian-built planes were reported in various actions during the day. The South African pilots shot down seven of them, but lost three Buccaneers and two Mirages in doing so. The rebel planes were painted with the flaming spear symbol of the APRA. South African defence analysts, however, considered they were almost certainly from Tanzania or Angola— or both.

But the air losses in dog-fights with MIG aircraft were small compared to those sustained by the South African Air Force as a result of the widespread use of light, ground-to-air missiles by the rebel troops. These were, the South Africans quickly discovered, a new, highly effective version of the Russian SA-7 Grail anti-aircraft missile and the rebel army units crossing the borders were carrying them by the hundreds.

Of sixteen Mirage III aircraft used during the day against the forces in the Mafeking area, six had been brought down by the guided missiles and three had been so badly damaged that, although they made it back to their base, just outside Pretoria, they would not be flying again for some time. This pattern was repeated on several fronts. The faster Mirages were slightly more lucky than the ageing Canadair Sabres and Vampires which had been brought out of mothballs during the past six months. They had been badly hit. Out of a total of sixty Sabres and Vampires, the SAAF had lost nine Vampires and eight Sabres. An additional six Mirages had been either destroyed or disabled by surface-to-air missiles. Seven Buccaneers and ten Aermacchi MB 326 converted jet trainers were also downed.

The heavy air losses stunned the South African defence staff— a significant proportion of their strike aircraft lost in one day. Similar heavy losses were experienced by the army with its helicopters; a total of nineteen Alouette II and Sud SA.330 helicopters were lost in seven different engagements. There were now serious doubts, after only one day of fighting, of the air force's ability to maintain the same degree of protective air cover for the ground forces. At this rate, the air superiority factor for South Africa would soon disappear.

When it came to combat on the ground, however, the South African forces were, in most cases, superior. The training and discipline of the regular troops clearly won the day for them in a number of bitter engagements along the Mozambique frontier. But the Citizen Force units did not fare so well, wherever they had been put into battle. There had not been enough time for them to be moulded into a cohesive fighting force. They all had the basic training and the knowledge of what it was all about, from two years' compulsory military service; but for many of them several years had passed since that training, and now that they had been suddenly called up again, they found that they still reacted as thousands of individuals, not as one body, with one purpose, one aim.

The only Citizen Force units that were asked to fight were those which had been called up weeks earlier in the partial mobilization programme set in train by the just-fallen Nationalist government. Those now assembling under the new government's call for total mobilization could not possibly have fought. It would be weeks before they could effectively be used and the rush to organise them in army camps across the country could only be described as chaotic.

While the regular South African units had been able to do well on the Mozambique border, their success, the army commanders had to admit, was largely to do with the training and fighting ability of the opposing forces, which, in the units encountered in the two engagements in the Kruger National Park, was not good. But in other areas, the South African forces had been surprised to come up against tenacious, well-trained units under intelligent leadership. For instance, the South African armour and infantry facing the troops advancing across the Botswana border at Grobler's Bridge had been outmanoeuvred by a lightning flanking movement that placed a second rebel armoured force behind the South African lines, isolating it on a thirty-mile stretch of road between the towns of Baltimore and Tom Burke and threatening it with a tightening pincer movement. There were avenues of escape for the South Africans, but they had been tactically disadvantaged and were in trouble.

President Van Essche's Security Council and the rest of the cabinet ministers were all grim-faced and serious as they gathered in the chambers of the Parliament buildings in Cape Town on the late afternoon of March 23. The rapidity of the developments and the unexpected swiftness of the chain reaction that swept the country in the form of the general strike and the rioting had caught the government off balance.

The president and his colleagues looked tired. They had all had, at best, only two or three hours sleep during the past twenty-four and were already feeling the strain. This was the fourth full cabinet meeting of the day and the crux of the matter they were now settling down to discuss was whether or not the vital scheme to partition the country into eight or nine black nations and one white one could possibly work. Under less desperate circumstances, they agreed, it could probably be done; but then the only reason they

322

were trying to do it at all was because the situation had become desperate.

It seemed clear to many of the ministers that it would not work, but the president persevered. "If we cannot do it the way we originally planned," he said, "then we will have to do it by force. If they destroy their passes, then we will simply move them to whichever homeland is nearest. They can sort out which homeland they belong to later. But what we *will* do is to clear every single black out of the white homelands!"

Several of the ministers exchanged glances between themselves and some spoke out against the scheme; the Minister for Bantu Administration, the Minister for the Interior, the Minister for Transport, and the Minister for Defence all opposed the continuation of the programme. But it was the Defence Minister and the Army Chief of Staff who finally convinced the president, not only of the impracticality—even impossibility—of carrying out the scheme, but of its extreme danger.

It was clear that a compulsory migration programme would take a massive force of tens of thousands of soldiers to put into effect. They would be facing violent opposition all the while and hundreds of people, both black and white, would almost certainly die or face injury if the programme was carried through on the president's terms. But, more serious than that, if the forced transmigration scheme was attempted, there would be insufficient military strength to hold back the rebel forces pressing in from all sides.

The Defence Minister, Hugo Retief, who at thirty-seven, was the youngest member of Van Essche's new cabinet, outlined an alternative plan. Retief, who basically shared his president's racial and political sentiments, had had a brilliant career in the South African Army, attaining the rank of brigadier by the age of thirty-five. His part in the Angolan and South-West African campaigns in 1975, 1976, and 1978 had earnt him considerable kudos within South African defence circles. His success in several major counter-insurgency operations in the guerilla war in Rhodesia, while attached to the Rhodesian defence forces in 1977 and 1978, had also added to his reputation.

But he had retired from the army in 1979 to run as a candidate in South Africa's general elections of that year, winning the seat of Oudtshoorn, some 260 miles east of Cape Town, for the Herstigte Nasionale Party. Now, with the dramatic collapse of the Botha government, he found himself suddenly elevated to ministerial rank in Van Essche's cabinet.

The position, however, held no fears for Hugo Retief. He felt he knew more than anyone else in Parliament about the realities of South Africa's defence situation. Of course, much of the top secret and classified information in the hands of the Department of Foreign Affairs—that relating to Russian and Chinese influence and to the extent of their aid to the revolutionary forces in the countries surrounding South Africa—had only just been placed at his disposal. Similarly, the classified information collected and collated by the Bureau for State Security, which had not been available to him either as a serving military officer or as a member of Parliament, was now given to him.

He had known for some years, for instance, as had most South Africans, that the big atomic research facility at Pelindaba, near Pretoria, had the technical ability to construct atomic weapons; but the facts of whether any had been produced, what type they were, and how many, were close secrets known only to a very few people. Now Hugo Retief was one of them.

The alternative plan he now presented to cabinet was, in many ways, as incredible a solution as the one proposed by the president. It was certainly just as dramatic—and traumatic—as the Van Essche scheme. Only, in Retief's programme, the traumas would be experienced by the whites. But, he hoped, they would only be temporary.

It was not, as he pointed out and as many of the other ministers knew, his own idea. It had been one of the many scenarios developed by South Africa's Institute for Strategic Studies, some years previously, for just such an occasion. Its general concept had not been top secret; in fact, when the idea had once been suggested by a foreign journalist in a feature article on the final cataclysm facing South Africa, it had been debated in Parliament. The Parliament of that time—only a few years ago—had dismissed the idea as a combination of fantasy and defeatism beyond the realm of possibility within the lifetimes of the members then discussing it. But now the ministers who listened to Hugo Retief listened attentively.

Firstly, he told them, there were several hard facts of life which white South Africans would have to face up to. The concept of an all-white, minority government ruling twenty million blacks was already untenable. It was an academic question to look ahead to the turn of the century, but by then, he pointed out, the ratio would be something like forty million blacks to seven or eight million whites. If the system of the past was untenable and the whites wished to remain masters of their own destinies, they would have to accept that they could no longer be masters of the black man's destiny also. The only solution, therefore, was separation—partition. Under Retief's plan, though, it would be the whites who moved.

"What I am saying," he thumped the big, oval cabinet-room table, "is that we will have to give up all of the Transvaal, Natal, and probably the Free State. We will give up the immense mineral and industrial wealth of these lands in order to survive as a white entity. It will involve tremendous hardships for hundreds of thousands of whites, but if we all move to the Cape, we will be able to survive."

There was silence in the room as he continued. "At the moment there are only two million blacks living in the Cape Province and one and a half million whites. If another three and a half million whites move from the other provinces, we will have superiority of numbers and a defensible position. We will be able to make the Cape into what it originally was when Jan Van Riebeeck brought the first white settlers—an all-white homeland in Africa. We will have lost a great deal, but we will have preserved the race. Eventually, we would be able to shift the remaining blacks out of the Cape and probably many of the coloureds too. But we have to choose now: to make the ultimate decision between survival of the white race in South Africa or integration, where we would disappear."

Retief's suggestion was so extreme, and conjured up visions of such hardship, that many of the other cabinet ministers could not accept it. Surely things weren't that bad was the general consensus. Events had moved too quickly for most of them to be able to believe or accept that such drastic and final measures need be taken just yet. Let's wait and see how things develop. It may not be necessary to go to such lengths, they said.

325

The president shared these more cautious sentiments, although he did accept the fact that Retief's suggested plan might ultimately be necessary if the situation deteriorated to disaster levels. In the meantime, he ordered that an urgent study be made of the proposal; of the logistics involved in transporting, feeding, and accommodating such numbers. It could be done, he knew that. India had handled ten million refugees from East Pakistan, back in 1971, but it had been a horrific job. South Africa could do it with three and a half million whites, but the cost and the economic disruption would be enormous and possibly catastrophic.

The president also ordered a temporary halt to the transmigration programme. It was purely a pragmatic decision on his part, with the realisation that the scheme was impossible to pursue at this stage without a massive and dangerous misdirection of military manpower. He did, however, issue another directive to his martial law administrators that major black population centres within white homelands were to be sealed off and that only food and essential supplies were to be permitted through the army and police barriers. He also sent out requests to provincial and local government authorities, to establish committees which would ensure that the supply of food and other goods were maintained to the hundreds of black townships throughout the land—already, to all intents and purposes, under siege.

Inside the major black towns, which in most parts of South Africa were sprinkled around the edges of the main white centres of population, a strange feeling of comradeship was growing. There were some clashes between different tribal groups and between the militants and the pacifists, and several blacks were killed by their own people; but overall, there had never before been such a sense of unity. The extent of the action taken against them as a whole had tended to pull groups together that would never have had anything to do with each other in the past. There seemed to be a certainty that they were involved in a climactic event; that things just wouldn't slip back into the old ways again. And this knowledge produced actions that many blacks, who had lived all their lives in one township, had never seen before.

Always, in the past, the whites had attempted to accentuate the

326

differences between the black tribal groups, and one black radical leader after another had called on the tribes to forget about their differences and to unite. But they had never done so . . . until now. Now anyone who promoted disharmony or inter-tribal friction was suddenly an outcast, or worse. In one incident in Soweto a Zulu youth was badly beaten by members of his own tribe for attempting to stir up trouble with the Xhosa tribe. And an edict had been passed by the APRA which could result in the death penalty for anyone stirring up inter-tribal trouble.

People in the townships began to pool their food and money and to help support other residents who were less fortunate. There was, in fact, a real siege mentality developing, and every report they heard on the rebel radio stations gave them nothing but encouragement to hang on.

During all of that day, the 23rd, Tony Bartlett and his captors had been totally unaware of these developments. In his darkened cell, where he had been taken in the late afternoon, Tony had slipped into a troubled sleep of absolute exhaustion. He had been dreaming of wolves and awoke to hear a dog howling in the distance and to find the cell flooded with an unearthly, pale light. It was moonlight coming through the window; not direct moonlight, because, although he shifted his position on the mattress, he could not see the moon itself. He recognised, however, a couple of stars of the Southern Cross and the recognition sent a wave of depression through him. The same constellation, he realised, had been shining down, only a few hours earlier, on Sydney. He wondered if Carol and Michael had looked up at it . . . or his mother and father. What did it matter anyway? The stars of the Southern Cross were hundreds of millions of miles away in space . . . and so might he just as well be for all the hope he ever had of laying eyes on his family or his friends again.

Tony thought vacantly of his childhood. His parents had moved around a great deal—his father had been a surveyor—and Tony had gone to a variety of schools in outback Queensland, New South Wales, and Victoria. But in the late fifties, his father had gone into the building business and the family had settled down to live in Sydney, so Tony had spent his last school years growing up there. God, they were happy years, too, Tony thought. He had surfed every one of the northern beaches and most of those south of the harbour too. But Harbord, North Narrabeen, and Bilgola were his favourites.

He closed his eyes and let his mind take over. He could see the big, clear swells of water coming in. He felt a surge of motion as if he were on his board, cornering hard to one side, the warm wind and spray whipping back over him. Or just swimming, treading water out beyond the line of breakers, waiting for the right one. Sometimes one would break early and he would dive under it. He saw it all in slow motion. Great, white crystal blobs floating through the air as the crest began to break, slowly, ever so slowly, and he was diving under, into the clear, blue-green water beneath the pounding white above, feeling the surge as the weight of water on top slowly increased, then passed away, and he would break out again into the surface sunlight.

God, what I wouldn't give to be back doing that right now, he thought, opening his eyes to the awful reality of his situation. He shifted his position. His body ached.

He wondered what time it was, but his watch and all of his other belongings, including his passport, cash, and travellers cheques, had been taken, with his security belt, when he had been first searched at the police station.

He remembered the time he had his passport stolen in Hong Kong. He wished he were there now. Transubstantiation, that was what he needed now—a little transubstantiation. Hong Kong had been good, too. His first job as a journalist—on the *South China Morning Post*. Everybody had thought he was crazy, back in Sydney, dropping out of the university arts course he'd been doing and taking off for Hong Kong; but things had worked out all right.

A couple of trips to Vietnam, and he had begun to work as a stringer for the *Guardian*. Funny how one thing leads to another, he thought. I suppose someone else looking at me with a degree of detachment could have predicted all this—could have predicted that I would end up here. It's just simply a matter of putting one foot in front of another. Surprising, really, that it hasn't happened sooner. There were some nasty scrapes in Vietnam, and then Bangla

Desh, the time in Dacca, the day after the Pakistan Army had surrendered to the victorious Indians, a few days before Christmas 1971. Jesus . . . almost ten years ago.

The picture, though, was as clear in his mind as if it were yesterday. He had left the others to walk to the telegraph office to see if he could get a cable out, but it and every other government facility was out of action. The streets were littered with bodies, which no-one was in a position to clear up. The capital was in a state of anarchy. There were no public facilities operating. Crowds of armed Mukti-Bahini guerillas roamed the streets cheering and chanting, firing their rifles in the air, and dispensing summary executions to anyone who had collaborated with the army in East Pakistan or with the hated Biharis. Near the telegraph office, Tony came across a group of civilians who had obviously been placed against a wall and machine-gunned only hours before. There were three of them; an old man, a middle-aged man, and a boy of eighteen or nineteen. They lay on the dusty footpath and pools of congealed blood lay around their bullet-riddled bodies. Two dogs tore at the flesh of the older men, while big black crows balanced on the head and chest of the boy, picking away. Pedestrians and cyclists passed them on the roadway, not twenty feet off, as though they were not there. There was nothing they could do.

At the telegraph office, Tony wandered through deserted telephone and teleprinter exchanges without seeing a soul. The doors were open and he walked in. Above the rows of telephone operators' desks there were signs saying "London," "New York," "Tokyo," "Calcutta," but not a single living person. All these mechanical connections sitting, waiting for a human to bring them to life, but no-one . . .

Suddenly, three armed Mukti-Bahini appeared from nowhere and grabbed him. One of them, shouting incoherent abuse at Tony in Bengali, had placed a .45 calibre automatic pistol at his temple. After three or four minutes of frantic explanation in English to one of the three men who understood, Tony was able to convince the guerillas that he was only a journalist and not some sort of spy trying to sabotage the telegraph office. He was allowed to go, but it had not been a pleasant experience.

Why hadn't he taken it as a lesson? Why hadn't he gone straight back home and taken a job on the subs desk at the Sydney *Morning Herald,* or something like that? Sold cameras maybe, or run a little fishing boat up in Cairns for charters out on the Barrier Reef? Why? Christ!

That situation in Dacca was as near as he'd ever come. He had been in the hands of a fanatic, with no recourse to any aid or justice whatever. The guerillas or freedom-fighters became a law unto themselves for a period—anything went. They exacted terrible retribution for their past oppression. And they *had* been brutally oppressed. Tony could see that happening here. And he would be just one of the statistics. Somebody must have eventually come and shovelled those bodies in Dacca away, into some mass grave for all the riddled and mutilated bodies that lay around the streets of the capital on those few days after the surrender. But who were they? What were they? Just statistics. Would he be one of the statistics of the South African situation? It wouldn't matter what side he was killed by, he would still be just a statistic. All because of hatred and mistrust . . . He remembered a book he had once read called *Children of Blindness,* about the conflict between blacks and whites in a small country town in Australia. "Hatred and mistrust are the children of blindness." Why did it have to be like that?

Tony slipped back again into blackness. It was sleep, but this time it was an absolutely dreamless sleep. He had no idea how long it lasted, but he was awoken by a light, a bright light, in the room. He shielded his eyes and eventually saw that, at the very top of one wall, there was a panel of white plastic, almost indistinguishable from the rest of the wall, behind which a fluorescent light now burned. Only a matter of seconds after the light came on, there were sounds of a key being fitted into the door from the outside. The door opened and Tony saw Colonel Starcke, Bruno, and the other man, Piet. A fourth man stood behind them in the corridor. It was immediately clear to Tony that Colonel Starcke had been drinking.

"Good evening Mr. Bartlctt," Colonel Starcke said, and then, looking at his watch, "Or, I should say, good morning."

Tony said nothing.

"How are you feeling? A little rested, I hope . . ."

Tony still said nothing.

". . . because you will need all your energy by the morning."

A brittle laugh emerged from Bruno Van Wyk's mouth as he stood in the doorway looking at Tony. He, of course, had not been drinking.

"There is someone I would like you to meet, Mr. Bartlett," Starcke said, turning towards the fourth man who was still standing in the corridor and, because of the light glaring in Tony's eyes, was almost in silhouette to him. "He has also expressed a desire to meet you," Starcke continued. The man moved forward. "This is Dirk Behrmann. He has just arrived from Johannesburg."

Tony felt his face go cold and his back crawl with gooseflesh. The man's face was a deathly white and his pin-prick black eyes were almost invisible in the shadow of two enormous, bushy eyebrows. Tony had only once before caught a fleeting glimpse of that face—for a few brief seconds—but he would never forget it.

"Hello, Mr. Bartlett," the man said. "Pleased to meet you."

Tony opened his mouth to say something, but no words came. He stared at the man, who returned the look with a cynical smile.

Slowly the sensation of fear slipped away from Tony, to be replaced by a feeling of disgust and burning hatred.

"Cat got your tongue, Mr. Bartlett?" Starcke said, and Bruno laughed his harsh laugh again.

"Mr. Bartlett . . ." Colonel Starcke moved further into the small room, his hands in his pockets, "you may or may not know, but I have been in charge of the security aspects of this operation— the operation which you have been attempting to undermine." He took his pipe out of his pocket and lit it with a match, puffing clouds of smoke into the air. "Within a very few hours, the operation will have been carried to a successful conclusion. Not a complete success, unfortunately, because of two incidents in which, I believe, you had a part. The hijacking of our plane and the kidnapping of Carl Verhoef . . ."

"That's ridiculous!" Tony said. "I . . ."

"There is little we can do about the plane. That is out of our hands. Although there is a great deal to answer for over the disappearance of that plane—a great deal—over one hundred million

Rand, Mr. Bartlett. One hundred million Rand! However, I am sure you can still help us with the question of Mr. Carl Verhoef's disappearance. If he is still alive, we intend to get him back."

Starcke's voice was raised slightly in anger. "This operation has run smoothly, except for the interference of people like you and Ingrid Hofmeyr, and possibly Miss Marta Van Sisseren. We are looking for her now—and also for your American friends."

"Howard Goldman?" Tony cried. "He . . . they have nothing to do with this, no more than I have."

"Not a very good choice of words, Mr. Bartlett, since you are quite obviously involved. In any event, we have already questioned Mr. Goldman and his colleague twice. We would like to see them again." He turned to the other men and back to Tony. "But, for the moment, we would like you to come with us."

Tony was grabbed by Bruno and Piet and pulled roughly to his feet.

"You have been permitted to rest because I was unwilling to have dinner with my friends interrupted. But we do not have much time. Come."

Tony was bundled out into the corridor and moved along it in the direction of the room in which he had been questioned during the day. A long, agonised groan came from one of the other cell-rooms along the hall. Tony was surprised and turned to look at Colonel Starcke.

Starcke smiled, but said nothing for several seconds as the group continued along the hallway. "You must not think, Mr. Bartlett," he said eventually, "that you are the only person important enough to warrant our interest. In fact, you would be amongst the least important of our guests in this establishment."

Other people here? Tony thought. Who are they? And what did he mean by we don't have much time?

They came again to the door of the chair room and Tony expected to be led into it, but he was hustled straight past to the next door and pushed into a room of roughly the same size as the first one but equipped with different "furniture."

There was a chair, similar to the one in which he'd been strapped during the previous day, but there was also a stainless-steel table,

332

something like an operating table. Tony shivered involuntarily at the sight of it. There was what appeared to be a sort of stainless-steel head-cradle at one end of it, with a plastic bucket underneath. A supporting framework next to the table held a clear, glass jar suspended above it. A rubber tube dangled loosely from the jar.

"Sit down, Mr. Bartlett," Colonel Starcke said, gesturing to the chair. The others stood around in a semi-circle behind Starcke, looking at Tony, but made no move to strap him down. Tony saw Behrmann's face clearly for the first time. He looked for all the world like a death's head. He had massive cheekbones and deeply recessed eyes. There were dark rings under them, which only heightened the skull-like effect and, when he smiled, which he did when he saw Tony looking at him, he exposed a huge set of irregular teeth.

If I ever get a chance, Tony thought, I'll kill you, you bastard.

Bruno shifted a spotlight, which was attached to a stainless-steel pole, and turned it on Tony. In its glare, Bruno, Piet, and Behrmann became vague forms standing behind it. Starcke, who stood a few paces in front of them, was lit only on his left side. The other side of him was in shadow.

"You, Mr. Bartlett, are one of the lowest forms of white scum on earth. If I had my way, people like you would never be allowed in to South Africa. There are too many like you here already and it is my opinion that they should be ruthlessly weeded out, so that only the pure remain."

Starcke moved a few paces to the side, blocking the light from Tony's eyes for a second. Then back again.

"It is mealy-mouthed white liberals like you," Starcke went on, "who have allowed the black races to ride rough-shod over the rest of Africa. To take everything that the white race has built up and just tear it down—like some prehistoric caveman rabble." He started to wave his hands about and to raise his voice again. "You come to this country, with your nigger-loving liberal attitudes, knowing nothing about the history of this place, nothing about the blacks, who could no sooner govern themselves than fly to the moon, and then you attempt to influence people outside South Africa against us."

Tony did not like the way the monologue was going; Starcke was letting himself go. Tony looked back at the half-silhouetted figure in dread silence.

"Oh yes, Mr. Bartlett," Starcke continued, pacing back and forth across the light. "We have read your articles. We know exactly what sort of person you are and . . ." his voice was raised now to a shout, ". . . we are not going to let Communist swine like you ruin this country. South Africa has never belonged to the blacks . . . never! Ever since the first white settlers came to this land more than three hundred years ago! There were no bloody kaffirs here! This land was ordained by God to be white!"

Tony could not believe his ears. But his disbelief only tended to increase his fear of Starcke.

"It was fought for by the Voortrekkers—men and women who laid down their lives for it. And we're not about to give it all up to a bunch of Communist-led apes. We will push the whole lot of them out of this country and let them make a mess of things by themselves. For my part, it can't be soon enough. I can't stand the sight of them."

The others had been standing, all the while, silently behind Starcke. A slight movement by Bruno Van Wyk prompted Starcke to turn around. "Anyway," he said, "we are wasting time. It is necessary for you now to cooperate with us to the fullest, if you value your life at all."

Suddenly, from a great distance, they all heard the sounds of automatic weapons firing. In the stillness of the night, the sounds came through clearly, although they were quite faint. Starcke turned to look at the others, who had also exchanged questioning glances.

"Probably someone breaking the curfew," Bruno said.

The firing continued for some minutes, but after the first thirty seconds or so, Colonel Starcke said, "It is a long way off. It will not interfere with us. As I was saying, Mr. Bartlett, information is what we want. In particular, the whereabouts of Mr. Johnathan Kapepwe and Carl Verhoef, and the names of the two men you drove south the other day. I will leave you with Mr. Van Wyk and Mr. Buchner," he turned and gestured towards Bruno and Piet, "as I personally cannot stand physical violence." Starcke grinned maliciously at Tony. "I trust, however, that you can, Mr. Bartlett. Goodnight."

He turned and walked to the door, followed by Behrmann. Tony was left, once again, with Bruno. In the distance there were more sounds of firing, but Tony did not hear them.

17

Confrontation

The automatic weapon fire continued. Before long it was accompanied by explosions. The sounds of what many people took to be a protracted battle with rebel army forces pressing down from the north were heard almost all over Durban in the early hours of March 24.

It was not, however, the revolutionary army, which was still 138 miles away at Mtubatuba, having broken through the South African defences and advanced a further thirty miles during the night, with reinforcements and tons of supplies pouring south from Mozambique and Swaziland behind it.

Most of the shooting the residents of Durban heard came from three different guerilla units in widely separated raids on the Umgeni power station at New Germany, the Durban port complex, and the railway yards in the centre of the city.

The question of containing blacks in the black townships had suddenly been proven impossible—in the Durban area at least—because the Kwazulu Homeland territories were so close to the city itself. Large quantities of arms and ammunition had now reached the homelands and African townships, and the prospect of universal uprising and anarchy was very real. The regular guerilla units were carrying out specific raids on chosen targets, but for the first time, scores of untrained and undisciplined blacks now had access to arms. The High Command of the Azanian Peoples Liberation Army expressed no concern at this development; in fact, it was encouraged. As a temporary situation, it was considered

336

the aims of the revolution would be furthered in this way by promoting chaos and terror within the white population. In this assessment, they were correct.

The night of March 23/24 was one of extreme terror for whites in at least two of Durban's suburbs, Clermont and Westville, as gangs of armed blacks rampaged on a killing and looting spree, which took the lives of thirteen whites—six men, three women, two children, and two policemen. Nine blacks also died. But the most significant factor for the whites was that the remainder of the black gangs—probably thirty or more men—got away.

Durban's security forces were in a state of uproar that night. Several army units had been rushed north to try to prevent the collapse of the force defending the coastal highway, and the police in Durban, who had to carry the main responsibility for the security of the city, had been so hard-pressed coping with the three organised guerilla attacks that they were unable to mount a proper attack on the gangs roaming through Clermont and Westville.

A fourth guerilla group, which saw no fighting action that night, was, however, also involved in a dangerous exercise. At 12.40, with the sounds of the first shooting across Durban Harbour, three trained frogmen, wearing black wet-suits and oxygen re-breathing scuba gear, slipped into the dark waters on the south-eastern side of the harbour.

They had cut their way through the high wire fence surrounding the bulk coal storage facility on the Bluff and slipped noiselessly into the water underneath a disused and rotting section of the wharf nearest to the harbour entrance. Two other guerillas, who were to remain on land underneath the old wharf, handed the three men their deadly cargo of six limpet mines which they attached to their belts; then they submerged into the water, setting off on a swim of more than a mile across the harbour towards the new Salisbury Island Pier.

In the moonlight, it was relatively easy for one to lead and the other two to follow close behind. They were travelling only two or three feet beneath the surface and their re-breathing apparatus left no tell-tale trail of bubbles. They hoped to be able to cover the distance in about forty to forty-five minutes, but the state of the tide and the currents moving in the channel would be crucial.

On the bridge of the *South Cape Aurora,* still standing at Pier One, Captain Martin Coetzee came to a decision. He had been awakened in his cabin, next to the bridge, by the sound of gunfire at 12.40. It was loud, and too close, to ignore. At 12.48 there was an explosion . . . and then another.

Captain Coetzee had thought that the shooting had been some way from the *South Cape Aurora,* probably at the container terminal at Pier Two. Now he saw the glare of the first explosion and estimated it was somewhere on the docks in the Island View Channel, he couldn't be sure. In any event, it seemed too close for comfort, and only eight minutes after he had been woken, he made the decision to leave.

The *South Cape Aurora* was scheduled to take on more cargo in the morning. But the main cargo, the most important cargo, was already securely deposited and battened down in the forward hold. He knew what the cargo was and the twelve-man team which was to accompany it was already on board. They had wanted to leave on the previous afternoon, but Coetzee had said that they should wait for the rest of their scheduled cargo, otherwise suspicions might be aroused. Now he changed his mind. He issued orders through the officer of the watch to wake all hands, for the engine room to get up steam, and that preparations be made to cast off and sail as soon as possible.

He went directly to the leader of the group in charge of the shipment and told him of his decision, which received immediate approval. Ernst Dingemans, a senior partner in one of Paul Trauseld's companies, required no urging. During the past few months, he had quietly and discreetly been selling off most of his assets in South Africa and converting them to diamonds, which he was now in the process of personally shipping out. His wife and family were already in Europe, ostensibly on holiday. He was to meet them there, after which he had no intention of coming back, although he would never, at this stage, have admitted as much to his colleagues.

The crew of the *South Cape Aurora* were all white; some South

African, but mostly Dutch and Danish. The night curfew imposed under the martial law regulations had prevented them from having overnight shore leave, although two men had been given permission to stay the night with relatives. The ship was leaving without them.

At about 1.20 AM, as the *Aurora* was ready to sail, several of the crew exchanged surprised and curious looks with each other at the sight of two of the passengers; a couple of the BOSS members of the guard group, carrying Sterling submachine guns, one on the deck and one on the wharf as the ship was casting off her lines. Under the circumstances, though, with automatic weapons fire and a series of explosions at the wharves nearby, perhaps it was not so unusual. For their part, the crew, without exception, were glad to be leaving.

The three frogmen crossing the harbour did encounter currents on their way. First they met an outward moving current coming from the Island View Channel, but strangely they found that it turned and was carried back into the harbour by the main tidal current, which was just beginning to flow into the harbour. Once they had crossed the outflow, they found themselves making reasonable time. They had surfaced every so often to check their bearings and had seen the night sky lit by big fires started at the old Salisbury Island piers further up the channel. By comparison, Pier One was in darkness. They had crossed the harbour in forty-five minutes and as they surfaced about two hundred yards from Pier One, they saw, to their amazement, that the *South Cape Aurora* was manouevring out of her berth. Her bow was already swinging out towards them and the entrance to the harbour. The three dark faces gazed through their masks at each other for a second above the surface of the water, and then set off again, swimming furiously towards the ship.

By five o'clock in the morning, Tony Bartlett was once more on the verge of total collapse. He felt close to insanity, if you can ever tell that you are close. He was, however, still alive, despite the terrifying methods of persuasion used by Bruno Van Wyk and Piet Buchner.

He had been strapped down, lying on his back on the steel table, his head locked into the frame at one end of it and tilted backwards over the edge. Then a special clamp had been fitted over his lips and mouth, so that he could only breathe through his nose. Bruno had stuffed cotton wool into each of Tony's nostrils so that, even if he was left like that, breathing was difficult. But then Bruno had stood at his side, holding the rubber hose from the glass jar suspended above, and began to slowly drip salt water onto the cotton wool in his nose. He told Tony as he was doing it that it was quite possible to drown a person with only a few drops of water.

Twice, during the night, Tony had been through the horrifying sensation of inhaling water into his lungs, struggling and losing consciousness. And in between times, after being brought round again, he was continually questioned. Very early on, he decided to give them what they wanted—names. He told them that the names of the two people he had driven south were Lennox Sengope and Joseph Ngala. They were the two names that came first into his head; the airport manager and the airport police chief in Nairobi. But Tony knew that the names would have to be checked first, and that would take time . . . time.

He couldn't tell them anything about Johnathan Kapepwe, except the truth; that he had recognised him at the American reception and spoken to him there. He had last seen Kapepwe before that on the TanZam Railway, but, Tony insisted desperately, they had fought. Kapepwe and he had argued bitterly and someone had tried to kill him. "I've never been involved with him in any way, believe me. It's true!" Tony had said over and over again. Bruno pressed him mercilessly about Verhoef's gun. "Where is Verhoef?" he shouted at him again and again. "You have seen him here in Durban, haven't you? Where have they got him? Where did you get his gun?" On several occasions in the face of continued denials by Tony, Bruno delivered a brutal karate chop to Tony's stomach as he lay on the table. Towards the end, when Tony had begun to feel that he had no more reserves to draw on, he began to sob, "Please, please, believe me."

There was a period, in the middle of his questioning, around 2.30 in the morning, when Tony had a brief respite from his tormentors. There had been several bursts of automatic fire within half a

340

mile of the house. Bruno and Piet left the room to see, with others in the building, what was happening. But they returned, some twenty minutes later, to continue their questioning. At 4.50, Bruno called it off. He was tired.

"I think you'll be all right here," he said to Tony. "We'll only be a few hours. Colonel Starcke will be in to see you later, I'm sure. If you want any water, just yell." Both Bruno and Piet laughed loudly as they walked out of the door, closed it, and locked it. They had taken the cotton wool out of Tony's nose and removed the clamp on his mouth, but his head was still locked down and his arms and legs strapped to the table.

The morning brought complete chaos to Durban. Thousands of whites were clamouring to leave. Many abandoned entire households of furniture, clothing, and other possessions to take only what they could realistically carry in their cars or in suitcases. They thronged the city centre, shipping offices, airline offices, and the port itself as they attempted to buy or bribe their way onto ships or planes. Hundreds of cars were taking off in convoys, heading for the Cape via the long northern route to Harrismith in the Orange Free State and then south: but gasoline supplies were a major problem. Gas had long since been rationed and only those who had somehow hoarded it, or saved enough coupons, could attempt the journey. Thousands also clamoured at army headquarters for permits to join the military convoys, but others formed their own and carried their own weapons for protection. In the face of such overwhelming panic, there was little the authorities could do. But Durban got off relatively lightly. In Klerksdorp, about one hundred miles west of Johannesburg, a mob of rioting blacks had killed more than seventy whites in their own homes during the night. When news of this was learnt in other parts of South Africa, it had a snowball effect on the panic sweeping the country.

For the first time, the city of Johannesburg had passed the night in almost total darkness; no power, no street lights, no lights anywhere, because of attacks on several key points of the ESCOM power grid.

In many places it was now impossible for blacks and whites to see each other without some conflict developing. The majority of black people, who would have preferred a peaceful settlement of the whole situation, stayed at home, either in the homelands or in the black townships. But thousands of other blacks now began to venture into white areas in large numbers. In many places the security forces were still sufficiently organised to prevent this, to contain blacks in their township areas and to stop them from congregating in groups of more than three, in accordance with the martial law regulations. But in other places everything was breaking down and the regulations were shown to be a farce. They were impossible to enforce and in some areas, where attempts were made to force blacks to comply, they only provoked riots and violence on a terrifying scale.

At eight o'clock in the morning, Colonel Starcke, Behrmann, and two attendants entered the room in which Tony had lain strapped to the table for more than seven hours. In the three hours since Bruno had left him, Tony had experienced brief periods of a kind of half-sleep, but he was desperately uncomfortable and his body ached all over. What sleep had come to him was a result of sheer exhaustion.

Colonel Starcke motioned to the attendants to untie Tony from the table. Tony struggled to bring himself to a sitting position, but found that it was so painful, he could not immediately accomplish the movement. His bones seemed to be locked into the positions they had been in all night. His neck, which had been bent backwards the whole time, was suddenly full of shooting pains, and both of his legs were without any feeling. He continued the effort and eventually managed to sit up on the edge of the table, his legs burning with pins and needles as the blood rushed more freely through them.

"Good morning, Mr. Bartlett," Starcke said. "I was not sure in what condition I would find you, but I see you have passed the night relatively easily." A mirthless grin passed over the face of Behrmann, who stood several paces back with his arms folded.

"I am in an expansive mood this morning," Starcke went on, smiling, "and, as a consequence, I am allowing you to spend the morning back in your room."

342

He chuckled to himself and then said, "Actually, to tell you the truth, we need this room for someone else. But you can count yourself doubly fortunate."

Tony looked blankly at Colonel Starcke and then down at the floor.

"Aren't you going to ask me why I'm in such a good mood? No? Well then, I'll tell you. Because we have just successfully completed the major part of our little operation."

Tony looked up again.

"Yes, Mr. Bartlett, the goods in which you seem to have been so interested are now safely on their way."

When Captain Coetzee had manoeuvred the *South Cape Aurora* out from her berth at 1.25 that morning and headed down Durban Harbour, he had no idea how close his ship came to disaster. The ship had sailed directly towards the three frogmen, who had frantically unhooked the limpet mines from their belts and attempted to reach the hull of the vessel and attach them while she was moving.

Only two of them had actually reached the ship as she was moving past, but although the *Aurora* had been travelling very slowly, the task of attaching the mines to the hull proved impossible. The swirling waters had prevented either of the frogmen from accomplishing what they had set out to do and had almost killed one of them. As the vessel moved over the top of them, the waters had sucked one of the men in towards the two huge bronze propellors. He had missed being decapitated by about a foot, but had been sent churning over and over helplessly in the ship's wake, which tore his mask and mouthpiece off and nearly drowned him.

The three men struggled to the surface, to watch gloomily as the dark hulk of the big freighter, the target they had missed by minutes, slowly gather headway moving towards the harbour mouth.

Once clear of the Bluff, the ship found a brilliantly moonlit sea. Behind her, a large section of the Durban docks was ablaze and the sound of shooting and rocket fire continued, slowly diminishing in level, as the vessel moved away. The captain ordered an almost 180-degree turn to starboard, which put the *Aurora* on a southwesterly heading down the coast of Natal. Coetzee had decided that he would stay well within the twelve-mile limit of South African

343

territorial waters for as long as possible and also to make up as much distance as he could. He ordered that the vessel hold a speed of twenty knots at least until dawn.

Captain Coetzee and the twelve special passengers he was carrying could not possibly have known that Captain Vladimir Serensky, commander of the Soviet Kresta II class guided missile cruiser *Marshal Voroshilov,* had been watching and waiting for the *South Cape Aurora* to leave Durban Harbour. The *Marshal Voroshilov* and two Kashin class destroyer escorts, the *Szerzhanny* and the *Ognevoy,* were cruising well below the horizon, some sixty miles to the north-east, at the time the *Aurora* left the harbour.

Captain Serensky was not personally watching and waiting at 1.45 AM when the *Aurora* cleared Durban's Bluff; he was sound asleep in his cabin. But one of the radar operators who had been specially assigned to keep a twenty-four-hour watch on the "high-sieve" surface search radar monitor spotted the *Aurora* leaving. Of course, he wasn't sure at that stage that it was the *Aurora,* but he was under instructions to inform the captain of any vessel, above a certain size, that left the harbour.

Serensky watched the movement of the bleep along the illuminated coastline on the radar screen and noted that it was following a course much closer in to shore than a ship of that size would normally steer. At 1.50 he ordered the *Voroshilov* and her escorts to follow the *Aurora,* but, for the moment, to stay well clear of South Africa's territorial waters.

Two hundred and seventy miles to the south-west, Commander Joseph Reilly, skipper of the American Charles F. Adams-class guided missile destroyer *Claude V. Rickets,* was also awoken by his officer of the watch and given details of the radio communications between the Soviet cruiser and her escorts, which had been monitored and decoded on the American ship.

For the past twenty-eight hours Reilly's ship had been averaging twenty-five knots, heading up the coast. Seven hundred miles ago he had been cruising in the Cape Sea lanes with two American frigates, tracking two Russian submarines. The crew of the *Claude V. Rickets* had, at times, been enjoying the game, although after

344

two days, it had begun to pall. But at 2200 hours on March 22 (exactly twenty-eight hours previously) Commander Reilly had received a top-priority communication from Naval Headquarters at the Pentagon, relayed via the DSCS-4 satellite, instructing him to proceed to an area off the Natal coast near Durban and to keep the coastline under surveillance for a South African vessel, the *South Cape Aurora.*

At almost the same time as the Russian and American warships began to close in on the *Aurora,* the threatened confrontation between the giant aircraft carrier *Dwight D. Eisenhower,* her two guided missile cruiser escorts, the *Texas* and the *Mississippi,* and the Russian freighters *Taseyeva* and *Berdyansk,* reached the moment of truth some two thousand miles away in the South Atlantic.

The American warships were within five miles of the two merchant vessels and had been signalling the ships to heave to or change course for twenty minutes as they closed in. Night fighters from the carrier had buzzed the two Russian vessels on several occasions, but there had been no change in course. Then, suddenly, at 0205 hours on March 24, the freighters made an abrupt change in direction and began heading due north.

The *South Cape Aurora,* after she had left Durban Harbour and begun her run down the coast, averaged over eighteen knots; by 6.00 AM, a little over four hours after her departure, she had covered almost eighty miles. The three Soviet vessels, however, had been sitting on over 30 knots and, although they had started more than 50 miles behind the *Aurora,* had covered almost 130 miles in the same four hours. They were now level with the South African freighter, but some fifteen miles due east of her.

The U.S.S. *Claude V. Rickets,* coming up from the south, had upped her speed to around 30 knots also and had covered about 120 miles, heading directly towards the Russian ships, so that at 6.00 AM the *Claude V. Rickets* and the *Marshal Voroshilov* were roughly 20 miles apart and closing on each other at a combined speed of 60 knots. Both the American and the Soviet ships were still in international waters, while the *Aurora* hugged the coastline.

Two South African destroyers, the *Simon Van Der Steel* and the *Jan Van Riebeeck,* which almost certainly would have been interested in the proceedings developing along the southern Natal coastline, were busy, during the early hours of March 24, shelling the revolutionary forces on the northern coast of Natal from a position off the St. Lucia estuary. Four of the South African Navy's six anti-submarine frigates were occupied off the Cape, while another two were in the East London area, well to the south of Durban.

The captains of the three Russian ships, the American destroyer, and the *South Cape Aurora* were all in their respective radar rooms, poring over the screens, watching the movements of the others and the information which came from their computers. During the run south, Captain Serensky had sent an urgent, coded message to Soviet Naval Headquarters in Leningrad. The request was passed immediately to the Defence Headquarters and the Foreign Ministry in the Kremlin. The Communist Party chief Mr. Brezhnev was consulted and within ten minutes, an answer was relayed back to Captain Serensky via the Molniya 7k military communications satellite in stationary orbit over the Indian Ocean.

For most of the morning of the 24th, Tony Bartlett slept. He had been given a plate of cheese and hard biscuits, the first food he had eaten since leaving the Mbatha house a little over twenty-four hours previously. He had eaten it greedily and fallen straight to sleep on the mattress in the corner of his room. He was woken at about 1.00 in the afternoon by the sound of shooting. It was much closer than the firing he had heard during the night. The shooting had stopped for an hour or so and then there had been more. He heard the sounds of running feet and voices at one stage, then there had been no more sounds for some time.

At about 3.30 in the afternoon, the door had opened and Bruno Van Wyk had been about to step into Tony's room to say something, when he had been called by someone further down the corridor. He had sneered at Tony, "I'll be back," locked the door again, and gone off.

Tony heard more automatic weapons fire in the distance and also the sound of voices raised to shouting level, which came through the small window at the top of his wall. The voices, which came

346

from the yard, were shouting in Afrikaans, however, so Tony could not understand. On two occasions, he also heard the sounds of trucks and cars revving their engines in the yard.

At 4.30, he heard shouting in the hallway and a key was rattled in the lock. The door was flung open and Colonel Starcke, Behrmann, and Bruno strode into the room. Starcke's face was red with rage. The pockmarks on his cheeks remained white, giving his face a bizarre, polka-dot effect.

He stood for a moment, speechless, looking at Tony, who could do nothing but return his look with a sinking feeling of apprehension.

"What . . . what's the matter?" Tony asked quietly.

"You filthy swine. You filthy swine. If there was some way of knowing whether this was because of information you passed on, I would personally tear you apart on the rack. As it is, there isn't time."

"What is it?" Tony said.

"Never mind," Starcke shouted furiously, "Bruno will deal with you. Goodbye, Mr. Bartlett." He turned and walked out past Bruno, saying as he went, "Be quick about it."

As Starcke and Behrmann disappeared, Bruno produced a pistol and pointed it at Tony. Tony raised his hands involuntarily in front of himself, but Bruno said, "Get up!" He waved the pistol towards the door. "Hurry. This way."

Tony staggered to his feet and was pushed back along the same corridor again. This time, though, Bruno stopped him at a different room. Only three or four doors from Tony's own cell-room at the head of the stairs.

"In here. Quickly." Bruno snarled.

This is it, Tony thought. This is it. He would have to do something quickly if he was going to try to stop Bruno from shooting him, but he felt as if he could hardly move one foot in front of the other, let alone tackle Bruno Van Wyk, who was too far away anyway.

"I should just shoot you right here and now," Bruno said. "But there's something I've been wanting to do for a long time. The only thing that kaffirs and kaffir-lovers like you can understand—

347

a good old-fashioned taste of the shamrock. Up against that wall!" He motioned to Tony to move towards one wall of the room on which two stainless-steel manacles hung from short chains.

Suddenly there was the sound of automatic weapons firing nearby.

"Put your left hand in that one," Bruno said, standing well back. Tony hesitated. "Quickly," Bruno shouted. "Unless you want a bullet right now." There was nothing Tony could do. He snapped the manacle shut on his left wrist.

"Now, hold your right arm up into the other one."

Tony did so and Bruno, in one quick movement, stepped forward and snapped the manacle shut.

"Ha!" He laughed derisively.

Another burst of automatic fire was heard. This time, Tony thought it could have been in the grounds of the house itself.

Bruno put his gun on the floor and dived for the short shamrock—the terrible rhinoceros-tail whip—which hung on another wall.

"This will have to be quick," he said, tearing Tony's shirt open and baring his back. "Oh God," he whispered, "how I've been waiting for this!"

There were several long bursts of gunfire and some shouting in the yard.

Bruno took a vicious slash at Tony and, for an instant, Tony felt as if a red-hot poker had been run across his back. He screamed.

Bruno let out a deranged laugh at the sound of Tony's scream. "More? Yes, more!"

He lashed at Tony's back again and, once again Tony screamed, but on the third stroke, there was a shout from the corridor. Bruno whirled to see a black man standing in the doorway with a PPS-43 submachine gun in his hands. He moved like lightning to pick up his own gun, but a burst of fire from the weapon in the doorway shattered his right knee and tore open both his thighs. He collapsed in a heap on the floor, gazing, horror-struck, at the blood spurting from the remains of his legs.

"Oh . . . Oh, please . . . please," he cried, holding his hands out towards the man in the doorway, who only closed his teeth tightly together as he pressed again on the trigger.

The second burst of fire hurled Bruno back against the wall, ripping off most of the top of his head. He slumped down beside Tony's feet, motionless.

Another black man appeared at the door. "Get him down . . . quickly," he ordered, moving on down the hall.

There was a key hanging on the wall next to the hook from which Bruno had taken the whip. The man with the submachine gun grabbed it and moved rapidly to free Tony from the manacles.

"Who are you?" he demanded.

"Tony Bartlett. I'm an Australian. They were holding me prisoner."

"Come quickly." He ran back to the corridor and looked out. Tony hobbled after him. In the hallway two other guerillas were in the process of freeing three more prisoners who had been occupying the other rooms in the corridor near Tony. They were all black; two of them, Tony noticed, were middle-aged men, while the third was a young man of about twenty-five. All of them looked as Tony felt; battered and exhausted. The guerillas motioned to Tony and the others to hurry down the stairs.

At the foot of the stairs, five more guerillas held nine whites at gunpoint. Some were white-coated attendants such as Tony had seen on the previous day, others were in civilian clothes. None of them spoke. They stood against a wall, with their hands in the air. Colonel Starcke and Piet Buchner were amongst them, trying to appear inconspicuous, but Tony could not see Behrmann.

The black who had ordered Tony to be released from his manacles walked up to the group and faced them.

"You!" he said sharply, pointing to Starcke. "This way!" Starcke began to shuffle his way out of the group, his hands still held high.

"Lock the others in here," the guerilla ordered, pointing to an open cell-room similar to the one Tony had occupied on the upper floor.

"There is another one," Tony said, as the cell door was being closed. "A tall man with . . . with bushy eyebrows."

Starcke turned a venomous glare on Tony, but said nothing.

"Never mind," the guerilla leader said. "We have Starcke. The other must have got away. We will deal with Colonel Starcke separately. Come. We must hurry."

"Wait," Tony said. "My passport and money. Can we check if they still have it?"

"We cannot waste time," the black man said, but then he turned to Colonel Starcke. "Starcke!" he shouted. "This man's papers?"

"In the office," Starcke muttered.

"Take them out to the vans, quickly," the guerilla leader said to the others. He grabbed Tony by the arm and led him hurriedly down another corridor, to the right, and into a small room with several desks in it. A number of filing cabinets were open and had obviously been rifled by the guerillas, who evidently knew what they were looking for.

But Tony also had no trouble finding what he wanted. A large brown, manila envelope lay on the top of one of the desks, with BARTLETT printed on it in capital letters.

"This is it," he said excitedly, beginning to open it to see if everything was there.

"Quickly!" the guerilla said. "There's no time for that now. We must go."

They hurried out into the hallway and began to make for the back yard, where the others were waiting. Suddenly a cupboard door opened just in front of them and Dirk Behrmann stepped out, holding a pistol in his hand.

He had left his hideout thinking that all the guerillas had gone from the building, and he was just as surprised at their sudden meeting as Tony and the guerilla leader. Tony instinctively dived at him, but Behrmann reacted like lightning. He swung around, squeezing the trigger of his pistol twice as he did so. The first bullet ripped into the guerilla leader's left arm. The second, which was fired an instant after Tony's weight hurtled into the man, went wild. Tony grabbed frantically for Behrmann's gun hand and held his wrist with both hands.

For several moments, all of the pains in Tony's wracked body were gone as he rolled over and over on the ground, desperately struggling to avoid the pistol being pointed at him. For a brief second, Behrmann's skull-like face was within inches of Tony's and a picture of Ingrid's broken body lying on that rain-swept street flashed before his eyes. With a terrible scream of anger and despair, using all his strength, Tony turned Behrmann's wrist backwards so that he was forced to drop the gun. Tony grabbed it, leapt back away from the man, and pointed the pistol at him.

A burst of automatic fire from beside him cut across Behrmann's chest, killing him instantly. Tony turned and, for a moment, felt confusion. At first it was anger and disappointment at having revenge denied him—then a feeling of thankfulness that the opportunity had been snatched from him.

"Come . . . we must go," the guerilla said.

When Captain Serensky had suddenly changed the course of the cruiser *Voroshilov* and her destroyer escorts to head west-south-west, on a line that would intercept the *South Cape Aurora* inside South African waters, Commander Joseph Reilly, watching on the radar screens aboard the *Claude V. Rickets,* could not believe his eyes.

"They're going into territorial waters! They can't do that," he said. He pulled a pack of White Owl cigars from his pocket, clamped on the plastic mouthpiece between his teeth, and lit the cigar. "Jesus Christ!"

He relayed an urgent message to the Second Fleet's South Atlantic Task Force commander, Admiral Stone, on board the aircraft carrier *Dwight D. Eisenhower* in the South Atlantic. Admiral Stone instructed the *Claude V. Rickets* to hold for several minutes while urgent communications were put in train between the carrier *Eisenhower* and the Pentagon.

The President was informed. Already American forces throughout the world, the Strategic Air Command, a thousand ICBM silos across the continental United States, and forty-one Polaris and Poseidon missile-firing submarines cruising beneath the seas at various positions around the globe had been on full alert for more than seventy-two hours as a result of the threatened American naval blockade of the Russian arms ships. The confrontation over the *South Cape Aurora* was a new development, but for the defence chiefs in the Pentagon, it was nothing to what they had just been through with the *Taseyeva,* the *Berdyansk,* and the three freighters in the Mozambique Channel.

The message was relayed back to Commander Reilly that the *Claude V. Rickets* was also to proceed into South African waters and that Russian interference with the *South Cape Aurora* was to be prevented at all costs. At the same time, however, the South African vessel was not to be allowed to proceed.

"What the hell is so goddam important about this goddam *South Cape Aurora* . . ." Commander Reilly shouted, chomping on his cigar, as he gave the order to change course, ". . . that it's got the goddam Russian Navy and the U.S. Navy violating territorial waters and creating an international incident?"

For the past month, Joseph Reilly had been trying to give up smoking. He was thirty-eight and for almost twenty of those thirty-eight years he had smoked too much. He had not had a cigar now for two weeks, but this morning, during the run up the coast, as they were heading straight for the three Russian ships, he had stepped back into his cabin and pulled the packet from one of his drawers. He felt some tension rising. He wondered if this could be anything like the Baltic incident. Joseph Reilly had earned quite a reputation in the U.S. Navy as a result of the Baltic incident, as well as the nick-name "The Iron Man."

He was the only American naval officer in history to have achieved the singular distinction of sinking a Soviet naval vessel in peacetime. It had all been quite simple, really. They had been on NATO manoeuvres with elements of the British fleet and the German Navy in the Baltic, back in 1979, and the Russians were hassling them all the way. They had submarines and frigates and one or two cruisers which shadowed every move the NATO ships made, sometimes putting themselves on a collision course with the American ships.

Joseph Reilly had been commander of the guided missile destroyer *Lynde McCormack* at the time, a Charles F. Adams-class destroyer like his present ship. A Russian submarine, running on the surface, was heading straight across Reilly's path. The submarine could have changed course, but it held on—playing chicken.

"Fuck 'em," Reilly had said on the bridge, chewing the plastic tip of his cigar to shreds. "Hold course!"

The *Lynde McCormack* had ploughed into the rear section of the submarine, almost cutting it in two. It sank with the loss of seven lives, and the American taxpayers had a $2.5 million bill to foot for the repair of the *Lynde McCormack*. Of course there was an enquiry, but it was concluded that the Russian submarine had been at fault, and Commander Reilly was cleared of any blame.

The incident may have dubbed him "The Iron Man," but it had shot his nerves to hell.

Captain Serensky acted, at first, as if the American ship approaching at high speed did not exist. He had his orders and he acted on them as rapidly as he could. He steamed at full speed for the *South Cape Aurora*. After several minutes, he ordered one of the destroyer escorts, the *Ognevoy,* to change course and to stick with the *Claude V. Rickets,* but that she should only stay close to the American destroyer for surveillance and harassment purposes. In the meantime, the *Marshal Voroshilov* began operating her powerful radio-jamming equipment, with the intention of stopping any radio transmissions from the *Aurora* asking for assistance.

Captain Coetzee had, for some time, been aware of the four warships nearby—three Russian and one American—although he had not known their identity. He had been convinced they were naval vessels by the high speed they had all exhibited across his radar screens, but he had taken no action, thinking that they could have been South African naval ships. The thought did cross his mind that they were foreign warships, but he felt relatively secure in the knowledge that he was well within the twelve-mile limit of South African territorial waters, which they would not violate.

But when he saw the two blips of the *Marshal Voroshilov* and the *Szerzhanny* suddenly change to a course that would intercept him, he gave orders for a radio signal to be sent to the South African Defence Command at Silvermine, on the Cape Peninsula, advising them of the developments. The radio operator informed Captain Coetzee, only minutes later, that there was jamming on every frequency he tried.

Captain Serensky did not hesitate. His destroyer escort was two miles ahead of the big cruiser as they closed on the South African ship. He ordered the *Szerzhanny* to fire a shot across the bows of the *Aurora* and to signal her to heave to.

On board the *Aurora* urgent consultations now took place between the captain and the twelve men charged with the security of the cargo. The men were all armed, including Ernst Dingemans, who had never fired a pistol in his life, and the consensus seemed to be that they should fire on any party that attempted to board the ship. Although there was no indication yet of what the Russians intended to do, it was clear that they meant business. They might even sink the ship.

There were two amongst the twelve guardians of the cargo who considered that it would be better to have the ship sunk, or to scuttle her themselves, rather than let her fall into other hands; but the majority decided to see how things developed.

The *Marshal Voroshilov*, which was now drawing up about a mile off the *Aurora's* port bow, began sending a series of messages by Aldis lamp, and semaphore, instructing the *Aurora* to change her course to due east.

Captain Serensky's instructions from Moscow had been to escort the *Aurora* to the Mozambique capital of Maputo, some four hundred miles up the coast to the north. But first he wanted to get the *Aurora* out of her own territorial waters.

On board the South African freighter there was an air of defiance amongst the twelve passengers, but the crew were dumbfounded. They had no idea what was happening.

Then suddenly the U.S.S. *Claude V. Rickets* appeared on the horizon, barrelling in from the south-west at close to forty knots, accompanied by the Russian destroyer escort, *Ognevoy.*

Captain Serensky was now forced to divert his attention from the *Aurora* to the American destroyer and Commander Reilly who, having attempted radio communication and finding it jammed, now also moved in close to the three ships to begin communicating by semaphore. He informed the Russian ships that they should leave the area, but at the same time ordered the *Aurora* to proceed no further.

Anyone viewing the scene from the shore at Southport or Sunwich or Umtentweni, the same beaches at which Tony Bartlett had holidayed some two years previously, would hardly have believed their eyes: a South African freighter drifting, almost at a standstill, about three or four miles offshore, with a Soviet cruiser, two destroyer

354

escorts, and an American guided missile destroyer all manoeuvring around her like bees around honey.

The Russian captain, of course, took no notice of what Commander Reilly had said and proceeded again simply to order the *Aurora* to change course and head east. Nobody moved. It was 6.30 in the morning. The crew of the *Claude V. Rickets* was on full alert and the vessel's "harpoon" surface-to-surface missiles were armed and ready—but then, so were those of the Russian ships.

Commander Reilly and the *Claude V. Rickets* were, in effect, out on a limb, because there was no other American warship within hundreds of miles. The ships of the Indian Ocean Task Force, led by the nuclear-powered aircraft carrier *Carl Vinson* (which was on her first operational mission, having been launched only two months previously), were 1,200 miles away in the Mozambique Channel escorting the three Soviet freighter-loads of arms away from Maputo. They had to travel with them as it was believed the Soviet vessels would attempt to land their cargoes at Dar es Salaam.

When the first news of the developments south of Durban had reached the Chief of Naval Operations in Washington, he ordered the Indian Ocean Task Force commander to send four ships to the aid of the *Claude V. Rickets*.

The missile cruiser *Bainbridge* and three destroyers were now heading south at full speed, but it would be well over twenty-four hours before they could reach the *Claude V. Rickets*.

Captain Serensky was also in constant communication with Moscow, and it was clear that the confrontation off the coast of Natal could very easily escalate. Moscow was already fuming at having been forced to back down as a result of the arms shipment blockade by the Americans, and there were senior members of the Soviet Navy and the Defence Command who advocated a tougher stand against the United States—no backing down.

The American President had already spoken on the Moscow hotline, on three occasions, to the Soviet President and Communist Party chief, Brezhnev, on the blockade issue. Now it was possible that an American destroyer and three Soviet warships could start trying to shoot each other up to force the issue and bring everything tumbling down around them. While Washington and Moscow tried to sort it all out, the five ships wallowed around in the heaving swell off the south coast of Natal for almost four hours.

The South African defence forces, which had learnt of the situation of their own accord within minutes of the Russian and American ships stopping the *Aurora,* had sent a flight of Mirage jets swooping low over the five vessels and issued a warning to the intruders to clear out. With the arrival of the jets, there was no longer any need for radio jamming, so the *Marshal Voroshilov* had stopped it, leaving the air-waves clear for communication.

The South African Air Force pilots, who had no idea why the *South Cape Aurora* had been stopped by the American and Russian ships, were at a loss over what to do when both the Russians and the Americans refused to cooperate. Should they attempt to blast all of the foreign vessels out of the water? No! was the reply they received from the defence command headquarters buried deep in the rock at Silvermine. The various South African service chiefs who were presented with this super-power confrontation within South African waters at about 7.00 AM on the morning of March 24 were also in the dark about why the *South Cape Aurora* was of so much interest. But to them, the question was academic. They were in the midst of trying to hold their country together in the face of disaster. The Mirages were desperately needed in the north for use against the revolutionary forces now advancing on the big port complex at Richards Bay, just over one hundred miles from Durban.

They ordered the Mirages to return to base, but at the same time to pass on instructions to the *South Cape Aurora* to return to Durban. The SAS *President Pretorius,* one of the two South African Navy frigates in East London, some 250 miles to the south, was ordered to proceed north and to intercept the *South Cape Aurora,* if she did not comply.

Four hours and ten minutes were spent attempting to resolve the stalemate. But eventually, with the prospect of being boarded by the South African Navy looming in the next few hours if they stayed where they were, Captain Coetzee decided to return to Durban. Those of the group who had earlier favoured scuttling the

356

ship now spoke again, but Ernst Dingemans reasoned that, if things were still under control in Durban, they could try another way.

At 10.40 AM the *South Cape Aurora* got under way again and began heading back up the coast of Natal for Durban. The cruiser *Voroshilov,* her destroyer escorts, and the U.S.S. *Claude V. Rickets* all cruised along behind her, but some five or six miles to the east, sitting on the imaginary line marking the difference between international and South African waters.

At 3.30 in the afternoon the *South Cape Aurora* re-entered Durban Harbour. She did not, however, return to her previous berth at Pier One, but dropped anchor in the middle of the harbour.

At 4.15—roughly the same time that Colonel Starcke learnt, with horror and disbelief, of the ship's return—the same three frogmen who had failed in their efforts to mine the ship during the previous night re-entered the waters of Durban harbour from beneath the disused wharf in the coal-loading facility and began swimming again towards the *Aurora.*

Their task was far more difficult on this occasion, as it was daylight and they could not surface to get their bearings. But when it had been learnt by the revolutionary leaders, with similar disbelief, that the ship was returning, the leader of the group originally charged with mining the ship decided that the risk must be taken now; they could not wait for dark.

It was a complex navigational feat for the three frogmen to get to the ship. She was slightly closer to them, but they would have to swim much deeper in the harbour waters to avoid detection and would have to do the whole trip by compass bearing, making allowance for tidal currents in the middle of the route they had mapped out. As it happened, they were off-target and one of the group had to surface, next to a big iron buoy, to get their bearings again. But the buoy was only one hundred yards from the *Aurora,* and by five o'clock they had reached the vessel's hull and planted a string of their six limpet mines around the bottom immediately beneath the engine room. At 6.00 PM, by which time they had returned to their concealed position beneath the old wharf, the charges detonated, ripping huge holes in the *Aurora* amidships.

The ship sank within fifteen minutes, with a loss of six lives—

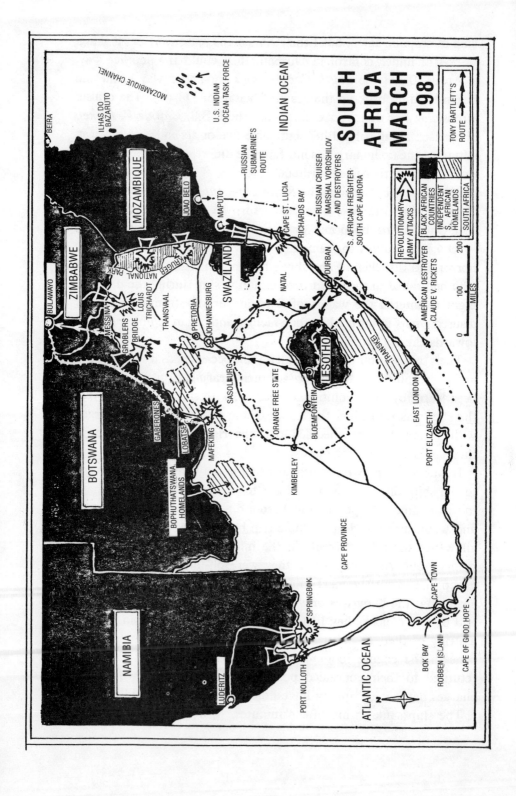

SOUTH AFRICA MARCH 1981

TONY BARTLETT'S ROUTE

REVOLUTIONARY ARMY ATTACKS

BLACK AFRICAN COUNTRIES

INDEPENDENT S. AFRICAN HOMELANDS

SOUTH AFRICA

MILES
0   100   200

INDIAN OCEAN

ATLANTIC OCEAN

MOZAMBIQUE CHANNEL

MOZAMBIQUE

ZIMBABWE

BOTSWANA

NAMIBIA

SWAZILAND

LESOTHO

TRANSKEI

NATAL

TRANSVAAL

ORANGE FREE STATE

CAPE PROVINCE

BOPHUTHATSWANA HOMELANDS

BEIRA

ILHAS DO BAZARUTO

JOAO BELO

MAPUTO

CAPE ST. LUCIA

RICHARDS BAY

DURBAN

EAST LONDON

PORT ELIZABETH

CAPE TOWN

CAPE OF GOOD HOPE

ROBBEN ISLAND

BOK BAY

PORT NOLLOTH

SPRINGBOK

LUDERITZ

KIMBERLEY

BLOEMFONTEIN

SASOLBURG

JOHANNESBURG

PRETORIA

MAFEKING

LOBATSE

GABERONES

BULAWAYO

MESSINA

GROBLERS BRIDGE

LOUIS TRICHARDT

KRUGER NATIONAL PARK

U.S. INDIAN OCEAN TASK FORCE

RUSSIAN SUBMARINE'S ROUTE

RUSSIAN CRUISER MARSHAL VOROSHILOV AND DESTROYERS

S. AFRICAN FREIGHTER SOUTH CAPE AURORA

AMERICAN DESTROYER CLAUDE V. RICKETS

N

four of the crew and two of the twelve guardians, who in the panic and confusion were trapped by raging waters pouring into the sinking vessel.

Ernst Dingemans, who was on the bridge at the time of the explosions, had run frantically to his cabin to try to retrieve some of the fortune in cut and uncut diamonds he had planned to spirit away from South Africa. Unfortunately, as he had placed them in different, secure places about the cabin, they took some time to retrieve.

His wife and family, who were waiting on the Italian Riviera, never knew what happened to Ernst Dingemans, who became one of the six casualties of the *South Cape Aurora* when she sank.

The stricken freighter, her back broken, had settled slowly, with her immense treasure intact, into the mud and silt of Durban Harbour, coming to rest, in sixty-five feet of water, at exactly 6.16 on the evening of March 24.

18

Escape

Even while the *South Cape Aurora* was still in her final death throes, Tony Bartlett was shown into an underground room, beneath a house in the African township near Umlazi on the southern outskirts of the Durban metropolitan area. He had been taken there with the three other prisoners who had been released from the old house at the same time as he had. Where Colonel Starcke was taken, or what happened to him, Tony had no idea. He never saw or heard of him again.

The three black men who had been released with him, Tony discovered, were all revolutionaries, but in different categories. The younger man was evidently an important member of the APRA, a South African black who had been captured by security forces during a guerilla raid from across the Mozambique border into northern Natal. One of the older men was a former leader of the banned Pan African Congress in the Durban area, who had been living in exile in Zambia for many years, but who had recently returned undetected to South Africa. The third man was a member of the also-outlawed African National Congress, who had been living under a banning order which had kept him under virtual house arrest for the past five years, in Pietermaritzburg. During the past few months, he had broken the rules applied to him under the order that prohibited him from associating with certain people, from meeting with more than two people, or from participating in any meetings of an even remotely political nature. He had naturally attempted to be discreet in these violations of the law, but he was discovered and had been undergoing questioning regarding the other people with whom he had been in contact.

There had been four more black people in the house when the raid was planned and the guerillas had been surprised to find that they were not there. They could only now be presumed to be dead. They were also surprised to find a white man a prisoner in the house; some of the guerillas, had the circumstances of Tony's rescue and his struggle with Behrmann been any different, would have been suspicious of him. In response to early questioning, however, Tony had mentioned Johnathan Kapepwe's name, which resulted in further surprise on the part of the guerillas.

Kapepwe had come to Durban secretly within the last twenty-four hours and had been in charge of the hastily organised scheme to launch the frogman attack on the *South Cape Aurora*. He had not been one of the swimmers, but the basic plan had been his. At two o'clock that morning, he had been faced with the complete failure of the project and months of wasted effort. The ship and the gold had gone. Now, in the evening of the same day, the situation had been totally reversed. If the gold was still on board the devastated *Aurora*, and there was no reason to believe that it wasn't, then they were close to success. They would make it impossible for any salvage operations to begin until after the war had been won.

When Kapepwe had been informed that there was a white man called Bartlett at the southern Durban headquarters of the APRA, who claimed to know him, he was undecided about what he should do. He didn't particularly want to see Bartlett. The Australian had stuck his nose in where it didn't belong in Tanzania, and almost ruined the attack on the American Consulate residence when he recognised Kapepwe. True, he had passed on the information about the mines and the *Aurora*, which had been vitally important. The mines weren't saved yet, but it seemed, at this moment, as if the gold had been. Now, the APRA people were not sure what to do with Tony Bartlett. Kapepwe decided that he would talk to him.

Kapepwe's beard was growing again, but it looked ragged and untidy when he came through the doorway into the underground room of the house near Umlazi.

Tony was sitting in a chair. His face was badly bruised and had several plasters stuck on it where the skin had been broken. He had two black eyes. His whole body ached and he had to lean forward in order to keep the back of the chair from touching the three open slash-wounds across his back. The wounds had been treated with antiseptic, as well as anaesthetic creams, so that he now felt considerably better than when he had been released from the clutches of Bruno and Colonel Starcke; but it was still raw and painful.

"You seem to have got yourself into a spot of trouble," Kapepwe said.

"Yes. I'm developing a penchant for it," Tony replied cautiously. He felt he wasn't out of the woods yet and he didn't really know what to expect from Kapepwe. Their last two meetings had hardly been friendly.

"They tell me you were whipped," Kapepwe smiled. "Well, at least we have one thing in common."

Tony remained silent.

"Why did you become so involved?" Kapepwe said.

Tony looked at him in surprise, as if the answer was self-evident. "Because of the story, of course! That's all. It was a good story."

For a moment Kapepwe smiled patronisingly. "Then why did you pass on the information to us about the mines and the *South Cape Aurora?* You needn't have done that."

"I know. And I'm still not sure why," Tony said, "because I certainly don't believe in your methods. I find them abhorrent." Kapepwe's face hardened, but Tony went on, "You have made yourself into a brutal killer . . . I don't even believe in your political ideology."

Tony suddenly felt the need to vocalise the motives behind his actions; to sort them out for himself, as much as for anyone else.

"But then," Tony continued, "I don't accept the ideology under which this country has been run up until now, either. That is probably the only area where the two of us might find agreement. I believe there has been oppression of the most sinister kind. But what I am afraid of now, is that you and your revolutionary army will just replace one form of oppression with another; a white dictatorship with a black one. All I hope is that somewhere within your

362

organisation there are enough moderate voices, with enough influence, to give the people of this country a chance to experience real freedom, instead of mock freedom."

"Once the white government is gone, we will be free," Kapepwe said.

"That's just it." Tony looked up at him. "You know as well as I do, that that's not true. It doesn't mean a thing to be free of white rule, so as to be ruled by someone who might have the right colour skin, but who is just as bad—or worse—than the whites."

"It will not be like that," Kapepwe said hotly. There was something about this Bartlett which always seemed to irritate him. "It will be a true dictatorship of the proletariat."

"Come on now," Tony said facetiously. "Do you really believe that in any of the Communist countries around the world, there is any such thing as a true dictatorship of the proletariat? A dictatorship of the privileged intellectual hierarchy is more like it. Where is there a dictatorship of the proletariat?"

"China!"

"China, perhaps. Certainly more than anywhere else," Tony agreed. "But it is still the hierarchy that has struggled to the top which makes the decisions, not the people. Is there any way for them to kick out their leaders if they don't like them? No. So what power lies with the proletariat? None. In China, maybe—but nowhere else."

Kapepwe restrained himself. "I see no reason why I should even discuss it with you, Bartlett. It is no longer a matter of debate. It is almost an accomplished fact. Only time will tell."

"Where is Carl Verhoef now?" Tony asked, taking Kapepwe by surprise.

There was an uncomfortable pause. Kapepwe looked back at Tony in silence for a few seconds, deciding whether to answer the question or not. His mouth seemed firmly set.

"He's dead."

Tony said nothing for a moment or two and then, turning his head slightly to one side, smiled and nodded cynically. "Of course," he said. "Why should I have expected anything else from a bunch of killers like you?"

"He was worse than a killer," Kapepwe whispered vehemently.

363

"Is that the sort of thing that the rest of the whites in this country can look forward to in this new order of yours?" Tony said.

"Of course not. People will be taken at face value and judged on their merits, not by the colour of their skin. Those who wish to remain and work within the framework of a revolutionary society can do so. Those who do not, can leave. Simple."

"If only it were as simple as that." Tony smiled. "In fact, the handling of whites in South Africa—Azania, if you like—will be the most crucial test of your revolution, because whether you like it or not, all of the industrial, technological, and managerial expertise lies with the whites and you will need to make use of it, unless you just want to throw your economy down the drain."

"We will not be beholden to whites any more! We will not be blackmailed. We can get the expertise from elsewhere, if necessary."

Tony shrugged. "I'm not suggesting that you're over a barrel. I'm just saying that, if it were possible to have cooperation, instead of friction and conflict, you could achieve wonders. After all, you are all South Africans—sorry, Azanians—whether you're black or white."

"Some of them . . . us . . . are," Kapepwe said slowly. "Some . . . but not many."

"Tell me," Tony said. "The plane? What about the passengers on the plane at Mbeya, what happened to them? And the gold? . . . And the plane itself?"

Kapepwe stretched his arms into the air and then clasped them behind his head in an almost detached air. "Why do you ask?" he said. "Surely it is of no interest now?"

"It is," Tony said, "to me."

Kapepwe paused for a few moments and then said, "The gold is safe with us."

"It was unloaded in Mbeya?"

Another pause. Then, "Yes."

"And carried on the train?"

"Yes."

"And taken off at that siding in the middle of the night?"

"Yes."

"And the passengers?"

"Four of them are still hostages. They will be released at the appropriate time . . . if certain conditions are fulfilled."

"And the other two?"

"They met with unfortunate accidents."

"Like Verhoef," Tony said sarcastically.

"Yes," Kapepwe replied without emotion.

"And the plane?"

"It also had an unfortunate accident. It was intended to be ransomed, but the pilot, the Tanzanian pilot, was inexperienced. It crashed as he was trying to land on a rough strip in southern Tanzania. There were only four people on board. Nobody got out of it. So you see . . ."

There was a knock on the door and the guerilla leader who had rescued Tony from the old house came in to speak a few words to Kapepwe. His left arm, where Behrmann's bullet had caught him, was wrapped in a blood-stained bandage. After a brief conversation with Kapepwe, which Tony was unable to hear, he left. Kapepwe sat down in a battered old lounge chair in one corner of the room.

"You are a strange person," he said to Tony. "Politically, I regard you as a wishy-washy, ineffectual liberal. I met them by the hundreds in London and despised them. But there's something about you that I like. You outmanoeuvred us in Tanzania on the train, you gave us the information about the mines and the *South Cape Aurora,* you saved those two boys in Durban . . . and this afternoon you almost certainly saved Simon Sekoto's life. Because of this, we are going to get you out of the country. That is . . . unless you want to stay any longer?"

"No thank you very much," Tony said.

"Right," Kapepwe went on. "Preparations are being made now to take you across the mountains into Lesotho. It will be a dangerous journey—roughly 180 miles from here to the frontier—over some very difficult roads. The only thing in your favour is that we now control most of the territory between here and the Drakensberg. But there are still several towns and areas where there could be trouble."

Tony was surprised. He had not been expecting any offers from

365

Kapepwe at all. Although he was free from the clutches of BOSS, he still had the feeling that he was some sort of prisoner and that he would have to go along with whatever happened to him. But now, suddenly, there was the real possibility of his getting out—getting away from it all.

"Are you coming?" he asked Kapepwe.

"No, but I will send three men with you. All of whom I trust. They will get you through to the border safely."

"And then?"

"You are on your own."

"How will we get there?"

"By car."

"When?"

"You will leave tonight. Simon is arranging it all. He will let you know. Now . . ." Kapepwe stood up. "I am going." He held out his hand to Tony. Tony hesitated, then took it. "There is a whole world between us," Kapepwe said, "and I believe that you can never really understand what has driven us to this . . . because you are white. But at least you try." He turned to walk to the door. "Goodbye."

"Wait," Tony said, "I . . . I wanted to ask you . . . Marta Van Sisseren, is she. . . ?"

"She is dead. She was a double agent. She helped us up to a point. But she turned against us. She was Russian, not Dutch, and there were Russian ships waiting for the *South Cape Aurora,* when it left Durban, because of her."

"And what happened to the *Aurora?*"

Kapepwe told Tony of the sinking and of the American and Russian ships off the coast of Natal that morning. The news had been passed on to the revolutionary headquarters via the short-wave radio links the APRA operated throughout Natal, by two separate rebel groups on the south coast which had witnessed the extraordinary developments just offshore.

"The Americans too?" Tony said. "How did they know?"

"Your guess is as good as mine," Kapepwe said. Then, turning again for the door, he left.

At 9.00 PM the guerilla leader, Simon Sekoto, entered the room

366

again with three other men. He handed a khaki shirt and a heavy blue jacket to Tony. The jacket was similar to an American Navy pea-jacket.

"You will need this. It is cold in the mountains of Lesotho." He turned. "These men will go with you. This is Louis Soyinka. He released you this morning . . . and these are two of Johnathan Kapepwe's men, Joseph Mfulu and Zak Molako."

The names meant nothing to Tony, but he instantly recognized Zak as one of the two men who had entered the dining room of the American Consulate residence during the reception. He had not seen Joseph during the proceedings, because he had stayed on the terrace the whole time. Tony was swept with a sudden fealing of fear. Did either of them realise that it was he who had caused the death of the other terrorist that night, by tripping him as he was running from the room? He had no way of knowing. He couldn't be sure if Zak Molako recognised him, or if either of them even knew that he had been there. They gave no indication. They just nodded silently and unsmilingly at Tony as they were introduced. Tony nodded back.

"You will have to walk four or five miles to reach the vehicle, which is waiting near the same road you travelled on the other day to Umbumbulu. We cannot travel on the coast road through Isipingo to get there, but you can go through the bush and across the river to reach it. Once you reach the vehicle, you should be safe for some time, because most of the Umbumbulu road is in our control."

Tony said goodbye and was taken out of the house, down a long, dirt road, past rows of tin shanty-houses, and into some dense bush that bordered on the edge of the township. They followed a winding path, but soon emerged into rolling open country for a while. It was full of small holdings and farmlands and on several occasions, dogs barked as they climbed over low fences to continue on their way.

Patches of bright moonlight would suddenly illuminate the landscape with an eerie grey light, but for most of their journey, clouds obscured the moon and they travelled in almost total darkness. The local man, Louis Soyinka, led the way. Tony followed, and

Zak and Joseph came up behind. All of them, except Tony, were armed with automatic rifles and Tony could not avoid the tingling sensation that they might suddenly turn on him and kill him, but there was no such move made against him. The worst thing he had to contend with was exhaustion. He had no broken bones as a result of his incarceration with Bruno and Colonel Starcke, nor any sprains. But he was badly bruised in many parts of his body and he felt an immense weariness as they trudged over the difficult tracks, sometimes slipping and stumbling over hidden obstacles.

After they had crossed the Umbogintwini River, the track began to climb and, although it was only a relatively easy slope, it was still uphill. Tony found the going tough. He asked if they could rest for a while and Louis Soyinka called a halt, but only for two minutes, while Tony got his breath.

A little more than an hour and a half after they had left the house, they reached the roadway. They were about a half a mile below the arranged rendezvous position, but quickly covered the distance along the deserted road, to find the car and two other men waiting in the bushes some twenty yards from the road itself. There was a whispered conversation in Zulu between Louis Soyinka and the two men, and then Tony, Zak, and Joseph were told to get into the car, which Tony saw, to his surprise, was an almost brand-new Range Rover.

The two men who had brought the car there and waited now disappeared into the bush. They had not even said hello or goodbye to Tony and the other two . . . they just vanished like shadows.

Louis Soyinka drove, while Tony sat in the front seat with him. Zak sat in the back seat and Joseph positioned himself in the rear compartment, so that he could more easily shoot from the rear window, if that became necessary.

During the three and a half hours they drove that night, they were stopped by terrorist roadblocks on four occasions, but each time Louis prevented the car from being summarily shot up by flicking the car lights in a sort of visual password signal, the moment he saw a roadblock in front of him.

At each stop, Tony was ordered to lie low until the explanations were made. The car would remain still, while powerful spotlights played over it for a few moments. Louis would shout something in Zulu, explaining that they were carrying a white man in the car. There would be more shouting and Louis would tell Tony to sit up so that he could be seen. On each occasion Tony felt he would get a bullet as he sat up. After he was sitting upright, a group of terrorists, sometimes half a dozen, would advance on the car slowly from the darkness of the roadside, their guns at the ready. More talking while Tony was inspected and Louis, Zak, and Joseph's credentials verified. Then they would be permitted to proceed.

At three of the four stops, the terrorists had had prior knowledge that the car would be coming, but went through the process of checking everything, just to be sure. On the fourth, there was nearly disaster, when one of the members of the terrorist group wanted to haul Tony out of the car and shoot him on the spot. The only good white man was a dead one, he had insisted in a rage. But he had been quietened down and, once again, the car had been allowed to pass.

They had been travelling along rough, unsealed back roads, passing occasionally through little towns like Eston and Rosebank. The first roadblock had been at the town of Richmond, which was now completely black, Soyinka told Tony. All of the five hundred or so whites who had lived there had fled to Durban or Pietermaritzburg—except for seventeen, who had been killed in a bloody clash when the government's partitioning edict had first been announced.

From Richmond, they travelled on the Eastwolds road through some of the most stunningly beautiful and lush countryside in South Africa, down into the valley of the Umkomaas River and the huge sandstone cliffs of Hela Hela. In the darkness, however, it was all lost.

By shortly after two in the morning, they had reached Underberg. Despite the tension of the trip and the four roadblocks, Tony had slipped into a shallow sleep during the past three-quarters of an hour, his head alternately knocking against the side window, sagging onto his chest, or snapping up as some movement of the car jerked him awake.

Just before they entered Underberg, they drove off the road to a small farmhouse. Underberg was apparently in the hands of the rebels, but there were still at least fifty whites in the town. No police, or white officials, just residents and farmers who had decided to stay on and take their chances. The blacks in the town had not attacked or abused them, largely because a reasonable relationship on a friendly basis had existed between many blacks and whites in the Underberg area for some time and the whites that stayed were those who had nothing to fear from blacks on the grounds of past discrimination.

"We will stay here tonight," Louis said, as they drove up to the farmhouse. "In the morning we shall climb to the Sani Pass, but I do not want to drive that road at night."

A group of blacks met them as they drove up. The Range Rover was put into a small barn and, after cups of tea prepared by a large black woman, Tony and the others found places in the hay in which to sleep.

When Tony was awoken, just before dawn, the air was crisp and cold. He could easily have slept for many hours more and he had to be shaken awake by Louis Soyinka. They had had only three hours sleep and Tony felt he desperately needed more. But slowly he came to his senses. He felt grubby and cold. The big woman came from the farmhouse again with tea in large, metal mugs and hot mealies, burnt brown on some of the kernels over a charcoal fire. Tony ate hungrily and drank the strong, dark tea as if it was the best he had ever tasted. As soon as they had finished eating, Louis Soyinka ordered everyone into the car and they set off again.

Underberg appeared deserted as they drove through the town, just after first light. It brought a pang of nostalgia to Tony. It had been near Underberg that he and Carol and Michael had spent several days during their holiday in Natal two years ago.

They had stayed on the farm of Bruce and Barbara Gill, near Bushman's Nek, about fifteen miles west of the town. Bruce and Barbara had built the gleaming white farmhouse, which sat at the foot of the massive wall of the Drakensberg Mountains, with their own hands. They used no native labour, except when a neighbouring black farmer helped them to thatch the roof. The walls, which

370

were made of sun-hardened mud, reinforced with saplings and chicken-wire, then white-washed, they made themselves, over a period of two years, during most of which time they had lived in a tiny rondavel.

The house had earthen floors made of a mixture of cow-dung and ox-blood, which compacted into a solid mass, so hard it could be polished. They had a few animals and grew enough crops to subsist on, but their main activities revolved around sculpting and potting. Bruce was the sculptor and Barbara potted in a kiln which she had made herself. They had spent several years living in England and in Europe, but had returned to South Africa some four years prior to Tony's visit, to live permanently in the Underberg region and to build their farm.

"We were born here and we love the country," Bruce had said. "We love the people too. It's only the terrible policies of a bigoted white government that we hate."

Bruce and Barbara Gill had insisted to Tony that they were typical of many thousands of whites in South Africa whose attitudes and feelings had been swamped by the overall effect of the government's policies.

"We tried to live away from the place, because we couldn't accept the things that were happening, but then we just got too homesick and decided to come back and live within the system, but do what we could to change it. There was precious little, of course, that we could do, but within our own little environment, we try to set an example to both the whites and blacks around us."

Tony wondered if Bruce and Barbara were still on their farm, only a few miles away, and if they were, how they were being affected by all this mess. He felt frustrated at being so near and yet unable to see them.

The car sped on through green fields and rolling hills and, after only three miles, passed through the small rural centre of Himeville. Half a dozen early-rising black people turned and stared as the Range Rover roared past, but Tony saw no whites. Two miles further on, Louis made a turn to the left and began driving westwards into the foothills of the Umkomazana Valley. They were at the start of the twenty-three-mile climb to the border post at the Sani

Pass, where Tony would hopefully be able to cross into Lesotho.

He gazed out of the window of the car at the breathtakingly beautiful scenery; a wild jumble of giant boulders, scores of streams, cascades, and waterfalls, and rich vegetation, from which towering sandstone cliffs sprang on all sides. The tops of the cliffs in the gorge were tinged yellow and orange by the first rays of the rising sun, but down on the road, where the car was winding its way upwards, there was still deep shade and it was cold. No-one in the car said anything. They all occupied the same positions as on the previous night and gazed silently out of the windows.

Tony attempted to make conversation.

"The other people you took from the old house, yesterday, were they important people?" he asked Louis Soyinka.

"Yes. But there were others . . . others who we missed. We were too late. Also the director of the asylum escaped us."

"Asylum?"

"Yes. It was supposed to be a mental asylum, but we have known for some time that it was being used by BOSS."

"Did you know Johnathan Kapepwe before this?"

"Oh yes. He is well known within our movement. It was he who established our communications network around the country, several years ago. He is quite famous. He is very important."

Joseph and Zak said nothing. Occasionally they would speak to each other or to Louis in Zulu, but apart from a few brief words, they remained silent.

Seven or eight miles into the valley, they approached the Sani Pass Hotel and Soyinka muttered a few words to the other two, who wound down the windows and checked their guns. He explained to Tony that there had been trouble at the hotel during the past few days; a clash between whites and blacks Now, as they drove up to and past the big hotel, there was no sign of life. There may have been people inside, but the car drove quickly past and on up into the gorge, slowly climbing the great Drakensberg wall.

Tony caught a glimpse of snow on the slopes above him. It was unusual for there to be snow so early and it would probably disappear within a few days, but in the meantime, it could make the going more difficult near the top of the pass.

372

The towering tip of Hodgson's Peak came into view for a few moments as the Range Rover wound its way upwards over the steadily worsening road. The snow on the 10,700-foot peak shone brilliantly in the morning sun. Then, within minutes, Tony saw to the north the snow-capped top of Thabana Ntlenyana, at 11,500 feet the highest point in Southern Africa. Tony was not aware of these details at the time, and it is doubtful whether the statistics would have made any impression on him, but he was, without question, impressed by the stark and rugged beauty of the two giant peaks between which the Sani Pass road climbed ever more tortuously.

The physical beauty of the country as a whole was something Tony felt he would never forget. But if he got out of this in one piece, he thought, it might be some considerable time before he would get a chance to appreciate it again—if he ever could. The beautiful Tsitsikama Forest and Storms River, the grandeur of Table Mountain and the Cape Peninsula, the harsh, dry beauty of the mesa-desert country in the Karoo, the plunging green cliffs of the Blyde River Canyon, Kruger National Park—would all this be lost? No, of course it wouldn't be lost. It had been there for millions of years. It would only be lost to those people who, while perhaps appreciating the country's physical beauty and potential, had sorely abused its human resources.

But what future, he thought, could the country have, gaining freedom in this way? The people who would now control it were murderers, like the three men with whom he was travelling—like Johnathan Kapepwe. But then, so, in many cases, were the people who had controlled it before. The history of the whites' struggle for control of Southern Africa had hardly been bloodless, or one of enlightened democracy. The American Revolution, the French Revolution, the Russian Revolution, the Chinese Revolution—they were all horrible and bloody. Was it the end result that counted? Did the end justify the means? Tony thought he could never support that concept. So what was the answer? Was he really the wishy-washy, ineffectual liberal that Kapepwe had called him? And was it necessary to become a killer to win the sort of freedom and dignity that the black people were supposedly fighting for here?

373

In some cases, perhaps it was. People like Bruno Van Wyk and Colonel Starcke and Dirk Behrmann had to be fought with methods they understood; fighting fire with fire. But the brutalising influence on the individuals involved could linger for the rest of their lives— if they lived—and the racial hatred coming from such violent upheaval might last for generations, souring any attempts at reconciliation.

But then, he thought, soldiers had come out of the blood and terror of World War II, the Korean War, and Vietnam as avowed pacifists—many of them, anyway. Perhaps that could happen here. He remembered Bruce and Barbara Gill saying to him, only two years ago, that despite generations of mistreatment by whites, there was still an immense reservoir of goodwill amongst blacks for white people in South Africa. Tony had found that hard to understand, but maybe it was true . . . maybe. He was sure of one thing: if the country was to come out of the other side of this holocaust, then every scrap of goodwill there was would be needed.

Tony looked at Zak Molako and Joseph Mfulu. Their faces told him nothing. He thought again of that instant when he had stuck out his foot and sent the terrorist sprawling to his death in the consulate residence. That man had been a friend of these men sitting with me now, Tony thought. At least of one of them, anyway. And I killed him, just as surely as if I'd pulled the trigger. But then, he had just killed three people before my eyes . . .

He had started again on the whole mental process, back at square one, wondering, how can killers like this run a country, when suddenly he was jerked sideways as the car slipped on a large rock and slithered towards the edge of the road. There was a drop of at least five hundred feet below them. Louis Soyinka put his foot on the clutch and the brake at the same time. The car stopped moving forwards, but it continued to slowly slide sideways in the mud, towards the chasm.

"Out!" he shouted, and everybody scrambled for the doors. Soyinka could not get out of his door because it was now less than a foot from the edge. He clambered out of Tony's door after him. Within seconds, the four men were out of the vehicle and both Tony and Zak grabbed desperately at the rear bumper, trying to

374

prevent it from slipping further, but the right rear wheel slipped over and the back of the Range Rover tilted downwards.

"Look out!" Soyinka yelled, but the car slid no further. It rested precariously on the edge of an almost vertical slope.

The vehicle was fitted with a metal tow-rope attached to the front, which was operated by a gearing system from the car's engine. They set to work, frantically uncoiling the wire rope from the front, trying to find a rock on the other side of the road sufficiently massive to take the weight of the car as they tried to haul it back towards the centre of the road.

On the first try, the rock to which the cable was attached was pulled out of the ground and the car slipped another six inches sideways to an even more precarious angle; but after more than an hour, they eventually managed to get the vehicle back onto the road and safer ground. Louis Soyinka stayed well clear of the edge for the rest of the drive to the border.

They were now in the last stages of the ascent to the top of the pass at 6,500 feet. The car had been on four-wheel drive since just after they left the Sani Pass Hotel, but the going had been so rough and the track so strewn with boulders that it was impossible to average more than four or five miles an hour. There was now plenty of snow on the slopes surrounding them, but none on the road. It was extremely wet, though, and because of the wrong camber of the road, conditions often threatened to send them sliding to the edge again.

Eventually the road levelled out and, after negotiating a few turns, they came up to the border post between South Africa and Lesotho. There was no-one manning the South African post, which had been forced open and looted. One hundred yards further on, they came to the Lesotho immigration post, from which two men in uniform emerged.

Soyinka spoke rapidly to them in Zulu, but they indicated that they could not speak Zulu, so Joseph spoke to them in Sotho, explaining the details of Tony's position and asking that he be allowed entry. They might just as well have spoken English in the first place, because one of the two officials turned to Tony and said, "Do you have a passport?"

"Yes," he replied, and handed it to the man.

"Come inside." He motioned to the small hut.

"We will go now," Louis Soyinka said.

Tony turned and looked at the three men. Joseph Mfulu, who specialised in killing policemen; Zak Molako, the knife expert; and Louis Soyinka, who had shot Bruno Van Wyk. He was about to hold out his hand, but he raised it in a sort of half-wave. "Thank you . . . I . . ." he began, but the men were already walking away.

"Goodbye," Tony called. "Thank you."

At eleven o'clock on the morning of March 26, Tony clambered down off the back of a truck onto the sidewalk of the main street of Maseru, having come some two hundred miles from the border post at Sani Pass across the roof of Southern Africa. He had waited three hours at the remote border post in the hope of a lift, but not a single vehicle arrived. The officials at the post informed him that no cars had come to the border in either direction for three days. At noon, however, one of the men offered to drive Tony to Mokhotlong, an isolated administrative post some thirty-five miles away in the mountains.

Mokhotlong, which, the official told Tony, meant Place of the Bald-headed Ibis, had long been renowned as one of the loneliest villages in Southern Africa. For many years it could only be reached by horses and pack animals. Now, trucks carrying supplies and trade goods regularly made the journey from the capital, Maseru, to Mokhotlong and other mountain villages. But the horse, Tony noticed before long, was still the most common, and in many ways the most sensible, form of transportation in Lesotho. From the back of the truck on which he negotiated a lift from Mokhotlong for a fee of U.S. $10, he saw dozens of Basotho men on horseback, all of them wrapped in beautifully woven blankets and wearing the traditional cone-shaped straw hats.

Strange, Tony thought, to be suddenly in a country where there is no civil war—and yet this country, Lesotho, is completely surrounded by South Africa.

The anachronism of landlocked Lesotho, created from the former British Protectorate of Basutoland, had long been a thorn in South

376

Africa's side. A politically independent Lesotho was all right with Pretoria, so long as it remained economically dependent on South Africa—which it had until a few years ago. But then, with outside help from several black African states, Lesotho had begun to behave as if it really were independent.

There had never been any guerilla training camps established in Lesotho, as there had been in Mozambique, Zimbabwe, and Botswana, but Lesotho had begun giving refuge and asylum to many terrorists who had fled across the border from South Africa. But most important was its propaganda support for the rebels . . . unofficial support, of course. South Africa had pinpointed many of the clandestine radio stations broadcasting into South Africa in the rugged mountains which completely rimmed the 12,000-square-mile territory. Lesotho denied their existence and there was nothing South Africa could do, unless it went to war with Lesotho, which had so far not happened. That was a definite possibility, though, now that the white government was faced with disaster and had its back against the wall.

Tony wanted to get to Maseru as fast as possible and out from there as soon as he could. How he was going to accomplish it, he had no idea. No ships, because it was landlocked. No road or rail, because that would mean reentering South Africa. Only by air. But how?

On the road between Thaba Tseka and Marakabei Tony's truck-driver went to sleep and the truck almost plunged hundreds of feet into a fast-flowing river in the valley below. But his eyelids fluttered open and he swerved just in time to avoid it. He was sufficiently shaken to stop the vehicle in a cutting, telling Tony he was going to sleep. The other passengers in the front seat, his wife and young son, who had also been asleep when the incident occurred, were only too happy to stop.

Tony almost froze on the back of the truck, where he tried to get some sleep. He was able to huddle under a folded canvas awning, which at least kept out the wind and a light rain that began falling at about two in the morning; but the temperature dropped almost to freezing and he was miserably cold.

At first light the truck was on its way again, but the ninety-mile run into Maseru took almost five hours because of the winding and sometimes dangerous road they had to travel on through the Blue Mountains.

Tony found Maseru, although it was the capital of Lesotho, not much more than a straggling, unattractive village; but he was surprised as they drove into the main street to see a big sign proclaiming, complete with stars and gaudy colours: HOLIDAY INN.

"Here," he shouted to the driver, "let me off here. This will do." Tony thanked the driver, said goodbye to him and his family, and ran across the road towards the hotel, visions of hot baths dancing in front of his eyes.

At the desk he was given a curious stare by the clerk and realised, glancing down at himself and feeling the stubble on his chin, that he must appear a bit of a mess. His clothes were all dirty and rumpled and he hadn't shaved or showered since he'd left the army barracks in Durban, four days ago.

"Sorry," he said with a smile. "Bit of mess. Been travelling."

"That's quite all right, sir," the clerk said. "Single room?"

"Eh? Oh yes. Thank you."

The clerk handed Tony a key and then turned the hotel register around on the desk. "If you'll just fill in the details and sign here . . ."

"Goldman!" Tony suddenly shouted. "Howard Goldman!"

The desk clerk jumped at Tony's outburst.

"This Goldman . . . here," Tony pointed to an entry in the register about four or five lines above his own. "Is he American?"

"Yes. Mr. Howard Goldman. He is in Room 27. But I am sorry, sir, he is not in at the moment. He went out of the hotel at nine o'clock."

"Can you leave a message for him to contact me in my room as soon as he returns?"

"Yes, sir."

Howard Goldman did not return to the hotel until 3.30 in the afternoon. In the meantime, Tony had showered and fallen straight to sleep between the clean sheets of the bed. He had intended only to sleep for an hour or so, and then to try to telephone through to London, but he didn't wake until Howard Goldman arrived in the mid-afternoon and began battering on his door.

"Tony . . . Tony," he called out. "It's me . . . Howard. Let me in."

Tony staggered to the door and greeted Howard with a smile.

"Holy Jeeesus, Tony! Where the hell have you been, for Chrissake? I really thought you'd had it. Goddam!" Howard slapped his knee. "How in hell did you get here?"

"Hitch-hiked on a truckload of goat-skins from Mokhotlong." Tony laughed.

"Yeah? And where the hell is Mokhotlong?"

Tony told him and then began the rest of the story. Goldman sat quietly on the edge of the bed offering only an occasional "Holy Jeesus!" as Tony told him of his capture by BOSS and his treatment in the "asylum." He showed him the three unhealed weals left by the whiplashes across his back.

"And the gold is still sitting on the bottom of Durban Harbour now?" Howard asked, when Tony had finished talking.

"That's right. And I've got to get on the phone to London about it right away."

"No way!" Howard said. "You can forget it."

"Why?"

"Because all of the normal phone lines go through South Africa and they've simply cut them off. They've been trying a radio-telephone link-up to Mozambique, and then, theoretically, it should be possible to get an international call through, but," he shook his head and held out his hands, "believe me, it's impossible. I've tried." Goldman stood up from the bed and spoke seriously.

"It's bad enough being cut off from the outside world like that, but the real problem is that this place is likely to be invaded by South Africa at any moment. There's no way they could stop it. Lesotho has no army and South Africa could just walk straight in."

"But why should it bother?"

"Because of the rebel radio stations and the fact that the guerillas are running here for cover all the time. And also because there seem to be quite a few Russians suddenly on the scene here. I mean, we're goddam lucky to be here ourselves. They're not letting any South African whites come across the borders. Only foreigners. Even then, we had some problems."

Suddenly Tony remembered Marty and asked about him.

"He's still out at the airport. That's where I've been all day, trying to sort this deal out with this kraut pilot guy. I think it's all okay now and tonight we're getting out. And you," he pointed his finger at Tony and smiled, "are coming with us, let me tell you . . ."

"Hold on, hold on," Tony said. "Slow down. Start at the beginning. First of all, how did you get here?"

"Don't you want to come with us?"

"Of course I do," Tony said, "but first I want to know all the rest of it. Like, what happened with those BOSS guys in my room, and did you see Keneally?"

"Yes. Sure we did—but not until the following evening," Goldman said. "'Course, it took us ages to get out of the thing with those BOSS guys after you ran off. We pretended we thought they were hoods. They took us off and questioned us for hours. But it worked out okay. Well, then, in the morning, the Australian Trade Commissioner telephoned us and asked us to come out to his place for lunch. We realised something was up—in fact, we thought you were there, and we were going out there—but then these BOSS guys put us on the mat again for several hours, so, like I said, we didn't get out to see Keneally until late in the evening. And, Christ, that was the day the Robben Island prison thing broke. Jesus! The network was screaming for stuff from us and there was nothing we could do. Those bastards had us over a barrel, questioning . . ."

"I'm sorry," Tony said. "It was all my . . ."

"Oh, for Christ's sake, don't worry about it . . . forget it. You'd have done the same for us." Howard paused and smiled at Tony. "At least I hope you would.

"Anyway," Goldman continued, "eventually, when we made it out to Keneally's house, he told us what had happened with you, and about the letter and the fact that you had gone to Durban. Incidentally, there was no way we could get your gear from the hotel. Those BOSS characters were going through your room with a fine-tooth comb and we wanted to stay well clear of them . . ."

There was a knock on the door and Tony answered it to find Marty standing outside. He greeted Tony with a big smile and a heavy slap on the back which made Tony yelp in pain.

"Jeeez, sorry, Tony," Marty said. "Sorry," after Tony had explained. "Hell, we *thought* you were looking for trouble. It sure sounds as though you found it."

They talked again about Tony's experiences, then Tony asked Howard, "So what happened after you saw Keneally? Did they get on to you too? How come you're here now?"

"Well," Goldman said, "nothing much more happened after that. We started thinking about heading for Durban also, and . . ."

"Hold on, Howard," Marty said. "You didn't tell him about the research we did on the ship."

"The ship?" Tony said.

"Oh . . . er . . . yes," Goldman hesitated. "The next morning, that is, the 22nd, we started on a little research at the library and began looking into Trauseld's companies, just as you did, trying to find out what ships he owned."

"God," Tony muttered, "we were doing the same bloody research four hundred miles apart. I don't know why I just didn't leave it all to you in the first place. Did you find anything?"

"Well, I . . . not really," Howard said, a little awkwardly.

"The hell we didn't!" Marty put in, looking at Howard curiously. "We found out about his three ships and decided that the *South Cape Aurora* must be the one, because she was in Durban at the time."

Tony looked at Goldman. He seemed strangely on edge.

"So what did you do then?" Tony asked, sensing some tension in Goldman. "Did you file anything on that?"

"No," Howard said. "We decided that we were going to head for Durban . . . to follow you. To see if we could pick up the story there; but it didn't quite work out that way. We got word from the consulate that BOSS was going to get a bit heavy with us, maybe even try to can us. And we figured that it must be because they'd worked it out that you'd told Keneally and Keneally had told us about the letter, which meant that we were the only other ones who knew about it."

"And the only ones who knew about the *South Cape Aurora,*"

Tony said, looking at Howard. Strange, he thought. There was suddenly a feeling of mistrust between him and Howard Goldman. Tony didn't understand it.

"Well, yes," Howard answered. "Although *they* couldn't have known that we knew the actual ship. Anyway, the advice we got from the consulate was to get out—quickly. We had to go down to Sasolburg on the afternoon of the 23rd, to do some filming there of the damage done by another rocket attack on the refinery, and when we'd finished, we just kept on driving south to here. Arrived here at seven o'clock the same night. Been here ever since. Three days."

Tony was silent.

"Well, that's it," Howard said, trying to be jovial. "And tonight we're leaving!" He stood up and began pacing the room with his hands clasped behind his back. "We don't sit on our asses around here . . . no, sir! We . . . are . . . going . . . to . . . fly . . . out . . . of . . . here . . .", Howard spaced his words out for emphasis and gave exaggerated movements to his eyebrows and lips as he told Tony, ". . . in . . . a . . . light . . . airplane . . . at . . . midnight . . . *tonight!*" On the last word, he slammed his hand onto the small wooden desk table against the wall and adopted a triumphant pose.

"And if y'all want to come along, why you're very welcome, sir, as we just do happen to have a seat available."

"A light aeroplane," Tony said, "but . . ."

"But me no buts, Mr. Bartlett," Howard said. "This is the one and only chance you'll have." Then he became suddenly serious again. "No joking, Tony, if this place is invaded, we'd be in big trouble. As far as I can see it, this is the only way for us to go. And it'll work! Christ, it'd better work. We're paying three thousand bucks to hire the goddam plane!"

"But how are you going to do it?" Tony asked. "Where are you going to?"

"We're going to Zimbabwe—to Bulawayo," Goldman said. "We've got a Cessna 310 and we figure it will only take about three and a half hours."

"How far is it?" Tony asked.

"650 miles."

"All South African territory."

"I know. But we're going to fly at tree-top level all the way, so their radar won't pick us up."

"At night!"

"Yep."

"Who's flying it?"

"German guy we met here. It's his own plane. He operates all over Central Africa. He flew a bunch of Russians in here the other day—or night, rather."

"And what about the air traffic control people here? Do they know about it?"

"Officially, no. They're going to shout and jump up and down about it in the morning, but it's got the unofficial nod, because of what he's done for them in the past. Apparently he's ferried a few interesting people in and out of here during the past few months."

Goldman stood in front of Tony's chair, looking down at him. "Anyway, we're going. There's no way we're going to stick around here, waiting for something to happen. You coming?"

Tony looked back at Howard Goldman. "Of course," he said.

At exactly midnight, Hans Hoefer gunned the starboard engine of the Cessna to life. Two minutes later, the port engine sputtered to life as the starter button was held down for three or four seconds. Howard Goldman sat in the co-pilot's seat next to Hoefer. Tony and Marty were in the two seats immediately behind them. The back seat was piled up with camera equipment.

Hoefer taxied the aircraft out to the head of the darkened runway, checking his instruments as he went. There was no communication with the tower, which was also in darkness. At any minute Tony expected flashing lights and sirens, with police cars tearing out onto the tarmac shooting at them; but Howard assured him that there would be no problems. Apparently the pilot's share of the $3,000 fee had only been $2,000. The balance had gone to the right people on the ground to ensure that there would be no interference with their take-off. The only proviso made by the officials that Howard Goldman had dealt with was that they should waste no time.

The runway was not lit, but there was enough moonlight coming through the thin cloud cover for Hoefer to see as much of the runway as he needed. However, he knew he would have to rely heavily on his instruments for the rest of the flight.

A straight line drawn on the map, from Maseru to Bulawayo, runs almost due north and passes only a few miles to the west of Johannesburg and Pretoria. If there were to be any problems, that was where they would be.

They had discussed with Hoefer the possibility of making a wide, sweeping arc, to avoid the Johannesburg–Pretoria area and the likelihood of being detected and chased by fighter aircraft, or hit by surface-to-air missiles. But Hoefer had decided that the disadvantages of the more indirect route outweighed the advantages. For one thing, it would increase the distance and therefore tax their fuel supplies, possibly dangerously; and secondly, it would mean that they would be much longer in the air and more likely to be discovered and either shot down or forced down by South African aircraft.

There was also the possibility, if they flew a wide arc to the west of Johannesburg, that they would cross territory in which fighting was going on and could come under rebel fire as well. So they finally decided on a direct flight past the Johannesburg area, in the hope that speed and surprise would get them through.

The take-off was without incident and Hoefer levelled the aircraft off after climbing to only two hundred feet. Almost immediately, they crossed the invisible border dividing Lesotho from South Africa and within minutes had passed over the small town of Clocolan, flying to the left of the 6,000-foot Mount Hlohlowane, which rose out of the dark landscape just to the north of the town.

After another twenty minutes they passed near Senekal. There were no lights in the town, but they had been looking out for it and just caught sight of a dark cluster of houses which was there one minute and gone almost before they realised it. Clocolan and Senekal were the only two towns of any size that they would pass before reaching the big industrial areas to the south of Johannesburg, at least another forty minutes away. Hoefer said he hoped that, in addition to the power being off in the two towns, the phone lines might also be out. If that was the case, they could still hope to arrive at the most dangerous part of the journey unannounced.

The little craft sped on over the vast flatlands of the Orange Free State's central plains with no real or threatened interference. The aircraft was flying at roughly two hundred knots and Hoefer was maintaining an altitude of less than two hundred feet. When the moon was clear, the endless miles of maize and sunflower fields looked like a carpet. But when the moon moved behind a heavy cloud, it would all disappear and Hoefer would take the aircraft slightly higher, watching his instruments and radar continuously.

As the first hour in the air came to an end, they were all straining to see the lights of Johannesburg; but there were none. Suddenly they came off the great plains and found themselves flying over a densely populated area, but all in eerie darkness. Over to their right they could see lights and there were flames coming from two chimneys. They decided that they were from the Sasolburg oil refinery, which was evidently operating under its own emergency power-generating system. The moon was out now and they could see clearly, but it was necessary to climb again because of the increasing number of high-tension wires, suspended by large, steel-framed towers, that spread about the area.

Soon the big steelworks at Van der Bijl Park passed beneath them. It was also in darkness. Then they saw the wide, sprawling black township of Soweto immediately below and, at the same time, off to their right, the towering buildings of Johannesburg, some ten or twelve miles away.

Tony could hardly believe his eyes. The city was like a black, lifeless pile of blocks; no lights anywhere. The entire city was in darkness, except for two large fires burning. One was to the north and the other to the east, which, as they flew on, threw the fifty- and sixty-storey skyscrapers of the city into weird black silhouettes.

It was like something from a science fiction movie, in which everyone in the world had suddenly died from radiation poisoning or some strange virus and the cities were left to rot as giant, empty, concrete canyons. And they, flying past in their little steel cocoon, were the only survivors.

Tony knew that this was not the case in Johannesburg; that there were hundreds of thousands of people alive in that city right now—

385

almost two million, to be exact. He imagined the terror, the stark terror, that this complete darkness must have brought, and still be bringing, to many people there.

Looking at the black, lifeless towers, it was difficult to think of Johannesburg as an immense castle, built on a mountain of gold— thousands of millions of dollars worth of gold. A vast, modern, sophisticated, industrialized city. And yet ninety-five years ago, within a human lifetime, Tony thought, there was nothing there— nothing but flat, open veld, until George Harrison found the reef; the richest reef of gold the world has ever seen. George Harrison, the itinerant Australian prospector who set the whole thing going. Wonder what he'd think of it all now, if he was alive? He didn't last long, though. Never got to enjoy any of it . . . eaten by a lion.

Tony's thoughts were interrupted as Hoefer banked the aircraft to the left and began flying a different course.

"What's happening?" Tony asked Howard Goldman, who shrugged his shoulders, then tapped the pilot on the arm to ask the same question.

Hoefer spoke a few words to Goldman, who passed it back to Tony and Marty.

"He's going to fly to the west a little, over the Hartbeespoort Dam. Otherwise we'd be flying right over the South African Air Force base at Swartkop and there's no sense in pushing our luck too far."

Suddenly the pilot stiffened. He pressed a switch and the radio channel connected to his earphones became audible in the cabin through a small speaker.

". . . Defence Control. Attention! Aircraft flying in position, bearing 225 degrees, 10 nautical miles from Johannesburg VOR, squawk code 23. Squawk code 23, immediate please."

"What the hell does that mean?" Goldman said to Hoefer.

Tony leant forward to hear the reply. "He wants us to operate our transponder," Hoefer said, leaning over towards Goldman. "Secondary surveillance radar. It would give them a proper fix on us."

"Do you think they've got us on their radar now?" Tony said.

"No," the pilot said, turning back towards Tony and raising

his voice to be heard above the sound of the engines. "I think we've probably come in and out of their radar net and been spotted a couple of times, but we are too low to be located definitely."

". . . Squawk code 23. This is Johannesburg Area Defence Command. If you do not identify, we will intercept. Operate transponder please."

Everybody in the plane now went silent and became totally alert. Tony began to scan the sky around him. Hoefer took the plane down as close as possible to the ground, sometimes to within fifty feet. They all knew how dangerous this was, because of the power grids which criss-crossed the country, but there was no alternative if they wanted to escape detection.

Finally, after passing over the Magaliesberg range of hills to the north-west of Pretoria, endless miles of flat bush-veld opened up before them and, on a direct line of flight, there was virtually nothing between them and the Botswana border. A few miles beyond that was the Zimbabwe border and Bulawayo. They had been in the air for one and a half hours.

The plane was not challenged again, either on the radio or by another aircraft, and, as the time slipped by and the distance from Johannesburg and Pretoria increased, the tension in the cabin relaxed slightly. Hoefer took the aircraft up to five hundred feet after half an hour and, fifteen minutes later, as they crossed the Botswana border, near the tiny village of Zanzibar, he climbed to two thousand feet.

Tony sat back in his seat, flinching slightly from the wounds on his back, to try to sleep. He felt a wave of tiredness sweep over him. He dozed for short periods, but then found he was wide awake, turning things over in his mind. He kept thinking about Howard Goldman and the conversation they had, back in the hotel at Maseru. Why had he been so on edge?

Fifty minutes after they crossed the Zimbabwe border, Hoefer found the Bulawayo airport, which was in total darkness. The moon was out, however, and he circled the strip three times, getting his bearings, estimating distances and heights. He looked again at the moon and a cloud which was approaching it from the south-east, then lined the aircraft up on its final approach to the runway.

Tony had to find out. He leant forward to Howard, tapping him on the shoulder. Howard leant back. "That American warship which met the *South Cape Aurora*," Tony said, "it was there because you told them, wasn't it?"

Howard looked around at Tony. He said nothing for a second or two, then simply nodded.

Tony hesitated a moment. "Are you . . . CIA?" he asked.

Howard Goldman turned to the front without answering.

The plane touched down bumpily on the moonlit runway and began taxiing towards the Bulawayo terminal, where lights started to come on in different parts of the building.

19
"Where's
Tony?"

"If you see a suspicious parcel," the sign read, "do NOT pull the emergency cord immediately. Wait until the train stops at a station and inform the guard as soon as possible."

Tony looked at the faces around him—a sea of faces moving gently to and fro with the motion of the train as it plunged on through the darkened tunnel. They seemed blank to him. No-one spoke to anyone else. Some read newspapers, but most just sat, looking straight ahead.

Tony was standing, because there were no more seats available. He wondered what all of these people had been doing during the past few weeks, but he knew, even as he wondered. They were doing just what they are doing now . . . travelling on the train. Silent, immovable passengers through life. They get on the train as babies and when it reaches the end of the line, they are old. That is their life—in the train.

He shifted his position and changed hands to hang onto the strap above his head with his left hand. The movement tore at the healing skin along one of the whiplashes on his back. His shirt had stuck lightly to it and Tony winced as it came unstuck again. A man in a grey raincoat gave him a puzzled stare for an instant and then re-submerged himself in the gardening column of the *Herald*.

Tony looked again at the route map above the heads of the other passengers. Gloucester Road next, then High Street Kensington.

Bit different from the TanZam, he thought. The doors opened and shut. His mind flew back to the terrifying instant in the door of that first-class carriage, when—clickety-clack, clickety-clack, the same sound—it's international. Bit more muffled here, that's all.

The Circle Line train pulled in to High Street Kensington station. Tony disembarked and two minutes later walked out into the cold and drizzly night air on Kensington High Street. He wasn't really sure why he was going to this party. He didn't feel in the least like socialising, but somehow it had just happened; walking down Fleet Street after leaving the *Herald* office and bumping into David North.

"Tony! For God's sake! Fancy seeing you here. It's been years. What have you been doing with yourself? How are Carol and Michael?"

Tony told him.

"Oh . . . well, that's too bad. Sorry. I didn't know. The last I heard of you, you were floating around in Hong Kong or Vietnam or somewhere like that."

You obviously don't read the *Herald,* Tony thought, but said nothing. Tony's articles for his paper on the South African Revolution and the gold conspiracy had created something of a minor sensation. The news from South Africa had been dominating the headlines anyway; the dramatic military developments, the impending collapse of the Van Essche régime, the headlong flight of hundreds of thousands of whites to the Cape, and the apparent ascendancy of the revolutionary forces throughout much of the country, occupied most of the front pages.

But the *Herald* had Tony's story of the gold conspiracy on its own, both in their front-page news coverage and in the longer, feature articles which Tony wrote for the inside pages. They were also well in front on the details of the U.S.–Soviet naval confrontation off the coast of Natal. Tony didn't have the actual details of what happened there, but when he informed the paper of it, the *Herald*'s Washington correspondent was able to get the full story from a Pentagon spokesman.

It had been just a week since Tony had flown out from Bulawayo, via Salisbury and Nairobi, to London. His editor, Peregrine Childers, had at first chided Tony over the long period he had been out of contact with the paper. But his physical condition left no doubt in Childers' mind of what Tony had been through. His face was still bruised and he carried the fading remnants of two black eyes. It was also evident from the way he walked, when he first arrived in London, that he was still feeling pain from the other bruises. But Tony's cabled stories and the reams of feature material he began producing on his arrival made him Childers' and the paper's blue-eyed boy within a couple of days. Childers offered him a raise and the *Herald*'s plum South American posting in Buenos Aires, to which Tony replied, "I'll give it some thought."

"Are you still in Hong Kong?" North had said.

"No. I've been in Africa for the past three years," Tony replied.

"Oh? Really? That must have been exciting. Doing the same sort of thing?"

"Yes. That's right."

Tony wanted to get away. "Look," he said, "it's been nice . . ."

"No, you must tell us all about it. Really. Tonight. We're having a party at our place and Anne and I would really love you to come along. Anne will be delighted to see you again and you must give her Carol's address. I'm sure she'd like to write to her. They were good friends years ago, you know."

"I'm sorry," Tony said. "I don't think I'll be able to make it. I'm going to Greece tomorrow for a little rest and recuperation, and I'm having dinner tonight with my editor, so . . ."

"Come along after, then. It won't be getting started until at least nine or ten anyway. There'll just be a few BBC and ITN bods there . . . and a few birds, of course. One or two of them on the loose, I think. They're from the show . . ." Tony looked blank. "I'm producing the Harry Martin Show, you know."

"Oh . . ." Tony said.

North produced a card, which he gave to Tony. "That's got the home address on it there—Kensington. Come any time."

Tony had no intention of going to the party. He shuddered at the thought of a room full of pretentious bores like David North, all feeding incestuously on their own inflated egos.

391

Tony took his time and walked all the way back along Fleet Street and the Strand to the Savoy, where he was staying. He knew the Savoy was extravagant, but he liked the idea of the contrast, after a period of deprivation. That was it. He knew that that was how he wanted his life to be. Not permanent luxury; you don't really appreciate it when you have it all the time. Just every now and then, he decided.

The dinner with Perry had been pleasant. They had dined elegantly at Quaglinos. It was a Saturday and as Perry was not responsible for the Sunday paper, he could take the evening off. His wife Marilyn had planned to come too, but her eighty-three-year-old mother, who lived with the Childerses, had become ill so Marilyn had stayed at home.

Perry had talked about how much he wished he was still out in the field, working as a correspondent, how he envied Tony, and that the editor's job was too sedentary; locked in that office all day, gazing out onto rain-swept, dreary grey streets.

"Why don't you just get out then?" Tony had said.

"Oh, I'm too senior now. That's the trouble," Perry had said. "And we've got our house out at Wimbledon, kids just finishing school and at university. It creeps up on you, you know."

Tony made a mental note not to let it creep up on him. He liked Perry, and he didn't like to see him unhappy.

"Not that I'm really unhappy," Perry said, "because I love London, I really do. It's just that—well, it's just a vague sort of dissatisfaction, I suppose, to know that it's all happening out there. It's worse for me, really, because I've spent so many years in the midst of it."

He sat back, as the coffee and liqueur were brought to the table, and lit a cigar. "Incidentally, they've started salvage work on the *South Cape Aurora* today. The rebels, that is. They're in full control of Durban and most of Natal now—and the gold *is* there!"

"What about Trauseld?" Tony asked. "Have they tracked him down?"

"No trace of him. He's disappeared completely. Out of the country, apparently. But Kapepwe seems to be emerging as a pretty important character in the overall scheme of things. Already they're talking about him holding some sort of cabinet post in any black government they try to put together."

"But they've had a provisional government for some time," Tony said.

"Yes, but the different factions are already starting to angle for a bigger slice of the cake—and he's evidently hopping in for his share."

They talked until about ten and then parted. Tony planned to return to London, after spending two weeks on the island of Ios, to make a decision about whether to return to Nairobi or take the new posting that had been offered to him.

For the moment, however, he was looking forward to the clear blue skies and harsh beauty of those arid hills running down to the Aegean Sea. In April it would be a little cold for swimming, perhaps, but Tony knew the sun would be there and that it would be free of the summer tourist rush. He could sunbathe and read during the day and sit quietly in the village square in the evenings, sipping ouzo or retsina and talking to people.

He patted the tickets in his inside pocket—ten o'clock in the morning, from London Airport. If only, he thought, if only Ingrid was coming with me. He thought of her straightforward friendliness and warmth. He wished she were here with him now. He missed her. He felt lonely.

On the spur of the moment, he had decided that he would go to David North's party after all. He should go back to the hotel, to sleep, but he wasn't tired. Something to do.

Tony knocked on the door of the ground-floor flat in Duchess of Bedford Walk. It was opened by David North's wife Anne.

"Hello, Tony," she exclaimed. "David told me you were coming. I'm so glad you could make it. Come in and meet some people."

"George Arrowsmith, the director of so-and-so, Adrian Bell, who produces such-and-such, Jennifer Adams. She writes scripts for the blah-blah series, you know." The names came and went.

Tony was introduced as a journalist.

He was definitely small fry compared to these extremely important people—in their eyes, anyway.

"A journalist? You mean you work for a newspaper?"

"The *Herald*."

"Oh . . . I see. How interesting." Then they would continue talking to their friends.

Tony was only mildly put out by this sort of reception, because he had to admit that he wasn't really in a very expansive or extrovert mood himself; but he felt that there was a vast gulf between him and the people milling around him. He knew that it didn't really matter that they were so shallow, except that they were the norm and he was outside that norm. It made him feel even more isolated and lonely. He felt, to some extent, as if he had been used—put through a wringer.

They don't give a stuff about what happens outside their own little world, he thought. Thousands of people could die in South Africa, or in an earthquake in Turkey, or in a tidal wave in Peru, but after the flash of momentary interest, they'd be wanting to know what the next story was, or the much more important question of how much video-recording time was available for the Harry Martin Show, or whether three cameras had been provided on the floor instead of two.

I could have been killed by Bruno Van Wyk, Tony thought, leaning up against the mantelpiece, sipping his whisky and watching the people around him . . . and it wouldn't have meant a damn thing. It wouldn't have made the slightest ripple here. He began to feel depressed. Maybe I'm just tired and a rest on Ios will make all the difference.

"I see the blacks look like taking over in South Africa now," someone said. "Going to call it Azania."

"Not all of it," another put in. "Apparently the whites still control the Cape Province, which is fifty percent of the whole country."

Tony stood to one side, listening. He felt completely detached.

"Yes, but they've lost the gold mines to the blacks now . . ."

"I think it's just terrible," a young woman said. "I was there five years ago. It's such a beautiful country and they're just going to mess it all up."

"How do you know they're going to mess it all up?" the first man said.

"Well, you've only got to look around you, haven't you?" she

394

replied. "They haven't made much of a success of things anywhere else, have they?"

There it is again, Tony thought, "them" and "us." He edged himself along the wall, slipped through the door into the hallway, and began walking quietly towards the front door, just as David North, who had been standing in one corner of the room, said, "Why don't you ask Tony Bartlett about this? He's just come back from Africa. Where's Tony? He was here just a minute ago."

Tony took his coat off the hook, closed the front door behind him, and walked out into the still-falling rain. As he made his way through the empty streets back towards Kensington High Street tube station, the fine drizzle formed beautiful, rainbow-coloured haloes around the street lights above him. But Tony didn't even notice them.